Jeena clasped her hands over her ears, screaming for him to stop and the voices to go away, but the clamor rose until it sounded like laughter. Lurching from the tent, she grabbed the shotgun and leveled it through tear-blinded eyes at the tormentor in her mind.

"Stay away from me, goddam you! Don't touch me!"

SAMSON JUMPED AT THE SHOUT, CAUSING THE CRATES AND CANS to tumble around him, pinning him in. He saw the tear-streaked face staggering toward him, and sensed her anger. Whether in a burst of sudden insight or from an instinct for survival, he understood his danger and began desperately clawing at the debris keeping him prisoner. He watched helplessly as she raised the weapon. Unable to move, he began to whine and cry, and then suddenly in a high-pitched voice, he cried out a single word.

"No!"

THE RAGING STORM IN JEENA'S MIND WAS DISTURBED. A SOUND she couldn't quite identify drew her attention away from the laughing face before her. It began to shift and fade. Confused, she lowered her weapon and wiped her eyes, a simple action that seemed to still the voices in her head. Now, she could see Samson partially buried under a pile, repeating his pitiable cry over and over: "No! No! No!"

Comprehension suddenly returned.

"It can't be. It's...not possible," she whispered. She took one halting step toward him and fell, collapsing into darkness on the yellow sands of Ararat.

If you enjoy this book...

Metered Space by M. D. Benoit
Kiyama by Diana Kemp-Jones
Deem by Barry Tomkins

TIGRA

BY

R. J. LEAHY

ZUMAYA OTHERWORLDS   AUSTIN TX

2006

This book is a work of fiction. Names, characters, places and incidents are products of the author's imagination or are used fictitiously. Any resemblance to actual persons or events is purely coincidental.

TIGRA

© 2006 by Richard J. Leahy
ISBN 13: 978-1-934135-21-1
ISBN 10: 1-934135-21-6

Cover art by Brian Hamner

Cover design by Martine Jardin

All rights reserved. Except for use in review, the reproduction or utilization of this work in whole or in part in any form by any electronic, mechanical or other means now known or hereafter invented, is prohibited without the written permission of the author or publisher.

Look for us online at http://www.zumayapublications.com

Library of Congress Cataloging-in-Publication Data

Leahy, R. J., 1960-
 Tigra / by R. J. Leahy. -- 1st Otherworlds ed.
   p. cm.
 ISBN-13: 978-1-934135-21-1
 ISBN-10: 1-934135-21-6
 I. Title.
 PS3612.E215T54 2006
 813'.6--dc22

2006033914

Printed in the United States of America

ACKNOWLEDGMENTS

Thanks to all and everyone who have helped and guided me in this. Too many to name here, but you know who you are. My everlasting thanks and love to Racine, who puts up with me, God knows how.

Prologue

SHE MIGHT HAVE BEEN PRETTY AT ONE TIME; PERHAPS SHE STILL WAS. IT WAS impossible to tell through the layers of grime that covered her. Not that the guards cared. They weren't bothered by filth, nor the mildly crazed look in her eyes. She was everything they wanted her to be. She was theirs.

The guard-sergeant led the men into her cell and brusquely ordered her to strip. She didn't fight, she didn't cry out, just silently and mechanically removed her flight suit to stand naked before them. Her breath misted slightly in the cold as she waited, shivering.

The sergeant grunted orders to his men before collecting money from those who had not yet paid. A battered mattress was pulled to the center of the cell.

Ignored for the moment, the woman began humming and slowly swaying to a half-remembered tune.

"My bonny lies over the ocean, my bonny lies over the sea…" She giggled at the silliness of the song but, when she tried to continue, found she had forgotten the rest of the words.

She shuffled her feet. She felt hungry and reached into her pocket for the bone she had been chewing on earlier in the day, only to find she had lost both the bone and her pockets. *Where are my pockets?* she wondered.

She looked down in search of them and saw the worn and tattered flight suit lying at her feet. It was covered in the accumulated filth of sixteen months of continuous wear, but the ID stenciling could still be made out, the white letters just visible against the jet-black of the suit.

"Cap-tain...Jeen-a...Gar-za," she whispered, carefully enunciating each syllable. She puzzled over the words for a moment then smiled. She remembered the name. It was hers.

At least, that had been her name, in that rapidly fading memory of a past that was once her life—a life before her crash and capture, before the prison and the torture and the rapes. She'd still been a pilot then, and a soldier, and human. She'd had a name. What was it again? She frowned. Lately, she found thoughts difficult to hold on to.

The ID came back into focus.

Jeena. I remember now. My *name was Jeena.*

But it was a hard thing to remember. Here in the prison she had no name. Here she was only a number: F548666. The F was for female, she assumed; the other numbers were meaningless. Not even the guards bothered with them anymore; to them she was simply Sixty-six.

Sixty-six! Sixty-six, come here, you bitch! They screamed it at her day and night—especially at night. It was at night they most wanted her, like they wanted her now.

They pushed her roughly onto the soiled mattress, and she let them, offering no resistance. Early in her capture she had fought hard against every violation, but the end had always been the same. Then, after they used her they would torture her for her disobedience, and she was now too weak to withstand any more torture.

She twisted a strand of hair absently between her fingers, still humming softly. Some of the other women had not learned the lesson. They had fought too long or too hard. Bad girls. Bad, bad girls. Eventually, the men tired of them, taking their clothes and food and leaving them to slowly freeze and starve in the bitter-cold cells.

But Jeena had learned. She would not fight back, for fighting back meant death; and despite the unspeakable horror her life had become, she could not yet bring herself to end it.

She'd been through this all before—God, how many times? All the other women were gone now. Dead, maybe...she didn't know. For the last five months only she remained, and they came for her nightly, laughing and drunk, no more than animals in rut.

Sixty-six!

Sometimes there would be only one or two, other times many, many more. Always there was the guard-sergeant. He had claimed her early in her capture, and now she was his—his property, his animal. Deep down in a place that was still Jeena Garza she knew her time was running out, and that he would soon grow weary of her, too.

The first soldier fumbled with his belt, cursing as the others laughed. Jeena stared at the flight suit, and at the name that once again had become meaningless, and felt nothing.

Chapter 1

The Coalition: Name adopted by the first four planets to break with the Union of Democratic Planets at the beginning of the Galactic Civil War. Now numbering twenty-two separate worlds, it is more often referred to as the Coalition Empire.

Encyclopedic History of the Union, 22nd ed.

Jeena woke with her fist buried in the pillow, sobbing and clutching at her stomach, fighting off the pain and nausea that accompanied her back to the waking world. The nightmare images of the prison faded, but she could still smell the men, still hear the echoes of her own screams.

With great effort, she opened her swollen and bleary eyes to a room eerily illuminated by flashing red lights, pulsating in rhythm to the modulated shriek of a klaxon. It took a moment for her to register the sound as the ship's main system alarm.

She was suddenly alert and leapt from the bunk, only to reel and fall to the floor. Something was terribly wrong. The walls of her sleeping quarters were shuddering, and there was an odor of smoke in the air. Grabbing the bulkhead for support, she forced herself up. The metal wall was hot to the touch.

Staggering, fighting to maintain her balance, she moved toward the cockpit door. She caught sight of her bloody flight suit on the floor just as she reached it. There was no time.

She hit the door panel, and it opened with a hiss. Naked, she stumbled into the cockpit.

A deafening roar like the inside of a blast furnace struck her, enveloping her in a ragged blanket of noise that made her cringe and cover her ears. The source of the noise was readily apparent. Through the cockpit window she saw angry, red-hot flames engulfing the hull of the ship. The smell of smoldering insulation was thick in the room, and white-gray smoke rose in twisting columns from the conn.

With a sudden sick fear Jeena realized her ship was burning up in an uncontrolled re-entry. The question of how that was possible would have to wait—she had to get control of the ship.

Lunging toward the conn, she swayed, falling again as the ship careened madly. She grabbed the back of the chair, pulling herself up. A reinforcement cable tore loose from its mooring and whipped through the cabin, the jagged tip slashing her left thigh and leaving a six-inch bleeding gash. Screaming, she fell into the conn chair.

Ignoring the wound, she scanned the instrument panel, quickly assessing the situation. Drive and main engines were offline; hydraulics were bleeding; external hull temperature was twelve hundred degrees and rising, angle of declination...fifty degrees. Too steep!

There was a sound like the firing of a gun beneath her, followed by a loud hiss of escaping air. A violent shudder ran through the hull. The ship was coming apart.

The air brakes had automatically engaged on entering the atmosphere but were doing little to slow the momentum. She needed power to pull out. She slammed her fist on the main engine switch, but the indicator remained dark. She hit it again then tried the auxiliary override. Nothing. The engines were dead.

The ship groaned, and the fire before her was now a searing wall of white heat. She quickly went over her options. *If I can't start the engines, at least I have to dump the Drive.* The Drive was enormous, and was not built to withstand an atmosphere, intended only for interstellar flight.

She gripped the double-level crossbar in both hands and pulled it down. The separation alarm sounded as a green warning light swept the cockpit. There was a jarring sensation and a deep grinding from behind her, followed immediately by a second alarm—separation failure. Dammit! The heat of re-entry must have fused the couplings; she would not be able to disengage the Drive. She would have to bring the huge transport down in one piece.

She gripped the flight stick between her legs she pulled back hard, sweating profusely as the cabin temperature climbed. Her right thumb toggled power to the tram's forward thrusters, and she felt some relief as the indicator light came on; but the stick was still buried forward, and she was unable to pull it back. Grunting with effort, her sight blurred by sweat she strained against it, fighting both the planet's gravitational pull and the inertia of the ship.

She cursed the lack of response. *Rigel's rings, it's like trying to fly a burning brick!* This wasn't a sleek frontline fighter; it was a beat-up cargo vessel with its Drive still attached. Theoretically, it might be possible to land the giant ship in one piece, but she'd never done it, or ever heard of it being done.

The forces against her were enormous. If the thrusters could not decrease the angle of descent, the ship would disintegrate, falling to the planet below in a fiery rain of burning debris.

The vibrations were so violent she could barely read the instruments. Smoke filled the cabin. Declination still read fifty degrees; hull temperature was now over nineteen hundred. The situation was deteriorating. She was losing the ship.

No, not now! Goddammit, not now! All those months of torture; all that pain. I won't die now. Not like this. Not after so much.

In a rage, she threw her body against the stick, the sinews of her arms screaming in protest.

"Help me!" she cried out to the ship. "Help me, you *bitch*!"

As if in answer, the ship shuddered and yawed, nearly wrenching the controls from her hands. Teeth gritted, knuckles white, she held on, fighting for control. She frantically sought out the declination gauge—forty-nine degrees.

She was gaining. Against the almost unimaginable dual forces of wind shear and gravitational pull, she was gaining. But external temperature was now three thousand degrees. There was a popping sound in front of her, and a small crack appeared in the center of the windshield.

"C'mon, baby," she pleaded.

Amid the noise around her, she could just make out the synthetic voice of the flight computer.

"Fifty-two seconds of thrust remaining," it announced calmly.

"Damn you, Vicki!" she cursed to the empty cabin. She had less then a minute in which to pull the ship out.

Bracing herself, heaving against the stick, she watched the numbers slowly recede as the seconds ticked agonizingly by. At forty-five degrees she could feel the vibrations lessen, but she was weakening, her muscles beginning to tremble. Her arms felt on fire, burning from the buildup of lactic acid as she pushed them beyond her limits.

"C'mon, c'mon," she grunted, but the stick felt as though it was moving through thick cement.

The air inside the cabin was searing, and she labored to breath. The small crack in the windshield began to enlarge, snaking in a twisted curve through the reinforced glass. Sweat poured from her. Declination was now thirty-five degrees.

Jeena closed her eyes and focused her energy, willing her tortured arms to maintain contraction. They finally reached their limit and the muscle fibers began to tear, then to shred as her strength finally gave out. Her eyes flew open as she gave another scream.

The wall of fire before her had thinned, the flames losing energy. Soon they fluttered and went out. With their loss the horrible roaring in her ears died as well. Jeena checked the declination gauge: twenty-eight degrees. She was in a stable glide pattern.

She released the thruster toggle and painfully pried her fingers away from the stick. Four seconds of thrust remained.

Slowly, her left arm throbbing, she reached out and canceled the red alert. The cabin was now still, save for the barely audible sound of rushing wind as they soared through the sky. Her body ached terribly, and her left bicep was already turning an angry shade of purple. There was the salty taste of blood in her mouth—she must have bitten through her tongue. She took a brief glance at the gash in her right inner thigh. The wound gaped but was only bleeding slightly.

Jeena sank back into the seat, trembling from exertion and the adrenaline still coursing through her body. She took a few steadying breaths as she watched the wispy, whirling patterns of clouds dance before her, and allowed one question to occupy her mind.

Where the hell am I?

She had been on a pre-plotted course to Earth when she left Mizar 3. She had chosen a flight pattern well away from all known Coalition military outposts and recent battle sites. The flight plan had been calculated and re-checked by the ship's navigation computer. She should still be in hyperspace. So where was she?

She puzzled over the question as the ship's computer droned on, giving her technical information on her glide path and the ship's status, but she had stopped listening. The sky before her had caught her attention, and she realized she could not recall the last time she had seen blue skies and white clouds. When was that? Earth? Yes, it must have been on Earth.

The military preferred low-gravity, moonlike worlds for their bases, and Jeena had spent most of her life in the Star Corps. Her last visit to Earth had been...almost ten years ago.

Can it have really been so long ago?

Looking out at the sky, she felt a sudden pang of regret and a deep feeling of loss for what she had missed. It was a life she had chosen, but in reality, there had been little true choice. You play the hand you're dealt the best you can, she had said often. Abandoned as an infant, she had cut her own way in the world. She had done the best she could. Still...

Jeena stiffened, loathing the feelings of self-pity that had crept up on her. The months in the prison must have softened her. She was a soldier, a decorated officer in an elite SAG unit. She had crawled and fought her way up the chain of command and if not for her capture might have made major by now. What more did she want?

Before she could explore that question, the clouds thinned then abruptly disappeared, replaced by an impossibly bright, blazing blue sky. Below her, expanding out to the horizon, lay a panoramic view of a new and alien world.

With land now in view Jeena activated AL—approach and landing. Using a combination of sophisticated radar and laser scanning, it would evaluate the condition of the surface below and recommend a site with the highest probability of her surviving an emergency landing.

"Okay, AL, what have you got for me?" she whispered.

Static crackled from the comm and a topographical grid map appeared on the heads-up display, floating like a phantom in the space between her and the windshield. The entire map was lit a dull red—probability of survival less than ten percent.

"Keep looking," she said, switching to a wider view. The display expanded its area, but all was still red. Jeena glanced at the altimeter. "C'mon, I've got to put her down soon. Give me something I can live with."

A moment later, a small patch of yellow appeared in the left lower corner of the grid—chance of survival greater than fifty percent.

"Nothing in blue or green today, huh?"

The screen remained unchanged. Glancing again at the altimeter, she set a course for the small area of yellow ahead and strapped herself into her seat, suddenly reminded of her nakedness as the stiff restraints bit into her skin.

She soared above a wide savanna, descending rapidly. She watched as the ship aligned itself with the area AL had chosen as giving the best chance of surviving an emergency ditch—*best* being a relative term, she reminded herself.

The plain was coming up fast, the ground now racing past her. Airspeed was still over five hundred knots, but four seconds of full forward thrust would slow that down significantly. Jeena quickly went over her mental checklist for emergency landings—everything seemed ready. Breathing deeply, her hands gripping the stick, she put the big ship down.

The rear Drive section hit the ground first, almost tearing the controls from her grasp. The great ship shook and shuddered as it thundered over the broken terrain. Jeena hit the forward thrusters and was slammed against the restraining straps. Four...three...two...one. That was it. The thrusters were gone. Now it was up to Newton.

She released the stick and gripped the restraints as the land rushed by. The momentum of the ship was enormous; she was still moving at over two hundred knots. She watched the grid map as the yellow patch disappeared; beyond all was ominously red. Still the ship raced on.

There was a terrible jolt and the sound of shearing metal as the tram's forward landing gear tore away. With a violent lurch, the nose pitched forward, plowing into the ground. Dirt and vegetation blasted into the air as the belly of the ship gouged a rut in the earth. The windshield shattered, the pieces held in place only by the layer of plastek running through it. Bolts from the rear of the ship tore loose and shot forward, crashing into the control panel. Sparks flew, and the smell of smoldering insulation filled the cabin.

Then all was silent.

Jeena slowly lifted her head. The cockpit windshield was dark under a blanket of dirt. Tiny sparks popped and fizzed from the conn. She sat for a moment, listening to the sputtering of the control panel. A drop of blood fell from her nose and splattered on her thigh. The edges of the restraints had cut into her flesh, and there was a sharp pain under her left breast that made breathing difficult.

But she was alive.

Wincing, she carefully disengaged from the restraints. Another drop of blood formed on her nose, and she wiped it away absently, leaving a bloody smear across her cheek. She took a trembling breath and sank back into the chair.

"Thanks, AL," she said hoarsely.

She allowed herself a few minutes to quell her nerves before punching up the ship's main computer.

"Vicki," she said aloud, "where am I?"

All interstellar ship's central computers were known collectively as "Vicki," a tradition dating back to the first flights some four hundred earlier. Few remembered that the designation originally stood for VICI, or Voice-Integrated Conn Interface, but the tradition was handed down through each generation of pilots, reinforced by the fact that conns were given feminine voices, the military psyches having shown time and again that was more soothing to the human ear than its masculine counterpart.

A sweetly feminine, slightly lilting voice answered.

"The ship is presently on the surface of Ararat, second planet of the Arcturus system."

Jeena frowned. *Arcturus? We shouldn't even be in the same quadrant as that system.*

"Did you change the flight plan?"

"Negative."

"Why was the Drive taken offline?"

"A collision with a large gravitational object was deemed imminent."

A reference to the planet, Jeena assumed. That was a non-answer. The planet shouldn't have been there because *they* shouldn't have been *here.*

"Our flight plan didn't take us through Arcturus."

"That is correct."

"Dammit, just give me a schematic of the hyperspace flight," Jeena snapped.

A holographic image appeared on the heads-up, representing the flight plan she had laid out prior to making the jump from Mizar 3. A faint line began there and followed a slightly irregular curved path toward her destination: Earth. This was a Hawking line, and should not intersect any stellar object.

She studied the line closely. The Arcturus system wasn't even close.

It made no sense. Her hyperspace flight took her nowhere near Arcturus, yet here she was.

She gnawed on her lower lip. "Was there a course deviation during flight?"

"Negative."

"Any sign of Drive malfunction?"

"Negative."

"What about a gravitational anomaly along our flight path?"

"Negative."

"Well, did the goddamn planet just jump in our way?" she demanded.

The machine maintained a dignified silence.

Jeena sat back in disgust. Her body throbbed, and her head was pounding. And she was hungry—she realized she hadn't eaten since she first lay down on the bunk after taking the ship out of orbit, almost two days ago.

Well, I may be lost, but at least I won't starve. Whoever the pilot of this cargo ship was, he was also quite obviously a smuggler. She remembered her shock at finding all the contraband goods in the cargo hold.

Probably had a good deal of his money invested in that hold, she thought. That'll teach him not to keep his ship hot on a prison tarmac. Although losing his ship might have been the best thing for him. If the Coalition discovered he was smuggling, he would have spent the next several years in a pain cell.

Whoever he was, he was either very brave or very stupid. Didn't he know all interstellar flights were logged? How did he figure on covering up all the extra Drive use?

Jeena sat up. Wait a minute, how *would* he cover them up? The CCOMS would document any trips to unapproved sectors. An answer slowly came to her, along with a sick feeling in the pit of her stomach.

"Vicki, has the central coordinate system of this ship been tampered with?"

"Affirmative. The CCOMS of this ship does not correspond to the local observable star pattern."

A shudder went through her. So, that's how he did it.

Navigation through hyperspace was guided by the CCOMS, or Central Coordinate Mapping System. Using Polaris as the origin, all known stellar bodies were plotted in four vectors—three for spatial position and the fourth for gravitational density. Orbital and linear motions were also recorded.

In hyperspace, since you were, in effect, skirting the normal dimensions of space, no directional readings were possible. It was only through such a system as CCOMS that interstellar flight had been made practical. It was also why every flight had to be plotted and calculated in advance, for once you were in hyperspace you could never be exactly sure of where you were at any given moment. In fact, the entire concept of "where"—at least in regards to three-dimensional space—lost all meaning entirely, and even gravitational fields could only be detected when you were almost right on top of them. Without a system like CCOMS, any hyperspace ship had a better than average chance of ending up passing through some immovable galactic object—usually with spectacular, if generally fatal, results.

The pilot of this ship, this smuggler, must have realigned the CCOMS prior to each of his smuggling runs in such a way that they would be recorded as ordinary supply trips in the log. Jeena was impressed. What balls! Even assuming he had a portable unit programmed with the actual CCOMS, it was a combination of guts and insanity she could admire.

"Vicki, is there a copy of the original CCOMS in ship's memory?"

"Affirmative."

"Re-up the original coordinate system and overlay my flight plan."

There it was. Plotted against the true CCOMS, her flight path took her right through the Arcturus system. She took a closer look. The line passed directly through the system's sun. She sank back into the chair. Good thing this planet was in the way.

She allowed herself a few more minutes to rest before slowly standing and making her way around the cabin. She needed to dress her wounds, particularly the gash to her thigh, but first she needed to locate the med kit.

Everything had been thrown about the cabin during the landing, and she had to pick through the debris. She eventually found it wedged under the conn seat and picked it up, limping back to the dayroom.

Sitting gingerly on the bunk, she placed the med kit next to her and broke the seal. The pain under her left breast was worse now and intensified with each breath—a cracked rib, she guessed. Taking the trans-hypo out of the kit, she loaded it with a cylinder of psuedomorph. Checking the dosage twice, she placed the instrument against her neck and pushed. Instantly, three milligrams of the painkilling drug pulsed through her skin and into her carotid artery, carried on a burst of ultrasonic waves. She waited a moment then attempted a breath—much better. The pain was still there, but much reduced.

She now examined the laceration to her thigh. It appeared deep, but there was not enough blood to indicate an arterial bleed. Taking a small atomizer from the kit, she sprayed the edges of the wound, instantly anesthetizing it.

With the wound numb, she could explore it more thoroughly. The edges were straight and clean, and she pulled them slightly apart, gazing into the gash. What bleeding there was, was coming from a small venous plexus—that should not be a problem.

Although the risk of infection was small, she decided not to take any chances. She took a vial from the kit and broke it open, pouring the bluish liquid into the wound. She watched dispassionately as it foamed and frothed. It contained an antibiotic as well as growth factors that would accelerate the healing process.

She now removed a pistol-shaped instrument from the kit and pressed the trigger, laying the glowing red tip at the uppermost margin of the wound. Holding the edges of the gash together with her thumb and index finger, she moved the skin welder down the wound, the abutted edges fusing together as she went. There was a slight sickly-sweet smell of burning flesh as she worked. She stopped just before reaching the end of the laceration, leaving a small opening for drainage.

Her wounds now cared for, she entered the adjoining shower stall, a small, slightly rusted metal cubicle set in the corner of the dayroom. Dialing up a warm spray, she stepped into it, grateful it still worked after the hard landing, and letting the clean water wash over her. She luxuriated in the feel of it, scrubbing away the dirt and filth of sixteen months of confinement and the more recent layer of splattered blood. It was the first real shower she had had since her crash and capture, the memory of which made her wonder fleetingly if anyone had missed her when she didn't return from the last mission.

Not the Star Corps brass, certainly. They would have logged her as dead or captured—the distinction being moot—and not given her a second thought. There was no Geneva Convention in this war to ensure the decent treatment of POW's, and no prisoner exchanges. The difference between being killed in battle and being taken prisoner was simply one of time—few prisoners lived long on either side. Soldiers were expendable, like the machinery they used.

Had any of *them* missed her, she wondered—the men and women of her unit? She didn't think so. SAG commandos were trained to keep emotionally detached, and no one had been more detached than Jeena Garza.

She respected her fellow soldiers, but that was where it ended. She would fight with them and drink with them and even make love with them in fast, furious, loveless couplings, but she could never love them, or they her. She was a loner among loners, and had never needed or sought their friendship. No, she would not be missed.

Tears suddenly appeared and began to flow without warning, washed away by the streaming water. Slowly, she sank to her knees on the cold metal floor, crying in great heaving sobs and pounding her fist impotently against the wall.

Chapter 2

If captured, you can expect to be tortured. It is inevitable. Do not worry that you may divulge miltary secrets. You will not be given any. Nothing you may tell your captures will help them in slightest, nor you.

Excerpt from *SAG Survival Manual*

JEENA STEPPED DRIPPING FROM THE SHOWER, HER EYES BLOATED AND RED, AND DRIED with a small towel as she crossed to the conn. The long-range scanners were still silent—there was no Union or Coalition communication in the area. She was safe for now.

"Vicki, what is the local time?"

"It is now dusk on the planet, equivalent to nineteen hundred hours Greenwich Mean Time."

It was too late to investigate the planet tonight. She'd wait till morning.

"Set a wakeup alarm for 0600 Greenwich Mean."

"Yes, sir."

She turned toward the day room. "Vicki, is there a music library on board?"

"Yes, sir. I carry an extensive catalogue of musical styles. These include..."

"Save it."

The voice stopped abruptly.

"Classical. Holst. *The Planets.* Begin." She lay on the bunk just as the first subtle strings of "Mercury" began.

Jeena closed her eyes, feeling weak. The months in the prison had taken a heavy toll on her. The episode in the shower had released a cascade of memories and emotions, and she was too worn out to fight them. As the music played, the events leading up to her imprisonment came drifting back to her.

She had been leading her SAG unit on a retaliatory strike against Cynos 7, one of the most heavily defended Coalition outposts. The laser cannons were firing all around as she swept in, the blasts lighting up the sky as they struck her shields. As usual her unit was the first into battle—they were the Union's elite shock troops, sent in to soften up the enemy before the main army group arrived.

She had just hit the generator-housing unit and was climbing out of atmosphere when her engines took a full cannon barrage. She could still taste the fear in her mouth as her ship tumbled back to the planet, her engines on fire. She had waited until the last possible moment, but when it came she bailed out.

Why did I do that? It was a question she had asked herself many times in the prison. She had always sworn she would never bail, would never risk being captured. The stories of the Coalition prison camps were too terrible to contemplate. Better to die quickly than to face that, she had said often.

Yet bail out she did. A Coalition cruiser found her half-drowned, still floating in the conn chair. They had thrown her in the brig, but at least they had fed her. And they had left her alone. Two days later she was transferred to a stellar transport bound for the prison world of Mizar 3.

She was in one of the first groups boarded on the transport. They were held in a rusted-out cargo hold that still stank of the livestock it once carried. She stepped through pools of stagnant water that had collected on the ship's floor and made her way to the rear of the hold.

There was little light, and Jeena could just make out the other prisoners. Their faces were blank, devoid of any emotion save resignation as they paced slowly, their movements creating echoes in the dank, cavernous space. They were all soldiers, and none had any illusions about their chances for survival.

She passed them in silence. There was nothing to say.

She found a spot near the far wall next to a bracing beam that ran across the ceiling to the other side. The beam and wall formed a little niche, a definitive space that gave her a tiny sense of security in the open and hostile environment of the hold. It was a completely illogical, yet totally human feeling, she knew; and she stood in her little nook, her feet in several inches of stagnant water, and watched as the hold slowly filled.

Within the hour the room had become impossibly crowded, with prisoners standing shoulder to shoulder. Ventilation was via a large, creaking, slowly rotating fan situated high on the back wall.

The cargo hold was never intended for this many living, breathing animals, and soon it was sweltering. Jeena was pressed tight into her little corner, directly behind a young woman in a Star Corps uniform. She was roughly Jeena's age, and the two exchanged whispered hellos. The woman was sweating profusely and seemed to be in pain. Jeena noticed she was holding her hand over her chest, the shirt under it soaked in blood.

Finally, the last prisoner entered, and the hatch was sealed with a loud clang. The room was still; then from the center of the mass of people a loud voice boomed.

"Join the service, they said," he mocked. "See the galaxy. Right. I tell ya, the first thing I'm gonna do when I get home is kill my recruiter."

There was laughter throughout the hold, and Jeena joined in.

The morose gloom now broken, conversations broke out, and soon the room came alive with voices. Jeena introduced herself to the injured woman. Her name was Maggie Fletcher, and she was a corporal assigned to the support team for the main army group. She had been part of the ground operations that were overrun following the failure of the Union's air attack on Cynos. Many in the hold were from the same battle.

At Jeena's insistence, Maggie allowed her to examine her injury. There was a small puncture wound below her right breast. It looked little bigger than a pinhole, but it would not stop bleeding, not even after Jeena applied direct pressure for more than an hour. It was a bad sign—she knew it was an indication of an arterial bleed into the chest, but said nothing to the girl.

Some of the higher-ranking officers organized the other prisoners into sleeping groups—there was not enough floor space for them all to lie down at the same time so they would sleep in shifts, four hours at a time. Maggie grew progressively weaker as the days passed, and often Jeena shortchanged herself in order to let her rest.

Sanitation was something their Coalition captors had given no thought to. Perhaps they had not expected so many prisoners, or perhaps they did not realize it would take the ancient freighter three times as long to make the trip as usual. Whatever the reason, they were forced to use two of the deeper pools of standing water in the corners as latrines—this for five thousand people.

Both of the sites were on the opposite wall from Jeena's corner. It was an arduous task, walking over the scattered bodies and invariably stepping on some, but for a while at least the offending odors were less pungent. As their stay in the hold lengthened, the stench permeated the room.

Food and water were lowered through a ceiling hatch twice a day. The food consisted of dehydrated military rations, much of it old and contaminated. The water was given out sparingly—one quart per person per day. In the suffocating heat of the hold, this was barely enough to keep one alive, and thirst was a constant companion.

The poor food and lack of adequate sanitation took its toll on the already weak and exhausted prisoners. Many had been injured during their capture, and like Maggie, none had received even cursory medical care. The first death occurred four days out.

They discovered the body at the morning sleep-shift change and screamed and pleaded at the guards lowering the morning food, but were ignored. They repeated their pleas that evening, but it was apparent their captors had no intention of removing the body. More dead were discovered the following day.

Jeena had never known such horror. A corner near her was chosen as a makeshift morgue; but as the days passed, the survivors became too weak and disheartened and soon the dead were left where they lay. The stench of the decomposing bodies was overwhelming—more than many could endure. There would be a cry in the dark, and suddenly, someone would be clawing at the bulkhead, screaming hysterically until they were finally subdued, or mercifully knocked unconscious by those near them.

Jeena knew it would not be long before she became one of them. Maggie had died two days earlier after days of gurgling in her own fluids, and Jeena had not slept in that time. The body of the girl lay at her feet, and she was too weak and too sick to move her. She was near collapse, her legs trembling with effort as she clung to the bracing beam, yet she would not lie down, could not lie down next to the bloated body. She knew that to do so would shatter her sanity, sending her screaming blindly into the night, and that she might never recover.

She had reached the end of her strength when the ship finally arrived at its destination. Her legs cramped painfully as she shuffled toward the light streaming in through the hatchway. Of the original five thousand captives, more than three hundred did not survive the trip. The survivors were assembled on the tarmac for their first view of Mizar 3.

It was a bleak, barren world. Huge ore smelters belched black smoke that blanketed the sky and fell back onto the planet in an oily rain. There was a foul, sulfurous odor in the air that burned the lungs. The sun was distant and dim, and the air was bitter cold, yet such was the unimaginable horror of the ship that many wept openly to be there.

They were forced to stand in the frigid cold for some time before transports finally arrived to take them to the prison camps. Some were taken to the nearby train stations to be shipped to distant colonies. Most would be used as slave labor in the many smelters and factories that dotted the planet. Mizar 3 was a lifeless rock, but it had a wealth of ore and mineral deposits the Coalition was exploiting to fuel its war machine.

The prisoners were segregated by sex, the captured women taken by open truck to the penal colony nearest the starport. The prison—or "camp," as the guards referred to it—was a collection of thick gray syncrete structures behind razor wire and plasma-field fences. They were divided into small groups and herded into the bunkers. Jeena was placed in a cell with six other female prisoners.

She was not there for long—the guards came for her within the hour for her "interrogation." For four days they questioned her, keeping her alone in a small, isolated cell they called the green room. By whatever euphemism they chose to call it, its purpose was clear—it was their torture chamber.

Interrogation methods had changed little over the centuries; they were not meant to retrieve information so much as to instill fear and intimidation. Jeena knew little that could be of use to the Coalition, something her captors were well aware of; but as a SAG officer she was a special prize, and they took to their work with unbridled enthusiasm.

She was stripped naked and searched thoroughly then forced to stand at attention during the long hours of tedious questioning. Weak from hunger and exhaustion, she inevitably collapsed, only to be dragged back to her feet. This was repeated again and again, until she could no longer support her own weight, even for few moments.

A chain descended from the ceiling, and her wrists were lashed together. She was hoisted up and suspended from the ceiling with her toes just touching the floor. The questioning began again, this time accompanied by blows to her back with a thin, flexible rod. The process continued day and night.

By the fourth day she was in a state of more or less steady unconsciousness, and her tormentors had determined they could get no more from her. Satisfied with their work, they dragged her back to her cell and threw her in with the other women.

She was the highest-ranking officer in the cell; and although the others tried to comfort her and dress her wounds, it was obvious they were looking to her for leadership. It was not a role Jeena was up to. She was in great pain, and only wanted to crawl into a corner and leave the decisions to someone else.

But there was no one else, so as the days passed she tried to calm and encourage the others as best she could, speaking more bravely and hopefully than she felt. They were left unmolested for a week.

Then, four guards entered the cell carrying small, dirty bedrolls, the guard-sergeant trailing them. They threw them onto the muddy floor, opening one and placing it in the center of the cell. There was no introduction, no warning. They grabbed the nearest woman, the most junior and youngest among them, and pulled her toward them. She was ordered to strip.

The frightened girl refused, instinctively wrapping her arms around herself. The sergeant held his rifle on the rest, smiling as the other men began tearing the uniform off the screaming and terrified girl. Although she knew it was futile, Jeena lunged at one of them.

When she came to she was on the mattress, bound hand and foot, and was being raped. The other women trembled and huddled in the corner, refusing to witness her debasement—all but the young girl. She was nowhere in sight.

When they finished with Jeena they left, but they also left her flight suit.

That night they could hear the pitiful cries of the girl. She had been chained naked outside in the bitter cold. Even in the cells the temperature dropped with the sun and those remaining had to huddle together for warmth. There was no warmth for the girl. It took three days for her to die of exposure. The fate was the same for any who resisted too much.

As the weeks and months went by those who remained were given better food and a small heater, but many still became ill. Eventually, the guards would come and take the sick woman away. Whether they were taken to work in the smelters or simply killed, Jeena never knew.

Finally, there was only her.

The soft, haunting sounds of "Venus" floated through the ship. Jeena wiped away a final tear that had run down her cheek. Sighing, she pushed the memories back and sank into a dark and fitful sleep.

Chapter 3

Tigra *n.* (The name is an apparent derivation of the species' zoological classification, *Tigerius rabidus araratus*, or as it was usually abbreviated in scientific papers, *tig. ra.*

Encyclopedic History of the Union, 22nd ed

The alarm buzzer sounded, startling Jeena awake. The phantom laughing faces dissolved into the shadows of the dayroom.

"It is 0600 Greenwich Mean Time, Captain," Vicki reported.

"Yes, all right. Thank you, Vicki," Jeena croaked. She sat up in the bunk and ran her hand through her hair, wincing. Her arms were stiff and sore, the left bicep swollen and almost black. The pain in her ribs was back again, and her eyes felt dry and swollen.

She limped to the head and sat on the latrine, catching sight of her reflection in the shiny metal wall. It was a face only vaguely familiar to her. The thick dark hair, full sensuous mouth and slightly olive complexion were only hinted at in the thin, emaciated image that stared back at her. Not even her eyes were the eyes she remembered—they were dull and lifeless. Not surprising, considering I have come from the planet of the dead, she thought. Turning away from the reflection, she finished her toilet and went back to the dayroom.

Once the ship had safely made the jump into hyperspace, she had torn off her soiled and bloody flight suit and thrown it on the floor. It lay there still, a small red puddle beneath it. She would not put the filthy thing back on now.

Searching through the pilot's private locker, she found some over-large T-shirts, the collars stenciled with *Capt. J.C. McCullough.* Throwing on one of these and her prison sandals, she went back to the cockpit.

The sensors still showed no activity. *Good. Maybe they think the ship was destroyed in the raid.* Even if they suspected she had managed to escape, there was little chance of them looking for her in this isolated sector—thanks to the CCOMS modifications of Capt. J.C. McCullough.

Tripping over a mess pack, she rummaged through it and found a food cylinder. After checking its label she tore off the lid, setting off a chemical reaction that soon had the contents steaming. Armed with the hot coffee, she sat back in the conn chair and had Vicki give her a short tutorial on the planet on which she was stranded.

Ararat was the second of four planets orbiting Arcturus, a Sol-standard star in the Aleph-prime sector—a sector, Jeena noted grimly, that had recently fallen under Coalition control. Of the remaining planets, the first was a barren moon-sized world in a close solar orbit and the last two were gas giants. The third planet, Leviathan, was enormous, even by the standards of these huge worlds—the largest planetary body ever discovered. In times of conjunction these behemoths were capable of playing havoc with Ararat's geo-activity but luckily this occurred only every few millennia.

Discovered slightly more than two hundred and fifty years earlier, at the beginning of an era in human exploration known as the Second Migration, Ararat was a beautiful if somewhat isolated world. Four-fifths the size of Earth, it had a single continental land mass and several oceanic islands. It hosted a breathable atmosphere and a variety of plant and animal life.

The official Five-Year Survey was completed in 2351, with no sign of either harmful microorganisms or sentient life; and the world was sanctioned for colonization by CAIO, the Council for Alien Immigration and Occupation, four years later. It was given a zed-tech designation.

Jeena interrupted the tutorial.

"Zed-tech? I thought you said this world had abundant energy stores?"

"That is affirmative."

She frowned. A zed-tech designation quarantined a planet from all advanced technology, allowing only agrarian colonies. The Union seldom used it, except in cases where the planet was deemed too poor in resources to support large populations or industry. Ararat certainly didn't appear to qualify.

"Your information must be incorrect."

There was only a slight pause.

"The designation does not correspond to usual Union standards; however, there may have been extenuating circumstances."

"I'm listening."

"I have several reports catalogued during this time period of a schism within CAIO concerning Ararat's eventual designation. There were rumors of external pressure brought on individual members of the CAIO directorate. Accusations of blackmail were apparently voiced. It is possible CAIO was compromised concerning Ararat."

"Compromised? By whom, and for what reason?"

"I do not have enough information to formulate an answer."

Jeena considered the possibility. CAIO directors were elected for life in an effort to immunize them from just this sort of political pressure. They were more powerful in many ways than even the members of the Supreme Union Court, with whom they shared the benefits of lifetime commissions. It was hard to imagine what pressure could be brought to bear on any seated director, let alone a majority, that could influence a vote on tech designation. And why Ararat?

Still, there was no denying the oddity of it. A world with geo as well as chemical energy stores left to a bunch of farmers? Of course, this Vicki was Coalition-programmed so this could all be nothing more than propaganda.

Jeena gave a mental shrug. However it came about, it would be an unlooked-for blessing. A zed world would hold little interest for the technology-obsessed Coalition, and its isolation would make it impractical even as a military outpost.

"You mentioned energy stores. What about mineral deposits?" She wanted to make sure there was nothing of value to lure the Coalition.

"Information concerning Ararat's internal makeup is incomplete."

"Why?"

"Ararat's magnetic field prevented detailed analysis at the time of the Five-Year Survey."

"Explain."

"Ararat's magnetic field is highly unstable and in a constant flux state, which interferes with long distance metallurgic detection. The technology did not exist at the time of the Five-Year Survey to overcome this interference."

"All right. What about people? Is the planet colonized?"

Two colonies had been given charter before the outbreak of the Galactic Civil War, both of which were followers of primitivism—odd back-to-nature movements that occasionally swept through mankind. There had been little contact with the Union by either even before the war; the colonists paid their taxes as required and on time, and for that they were pretty much left alone. Since the war began there had been no contact at all.

Vicki projected a map of the last known population centers for both colonies, but as these were almost a century old, they were probably useless. Most agrarian societies lasted no more than a few generations even with continued support from the Union—the dream of a simpler life that drove the colonists to the edges of civilization was seldom passed on to their children. With no contact in more than ninety years, it was doubtful either colony had survived.

Vicki began an overview of their societies, but Jeena cut her off and fast-forwarded to flora and fauna.

Animal life was abundant on Ararat and included several large carnivores, the most fearsome of which was reported to be the large cat-like animals the locals referred to as tigras. The holo-image Vicki projected showed a large cat much like an earth tiger but without the stripes. It had a beautiful golden-yellow coat, its eyes as golden as its fur. Interestingly, its fangs were retractable and projected only during times of stress or when it was bringing down prey. It was a truly gorgeous animal, and apparently quite dangerous, although one of the colonies had reported the species was nearing extinction.

Intrigued, she had Vicki run a short video on the animal. As the clip began, the tigra was circling a large bear-like animal the computer identified as an usk. It seemed to Jeena the cat had picked the wrong fight—the usk was huge, towering over its smaller antagonist and possessing claws she conservatively estimated at nine inches.

She watched as the tigra crept closer, trying to get inside, only to be driven back by the bigger animal's greater reach. After several unsuccessful attempts, the tigra reared up on its hind legs. Where this would have proved unsteady and awkward for an Earth cat, the tigra looked strangely stable in this position.

Then it faltered. The usk, sensing the feline's mistake, drove in for the kill. At that instant, the tigra sprang, sweeping its right foreleg to the left, straight at the big animal's neck. Five razor-sharp claws found their mark, tearing into the usk's throat. Blood flew. The holo ended with the great ursine crashing to the ground.

Jeena watched the clip again—there had been something not quite right about the tigra's actions. As the scene neared the attack, she had Vicki slow the speed two-thirds.

The cat was in its strange upright position. The usk's right arm muscles tensed to strike. The tigra swayed to the right.

There!

She backed it up a little and played it again, watching intently. She was an elite combat soldier, academy-trained and an expert in hand-to-hand combat. There had been no mistake. The tigra hadn't faltered. It had deliberately feinted to one side to pull the usk's blow wide, opening it up. The cat had set all its weight on its left hind leg. As soon as it had created the opening, it leapt straight at the throat.

She let the clip run out. No wonder the colonists feared this animal—it fought with the guile of a man and the speed of a coiled snake. She'd remember to give it a wide berth if she ever had the misfortune of meeting one.

Vicki continued her discussion of Ararat's animal life, but Jeena stopped the lecture. She could stay here for weeks studying the planet, but to what end? With her ship out of commission this was going to be her home for a while— at least until she could figure out how to contact the Union forces. This ship had no direct subspace link to Union Command, and her general access codes were more than six months old and therefore useless. The planet had passed the Five-Year Survey; it had to at least be livable.

She swallowed the last of the coffee and stood, testing her legs. It would take months of rehabilitation to fully recover from her imprisonment, but it was time to look around. Opening the weapons cabinet, she withdrew an eight-gauge shotgun and slung it over her shoulder. She considered taking the .44-caliber handgun but decided against it. If there was anything out there the shotgun couldn't handle, the pistol wasn't going to help.

These were the standard weapons for most transport vehicles and ground troops on both sides of the war. Laser and plasma hand weapons had been available for many years; but they were expensive and needed regular high-tech maintenance, and were generally assigned only to personnel on the larger battleships and carriers. Projectile weapons were dependable, easy to use and repair, and killed just as readily as lasers. They were also cheap to produce— an advantage not overlooked in a war that had spanned a century.

Armed with the shotgun, Jeena opened the ship's outer hatch. There was a rush of escaping air and plumes of white mist as the cabin pressure equilibrated with the planet's atmosphere. Squinting in the brightness, she looked out on Ararat.

The sun that greeted her was low on the horizon—it was still morning on the planet. The area immediately surrounding her ship was scrub—mainly dirt and twiggy bushes—that became an expanse of grass a hundred yards distant. The knee-high grass shifted softly in the warm breeze, a sea of yellow extending to the distant pale mountains to the north.

To the west lay a vast desert, the sands rolling in undulating hills toward the horizon. The sky above her was less blue than she remembered on Earth, yet still imbued with that subtle aqua hue so intimately associated with all habitable worlds that it took an effort of will just to see it. A flock of alien birds, their forms unclear in the hazy sky, flew silently above her, heading off to the north.

Jeena observed that the sky, like the horizon, seemed closer than they would have appeared on Earth—a visual confirmation that the planet was, indeed, smaller. Impulsively, she jumped from the ship, leaping over the steps and landing lightly on the ground. She felt a stab of pain shoot through her body. That was stupid, she thought, but the gravity was weaker.

Standing on the soft yellow soil, she scanned the immediate area and breathed in the air of this new planet. The act made her cough and wince. There were no animals to be seen, but the air was heavy with the rich odors of life. The sweet scent of flowers mingled with the muskier, acrid smell of animals in a combination that was almost nauseating to someone used to filtered air and sterile environments.

And yet...there was something oddly familiar about it, a sense of déjà vu that brought her back to the Home, and the stables she had known as a child. It was not an unpleasant feeling, but she did not have time to dwell on it and turned her attention back to her ship.

It had the general shape of a wedge, with the tram the forward tip. Behind it, the huge engines and Drive extended two hundred feet and rose steadily to a height of forty feet at the engine exhausts. The Earth weight of the transport was fifty thousand tons, forty-five thousand of which was the singularity cell—a miniscule ball of incomprehensively dense matter the size of a grain of sand buried within the Drive. It was the manipulation of the singularity that produced the "warp" in the space-time continuum that made interstellar travel possible.

The hull of the vessel was charred black and steaming, the heat of re-entry still radiating from it. The nose of the tram was buried in the ground, the windshield covered by a thick layer of dirt. There was no sign of fore or aft landing gear. The immense engines and Drive lay in a deep furrow that extended half a mile behind.

The hull itself appeared intact, and there was little other external damage that she could see. Reaching the rear of the ship, she gingerly opened a small panel, burning her fingers slightly in the process. Behind the panel was an array of instrument readouts. Jeena studied them closely. The engines and Drive were still intact—good. Not that she had any hope of powering them up again, but she didn't need a massive radiation leak just now.

Satisfied with the condition of the ship, she once again scanned the horizon for several minutes. The feeling of déjà vu was still there, as was the unsettling sense of being watched. She saw no movement, however, and after several minutes she was convinced there was no immediate danger.

Setting aside the weapon, she began to unload the cargo hold. She had examined its contents briefly while in flight, entering through the cockpit hatch, and knew the storage area was almost full. Using the levitation jack in the hold, she removed all the crates and containers, taking inventory.

There were twenty cases of cigars, thirty-five cases of Polarian whiskey, fifty crates of assorted gourmet foods, a case of old binoculars and ancient communicators and ten crates of various junk—pots, pans, hand tools and costume jewelry.

When she had removed everything she noticed a panel in the far wall that had torn lose during the crash. Prying it away, she discovered a container hidden in the space and carried it out into the light. The contents were wrapped in a layer of oiled rags. Jeena gasped at what lay underneath. It was a MAAD.

She lifted the weapon from its container, feeling its balanced weight in her hands. MAAD—for Mobile Attack And Destroy—was the most sophisticated and destructive handheld weapon ever developed. Essentially an electromagnetic pulse generator, it had been recently invented by Union scientists—a weapon the Coalition was not supposed to have. She had never seen one this close, but there was no mistaking it.

It had an over/under design, the upper part resembling a typical rifle barrel. She pulled out the clip and looked inside. There were thousands of small, hardened pellets aligned in neat rows. She knew the pellets were composed of ferrion, a highly charged metal. They were propelled through the barrel by the force of a traveling electromagnetic wave. Since the EM wave moved at the speed of light, it was able to accelerate the projectiles to enormous velocities. Ferrion had the added property of expanding on impact, making the weapon both incredibly accurate and brutally effective.

It was what lay below the rifle, however, that gave the weapon its true destructive force.

Jeena flipped it over and patted the hollow tube below the barrel. Called a sonic concussion cannon, it measured eight centimeters in diameter and thirty centimeters in length. A slight smile curved her lips. Twenty thousand ferrion bullets spitting out at three thousand rounds a minute could decimate an army, but the real power of the MAAD lay in that hollow tube.

Unlike the pulse rifle, the tube held no projectiles. The air within was charged, initiating a massive power surge. Once primed, this enormous store of energy was released down the length of the tube as a powerful electromagnetic pulse. The pulse carried the now-ionized air along with it, compressing and accelerating the molecules in the process. In the instant it took the air to reach the end of the tube, it obtained a velocity just below that of light, and the molecules reached a density beyond anything short of a neutron star.

This rapidly moving mass of unimaginably compressed air struck the normally dense air before it with the force of a small nuclear weapon, sending a concussion wave before it as an ever-expanding cone of pressure at relativistic speeds. Anything unlucky enough to be in front of it when it fired did not so much blow apart as vaporize.

Jeena shook her head in amazement. The MAAD was the most closely guarded weapon in the Union arsenal. Her own unit hadn't even been issued them, and yet here was one in the cargo hold of an old Coalition supply ship. Whoever he was, this smuggler was good.

Among the rest of the contraband, she had discovered a good-sized tent, and decided her first task would be to erect it. Using the detailed and well-diagramed military instructions that came with it, she managed, in the space of two hours, to build a precariously leaning wall of black cloth. Finally, tossing away the instructions and putting it up the way that looked right, she had an airy and stable tent in twenty minutes.

Standing before it she realized some things never changed. The military could build the most sophisticated and durable machines ever made then couldn't find one son of a bitch in the army able to write a readable manual on it.

She went back inside and powered down all unnecessary systems—she wanted to conserve as much battery life as possible for communications, and for Vicki. The computer's memory stores could prove invaluable. From the cargo hold she built a stores pile near the tent of canned food, liquor and cigars. The rest she put back into the hold and sealed it up. By the time she was finished, the sun was high and the day had turned hot and steamy.

Sitting on an empty crate, Jeena removed her sweat-drenched T-shirt and wrung it out, using it to wipe the dirt from her face. She tossed it on the tent to dry and lit a cigar, turning it over in her fingers and considering her next course of action.

Ararat was in Coalition-controlled space, and although long-range sensors were still showing no activity in the area, she was not going to risk sending out a distress signal just yet—not with a hospitable planet to rest on for a while.

Not with the memory of the Mizar 3 still fresh in her mind.

She would not risk being taken prisoner again. No, that was not quite right. *I will never be taken prisoner again—ever. I will die first.*

Pushing the thought away, she concentrated on the terrain before her. According to the map Vicki had provided, there was a stream about one mile to the north. She'd soon need a source of fresh water, so this seemed like a logical place to begin her recon of the planet. Hopping off the crate, the cigar between her teeth, she reached for the shotgun.

There was a rustling sound behind her, and she turned her head slowly, the cigar smoke curling up into her eyes. A lurking shape crouched in the shadow of the ship's wing. Two golden circles reflected light back at her.

Jeena glanced at the gun, trying not to move as beads of sweat appeared on her brow. She looked back at the animal—just as it sprang.

Leaping for the weapon, she grabbed it and rolled in a single fluid motion, firing blindly into the onrushing shadow. A huge weight slammed into her, knocking her down and pinning her. Cursing, she clawed at the animal, fighting out from under it. Her body was covered in blood as she finally pushed it off and struggled to her feet, panting hard and shaking.

Holding her ribs in pain, she examined the dead animal at her feet.

The tigra looked just like the one in the holo—or would have if not for the gaping hole running through its chest. The luxurious coat was a radiant yellow, slowly fading to snow-white on its paws. It was slightly smaller than an Earth tiger but more heavily muscled. The toes were different as well, longer and thinner. Delicate, she might have called them, if not for the five-inch claws at their tips.

She knelt and ran her hand through the fur. It was as soft as the Chimenian mink she had once felt on Tycho, but up close, she saw the animal was not as healthy as it first appeared. The fur had scattered bare spots, and the skin was loose over its bones. It was sick, starving probably, which could explain why it was not as silent as it might have been in its attack.

Jeena kept a wary eye out for others but neither saw nor heard anything else, and remembered Vicki mentioning something about them being solitary hunters. Still shaking, she picked up the burning cigar and brushed it off before sticking it back between her teeth. Taking one last look at the animal, she limped painfully back toward the tent. The recon could wait. It was time to open the liquor.

Chapter 4

"And they shall say, This land that was desolate is become like the garden of Eden; and the waste and desolate and ruined cities are become fenced, and are inhabited."

>Ezekiel 36:35
>*Arian Christian Bible*

JEENA AWOKE THE NEXT MORNING KICKING OUT AT DARK DREAMS. SHE OPENED HER EYES to the sun blazing through the flap of the tent, the whiskey bottle empty on the ground.

She groaned. She was nauseous, and her tongue felt thick and sticky. Her chest and arms were caked in dried blood. Through the tent flap she could see the carcass of the tigra, a swarm of flies buzzing around it.

She felt her bile rise and turned away, picking up a canteen of water. She gulped it down and felt better. Rummaging through the tent, she found a carbo-bar and chewed it slowly, considering the dead animal outside her door.

It'll take a good-size hole, she thought miserably, but the flies were getting thick. Sighing, her stomach still queasy, she went outside, making a mental note to never again kill anything bigger than a shovelhead near her tent.

She dug the hole under the ship's wing then slowly and painfully dragged the corpse to it and dumped it in. It was late afternoon by the time she threw the last shovel-full of dirt over the grave, and her hangover had dissolved into a minor headache. She lit another cigar and wiped herself down with the T-shirt—she had stopped wearing it, as it had no practical use and only became wet and heavy with sweat.

After a lunch of canned meat and water, she grabbed some synlamps and motion detectors from the ship and set up a perimeter—she wanted no more uninvited guests dropping by, particularly at night. Once the area was secured, she re-armed and headed north toward the stream, taking along a canteen equipped with a sterilization unit.

She found it in short order, just as shown on the map, and silently thanked AL for his good choice in picking this place to ditch. Walking upstream, she came to an abrupt rise in the terrain that resulted in a small waterfall. Placing her weapon carefully on the bank she ran under it, washing the dried blood and grime from her body and enjoying the feel of the cool water cascading over her. Afterward, she lay on the grass near the bank, letting the hot sun dry her and feeling clean in a way she had not felt in a long time. She closed her eyes and listened to the gurgling stream as it flowed by...

SHE YAWNED AND OPENED HER EYES THEN BOLTED UPRIGHT. SHE HAD FALLEN ASLEEP! THE sun was low and setting fast. Grabbing her weapon and the now-filled canteen, she hurried back to her camp, cursing herself the entire way.

It was fully nightfall when she finally arrived back at camp, triggering the perimeter lights as she did. *Well, at least they work,* she thought. She searched the area carefully, assuring herself it was unmolested, then set about building a fire. She had dug a shallow pit earlier in the day and now filled it with kindling and dead wood she found lying around. Soon, she had a warm blaze and, feeling more secure, killed the lamps.

It was a warm, clear night, with the sky an explosion of stars and wispy streaks of color. Although Vicki had mentioned Ararat's aurora in her summary of the planet's characteristics, Jeena was amazed at the brilliance and rapidly changing patterns of the nocturnal lightshow. All those she had seen on other worlds, including Earth's, paled in comparison. Keeping the shotgun close, she lay back near the fire, its heat warming her body, and stared out at the stars and lights as she examined her situation.

Through fate or dumb luck, she had escaped a hellish prison only to end up marooned on a distant and virtually uninhabited planet—a planet that, with the exception of the tigra, was beginning to resemble a Garden of Eden. The thought made her smile. *Does that make me Eve?* She looked down at her naked body. *I certainly have the right wardrobe for the part. Come to think of it, an apple would taste pretty good right now.*

She didn't find any apples among the smuggler's foodstuffs, but there were tins of sardines and Tychorian truffles that she placed on crackers and ate with gusto. She had tossed the tins aside and was just picking up a fiery brand to light a cigar when the perimeter lights suddenly burst on.

Dropping the stick, Jeena grabbed the shotgun, pumping the slide in the same motion. Moving with her back to the fire, she scanned the circle of light, peering into the darkness beyond. She could feel her heart pounding as she waited and listened.

There was a faint sound to her right, and she whirled toward it, aiming the gun into the shadows. She could make out two golden rings, glowing from just beyond the reach of the firelight. Her finger tensed around the trigger as something stepped out from the darkness.

Jeena lowered the weapon. Before her stood a tiny tigra cub, blinking in the harsh artificial light. She stood unmoving, blinking back at the animal, alert for any sign of another tigra. Surely, the cub's mother must be near. Then she recalled the mound beneath the ship's wing, and realized that this cub's mother would never return.

Well, that wasn't her fault. The tigra had attacked her, and she had only been defending herself. Besides, it had been half-dead anyway. Another week, two at the most, and she would have likely died, and the cub right behind her.

She raised the weapon again. It would be the merciful thing to do.

"Sorry, cat, but it was me or her. Nothing personal."

The tigra cocked its head curiously at the sound of her voice.

"I can't have you wandering around here tripping my alarm at all hours and maybe attracting other predators. You won't last long without momma anyway. It stinks, I know, but that's life."

She aimed carefully, not wanting the animal to suffer. A moment later she had still not fired, and found the gun was shaking in her hands. Angrily, she pulled the weapon from her shoulder and wiped the sweat that had appeared on her brow. *What the hell is wrong with you? How many thousands have you killed, men and women? It's just an animal. Pull yourself together and do what you have to do.*

Raising the weapon again she held the cub in her sights for another long minute before finally falling to her knees and vomiting hard and loud onto the dark sandy ground.

She wiped her mouth with the back of her hand. Battle sickness. She had heard of soldiers who, after years of bloody fighting, had suddenly awoken one day to find they could no longer kill. As conscription did not allow for psychological leave, it was most often a fatal disease.

The cub stood unmoving, and apparently unconcerned.

"So, what the hell am I supposed to do? I can't have you wandering around," she said, spitting the taste of bile from her mouth.

The cub made no reply.

"Right. And I guess you're just going to stand there till you get something to eat, huh?"

Keeping her eye on it, she groped behind her until she fumbled on a half-empty sardine tin. She set it in front of her.

"Is this what you smelled? Yeah, maybe you just want a little snack before you go," she said hopefully.

The cub sniffed the air and pricked up its ears. It hesitated, looking between Jeena and the food, as if debating with itself. Hunger won out, and it strode briskly and fearlessly toward the all-too-tempting food, bouncing slightly as it did. It sat in front of the tin and, taking one last look at her, began eating the remaining sardines in earnest.

Jeena found the cigar she had dropped and lit it. She sat back on her haunches and watched the cub eat, blowing smoke rings and considering what to do. The dead animal buried behind the tent was obviously this one's mother, probably just protecting her young, she thought with a pang of remorse. Left on its own, the cub would certainly die within a few days.

So?

So, you can't even kill it cleanly. You think you can just sit back and watch it die slowly of starvation while you eat?

But I can't keep feeding it. This is no pet. It's a wild animal and very dangerous.

The cub, finished with its meal, began to carefully lick its paws.

It doesn't look dangerous.

Don't be a fool! It's still a baby. When this thing grows up it will be as lethal as its mommy.

That's a long ways off. Besides, it will probably run away long before that.

Yeah, right.

Jeena shook her head, clearing the debate from her mind. She couldn't kill it or let it die of starvation. That left caring for it as the only option.

The decision made, she stood and tossed the cigar into the dying fire. She was tired, and it was late. She made her way to the tent. Maybe the thing really would be gone by morning.

Yeah, right.

At the tent flap she turned to check on the animal—and found it right at her feet.

"No, no. Go back. Shoo."

She waved her hands, feeling slightly foolish. The cat stood its ground. She pushed it away gently with her foot, but it sprang back. Since the cub seemed unmoved by her verbal dismissal, she picked him up and carried him back to the slowly fading fire.

"Stay," she said, for no reason she could think of, and raced back to the tent. At the doorway she wheeled around...and almost stepped on him in the process

"Fast little bugger, aren't you? All right, stay here if you want, but the fire would have been warmer."

She ducked into the tent and zipped up the flap. She lay down heavily on the cot and drew a light blanket over herself. Jeena Garza, lion tamer, she thought, just before falling into a deep sleep.

No! Please, no, not the baby!

Jeena awoke with her heart pounding in fear—fear that did not abate when she realized she had been dreaming. She could still hear the baby crying. She staggered to her feet, her body shaking. The cries were coming from just outside the tent, loud and incessant. She covered her ears with her hands. *No! Don't do this! She isn't there. She's dead, dammit. She's dead, and you can't bring her back.*

But the wailing did not stop.

Trembling, she stumbled to the tent flap and threw it open, fully prepared to see nothing but the empty air. Instead, she found the tigra cub, exactly where she had left it. Emanating from the tiny ball of fur was a high-pitched, shrieking wail. The sound resembled nothing like the whine of an Earth cat but was eerily reminiscent of the screaming cries of a human baby. As if to emphasize this point, a stream of tears ran down its furry face.

Jeena knelt down and stared open-mouthed at the cub. Fear was quickly replaced by incredulousness. *This is ridiculous. Cats don't cry—do they?* She was fairly certain they didn't. And she was sure they didn't shed tears. At least, she didn't think they did. Anyway, this definitely did not look right.

She picked up the cub and held it at arm's length, as if not trusting the strangeness of the animal. Oblivious as to whether it was behaving correctly or not, the cat continued to wail. She winced—the sound was piercing.

Still wary, but wanting to quiet the animal, she brought it close to her and gently stroked its back. There was no effect for some time, but eventually the crying decreased in both volume and intensity until it was replaced by quiet sniffling. Having a now-quiet tigra cub and wishing to keep it that way, she eased them both onto her cot, lying down with the cub next to her. It immediately snuggled up to her and closed its eyes, content and unconcerned.

Just before dozing off herself, Jeena opened one eye and peered at the animal.

"Piss the bed," she warned, "and you die."

THE NOISE, WHICH HAD EARLIER MADE A HAIRLINE CRACK IN JEENA'S CONSCIOUSNESS, NOW shattered it completely. With a start, she opened her eyes to see the cub digging itself out of a fallen pile of food cans.

"Making yourself at home?" she asked.

The cub stopped trying to extricate itself long enough to cock its head at her, then resumed.

"Fetch me the canteen," she mumbled.

Finally extracting itself from the pile, the cub loped over to the cot and looked up at her.

"Oh, well, it was worth a try. What were you looking for? Hungry again?"

The cat licked at the air.

"I'll take that as a yes. But what do you say we take a morning pee first? I'm guessing you have to, and I know I do."

Together, they strode up to the pit latrine she had dug a little way from the camp up in the high grass. There was a small wooden seat she had built from a crate, and she sat down on it. The tigra cub, watching her actions, seemed to grasp the purpose of this trip and lifted his leg.

"Ah, so you're a male. I was wondering about that."

Their morning toilet complete, they walked briskly back to camp.

"Hey," she said suddenly to the trotting cub beside her, "I thought only dogs raised their leg?"

They spent their first day together investigating some fruit trees Jeena had noticed growing near the riverbank. The trees resembled baobabs and bore fruit with a burnt-orange rind. Splitting open the husk with her thumb, she found a soft light-pink pulp with a scent and flavor that reminded her of banana. She gathered as many as she could and stuffed them into an old duffel bag she had found in the pilot's locker.

Heading on to the waterfall, she tossed the duffel on the riverbank and went in for a dip. The cub declined an invitation to join her, content to remain on the bank and guard the fruit.

It was while standing under the cascading water that Jeena noticed the red clay along the wall of the rise. She pried a handful away. It was heavy and thick, and molded well in her hands. She washed it off from her fingers and jumped out of the stream, picking up the fruit and heading back to camp, tigra in tow.

The fire pit had some flaws that had become apparent the first night. For one, it was too shallow, and sparks tended to fly all around. Also, the embers mixed with the loose, sandy dirt, making it difficult to clean. The clay could be the answer if she could make them into bricks.

Taking the levitation jack from the hold, she slid it under a small empty crate and pulled it to the waterfall. There she filled it with the soft clay and hauled it back, with the cub managing to get underfoot at every opportunity. He became curious at the sight of the jack floating effortlessly a few inches above the ground and made the mistake of trying to crawl under it. He let out a yelp as the reverse gravitational field kicked him several feet into the air. She checked him out—he seemed only startled, but he had learned his lesson and never again got near the jack.

Back at the camp she formed the clay into large, rectangular bricks, setting them in the hot sun to bake. Once dry she set them in the pit, starting in the center and spiraling out. The fire, she knew, would harden them even more.

Having clay left over, she tried her hand at pottery. Some hours later she had produced several less-than-round bowls and two precariously leaning drinking cups. Playing with the clay brought back an old childhood memory. She rolled out an oval-shaped piece of clay and flattened it, then pressed her palm into it, leaving an imprint. She stared at the cub for a moment before lifting him up and pressing his paw into the center of her palm print. The cub looked confused, but Jeena was pleased, and set the whole thing aside for firing later.

That night, she placed the pottery in the mound of ashes collecting below the flames; she kept the fire burning long into the night. The next morning she pulled the pieces from the still-smoldering embers. The method was crude, but it worked well enough. The hand-and-paw plaque she hung up as an ornament in the tent.

For the next several weeks Jeena spent her time improving the campsite and exploring the immediate area. She crafted a crude table and chair from discarded crates, formed a ring of large logs around the fire pit to sit on, filled a barrel from the hold with fresh water from the stream and created an awning over the tent door using a discarded piece of tarp.

She did a reconnaissance of the surrounding land for ten miles in each direction, recording her findings. There were few surprises. Vegetation consisted mainly of grasses and scrawny bushes. There were few true trees, and only those by the river bore fruit. There was ample animal life, from insects and birds to large herbivores, like the swift, deer-like creatures Vicki had identified as wolla. She also ran into a few usk foraging for game in the high grass, but they seemed to ignore her and she returned the favor.

In none of her travels did Jeena see any sign of other tigras. Although she knew they were solitary animals, she had half-expected to at least see some signs of their presence in the large area she had covered, and was surprised by their absence. Surely, the cub and his mother were not the only ones of their kind in all this savanna. The cub's presence alone implied at least one adult male of the species.

During all these activities, the cub was her constant companion. She awoke each morning unsure as to whether he would still be there, and lately found herself hoping he would be. She kept up a more-or-less constant one-sided conversation with him, out of a general human habit of speaking to pets as well as a basic need to communicate. He never spoke back, but then, he never argued, either—a fair trade-off as far as she was concerned.

Actually, he's probably the best company I could have right now, she realized. After the trauma of the prison, she needed time alone but not total isolation. To do that was to risk madness. Jeena knew that pets had played a part in psychotherapy for centuries, helping to heal invisible wounds by the simple act of their presence. The tigra had that effect on her, and although she loathed the idea that he had gained the status of "pet," there was no denying that, despite her best efforts, she was growing attached to him.

Chapter 5

"He who is unable to live in society, or who has no need because he is sufficient for himself, must be either a beast or a god."

        Aristotle, Ancient Earth Philosopher
        Encyclopedic History of the Union, 22nd ed.

JEENA STEPPED OUT OF THE SHOWER, DRYING HERSELF AND HUMMING ALONG TO STRAUSS'S "Tales from the Vienna Wood." To conserve ship's power, she allowed herself only one hot shower a week, at other times using the waterfall at the stream. As she dried, she examined her body in the mirror.

The exercise program she had initiated two months ago was starting to show results. Although she was still thin, her shape was returning. Her hips were no longer just bones draped with skin but now curved in a graceful line to her legs. These, too, had filled out and were now sleek and strong. Even her breasts had returned to their normal size. She cupped them in her hands.

"Welcome back, girls," she said to her reflection.

The cub stood looking at her curiously.

"Hey, these babies picked up their fair share of men in their day. Women, too, come to think of it."

The cub appeared unimpressed.

"Ah, what would you know?" She pulled her foot up to her buttocks and arched her back, stretching. "How 'bout going for a run, fur-butt?"

In answer, the cub began to bounce and prance around. Running was part of her daily regime, and he loved to accompany her. In Ararat's lighter gravity Jeena could run faster than she ever had on Earth, but she was still no match for him—even at his young age he had a speed she could scarcely believe.

She started off to the east along a ten-mile trail she had laid out a few weeks before, the cub running easily beside her. She loved this time of day, when it was warm but not yet hot and the air smelled clean and new, as though she was the first living thing to breathe it. She felt good today. Her body was responding to the workouts, and she reveled in the sensation of strength in her legs as they propelled her along. She ran quietly, listening to the sounds of the planet around her.

Having spent most of her life on the noisy high-tech worlds of the Union, she had at first thought Ararat impossibly quiet and still. As the months passed, she discovered her hearing had sharpened, and found that the planet actually hosted a chorus of life. Throwing her head back as she ran, she listened for the individual voices in that chorus.

There was the sound of rustling grass near her feet. Strange, alien birds cried faintly above her. Skittish grazing animals stomped and snorted as she ran by, sometimes bolting and triggering an entire herd to thunder across the savanna.

She had learned to distinguish those sounds and more: the light patter of the cub's paws as he ran beside her; small herbivores darting unseen in the tall grass; an occasional roll of distant thunder. And the smells. Both animal and vegetal, they were thick and heavy in the air. Where they had once seemed overpowering, they were now familiar and reassuring.

They made their way to the end of the trail, and Jeena paused for a moment to rest, sitting on a fallen tree trunk. The cub romped around her, full of energy and wanting to play. To Jeena's mind he behaved more like an Earth dog than a cat, but then, she had little real experience with either.

She picked up a stick and threw it down the path. The cub ran eagerly after it, grasping it in his jaws and bringing it back to her proudly. She threw it again, and this time it landed in the tall grass. The cub stood at the edge of the trail, looking into the dense blades and trying to locate the wayward stick.

Jeena knew from past experience that he hated going into the grass. It was thick and stiff, and he was too small to see over it. This caused him to become disorientated and occasionally lost, something that had happened to him on more than one occasion. Once she had heard him crying and went looking for him, eventually finding him shaken and scared in a thick patch near the latrine. He seldom now went into the grass without her there beside him.

This time he appeared to have made up his mind to face his fear and took a step forward in search of the stick. A moment later he jumped back onto the trail.

A kroll followed him.

Jeena froze. One of the few life forms on Ararat that Vicki had identified as poisonous, the kroll resembled a thick-armored lizard with powerful front and rear limbs ending in claws. It was not much smaller in size than the cub. The reptile faced the tigra, hissing and ready for a fight.

The cub had initially jumped back in surprise, but now he approached the lizard warily, his fangs and claws projecting. Jeena looked quickly for something to throw at the kroll. If she could distract it maybe the cub had a chance to escape—she did not see how he could survive a fight with this deadly foe.

She had picked up a stone and was prepared to hurl it when the kroll struck, its venom-dripping fangs aimed for the cub's face. In a movement too fast for Jeena to see clearly, the cub dodged the blow, twisting his body and bringing his jaws down on the lizard's head. The reptile tore at the air with its claws, slashing wildly and trying to reach the cub, but the cat was too quick. His movements were a blur as he jumped and spun, always keeping his body just out of reach of the kroll's claws, its head held firmly in his jaws.

Finally, the kroll went limp, and the cub halted his acrobatic display. Trotting proudly, he brought the dead lizard to Jeena, laying it at her feet.

She looked at the cub with renewed wonder—it was an awesome display of fighting ability in an animal so young. Gently picking him up, she examined him closely. He squirmed in her lap as she lifted his upper lip.

The fangs lay just inside his cheek, more lateral than the other teeth and folded back on a muscular hinge. She touched the tip of one with her finger and was rewarded with a pinprick. Like his retractable claws, they had snapped into position automatically, and were already returning back to their resting position.

Jeena put the cub back down. *This animal is not a pet*, she reminded herself again. *Take him out somewhere and let him go before he becomes too dangerous. He is strong enough now to care for himself.*

She stood and stretched then started back toward her camp, running at a leisurely pace, the cub trotting happily beside her. *It's time to let him go. Deal with it.*

But she did not deal with it. The months turned into more months, and still the cub showed no sign of wanting to leave. He even continued to sleep with her in the tent, although on a mat on the floor now he had grown too large to comfortably share the cot.

She had puzzled initially over what to feed him before finding the powdered milk in the ship's galley. Re-hydrated and used sparingly, there was enough to give him a milk meal every day for the first month or so. This was in addition to the sardines, herring and other canned fish she found in the ship's stores. She had no idea if this was a good diet for a tigra or not, but she remembered something about Earth cats liking fish and milk, and besides, he was getting bigger and he looked healthy.

Time passed, yet Jeena made no attempt to verify the existence of the colonies. She justified this by reminding herself that this sector of space was in Coalition hands, and that there was a good chance of one or both colonies—assuming they had managed to survive—being aligned with them.

Yet she knew this was simply an excuse. The real reason she didn't search out the colonies was that she didn't want to find them. Not now, not yet.

Linking up with the colonists might provide her with a way of contacting the Union, but it would also mean reassignment to her unit. She wasn't ready for that. If her time on Ararat had showed her anything, it was that she was not the same woman she had once been. Mizar 3 had broken her.

She remembered little of the last few months of her confinement and realized now that she had slipped into madness. The Union raid that gave her the opportunity of escape had jolted her back to reason, but the torture and degradation had taken the once-cocky soldier and twisted her, until everything inside her was sick and dying. Whatever else she might be, Jeena Garza was no longer a warrior. It was a sobering realization, since war was the only life she had ever known.

She had spent her youth in a group home run by the Arian Christians. When she was old enough to understand, the sisters at the orphanage explained that a young woman had come to them in the middle of the night. She was exhausted and frightened and obviously running from something or someone. With her, she carried a child only a few weeks old. She had given no explanation and left no name, just pushed the child into the arms of a matron and ran, never to return.

The orphanage was clean and comfortable and efficient—about as much as one could expect from a charity-run institution. The children were sent to a nearby public school, and as much as she could enjoy anything, Jeena enjoyed learning and buried herself in her studies.

From the very first she seemed to have difficulty forming relationships with the other children and grew into a lonely, somber child.

If there was one bright aspect to her life, it was the stables. They were not part of the orphanage but belonged to a wealthy landowner and sat on wooded acreage adjacent to it. He had agreed to allow a few of the children to ride on the weekends in exchange for them cleaning the stables and maintaining the horses. Most of the children soon tired of this arrangement, but Jeena never did, continuing to ride until the day she left.

She would gallop recklessly through the fields, loving the feel of the wind in her face and the sense of freedom it gave her. She pushed herself and the horses hard, but they instinctively trusted her, and she, in turn, treated them with respect and kindness. At the end of a day of riding she would clean and brush the animals, lingering as long as she could before walking slowly back to the home.

She was accepted into the Star Corps Academy at sixteen. The military's need for soldiers in the century-old civil war was insatiable, and orphanages like hers were always a reliable source of raw recruits. Although it was customary to have a small party when a child finally left the home, Jeena never attended them, and it was no surprise when no one thought to give her one.

The Academy was hard, both mentally and physically. Space was an unforgiving environment in which to fight a war, and only the smartest and toughest survived long. Jeena thrived on the competition and intense physical training and soon excelled, ending up near the top of her class at the end of her first semester. She was considered ruthless and distant by her classmates, but she took no notice, even when she bothered to listen to the whispers.

She was exposed to much that was new to her during this time, including, inevitably, her first sexual encounter—a male cadet and upperclassman. She had discovered the art of pleasing herself accidentally some years earlier, but this was vastly different. Following the initial encounter, she was immediately ready to repeat the experience and was disappointed to discover the limits of male performance—her partner had fallen asleep.

For a time, sex became an obsession, and she soon gained the reputation as an aggressive and passionate lover—as well as other descriptions that were not so kind. Jeena didn't care. She had many partners, both men and women, but made no close emotional bonds with any of them. She made it clear from the outset she was interested only in the physical side of relationships. There were few objections to this precondition, and she had little trouble satiating her often-ravenous sexual appetite.

In her third year at the Academy she opted for specialist training as an SAG commando. The SAG, for Space, Atmosphere and Ground, were the fiercest fighters in the Union military. They were schooled in all aspects of warfare, and were trained to fight in any environment. Their units were given the best weapons and most sophisticated attack ships, and yet they were just as deadly in hand-to-hand combat. To survive the training one had to be rugged, intelligent, adaptive—and brutal. Mercy and pity were expunged from a commando's vocabulary. When the Union wanted to punish the Coalition, they sent in SAG units.

If the weapons were sophisticated, the soldiers were somewhat less so. They might be the hardiest and best-trained of all the Union forces, but they prided themselves on being rude, crude social misfits. *Out-drink, out-fight, out-fuck*—that was their motto. Fatalities in SAG were the highest in the military, and the odds of returning home from a mission were never great. They took a certain macabre pride in this fact and openly flaunted their precarious existence, taking crazy chances and driving themselves and each other to their limits.

Jeena fit right in. She excelled in the physical demands of training and in battle felt invincible and invulnerable, always pushing herself and her team to their limits and loving the feel of the adrenaline that flowed during battle. A veteran of a dozen battles, she won numerous medals for valor and began to gain the attention of the military brass.

Then came her capture and the prison and all that had once made her strong was now a poison that was slowly eating away at her.

JEENA LIFTED THE LADLE TO HER LIPS AND TASTED THE STEW. SHE HAD BEEN TRYING HER hand at cooking during the last few months, and although she had little prior experience, she thought she was getting pretty good. The meat had come from a wolla she had brought down with the pulse rifle earlier in the week. The stew was ready, and she looked around the camp, calling for Samson.

She'd finally accepted that the cub was with her to stay, and reluctantly decided he needed a name. She settled on Samson as much for his predilection for knocking down everything in sight as for his beautiful golden fur.

He seemed quite intelligent, and she was able to teach him several commands, the most often used of which was "no." It was a word whose meaning he seemed to grasp only vaguely.

Hearing his named called, the cub came barreling up the hill, skidding to a stop just before knocking Jeena into the fire. She patted his head, smiling as he began to babble.

That was her word for it. It had begun three weeks earlier—a high-pitched series of sounds the cub repeated throughout the day. At first she worried he was choking or ill, but as the weeks passed he showed no sign of distress. Jeena had searched the records for any information concerning this odd behavior, but there was no mention of it in either the colonist's records or the FYS report. Vicki analyzed recordings Jeena made but was unable to shed any light.

Initially, the vocalizations had surprised and fascinated her, but lately had become monotonous and slightly irritating. Ignoring the sounds, she poured the stew into two bowls, setting Samson's on the ground. He stood over it and, as always, waited for it to cool.

Jeena ate slowly, shaking her head. I'm really spoiling this fur-ball, she thought. But what could she do? At some point, the cub had noticed she only ate cooked food and from then on steadfastly refused to eat raw meat, begging instead for hers.

What a strange animal he is. She had studied him carefully. His paws, which at first glance resembled an Earth cat's, were far more complex. The individual "fingers" were long and graceful, and he had a workable opposable thumb. He had even begun using his paws to grasp the ball she threw to him at times.

Vicki explained that Ararat had once been covered in dense jungles and offered the theory that, like man, the tigras may have developed thumbs to grasp limbs. It seemed plausible enough, but Jeena found the idea of big cats swinging through the trees a bit disconcerting.

Then there was his face. Although it had the general features of a feline, with its long nose and protruding whiskers, the muscles seemed ...well, *wrong*, as if there were too many of them. It gave him a plasticity of expression that seemed out of place for an animal—he could give a sort of smile when happy, or screw up his face when displeased. He had even tried to mimic her by sticking out his tongue, with acceptable results.

Jeena drank easily from the whiskey bottle as she ate. Some days were like that. She would awaken from dark, disturbing dreams she'd spend the rest of the day trying to forget. The alcohol helped, but it seemed to take more each time—it was not yet dusk, and her head was already spinning.

She rationalized her downward spiral to herself. *Why the hell shouldn't I get drunk? God knows I've earned it. In fact, what difference does it make if I get piss-drunk every night? I don't have to report to anyone.* She smiled grimly. *Unscheduled R-and-R, that's what this is—rest and rye.*

She lit a cigar and rubbed her forehead as the headache began.

Samson finished his meal and came to her, laying his head in her lap. He had grown fast these last few months and now stood almost as high as her waist. He had picked up a sense for her moods and seemed to understand she was not feeling well tonight.

Jeena stroked his head.

"It's all right, Samson. Whiskey is mankind's oldest painkiller," she said, slurring her words slightly. "Give a human enough booze and you could cut off his head with barely a word of protest." She took another drink and stood on wobbly legs, raising the bottle to the sky. *"Right, Sergeant?"* she screamed. *"C'mon, hurt me now, you bastard! I'm ten feet tall and laserproof!"*

The bottle slipped from her hand and smashed on the ground. Mumbling and cursing, she staggered to her tent, passing out as she hit the cot.

She awoke crying before the sun was up. It had been a long night of dirty, laughing faces and hard, grasping hands, of pain and stench and filth and helplessness. Her head was pounding, still full of memories that wouldn't fade, of voices that refused to die. And there was Samson, already outside the tent knocking over crates and cans and making a racket that blended with the noises in her head into a fugue of sound that threatened to engulf her.

Jeena clasped her hands over her ears, screaming for him to stop and the voices to go away, but the clamor rose until it sounded like laughter. Lurching from the tent, she grabbed the shotgun and leveled it through tear-blinded eyes at the tormentor in her mind.

"Stay away from me, goddam you! Don't touch me!"

SAMSON JUMPED AT THE SHOUT, CAUSING THE CRATES AND CANS TO TUMBLE AROUND HIM, pinning him in. He saw the tear-streaked face staggering toward him, and sensed her anger. Whether in a burst of sudden insight or from an instinct for survival, he understood his danger and began desperately clawing at the debris keeping him prisoner. He watched helplessly as she raised the weapon. Unable to move, he began to whine and cry, and then suddenly in a high-pitched voice, he cried out a single word.

"No!"

THE RAGING STORM IN JEENA'S MIND WAS DISTURBED. A SOUND SHE COULDN'T QUITE identify drew her attention away from the laughing face before her. It began to shift and fade. Confused, she lowered her weapon and wiped her eyes, a simple action that seemed to still the voices in her head. Now, she could see Samson partially buried under a pile, repeating his pitiable cry over and over:

"No! No! No!"

Comprehension suddenly returned.

"It can't be. It's…not possible," she whispered. She took one halting step toward him and fell, collapsing into darkness on the yellow sands of Ararat.

_Chapter 6

"Language shapes the way we think, and determines what we can think about."

> Benjamin Lee Whorf
> 20th century Earth linguist
> *Encyclopedic History of the Union*, 22nd ed.

J EENA CAME TO, CERTAIN SHE HAD BEEN DREAMING. THAT CERTAINTY EVAPORATED WHEN she found Samson cowering under the wing of the ship. His voice was high and squeaky, but there was no mistaking the word "No" when she tried to approach him.

She finally managed to grasp him and cradled his head in her arms, holding him there until he stopped struggling and settled down. She sat in the shade of the wing and let the enormity of the situation sink in.

It simply wasn't possible. Humans had been on Ararat for more than two hundred years. If tigras were sentient, surely it would have been discovered by the FYS and announced throughout the galaxy. Why wasn't it known? Or if it was, why had the knowledge been suppressed? Certainly, the colonists had given no indication that tigras were anything more than dumb beasts, and her only other encounter with them had affirmed that conclusion.

Then how to explain Samson?

Genetic mutation? She discarded the idea immediately. No realistic combination of genetic events could have taken a single brute animal and imbued him with sentience. It made no sense.

When she was sure Samson had begun to trust her again, and was convinced her own legs would not give out, she entered the ship, setting Samson on the floor.

"Vicki."

"Sir."

"Analyze everything you have in your memory concerning Ararat. Look for anything relating to the tigras and intelligence."

"Affirmative." There was a pause, then: "The Five-Year Survey calculated a mean intelligence rating for tigras of thirty-seven-point-five. No other information is available."

Thirty-seven? Well, that was high for an animal, but no more so than for an Earth chimp.

"What about speech? Anything about their ability to mimic human voices?"

"I have a paper written by an early settler concerning occasional crying sounds produced at times of stress by tigra cubs. The author concludes that it is a behavior only seen in the juveniles. Shall I print a hard copy for you?"

"No. Nothing else? Nothing on possible sentience?"

"I have no information concerning sentience in tigras. No sentient being other than man has ever been discovered."

Yes, yes I know. More than four hundred years of human exploration and mankind is still alone. There had been scattered traces of what some thought were the remains of ancient, dead civilizations found on a few worlds, but these had been fragmentary and inconclusive. It was an article of faith that mankind was the only sentient species in the galaxy, or at least in the quadrant that man had explored.

Jeena looked down at the cub.

"Well, now, I guess we're going to have to test that, won't we?"

IN TRUTH, JEENA WAS CERTAIN SHE WAS DEALING WITH A KIND OF MIMICRY, MUCH LIKE WHAT was seen in Earth parrots. Her certainty did not last long. Like the rupture of a dam, Samson's first utterance unleashed a torrent of words the number of which increased daily. It was more than a reflexive echo, she was sure. She was certain he was trying to communicate. True, it was primitive and clumsy—single words indicating something he wanted—but no more so than a human child.

As the weeks passed, she watched him struggle to pronounce new words, his face contorting to reproduce the alien, human sounds. His soft palate had yet to fully form so his pronunciation carried a slight lisp, giving his voice another eerie similarity to that of a small child.

His speed of advancement amazed her. It was as though his mind, long dormant in a dark sleep of ignorance, had been awakened and was now making up for lost time.

Jeena could come up with no reasonable explanation for this sudden intelligence, but once the initial shock wore off she became less concerned with finding an answer and more involved with helping him through the learning process.

SHE KNELT IN FRONT OF THE TENT, SAMSON SITTING BEFORE HER. SHE POINTED TO herself.

"Jeena," the cub answered in his high, singsong voice.

"Good," she said, and pointed to him.

"Samson."

"Very good." She reached behind her back and brought out a small ball.

"Ball!" he screeched, and began spinning excitedly in circles. "Ball ball ball ball," he repeated until she finally threw it.

At first nouns comprised his entire vocabulary, but he soon learned to modify them with simple verbs—"ball" became "play ball." It took only a few weeks for his sentences to increase in complexity by the addition of short prepositional phrases—"play ball" became "play ball with me."

The process continued.

Jeena understood that he was taking all his verbal clues from her, yet the idea that alien communication could develop along such human lines astonished her. She made extensive notes and holo recordings of his progress. Whenever she finally contacted the Union, this information could prove invaluable in answering the mind-boggling question of how this development was possible.

He had a child's natural curiosity, and eventually that led him to question his own beginnings. He listened intently to Jeena's rather graphic description of the entire reproductive process, not quite getting it all but fascinated nonetheless. He seemed to grasp instinctively that she was not his mother yet never asked for details concerning her or her whereabouts, something Jeena was silently grateful for. She still could not reconcile this incredibly human-like mind with the snarling animal she had been forced to kill.

If Samson was mimicking a human childhood, it was a childhood completely alien to Jeena. Where she had been a dark and sullen child, he was impossibly happy, awaking each day bouncing and singing the few children's songs she had taught him. She did not remember many. He was painfully anxious to please and would eagerly attempt any task she set him to. He would struggle and puzzle over each new problem, searching for a solution, and she could almost see the light go off over his head when he finally had it.

She soon realized Samson's growth was extending beyond his vocabulary. The logical and linear reasoning required for speech and problem-solving were having profound effects on other aspects his behavior as well.

I can see it in the way he moves, in the way he responds to his environment. Instinct is losing its grip on him. The more he learns, the more firmly his brain is becoming wired in a human pattern.

Then came the morning she awoke to find him playing dress-up in her T-shirt and sandals and suddenly understood that this *tigra* was no longer an animal at all. In his mind at least, he was human.

"Rrrrr...Jeena," Samson whispered. He still produced a soft purr prior to speaking, but even this was rapidly disappearing

Asleep on the cot, Jeena lifted one eyelid and found herself staring at an enormous wet black nose.

"What is it, Samson?" she muttered.

"Gotta pee," he pleaded.

"You little shit, it's not even light out," she groaned. "Go by yourself if you have to."

"Noooo," he whined. "You come with."

Jeena muttered a curse. Samson knew the way to the latrine, of course, but it was in the high grass out of direct sight of the camp. As she groggily put on her sandals, she considered the incongruity of a wild animal afraid of the outdoors. Except that Samson was in no way wild, and she had stopped thinking of him as an animal at all. She wasn't sure what she considered him—except a pain-in-the-ass prepubescent perhaps.

The sun was beginning to rise as they made their way back to the camp, and Jeena noticed a cloud of dust to the west. Samson noticed it, too.

"What's that, Jeena?"

She squinted, using her hand to shade her eyes from the sun's low rays.

"I'm not sure. Looks like horses."

The cloud was moving toward the south.

"What are horses?"

"Earth animals. People ride them sometimes."

"People? You mean more people like you?" he asked excitedly.

Jeena gnawed her lower lip. "Maybe. I'm not sure. Looks like they'll be coming close to us. I suppose we should check it out," she said uncertainly.

Samson was in full agreement. They stopped by the camp, and she grabbed the binoculars before the two of them headed in the direction of the moving cloud. Normally, Samson would race by her as he ran then slow down to let her catch up. Today he chose to stay close to her, caught between excitement and apprehension at the unknown.

"I didn't know there were more people besides you," he said as they ran.

"Of course, you did. I've told you about Earth."

Samson clicked his tongue. "Rrrrr...No, I meant here."

"Yes, there are a few. Some people came here a long time ago. Probably not many left."

"How come you don't live with them?"

"I wasn't sure there were any still here. Besides, I haven't had time to go look for them. I've been busy here with you."

"Oh." He considered that for a moment, then: "So are there more like me here, too? More tigras?"

Jeena did not break her stride. "I don't know. I hope not. Too many stinking animals on this planet as it is."

They'd gone about five miles, and she was just beginning to breathe hard when they came to a cliff overlooking a narrow gorge. Muffled voices drifted up to them. Crouching down and warning Samson to be quiet, she crawled to the edge of the cliff and peered over.

Below her were the three animals responsible for the dust cloud. They looked somewhat like large horses, slightly bigger, Jeena guessed, than the Clydesdales they resembled. She recognized them from Vicki's tutorial as kytars, an animal native to the planet. They were a deep crimson color with long, white fetlocks and were thick-boned, heavy animals. Their heads were odd-looking, with a beard like a goat's and a stumpy horn projecting from their foreheads. The overall look was not so much unicorn as rhinoceros.

The kytars were saddled, but their riders were on their feet, circling an animal they had cornered in the gorge. The animal was a tigra. It snarled and paced in the cleft of the gorge, swiping its claws at the approaching men. One of the men was swinging a loope roped and suddenly threw it over the animal's head, dragging it to the ground. A second man hurled a weighted bola against the animal's back legs, binding them together. Quickly, the men descended on the tigra, tying it expertly while carefully avoiding the flailing legs and snapping jaws. They obviously had experience in dealing with these animals.

The tigra now secured, they pulled the ropes taut, stretching its neck.

"Jeena..." Samson whispered.

"Shhh!" she warned, intent on the action below.

As they watched, a third man, who until now had stayed out of the fray, approached the bound animal, his hands raised heavenward. Like the others, he wore heavy black robes, a green crescent moon emblazoned across the chest. A large sword hung from his belt, and the hilt of a knife glinted from under his robes. He spoke in a low monotone, but Jeena could not make out the words. Peering through the binoculars, she studied the face of the speaker.

He was old, but how old she could not guess—the desert aged people prematurely, she knew, as did life in primitive agrarian societies. His hair and beard were dull dirty-silver, his beard reaching almost to his belt. His features were sharp and severe, his skin weathered and wrinkled. She tried to make out his eyes, but they were shadowed under heavy brows and sunk deep into his gaunt face. It was a hard face, almost inorganic in appearance, and its expression was grim.

The old man finished his recitation and pulled aside the heavy cloth tunic he was wearing, too heavy to be comfortable in Ararat's heat, she thought. He withdrew the dagger, its curved blade shimmering in the sun. Murmuring, he held it momentarily above his head then strode toward the cat, a thin smile appearing on his lips.

"Come here, Samson!" Jeena said urgently.

"But..."

"Come here now!" she repeated under her breath.

Samson crawled over to her, and she grabbed his head, pressing his face tight against her breasts and away from the scene below. She watched as the knife wielder put the blade to the struggling animal's neck and, with a flick of his wrist, calmly slit its throat.

Blood spurted high in the air as the tigra kicked weakly a few times then lay still. The old man kicked the limp body to ensure it was dead then signaled the others to untie the animal. They quickly remounted and rode away to the west, leaving the corpse to lie under the hot sun, the pool of blood slowly widening.

Jeena scrambled away from the cliff's edge holding Samson near her, not allowing him to see the dead tigra below.

"What happened, Jeena?" he asked as they made their way back to camp.

"Nothing."

"But, Jeena..."

"I don't know, dammit!" she screamed. She was nauseous, shaking in confusion and anger and unable to point to the source of either emotion. She had just witnessed the killing of an animal, but so what? Hadn't she killed one as well? Probably this one had been raiding their livestock or perhaps had even mauled one of their people. That tigra, like the one she had been forced to kill, was a wild animal, not like Samson at all.

Then why did she feel so ill?

Because it was like Samson. It was *just* like him, from his golden-speckled eyes to his snow-white paws. *And who's to say that Samson is unique? Maybe more are intelligent, maybe none are. God, I wish I had the answers!*

Then there was the killing itself. The men who killed the animal didn't seem intent on simply dispatching the tigra quickly and mercifully. It was as if they were performing some sort of long-rehearsed ritual. And those men did not look like half-starved farmers. They moved like a well-disciplined military unit.

But for whom? Why would a farming community commit the time and resources necessary to maintaining a standing army? *What the hell is happening on this planet?*

They reached their camp, and Jeena bounded up the gangway to her ship. She ordered Samson to remain outside.

"Vicki, on," she said, sliding into the com-chair.

"Ready."

"Two colonies were granted charter on Ararat, correct?"

"That is correct."

Jeena thought for a moment. "I saw a group of men today. They were wearing dark clothing decorated with the sign of a crescent moon. Speculate: from which colony would they most likely have come?"

"The crescent moon and star is the symbol of the Afridi, a sect of Judaslam. The Afridi were the first colonists to be granted charter on Ararat."

Judaslam? I thought mankind had seen the end of that silliness, she thought. "All right, I want everything you have on both colonies, starting with the Afridi—history, politics, religious beliefs—all of it."

It was late in the day when Vicki ended her tutorial. Jeena stood and stretched, looking out of the hatchway at Samson lying comfortably in the sun. If she had been reluctant to initiate contact with the colonists before, she was even more so now.

The Judaslamics she already knew about. Followers of a centuries-old fusion of Judaism and Islam, they had held great sway in Earth politics prior to the Second Migration. History had not been kind to their memory. They were intolerant and militaristic—religious fundamentalists who had used the

Obsidian Plague as justification for driving mankind into a hundred years of ignorance and persecution. Like all dark ages, this one eventually passed, and the reign of Judaslam was now little more than a dark chapter in mankind's history.

The Afridi were a particularly fanatical sect of Judaslamics who had migrated to Ararat almost two hundred years ago during their waning days of power. The original colony had been led by a charismatic zealot calling himself Caleb. Caleb preached an apocalyptic vision of the future wherein God would set up a holy realm in "the land of the righteous." He had apparently intended that place to be Ararat.

The colony was situated two hundred miles away, deep in Ararat's great western desert. Why? she wondered. As Ararat's first chartered colony, they had the whole planet to choose from. The southern hemisphere was much more temperate. Why settle in the least hospitable corner?

Whatever their reasons, they didn't have long to change their minds. A second colony was chartered only twenty years later. Calling themselves Babylonians, they had risen from the chaos left after the fall of the Judaslamics. Perhaps as a response to the years of repression under the old regime, they embraced the pan-deism of the ancient world, with its numerous gods and lesser deities. They were proponents of sexual freedom as well, even going so far as to hold public orgies until halted by the local government.

It seemed the Union was only too happy to be rid of them, and quickly approved their application for charter. They had settled some five hundred miles south of Jeena's position.

She took a cigar from her rapidly dwindling supply and leaned against the hatchway, smoking. Only a Union bureaucrat would see fit to place two such diametrically opposed groups on the same planet. It would be a minor miracle if they hadn't managed to kill each other off by now, although armed conflict against a chartered colony was a high crime and grounds for revocation of charter. Then again, who knew what had happened in the ninety years since the Union last had contact with Ararat.

Samson stirred and glanced up at her. He smiled and yawned.

Vicki had been unable to shed any light on the killing of the tigra. There was no modern tradition of sacrifice in the Judaslamic religion, although certainly there had been in the far past, dating back to prehistory. The Babylonians seemed harmless enough, so she would have considered visiting them and gathering more information if not for the distance involved.

No, whatever was happening on this planet it was not her concern. She and

Samson were comfortable and safe here. It made no sense to go looking for trouble. From her experience trouble, in time, came looking for you.

Chapter 7

Standing Order #17: Firing the concussion cannon without the wearing of body armor is strictly prohibited. Survivors will be subject to disciplinary action.

Excerpt from *MAAD Training Manual*

THREE WEEKS AFTER THE INCIDENT AT THE CLIFFS, THE RAINY SEASON BEGAN. BY THE third day of the deluge, Jeena and Samson were forced to seek shelter in the ship—while the tent was waterproof, the floor had become increasingly damp, and cooking was impossible. Also, she admitted to herself, she was getting very tired of the smell of wet cat.

So, they immured themselves in the belly of the ship, keeping the hatch open for ventilation on most days and closing it only when the rain became so severe it pitched in horizontally. It was cozy and pleasant, if a bit claustrophobic, and to pass the time Jeena decided to try and teach Samson to read.

It was a daunting task, and at times she wondered if she wasn't expecting too much from this alien feline. Samson, however, would not be discouraged. He threw himself at the task, burying his nose in the primers Vicki printed out for him and struggling over each new letter and word.

Jeena could only watch in awe. By the end of the first month of rain he had the entire alphabet memorized and could recognize simple words. By the third month he was devouring entire volumes in a single day. She made another important discovery about her ward then. Samson, it seemed, had a photographic memory.

She sat near the open hatch, listening to Vivaldi's *The Four Seasons* and gazing out over the landscape. The rain was still coming down in sheets, but it was not as thick as it had been the previous months. She was getting a case of cabin fever, and was glad the end of the season was near.

Samson sat near her, his head hanging low over his front paws, reading. His latest interest was human history, and he was studying a new holo Vicki had supplied him.

He twitched his whiskers and looked up. "I have a question."

"No kidding. So what else is new?"

He ignored the sarcasm. "What was the Obsidian Plague? The histories mention it a lot, but they never say much about it."

"It was a disease created by mankind. It happened a long time ago, just after we had started exploring the stars. It killed a lot of people."

"That doesn't make any sense. Why would humans make a disease?"

"It wasn't created on purpose, fur-head, it was an accident, or so they say. I still don't think we know the whole story, but according to the history holos a group of scientists on a planet called Obsidia 5 were working on something they shouldn't have. They were fooling around with our genetic code, creating humans in the lab, trying to make a more perfect person or some such silliness.

"Back then, mankind was still divided into different nations, and there weren't many safeguards on scientific research. It's said they created thousands of genetically engineered people over the ten years the project ran before the rest of mankind discovered what they were up to. By then it was too late. Somehow, one of their genetic transplantations went wrong, and the newborn child began expressing a virus our species had never seen before.

"Must have been one nasty little bug. It didn't hurt people right away, so you didn't even know you were infected for months. Freighters delivering supplies helped spread it to most of the inhabited worlds. Suddenly, people started dying—fast. They say it only took a few hours from the first symptoms until death."

"Did a lot of people die?"

"Something like five billion in seven months—one-third of the entire human population at the time. The planets quarantined themselves from each other in an attempt to stop the spread of the disease, but the damage had already been done. Even after the plague burned itself out, the quarantine continued. People were terrified it might start up again—they still are. It's why we insist on a complete survey of each new planet now before we allow colonization."

"Wow."

"Yeah, it was one of the worst times in our history."

"So, whatever happened to them?"

Jeena drew on her cigar. "Who?"

"The people. The ones the ones the scientists created."

Jeena sighed. "Oh, them. The horrors, that's what they were called. People panicked. No one could be certain they were safe. Try to understand, Samson, the whole human race had almost been wiped out. They were afraid any one of them could be capable of expressing a new virus."

"So, what happened to them?"

"They were killed. They were rounded up and killed—although *slaughtered* might be a better word, from what I've read. They burned the entire facility on Obsidia, and the planet has been off-limits ever since."

Samson shuddered. "How horrible. But why were those scientists trying to make humans better? How much better could they make you?"

She had to smile. In Samson's eyes humans were already perfect, or nearly so. To him Earth was a kind of Eden, the home planet of intelligent and noble beings who had colonized the stars. He thought much less of himself and his own species, and Jeena knew she was partly to blame for that.

In an effort to show him what other tigras were like, she had mistakenly showed him some nature holos of tigras hunting and living in the wild, but had to stop when he became visibly upset. Although she had explained many times how unique he was among his kind, he was unprepared for the impact of seeing mirror images of himself as nothing more than brute beasts. For the rest of that day he could not bring himself to look at her, and never again asked about his own species.

He was keenly interested in mankind, however, and saw in man's accomplishments a grandeur she knew was misplaced. She understood he had taken humanity as his adopted race, figuring, perhaps, that even if he didn't look like them, at least he reasoned like them. So, he elevated mankind in direct compensation for what he saw as the tigra's low state.

"We aren't perfect, Samson, not even close," she replied. "I keep telling you that. Anyway, it won't happen again. Genetic engineering has been universally banned ever since, at least in the Union. Who knows what those butchers in the Coalition are doing."

She sat up and leaned out into the rain, letting it beat gently on the back of her neck.

"You hate them, don't you?" he asked softly. "The Coalition, I mean."

Jeena did not answer immediately. "Yes, Samson, I hate them," she said finally. "And I will go on hating them for as long as I live."

The rainy season finally ended. After three days of sun and clear skies, Jeena moved them back into the tent. Samson had grown quite a bit during the preceding months, and it seemed the tent was smaller than she remembered, but they managed.

They had depleted their food stores during the rains, and one of the first things on her list was procuring meat. Samson was less than enthusiastic.

"Why can't we just eat what's left in the cans?" he asked.

"Because, dummy, there's nothing left but beans and cream soup."

He shrugged. "So?"

Jeena regarded him mournfully. Here was an animal born to bring down heavy game, and yet his favorite food was paté. It was pathetic.

"We need fresh meat, and besides, you need to learn how to hunt. Tell you what, you bring it down, and I'll skin and clean it. How about that?"

His eyes brightened. "You're going to teach me to use the rifle?"

"The rifle? No, I mean I want you to *hunt*. You know—naturally. C'mon, you have to learn sometime. It'll be fun."

Samson cocked his head suspiciously. "What are you talking about?"

"Don't act dense. You know what I mean. It's time you learn to hunt like the rest of your species."

His whiskers twitched. "Why?"

"Because you're a tigra. I've been treating you like a human being and it's not right."

"Why, because I'm just an animal?" he demanded angrily.

"No, dammit. I mean living like this is erasing all your instincts. You're losing all the skills evolution spent millions of years giving you, and I'm to blame."

"Oh, right, big important skills. What are we talking about here anyway—marking territory with my pee and licking myself clean? Is that what you mean?"

"I'm just saying I have no right to change you into something you're not."

"Well, it's a little late for that, don't you think?" He was now visibly angry. "Rrrr...I don't believe this. Do you really expect me to chase after some filthy animal you just know is going to be crapping all over itself, grab its neck in my jaws, pull it to the ground and kill it with my teeth?"

Jeena nodded. "Stop making a face. There's nothing wrong with hunting that way, it's perfectly natural."

Samson's eyes narrowed. "Then you do it."

"I can't, you little shit, I'm not built for it. That's why I have to use a gun."

"I'm more than willing to use the gun."

"That's not the point. You're a tigra, you're *supposed* to use your teeth. You wouldn't have fangs otherwise. They're there to be used."

"Is that a fact? And how's that appendix of yours working? Look, I'm not doing it, and that's final. It's sick and disgusting. Besides, hair makes me gag, you know that. I can't even stand it when my own fur gets in my mouth. I can't believe we're even having this discussion."

"Samson..."

"No. Forget it."

They stood staring each other down. Jeena blinked first.

"Oh, all right, you little shit, you want to throw away all your instincts, fine. I'll teach you to use the damn gun." She picked up the MAAD and stomped off to the east in a huff.

"Really?" Samson said, running up beside her. "That's great. But you'll still skin it and clean it, won't you?"

JEENA STOPPED AFTER ABOUT A MILE AND GAVE SAMSON HIS FIRST LESSON WITH THE PULSE rifle. The brush was just beginning to get heavy, and there were plenty of trees to use as targets.

"Watch closely," she said, and knelt on one knee. Shouldering the weapon, she aimed along the barrel and gently squeezed the trigger. There was a slight sound like a spark of static electricity. A hundred yards away a small branch flew from a tree.

"Were you aiming for that?" Samson asked.

She looked sidelong at him. "Yes, I was aiming for that."

"Just asking. You know, in the holos the guns are a lot noisier," he said informatively.

"This is a pulse rifle. It's very quiet. Here, now you try."

She had him sit and hold the gun much as a human would. She was surprised to find that it was a natural and comfortable position for him.

"Okay, now, close your left eye and look down the barrel. See the little projection at the end? Line it up with a branch. Got it?"

Samson had a little difficulty maneuvering his larger head into the right position, but finally, tilting his neck sharply, he said he was pretty sure he had it.

"Okay, now, slowly squeeze the trigger."

There was a burst of static, and a cloud of sand erupted twenty feet in front of them.

"How was that?" he asked.

"Pitiful."

Samson was undaunted. "You know, you should really work on your pep talks. Anyway, it was just my first try." He patted the tube below the rifle. "What's this for?"

"That's the concussion cannon. Don't worry, you won't ever be using it." She went on to explain its uses and effects.

"Rrrrr," he said when she had finished. "Sounds dangerous."

"It is, and not just to your enemy. It can cause internal damage to the user as well. It can't be used safely without wearing body armor."

They spent the rest of the day practicing and looking for game, without much luck. Neither was particularly upset about that, as the day was nice and they had brought along provisions for an overnight.

Jeena sat by the fire finishing up the last of the soup. A small blanket covered her shoulders, warming her against the cool of the night. Samson was pacing and nosing around, looking uncomfortable.

"You brought something to sleep on, I hope," he said, eying the blanket around her.

"Yes, you spoiled cat, there's a bedroll big enough for both of us in the pack."

Samson stared oddly at her for a moment before rummaging through the pack. He found the bedroll and unrolled it before the fire, lying down on it and gazing silently into the flames.

Jeena finished the soup and lay down next to him.

"What's wrong?" she asked.

"Nothing," he said, and she did not press him. After a few minutes he spoke again. "I'm not an animal, Jeena."

"No? You sure as hell smell like one."

Samson pulled away from her.

"Hey, I'm joking. I know you're not an animal. Don't you think I know that?"

"You wanted me to hunt like one," he said, and there was hurt in his voice.

"I just want you to be what you're supposed to be, dummy. I'm flying blind here. On the one hand, I want you to grow and learn as much as you can, but on the other I don't want you to lose your native culture in the process."

"Tigras don't have a culture!" he snapped. "They're just dirty, stupid animals."

"Don't say that."

"Why not? You say it all the time."

Jeena squirmed uncomfortably. "Yeah, well, sometimes I say things I don't mean."

"Why?"

"I don't know, just because."

"Because you're mean."

"Yeah, maybe I am. I guess I haven't had much experience in not being mean."

"I know. And I know you were really hurt on that bad planet, and that sometimes the nightmares make you say terrible things, but, Jeena…sometimes you make me feel so bad." He curled up in a ball and covered his eyes with a paw. "I don't want to be a tigra. I want to be like you."

Jeena cursed herself. *What do I say to that? I don't know how to be compassionate. I never learned.*

"All right, look, here's the deal. You can't pay attention to the things I say. I don't mean anything by them. I'm so used to treating people like shit that I guess I've just been treating you the same way. But I'm not going to do that anymore—or at least I'm going to really try. Okay?"

He did not reply.

"Understand?"

"No, I can't understand, I'm just an animal."

"No, you're not. I mean, yes, you are a tigra, but you are not just an animal and you are far from stupid. The truth is, Samson, you're brilliant."

He rolled over. "I am?"

"Yes, you are. You've managed to learn in just a few short months what it would have taken a human child a decade to learn."

"You're just saying that."

"It's the truth. You have an incredible mind."

He grew quiet again. Gently, he took her hand in his paw, touching it and examining it closely.

"I don't want to be brilliant. I want to be human," he whispered. "I wish I had hands instead of paws, and I didn't have this stupid tail, and this big dumb nose, and…"

"I like you fine just the way you are."

"I'm ugly."

Jeena smiled. "No, you're not. Actually, I think you're very handsome."

"Yeah, right."

"I mean it."

They watched the fire together in silence.

"Why aren't there any more like me, Jeena?" he asked finally.

It was a question she had asked herself many times.

"I don't know, Samson. I just don't know."

They awoke the next morning to a chill dawn, with Jeena thoroughly ensconced in Samson's fur. She had moved up against him during the night and wrapped her arms and legs around his body.

He disengaged from her and stomped around the dying embers of the fire, trying to get the circulation back in his legs.

"You know, it would be a lot easier if you just made a coat out of me." He stood on his hind legs and stretched, scratching his chest and belly. Like all tigras, he could stand and walk on his hind legs but found it awkward and much less efficient than walking on all fours, and only did it when he needed his front paws free. "So, what's for breakfast?"

Jeena shivered.

"Unless your aim gets better, dirt and grass." She stood and began folding the bedroll back into the pack. "Grab the MAAD, Buffalo Bill, it's time for more practice."

By late that day they had accomplished their mission and were back in camp with a prize wolla, a buck Jeena had bagged. They were not, however, back on speaking terms. This was due to an errant shot which had just missed Jeena's posterior, the firing of which was totally and completely not Samson's fault, and besides, if a "safety" was such an all-important thing to know why didn't she tell him about it before?

Chapter 8

Sing, children of Ibrahim! Let loose your voices to heaven! At last we are joined, and the lost tribe is found. Sing, children of Ibrahim! For we are all gathered again in our father's house.

32nd Psalm, Judaslam *Qatar*

SAMSON PACED OUTSIDE THE TENT. THE MORNING AIR WAS COOL AND SWEET, THE END OF summer was rapidly approaching; and while the days were still warm, there was a briskness in the air that had been missing just a few weeks before.

He was nearly full-grown now, more than twice Jeena's weight, and taller by a head if he stood on his hind legs. The small purring sounds that earlier had inflected his speech had completely disappeared. According to what Vicki had to say about tigras, Jeena put him at the young adult stage.

Over the last several months, their relationship had evolved from teacher/student to one of more-or-less equals, but he bowed to her age and experience on most decisions. Not that he was above throwing his weight around—literally. He once carried her all the way to the stream and threw her in to emphasize a point.

"Hurry up in there, I gotta go," he yelled into the tent.

Jeena stumbled out, tying up the laces of her moccasins. She had made them from a wolla hide after her prison sandals had finally disintegrated around her feet.

"I'm hurrying, I'm hurrying. Geez, I wish you'd learn to go by yourself."

Samson ignored her. He was staring intently out over the southern horizon. "Uh, Jeena..."

She followed his gaze. In the distance was a hazy cloud of sand. She went quickly into the tent and brought out the binoculars. She studied the oncoming cloud before handing them to Samson.

"Three riders on kytars," he said. "Dark clothes and beards. They're coming this way."

"Let's get to the ship."

Samson sat in the dayroom watching her slip into her flight suit. She had washed it thoroughly after landing so, although it was tattered, at least it was clean. She'd torn off all the Union insignia, leaving only her captain's bars and her name. Flight suits looked pretty much alike no matter which side of the war you were on, and she didn't think these people would notice any subtle differences. The ship itself was completely black, all its outer identifying marks having been burned away in re-entry.

"Why are you getting dressed?" Samson asked. The whole matter of clothing perplexed him. If they weren't worn to keep out the elements, what was their point?

"These are religious fundamentalists. I doubt they'd look kindly on greeting a naked woman." Jeena zipped up the suit. "All right, I'll go talk with them and find out what I can. I want you to stay here and keep still."

"Why?"

"Why? Well, because I'm not sure how they'll react. I mean, I don't think they're aware..." She sighed. "Samson, humans can sometimes act irrationally when faced with something new. I just want to size them up first, that's all."

"You mean about me."

"I mean including you."

"Does this have anything to do with what happened at the cliffs?"

Jeena paused at the door. They had never spoken of the events at the cliffs since that day.

"Please, just stay here."

He tapped his back paw. "I still have to go," he reminded her.

The sounds of hooves could be heard slowing outside the hatchway.

"Hold it," she said firmly, and walked out to meet the riders.

The three men had dismounted and were staring in wonder at the enormous, partially buried ship. They all wore the same dark, coarse robes as the men at the cliffs, with green crescent moons on their chests. Swords hung from leather scabbards around their waists. The hilts of their knives peeked from beneath their cloaks. Four kytars stood snorting and stomping in the brush nearby.

Jeena smiled warmly as she descended the steps, but it was a façade. She felt decidedly unfriendly toward these people, and not just because of what she had seen at the cliffs. *It's been almost two years since I last had contact with other human beings. If Samson has become more human during that time, I have not. I feel more like a wild animal than he does. I just want to be left alone.*

She reached the bottom of the steps and held out her hand.

"Welcome, gentlemen, I am Captain Jeena Garza, pilot of this vessel." She had deliberately omitted her affiliation and hoped the omission went unnoticed.

The tallest and sternest of the three stepped forward and bowed stiffly. He did not take the offered hand.

"I am Serug of New Jerusalem. This is Ibrahim, and Esau." He pointed to his left and right respectively. He stared up again at the huge ship towering above them. "We have not seen such as this in many a generation. We thought perhaps thy ship was a mirage—such things are frequent in the desert. But I see both thee and it are real." He returned his gaze to Jeena. "Has the Union, then, finally returned to Ararat?"

"You say the Union. Then you are not aligned with the Coalition?" she asked cautiously.

"Coalition?"

"Yes, in the war."

Serug appeared confused.

"The civil war," she added.

The one Serug had introduced as Ibrahim, the eldest of the three, spoke.

"Ah, yes, I remember stories of a great war, one that raged whilst my father was still a boy. But can it be that this is the same war of which thou speaks?"

"Yes," she answered, "it's the same war."

Serug shook his head. "I know naught of this. But the petty wars of mankind are of no concern to us. We are Afridi, people of God. We are aligned only with the Almighty."

"Why has the Union returned?" asked Esau. "We have no wish for outsiders on Ararat."

Jeena studied the man closely. He was of medium height and build and appeared young, perhaps early twenties. His unkempt hair and patchy beard were a dirty red, his teeth stained yellow. But it was his eyes that caught her attention. They were so dark they were almost black, and sunk deep into his skull. She had seen such eyes before, but on a much older face—in the gorge below the cliffs.

"My presence here is an accident," she explained. "My ship malfunctioned, and I was forced to make an emergency landing."

"So it seems," Serug replied, gazing at the small camp just beyond the wing of the ship. "Thou hast been here long?"

"Almost two full Ararat years."

"A long time to survive alone in the desert. Thou art alone, yes?" he asked.

Jeena hesitated only an instant. "Yes, I'm alone."

"And none have found thee until now?"

"No, you're the first human contact I've had since my crash. I was aware there were colonies on Ararat, but without knowing their locations, I thought it best not to wander randomly."

"Yes, that was wise," Ibrahim agreed. "We are the only colony near to thee, and we are across the western desert. It would be a difficult trek on foot. We ourselves seldom venture so far east. Only the cleansing brings us here today."

"The cleansing?"

"Yes, every year we of the Rosh-dan scour all of Ararat in search of tigra. We are just one of several such parties."

"Tigra?" Jeena asked in an innocent tone.

"Yes, tigra," Esau spat. "A cunning and vile devil in the shape of a stalking cat. Perhaps thou hast seen such an animal? Large and ferocious, golden of hair and of eye?"

She held her gaze steady on his. "No, I'm sorry. I haven't."

"Ah, well, there were never many in the south, and few remain in the western lands, thanks to our vigilance. Soon all of Ararat will be free of this unholy plague," Serug said.

"You hunt them?"

"They are unclean in the eyes of God," replied Ibrahim. "Like the snake in the Garden of Eden, they are the embodiment of evil on Ararat. It is our law that none should live. The Rosh-dan do not hunt them for sport. They are captured and sacrificed to the greater glory of Yahweh."

"And their corpses left to rot," said Esau, grinning.

Jeena fought her involuntary shudder.

"I see. And the Rosh-dan, what is that?"

"We are soldiers of the Rosh-dan, the Army of God," answered Serug. "The green crescent is our symbol."

An army? Then I was right in my assessment at the cliffs.

"I have never heard of a zed-tech colony requiring an army. Surely, there is little need?"

"We are an army against evil, Captain, and evil is to be found in all places where man refuses to accept God's will," Serug explained, "Ararat included."

"I assume by that you mean the other colony, the Babylonians? Then, they still exist as well?"

"Exist?" Serug snorted. "If that is what thou wishes to call it. They are warlike barbarians and infidels who live in total disregard of the laws of God. It is good they did not find thee. Such has been their descent into savagery it is rumored they practice cannibalism."

Ibrahim shuddered and made a sign over his chest.

"Well," continued Serug, "God in his infinite mercy has spared thee from the infidel and sent his servants to thy rescue. Come, gather what belongings thou may need and accompany us to New Jerusalem. We have an extra mount, as thou canst see."

"Yes, " Jeena replied. "I thought maybe you had lost a man."

"Nay. But the desert can be an unforgiving place. We always bring an extra mount when we venture away from our cities. Come, thou will have no difficulty riding him, though thou hast no experience. He is a gentle animal, strong and surefooted."

Suddenly, a sound like a stream of water flowing into a hollow bowl emanated from the hatchway. Jeena paled as the three men gazed up at the noise.

"Wastewater reclamation unit," she explained quickly.

The flowing sound stopped, replaced by the flush of the ship's toilet.

"Needs work," she added, her face reddening. *Good thing these people seem unfamiliar with indoor plumbing.* "As to my accompanying you," she continued quickly, turning their attention away from the ship, "I am very grateful, but I'm afraid I can't. I am a Union officer and must remain with my ship. I've sent a distress signal—I have to be here when the rescue ship arrives," she lied.

Esau leaned forward and whispered into Serug's ear. Serug nodded as the man finished.

"Yes, yes," he said impatiently. "Captain, thou art the first contact we have had with the outside in many generations. The Council of the Rosh-dan—the leaders of our order—will wish to speak with thee at more length. I am afraid I must insist that thou accompany us back to New Jerusalem. Surely, a message can be left for thy people, explaining where thou hast gone?"

"Thou hast done well, child, to have survived so long, but this land is fraught with many dangers. We cannot simply ride away and leave thee to fend for thyself alone here in the wilderness," added Ibrahim.

She studied the determined faces before her. *It's obvious they are not going to leave without me. Continuing to resist will only raise suspicions, and I can't risk exposing Samson. What would their reaction be to him, I wonder? Shock? Disbelief? Worse? Surely, they could not see him and hear him, and yet still regard him as a thing to be destroyed? But, I won't chance that yet. Not until I know more.*

"Very well," she said, trying to smile. "I would be honored to visit your city. I must secure the ship before we leave. I won't be long."

They bowed to her in unison, and Jeena returned the courtesy then hurried up the landing ramp and into the dayroom. She found Samson sitting quietly near the bed, his ears flat against his head and his whiskers twitching.

"What did you think you were doing?" she snapped. "My heart almost stopped!"

"I said I had to go," he replied. "Did you want me to use the floor?"

"No, I suppose not." She shuffled her feet nervously. "Listen, I, um…I have to go away for a while."

"I know. I heard. I heard everything," he said, his voice cracking. "They kill tigras."

"Samson…"

"You knew, didn't you? It's what they did to the tigra at the cliffs. You knew, and you didn't tell me. Why?"

She sat next to him. "I don't know. There was nothing I could do to stop it, and what good would telling you have done? I didn't want to hurt you. You were so young."

"I'm grown now."

She cocked her head at him and smiled. "Yes, you are."

"Please, don't go with them."

"Samson, I don't want to, but if you heard then you know I don't have a choice. I have to go, but I'll be back as soon as I can."

"Will you?" he asked. His eyes had grown red-rimmed and moist.

"Of course, I will. Why would you ask me that?"

"I don't know. You haven't been with other humans in a long time. You've been stuck out here all alone with me. Maybe when you get to their city you'll like it. Maybe you won't want to leave. Or maybe if you do come back, *you* won't like tigras, either." He laid his head in her lap and closed his eyes.

Jeena stroked him gently, and felt him trembling under her fingers.

"That could never happen. I will come back, I promise," she said, and was surprised that her own voice was tight.

"I'm scared."

"I know, but you don't have to be. I even think that once I learn more about them I could break the news about you. They're bound to change their minds about tigras once they meet you."

He lifted his head from her lap. The fur under his eyes was damp.

"Do you think so? Maybe I should talk to them now."

"I don't think that would be wise. Seeing you coming out of the ship would just frighten them."

"I would scare them?"

Jeena smiled. "Yes, you would. Hey, you're the big ferocious tigra, remember? Claws like steel, fangs like sharpened knives." She growled.

Samson laughed in spite of himself.

"Yeah, right," he said, and then became serious again. "Do you think, Jeena, that when they learn about me they'll stop hunting the other tigras?"

"Of course, they will."

"That's good, 'cause there could be more like me, couldn't there?"

"It's possible."

"Yeah." He took a deep breath. "Well, I guess you better go. They'll be wondering what's keeping you."

She had little in the way of clothes but gathered her few T-shirts and a spare pair of moccasins and threw them in the duffel bag along with a wide-brimmed hat she had woven from the fronds of a fruit tree. She picked up the MAAD and held it for a moment before stuffing it into the bag as well.

"I'll leave you the shotgun," she said. "You're no good with the MAAD anyway. Not that I think you'll need to do any hunting. There's plenty of meat left over from the last wolla."

"I'll be okay. You don't think you'll need that, do you?" he asked, pointing to the duffel, a hint of worry in his voice.

"No, of course not. I just like being prepared. I'm a soldier, remember?" She slung the bag over her shoulder. "Stay inside till we've left. I'll close the hatch, but once we're out of sight, you can open it and come out." She turned just inside the hatchway. "I'm not sure how long I'll be gone. It has to be at least ten days' travel to their city and another ten back. Better figure on three weeks, at least."

Samson only nodded, but his eyes grew wide.

Jeena set the duffel down and knelt next to him, taking his head in her hands.

"I'll be back. You can't get rid of me this easily. You and I are stuck together, pal." She stroked his fur one last time then rose and grabbed the pack, closing the hatch as she descended the ramp.

"All is ready?" asked Serug.

"Yes." She tossed her duffel over the horn of the spare kytar's saddle.

"Excellent. Allow me to help thee onto thy mount. It can be quite tricky to one who is unaccustomed to these creatures."

Jeena grasped the saddle horn and threw her leg over, mounting the animal in a single fluid motion.

"Thou hast ridden before," Serug observed.

"Yes. Earth horses. Very similar to these animals."

"Good. This will make for a speedy journey. I would like to present thee to the k'laq before the Festival of Martyrs."

"K'laq?"

"Leader of the Rosh-dan and head of the council," said Esau, riding up next to her. "Come, the time for talk is at night by the fire. The day slips away. Let us make haste."

They rode in relative silence, heading as near to due west as Jeena could reckon. Although the worst of the summer heat was over, the three men pulled the hoods of their cloaks over their heads to protect them from the sun's rays. Jeena soon followed suit, removing her hat carefully from the duffel bag so as not to expose the MAAD.

They traveled through the day without a pause. Serug and Ibrahim rode ahead, speaking seldom and then in muffled tones she couldn't hear. Behind her rode Esau, and though she seldom looked back, she could feel his eyes on her.

Not until the last rays of daylight dropped below the horizon did they stop and make camp.

Jeena squatted beside the crackling fire, holding the cup between her hands and sipping the hot coffee. Her three companions sat on the sandy ground near her, staring silently into the flames. The evening meal had consisted of a kind of gruel prepared by Ibrahim, tasteless but filling. They had spoken little to her but were polite and respectful when they broke their silence.

All except Esau. While he made no hostile gestures toward her, his lips twisted into an unpleasant smile when he spoke, and his eyes gleamed. She had seen that gleam in men's eyes before, and made it a point to speak to him as little as possible.

Serug slurped the last of the strong, bitter coffee in his cup noisily.

"Now, then, Captain," he said, placing the cup before him, "as thou knowest it has been many years since we Afridi last had contact with our brethren. We hunger for any information thou can give us."

"I would be pleased to tell you what I can," Jeena replied. "Let's see...the Union now consists of thirty-eight inhabited worlds; the Coalition Empire twenty-two. These numbers have been fairly stable for the last thirty years, as have the front lines. In spite of that fact, the battles continue.

"The Union center of government remains in The Hague, on Earth. Nothing much really has changed there. The Central Progressives still hold on to power, although they seem little different today than the Reform Conservatives they replaced. Exploration has all but halted due to the war, but there have been significant technological advancements, if you are interested in such things."

Ibrahim frowned. "I believe thou mayhap misunderstood brother Serug's question. We have no interest in the politics of the Union or in the conceit of their science. Rather, we were wondering if thou perhaps had knowledge of our Judaslamic brothers on other worlds, in particular Earth. Is the church strong? Are the temples filled with the faithful?"

Jeena was taken aback. *They don't care about the war or the government. A hundred years of isolation, and all they are interested in is their precious church.*

"I'm sorry, but I can't say that I know much about the Judaslam religion, other than historically. I do know they suffered some setbacks over the years. I don't think they play much of a part in people's lives anymore. You hear very little about them these days. I would say the Arian Christians are the dominant religion of most worlds."

"But thou art from the Union," Esau argued. "Perhaps we are more influential in this Coalition."

"Doubtful. The Coalition has all but outlawed religion on their worlds. They have a long and bloody history of religious persecution."

The three men grew silent, and Jeena wished now she had not been so forthcoming. Tact had never been her strong suit.

"Thy words are troublesome but not entirely unexpected. It was foreseen long ago that God's great works were ours to complete," said Ibrahim. "If mankind has fallen so far from the true path, then so much greater will be his redemption."

"And our glory," added Esau.

"It is not for glory we do this, Esau, remember that. The Rosh-dan are but the tools of God," Serug said.

Esau turned a hard stare to him.

"I do not need to be reminded of the purpose of the Rosh-dan," he said.

Serug returned the stare. Jeena sensed the tension between them. Although Serug was obviously the leader of this group, Esau appeared to hold a power unrelated to his age or position, a power neither Serug nor Ibrahim seemed willing to contest directly.

"It is late," Ibrahim said after the silence had grown uncomfortable. "We have many days' ride left. Let us retire to our sleep now that we may begin the morning that much earlier."

Jeena was asked few questions for the remainder of their journey. It was as though they had decided that since she could tell them nothing of Judaslam in the Union she had nothing of importance to tell them. The men still engaged in small talk as they made their way through the desert, and on the third day they met another traveling party; but Jeena was not included in their conversations.

The arrangement was fine by her. She had grown accustomed to long periods of solitude and the comfort of her own thoughts, and was still uneasy in the company of others. As the days wore on she found she enjoyed the peaceful, unchanging scenery of the desert and the rhythmic rocking of the kytar.

They had ridden for nine days and, according to Serug, were now only a day's ride from their principal city of New Jerusalem. Jeena sat by herself near the fire with Esau on the other side of the flames, his eyes unseen under his dark brows. But she felt his stare. Serug and Ibrahim were lost in the shadows, engaged in an animated debate over some issue of local importance. She would be glad when this visit was over.

In spite of what she had told Samson, she was less than certain she would divulge his true nature to these people. So far, she had seen little to convince her their reaction would be positive. Yet, she could not hide him forever.

So, what the hell am I going to do with him? Sooner or later, I have to return to Earth. Do I take him with me? What would life be for him then, the only alien sentient being ever discovered? But what other choice do I have except to leave him here alone, and I can't do that to him. Dammit, when did I start getting so maternal?

"Thy thoughts are pleasant?" Esau asked. He was leaning far toward the fire, as though to keep his words from the ears of the others.

Jeena looked up, startled from her musings. She could detect a faint scent of bitter coffee and half-digested gruel.

"What?"

"Thou dost smile. Thou remembers another? An old friend, perhaps?"

"Yes."

"A lover?" he leered.

"A friend," Jeena repeated curtly.

"Ahh…but *friend* can be interpreted in so many ways. In my culture it is hard for a man to befriend a woman not his wife. I have no wife, yet I would welcome a woman as…*friend*." He smiled, revealing rows of uneven yellow teeth.

"Then I hope you find one," she replied, and threw the last of her coffee in the sputtering flames.

She left the fire and removed the bedroll from her kytar. Esau hesitated for a moment then turned away, but not before Jeena caught a glimpse of the searing anger that flashed across his face.

Chapter 9

The greatest challenge for any soldier is to survive capture. In this, speed is of the essence. Remember that your odds of escape are inversely proportional to the amount of time you are held. These are the four cardinal rules of survival, should you find yourself in the hands of the enemy:

> 1) Memorize the terrain
> 2) Stay alert for opportunity
> 3) Avoid contention
> 4) Act swiftly
>
> Excerpt from *SAG Survival Manual*

IT WAS LATE IN THE AFTERNOON ON THE TENTH DAY OF THEIR JOURNEY WHEN JEENA FIRST caught sight of New Jerusalem. They were riding through a valley lying between the feet of two mountains. A pair of dark towers appeared on the horizon, rising to the sky like twin spears guarding the hills beyond.

"Prayer towers," said Serug, noticing the direction of her gaze. "From their balconies the priests call the people to service."

A wall now came into view, stretching across the plain. As they neared, she saw that it was formed of large stones, black as obsidian and expertly fitted. The wall crossed the entire pass, a distance, she guessed, of not less than a mile.

"Thou didst not expect so large a city, yes?" asked Serug, the pride evident in his voice.

Jeena shook her head. "What is the population?"

"In New Jerusalem, almost one million. But to the west lie many more communities of the faithful, though none so large. The total population of all our cities nears ten million."

Ten million. Jeena had never heard of an agrarian colony reaching such numbers. As a rule, they tended to stabilize at less than one million—assuming they survived at all.

But these aren't just simple farmers. Vicki described them as religious zealots, and I haven't seen or heard anything to contradict that opinion. And the power of religion can move people in ways other enticements cannot.

They rode to the center of the wall, to a large iron gate with a raised portcullis, its iron spikes just visible in the archway.

"Your fortifications are impressive," she observed. "And yet the need—"

"As I have said," Serug interrupted, "we live among infidels."

Above the wall stood two men wearing the black-and-green livery of the Rosh-dan. Esau called out to one of them.

"Open the gates, Ezechial."

"We have long watched thy coming, Esau," the guard shouted down. "Thou dost bring a stranger oddly dressed. Surely, she is an Apostate?"

"Nay," answered Esau with a warning hiss. "Speak not of this. She comes from a place strange entire. Open, for the k'laq himself will wish to have speech with her."

The guard disappeared from view, and Jeena heard him call down to the other side of the wall. A moment later, the iron gate creaked open. Steadying her kytar, she passed through the meters-thick stone walls into the city of New Jerusalem and into the heart of the Afridi realm.

They entered an open plaza paved with smooth sandstone. At the far end was a large open-air amphitheater; the many tiers of seats formed a half-circle, before which was a round dais, elevated about two meters and ringed by steps. In the center of the dais stood a slab of grey stone about a meter high—an altar, Jeena assumed. The stone was engraved with the sign of the crescent moon.

A rider approached them. He was young—she guessed early twenties—with curly brown hair and a thin beard. He wore no sword, and although his robes were dark, no crescent moon adorned his chest. There was something familiar in the twinkle of his hazel eyes she couldn't place.

He spoke to Serug, but his eyes were on her.

"Welcome home, Serug. The scouts reported thy approach two days ago, but they gave no mention of a stranger."

"No doubt they saved that information for the k'laq, as should be," Serug answered gruffly. "He will wish to speak with this woman at once, so if thou wouldst excuse me…"

"The k'laq has not yet returned from his visit to the west," the young man answered. "He is not expected back until the morning."

Serug frowned, turning his attention to Jeena.

"Well, Captain, I had hoped to present thee to the k'laq today, but it appears that must wait till morning."

"I understand. A day or two will make no difference, provided I return to my ship before long."

"Of course. We will need to find quarters for thee, and perhaps a guide, if thou wouldst like a tour of the city."

Esau rode next to her.

"I would be most happy to show Captain Garza the sights of New Jerusalem," he volunteered.

"We have duties to attend, Esau, or hast thou forgotten? Nay, Daniel will escort her." He spoke to the young man. "Thou art free from thy religious duties for the day?"

"Uh…yes. I mean, I believe so."

"It is a simple question, Daniel," Serug said with forced patience. "Yes or no."

"Yes, I am free for the day," Daniel answered, his face reddening.

"Good." He pointed to Jeena. "This is Captain Garza. She has recently come to Ararat on a ship from the Union. Yes," he said, seeing the wonder in the young man's eyes, "from off-world. Do not bother her with undue questions. Jacob will undoubtedly have more than enough of his own."

He turned to her. "Daniel will find quarters for thee, and anything else that thou requires."

He looked questioningly at Daniel.

"Uh…yes. Of course. The Maudrian have a small apartment that is unoccupied. It is in the northern quarter, across from the linen shop on Junamar Street."

Serug nodded. "I know of the place. Good. Thou willst take her there." He turned back to Jeena. "I will come tomorrow and escort thee to the k'laq."

With a curt bow to Daniel, he nudged his mount and led Ibrahim and Esau out of the plaza, Esau's gaze lingering on Jeena as they passed from view.

Daniel coughed nervously. "Well, then…thou art no doubt tired, Captain Garza. Perhaps thou wouldst like me to take thee to thy quarters first?"

"That's not necessary, and please, call me Jeena. I'm not tired and I'd be interested in seeing the city, if you would care to show me around."

Daniel beamed. "I would be most pleased to do so. And perhaps thou couldst tell me of Earth, and of the other planets thou hast seen as we ride."

"I'm afraid I don't know much about Judaslamics elsewhere."

"Oh, it is no matter," said Daniel, turning his kytar and leading the way around the amphitheater and into the city. "I wouldst love to hear of other worlds and the people who inhabit them, whatever their beliefs."

"Really? It's a deal, then. You show me the city and answer my questions, and I'll fill you in on the rest of the galaxy. If you like, you can start with this amphitheater here."

"Ah, yes. It is called the Nolstradium," he explained. "It was built in the early days of our colony. We use it for public meetings and as a temple on high holy days."

"And the altar? Is it…for sacrifice?"

"Of course," he said, and saw the unpleasant look on her face. "Thou dost not approve of sacrifice?"

"I guess I don't understand why any God would want a dead animal," she said. She reproached herself immediately. *Dammit, watch what you say! This man doesn't have to justify his beliefs to you.*

But Daniel only smiled. "Nay, thou misunderstands. The death of the animal is *our* sacrifice. We live austerely and take no more from the land than we need. The animal we sacrifice is the food we will not have. It is our hunger that is the true gift to God."

"I see. And you're right, I didn't understand. I'm sorry. I have another question, but it may be just as naive."

"Please, feel free to ask me anything. The prophets say we cannot learn if we do not ask."

"All right, then. What about the tigras? I understand you sacrifice them, as well, and yet surely, they're not food."

"Nay," he said sadly. His expression was pained, as though searching for the right words. "It was not always thus," he began slowly. "It is said that in the beginning the tigras were considered as many other wild animals on Ararat— dangerous but not evil. The command to destroy them came later, and was issued by the first K'laq of the Rosh-dan. They quote obscure scripture to justify their actions, but I must confess I do not see their reasoning."

"So, you are not a member of the Rosh-dan? I wondered that you weren't wearing a sword."

"Nay, I am an initiate of the Maudrian, the Judaslamic priesthood. All but the Rosh-dan are forbidden from carrying weapons. The Rosh-dan are..." He shook his head and sighed. "The Rosh-dan were created by Seth, son of Caleb, the prophet and founder of our colony. They were few in number in the beginning and were responsible only for seeing that our religious laws were followed, but their power has grown much of late, in especial since Jacob became k'laq."

"Jacob? I've heard his name mentioned before."

"Yes, Jacob is leader of the Rosh-dan. Thou hast met his son, Esau."

Jeena cringed inside. *So, Esau is the son of their military leader? That explains his haughtiness, and why Serug and Ibrahim seemed unwilling to confront him. I hate to imagine what the father of that one must be like. Well, just one more reason to finish up this visit quickly and get out of here.*

Daniel led them around the amphitheater and turned into a narrow, winding street. She observed that many of the buildings lining the way seemed pressed together and haphazardly erected—a sure sign of rapid population growth. Their nearness to one another blocked much of the sunlight from reaching the street, and the way was dim and shadowy. The thick stones the Afridi preferred for building muffled sounds, including the hoofbeats of their kytars, which together with the muted lighting created an atmosphere of gloom and foreboding.

The dimness did not seem to bother Daniel, who whistled softly as he navigated the maze of streets, occasionally stopping to point out some structure of interest. Finally, the way opened up, and Jeena found herself before a great tower, as black as the gates and rising to the sky. A small arched doorway was carved into its base, and a balcony ringed the top.

"This is the southern Tower of Holies," Daniel explained. "There is another identical to it to the north. The Maudrian call prayers from the towers every dawn and dusk. Thou will hear them tonight."

They passed under the shadow of the tower, continuing their journey into the heart of the city. Again narrow streets wound around grim, oppressive buildings, swallowed in artificial twilight. Daniel continued his tour, pointing out with obvious pride the various engineering accomplishments of New Jerusalem, including the extensive aqueducts that carried fresh water from the mountains, and the immense underground sewer system. Jeena smiled and tried to look impressed, although by late afternoon she was beginning to get bored and more than a little saddle-sore.

They came to a group of low buildings set in a row.

"These are the meal-houses for this section of the city. Art thou hungry?" Daniel asked.

"Yes, I could eat."

"Good," he said, smiling. "It is almost time for the evening meal, and I am famished."

As he spoke a loud gong sounded, echoing off the walls. This was answered by another, farther off. Soon, more joined in, until the city was alive with the sound.

"That is the signal. Come, follow me."

They dismounted, and she followed him to the nearest building.

"We are a communal society, and eat our meals together," he explained. "Each family is assigned to one of the meal-houses set throughout the city. As a bachelor and initiate of the Maudrian, I have somewhat more freedom then most, and have visited most of the houses."

He opened a door onto a large hall, lighted by many candles and filled with row upon row of long wooden tables. They moved aside the doorway as people pressed in behind them, and before long the hall was filled. Jeena observed that, while the men and small children quickly took seats at the tables, the women bustled in and out of doors at the far end of the hall, carrying platters of food and drink. As with all the others she had seen, the men wore dark clothes and untrimmed beards, and the women were covered in long, shapeless robes of rough cloth that wrapped them from head to foot so that only their eyes could be seen.

Daniel led her to one of the nearer tables. An elderly man sat at the head, staring openly at her with unfriendly eyes. Daniel introduced her, explaining in a hushed voice that she was a visitor from afar, brought to the city by Serug.

The man regarded him gravely.

"Those who have left may not dine in our halls, nor their generations, Daniel. Thou knowest the law."

"Nay, she is not an Apostate. She is from…" He pointed toward the sky. "…from the Union," he whispered.

The man's eyes widened in disbelief.

"It is true," Daniel said in answer to the unspoken skepticism. "Serug is to present her to the council in the morning."

The old man returned his attention to Jeena.

"The Union," he growled. "So, at last thou hast returned to our world. It has been long."

"Long, indeed," Daniel agreed. "But Serug wishes the announcement to be held until Jacob and the council have had a chance to make speech with her."

"If thou wishes to keep her presence a secret, thou wouldst do well to cover her. Her dress is immodest."

Daniel reddened. "She is not Judaslamic, Fareed, and is not required to wear the chador. She is a guest in our city and will be treated with all kindness, or Jacob will hear of it."

"Thou takest offense too easily, Daniel. I merely state the obvious. Calm thyself and share the blessings of our table," he said, bowing his head.

Jeena had come close to speaking up in her own defense but thought it best to let Daniel handle the situation. As they sat she whispered in his ear, "If my dress is going to cause a ruckus, maybe I should just leave."

"No, thou shall stay. Thou hast done no wrong. Fareed has made the offense—kindness to strangers is a holy command. But he is right—it is too long since we have had contact with the outside world. We have grown intolerant of other cultures. We are distrustful of them and scornful of their ways. The coming of the Union will be a blessing."

"Daniel…" Jeena began then stopped. *Stupid! Keep your mouth shut. You're here to gather information not dispense it. If they believe the Union is coming then let them. It may work in your favor. You know nothing about this man. Do not let your guard down.*

"Yes?" Daniel said.

"I'm sorry. I was going to say that you at least seem comfortable with outsiders. Have you had contact with the Babylonian colony?"

"Nay," he replied, a look of fright on his face. "Travel to the east is forbidden to all but the Rosh-dan, and even they avoid their lands." He lowered his voice. "It is said they practice human sacrifice and cannibalism. I have even heard it whispered that in days past they would often raid our cities, making off with our children. It is only by the continued vigilance of the Rosh-dan and our own stout walls that we have managed to keep them at bay."

Jeena said nothing. Cannibalism, human sacrifice, baby-snatching—how many times had these same outrageous crimes been charged against strange and alien cultures? Jews, North American Indians, native Africans, Secundus Resurrectors—the list was endless. In every case they had been proven to be outright lies, slanders initiated by those who had a stake in the accuseds' destruction. *Maybe it says something about us, that we are always so willing to believe the stories.* Even Daniel apparently believed them. The Afridi leaders were obviously propagating an atmosphere of fear and hatred toward the Babylonians. The question was why.

Fareed stood and offered a short prayer before the meal was served. The food was simple but nourishing, and well prepared. There was roasted meat and green vegetables, as well as nuts and fresh fruit. Jeena tried to initiate polite conversation with several of the people at her table but was rebuffed. The men openly ignored her comments while the women averted their eyes. Apparently, conversation at mealtime was another proscription of Afridi law.

When the meal ended they left the hall and remounted, and continued their journey north. They traveled less than an hour before Daniel halted.

"I hope this will suffice," he said, pointing to a small, single-story structure. "It is a spare apartment owned by the Maudrian."

"It will be fine, Daniel, thank you." She dismounted and slung her pack over her shoulder.

"Good. I must leave thee now—curfew begins after evening prayer. Serug will be here in the morning to escort thee to the council. I do not know thy schedule, but hopefully I will see thee again before thou leaves."

"I would like that. I have enjoyed your company."

He smiled at the compliment.

"Daniel, there was something I meant to ask you—if I'm not being too nosy. You and Serug bear a close resemblance. Are you...?"

"Serug is my brother."

She smiled. "I see. Well, goodnight, Daniel."

He bowed his head then turned his kytar into the shadows of the street and disappeared.

Jeena stepped into the small one-room apartment—the door had not been locked. It was sparsely furnished with a simple wooden table and two chairs. The table was bare save for an oily and blackened oil lamp. Finding some matches, she lit it, throwing harsh yellow light and sharp shadows across the walls.

Like the meal hall, there were no bright colors or ornamentation anywhere in the room. Against the far wall was a side table on which sat an ewer of water and a small bowl. Next to this was a simple slat bed covered with a coarse mattress. On the bed was a book.

Jeena rummaged through her pack and found a cigar. Lighting it, she sat on the bed and examined the book. It was bound in smooth but well-worn black leather and was embossed with a silver star and moon. The pages were yellow and curled with age, some of them falling out as she carefully turned the pages.

It was a Judaslam Bible. She opened the book randomly to Psalms, and read the text:

> And God the Merciful will come among you
> And sit among you
> In the house of the righteous He will sit
> And over all He will rule.
> Therefore prepare the place of His coming
> Make the holy ground ready
> For in His right hand sits truth
> And in His left hand is the sword of justice
> Over every living thing He will rule
> The birds in the sky
> The fish in the sea
> He will judge them good or evil
> Therefore suffer not the blasphemous among you
> Nor the evil beast to live
> For it speaketh like a man
> To spread its lies upon the world

She placed the book back on the bed and went to the one window in the small room to sit on the windowsill. Leaning her head back, she closed her eyes and listened to the lyrical sounds of the Maudrian prayer chants reverberating through the city. Tomorrow, she thought, should prove an interesting day.

THE BED WAS JUST AS UNCOMFORTABLE AS IT LOOKED, AND JEENA SLEPT FITFULLY. SHE WAS already awake and tying up her moccasins when Serug arrived. She grabbed the duffel bag on the way out then reconsidered and left it in the apartment. Automatically, she searched for a lock.

"Thy things will be perfectly safe," Serug said, sounding defensive. "Theft is unknown to us."

"Of course. I'm sorry. Old habit." She leapt on her kytar and followed as he headed toward the center of the city. "Do you know what will be expected of me at this meeting?"

Serug smiled. "The council simply wishes to make thy acquaintance. They may have some questions concerning this war thou speaks of, but not many.

Have no fear, Captain, it is not to an inquisition I take thee."

Jeena smiled back. *Well, that's reassuring, at least.*

They soon came upon a long, towering structure near the very center of the city. Its walls were made of an alabaster-white stone and its roof of dark wood, sloped like the bow of a ship. Two gleaming iron doors stood atop a dozen marble steps.

This will be the Rosh-dan headquarters, Jeena guessed. It's a building meant to impress. And it does.

They dismounted, and Serug led her up the steps. As they approached, the iron doors opened. *Of course—we're expected.*

The doorway opened to a single large hall, the interior lined in smooth marble. Narrow, slit-like windows of stained glass were set high in the walls. Along the length of the hall stone columns, beautifully carved, ran on either side of a central aisle. Set between the outer walls and the columns were rows of wooden pews. Thin shafts of colored light filtered in from the windows and fell across the floor in a rainbow of subtle hues. It all reminded Jeena of an ancient medieval cathedral.

At the end of the aisle was a long table of ebony wood, and behind it sat five grey-haired men—the Council of the Rosh-dan. A single chair had been placed before the table.

Serug escorted Jeena down the aisle. As they neared the table, the man in the centermost seat rose. Like the others, he was old, his long grey beard neatly combed against the black of his robes. On his head sat a square black hat, and around his neck a silver star and crescent moon hung from a thin silver chain.

But Jeena could only stare at his face. It was the same hard, leathery face she had seen through the binoculars at the cliffs.

Serug halted before the table and crossed his right arm over his chest in salute.

"K'laq, members of the council, may I present Captain Jeena Garza of the Union of Democratic Planets."

The familiar man rose. "I thank thee, Serug. Captain Garza, allow me to introduce myself. I am Jacob, K'laq of the Rosh-dan and leader of the Afridi of Ararat. Before thee sits the elder council of the Rosh-dan: Harun, Jabril, Zachariah and Ezekiel."

As he spoke each name, the man rose and bowed.

"It is with great pleasure that we welcome thee to our fair city."

Jeena tried to smile. "Thank you, K'laq, councilmen, and greetings from the UDP."

If possible, Jacob was even less lifelike in person than he had been in the binoculars. There was a grey tone to his skin, almost matching the color of his beard. Deep, chiseled lines were carved along the length of his face, and even this close she could not make out his eyes. They were lost within the dark caverns sunk deep into his skull and shadowed by projecting brows.

"Please be seated, Captain. As thou might imagine, we are anxious to learn all thou can tell us. A hundred years is a long time to be separated from the rest of mankind."

"Of course. I will be pleased to tell you all that I can," she said, sitting in the proffered chair.

Serug bowed once more to Jacob and the council and slipped quietly away into the shadows of the hall.

"I am told thee has not come to Ararat as an official emissary of the Union." Jacob said.

"Not officially, no. As your men may have informed you, my presence here is an accident of war."

The one introduced as Zachariah nodded.

"Yes, the war. I heard rumor of the Galactic Civil War in my youth. I had no idea it continued."

"I'm afraid so. It has been raging for almost a century."

Jacob raised his brows. "Quite a long time for continuous hostilities."

"Yes, it is," she agreed. "As you may be aware, historically, civil wars are often the longest and bloodiest. This one has proven no exception."

"These worlds which form your enemy, the Coalition, were they not once part of the Union?" asked Harun.

"Yes. The war began with the secession of four planets. They launched attacks on other worlds, steadily gaining territory, and now number twenty-two worlds."

Jacob leaned forward, studying her intently.

"I see. And has the Union been battling all these years to win them back? To force them back into the fold, as it were?"

Jeena shook her head. "No, sir. While the initial break with the Union was an obvious act of sedition, we were willing to work with them toward a compromise. The problems began when they started making territorial claims on other Union planets."

"And these conquered worlds have been unable to free themselves?"

"No. The Coalition Empire holds the populous in a tight grip."

"Empire?" asked Harun.

"The Coalition government is fashioned as a lineal monarchy. Power is centralized in an emperor and channeled to the planets through various royal houses. It's an antiquated system, I know, but very efficient in maintaining tight control."

"So it seems, as the Union has been unable to defeat them," said Jacob.

"Don't be misled by their archaic style of government, K'laq. The Coalition is a highly advanced technological society. While we have superiority in numbers, the Union has fought hard just to keep up with their scientific prowess. Lately, we have even obtained evidence that they are experimenting with the fusion of man and machine, in an effort to create a superior soldier."

Jacob sneered. "Man was created in the image of God. To tamper with that is to commit blasphemy. Did the lesson of the Obsidian Plague teach them nothing?"

"Apparently not. And I doubt they are troubled much by blasphemy. The Coalition practices an atheistic culture."

"Thou means they are godless," said Jabril.

"Yes. From the information we have, it is clear that religion is brutally suppressed on all of their worlds. Apparently, they see it as a challenge to their authority."

Jacob shook his head. "Thou paints a bleak picture of these heathens, Captain. The Union has done wisely to continue this war. Such people must not be allowed to rule."

"But surely even the Union cannot fight a war indefinitely," Jabril said. "How goes the war for thee?"

"Yes, Captain, what is the outlook for a Union victory? I ask for thy honest assessment," asked Jacob.

Jeena paused. These people were obviously not aligned with the Coalition, and could do little with the information if they were. *But how much am I prepared to tell them? The realization has been slow to dawn on us, but even the most strident hawks in the Union have accepted the truth. There will be no victory.*

After a century of war, each side was firmly entrenched in their respective sectors of space. Despite several all-out assaults in the last few years, the front lines had changed little. It was commonly accepted among the higher-ranking officers that a permanent truce was the only realistic end for the war.

It seemed impossible to conceive, but it appeared mankind would soon have to learn to exist as two separate, and mutually hostile, states.

No, there are still too many unanswered questions about these people and their loyalties. Until I can determine what, if any, risk they pose, it's better to operate from a position of strength.

"Victory is very near," she said. "It is inevitable. The Union is simply too large and too strong. The war has dragged on for so long only because of our initial underestimation of the enemy. We were unprepared for war. That mistake has been corrected."

Jacob seemed pleased by her answer.

"That is good news. And thou art correct about the need for preparation. It can mean the difference between a speedy victory and an agonizing defeat, as I must often remind my people."

Jeena saw the opening and jumped at it.

"Yes, as a military commander myself, I couldn't help but notice the impressive defenses of your city, but I am puzzled as to their purpose or need."

The council members glanced nervously at each other, but Jacob only spread his hands out.

"Captain, we are a peaceful people. Our lives are devoted to worship and the spreading of the word of the one true God. But we are besieged, I'm afraid, pressed upon by violent and bloodthirsty savages to our south."

"The Babylonians."

Jacob's eyes flashed, and for an instant Jeena thought she could see a smoldering fire in the black pits.

"Thou hast had contact with them?"

"No, I have simply heard rumors of them since entering your city."

"I see. Thou art correct, of course. In a terribly misguided move, the Union saw fit to give them charter here on Ararat. They were little better than animals when they arrived, cavorting unnaturally and sinfully and preaching all manner of blasphemies. I have often questioned the Union's reasoning behind settling them here. Perhaps they felt our proximity would have a civilizing affect on them."

"Perhaps." *More likely they felt those people had just as much right to their beliefs as you do and didn't give a damn what you thought.*

Jeena felt her pulse quicken. Jacob's air of superiority and condescending attitude was starting to irritate her.

"Alas," he continued, "that has not happened. They have rebuffed all our attempts to instill decency and righteousness in them, falling ever further into wickedness and depravity. Their leader is a witch, adept in the black arts. You smile, but it is true. It is said she can read the minds of men, and more."

"They are warlike savages, Captain. It is why we have spent much time and effort in building our defenses, although we pray always we will never have to test them. It is well they did not find thee first, alone and unprotected. But fear not, thou will be safe behind our walls."

"Thank you, K'laq." *Warlike? This sounds nothing like the over-sexed pacifists Vicki described.* "I am afraid, however, that I cannot stay long from my ship. I was recently able to repair my instruments enough to send a distress signal. Any rescue attempt is likely to be a rapid affair, and I would not want them to have to scour the planet looking for me." *All right, so I'm bluffing. But unless I'm wrong, whatever you've got planned I doubt you'd welcome a Union star cruiser orbiting overhead.*

"Yes," Jacob said thoughtfully, stroking his beard. "That is wise. I would not want to worry them unnecessarily. And in truth, we have been quite successful in keeping the savage Babylonians confined to their southern lands, so thou need not be overly concerned about thy personal safety. Tell me, dost thou have any idea as to when the rescue ship might arrive?"

He asks the question offhandedly, and yet he holds his breath in anticipation of my answer. "Not with any certainty. That is why I wish to remain near my ship. It could be a few days or several months."

"Several months...several months," Jacob repeated. "And in that time it is possible the war may be over?"

"It is possible."

He nodded and smiled. "Very good. As thou may be aware, we Afridi have always kept a discrete distance from the rest of the Union, even in the days before the war. It was necessary in the beginning in order to consolidate our population and to limit undue influence on our culture.

"But we have grown. Our people are many and devout, dedicated to the spreading of the Word. It has been prophesized that the day would come when we of Ararat would carry our message from our own small world to the rest of mankind and, in so doing, once again raise Judaslam to the days of its glory. I feel that day has come. Thy arrival is the sign we have been looking for. The time is nigh."

Careful. Be wary. Promise this man nothing.

"Time, K'laq?"

"Yes, the time of the prophecies nears. I wish to re-establish contact with the Union and meet with representatives of the Union government. Lately, I have puzzled over how to relay that information to them, but God, as always, has seen to my needs and sent thee to us. When thy rescue ship arrives, I would have thee pass on our request for an official meeting."

"I would be happy to inform the President and Congress of your interest in more open dialogue, K'laq."

"Excellent. If what thou sayest concerning Judaslam in the rest of the galaxy is true, then there is much work to do. A new age rapidly approaches, as was foretold. After so long a war the people will no doubt be hungry for purpose and direction. We will provide that direction. We have much to offer humanity, Captain. Most importantly, we have the truth—the word of the one true God and his laws. All of mankind can benefit from our teachings, even thee," he said with a smile.

"Do you think so?" she replied coolly.

"Of course. Consider—thou art a woman, yet a soldier in a great army. Now, it is common knowledge that this goes against thy gentle nature. More importantly, it goes against the laws of the Almighty. Women were created to nurture, not to kill. And certainly they should never raise their hands against men, who were chosen as their teachers and guides in this life. Under Judaslam, thou wouldst learn thy proper place and enjoy the peace and fulfillment that comes from following God's laws."

Jeena returned his smile with an icy stare.

"My proper place is anywhere I damn well choose to be."

Jacob reddened, his face twisting as a wave of anger washed over him.

Careful! He isn't used to a woman speaking to him like that. For a moment, Jeena thought he would lose out in his battle to control his rage, but finally he forced his lips into a tight smile. When he spoke his voice was controlled, though she could see the effort involved to keep it that way.

"Well, perhaps religion was a poor subject for a first meeting. I ask only that thou wouldst keep an open mind." He breathed deeply. "Now then, thou has answered our questions and we thank thee. Is there anything thou wouldst ask of us?"

Yes. I'd like to know what you're really planning, but I don't suppose I would get much more than lies.

"Actually, there is something I was curious about," she said. "Serug explained there is an order to kill the wild cats known as tigras. Might I ask why?"

"They are very dangerous and deadly creatures."

"Yes, of course, but no more so than many others on Ararat."

"Other dangerous animals there are on Ararat, but it is more than just their ferocity and strength that condemns them to death. Scripture is clear concerning them. They are evil in the sight of God."

No, there's more to it than that, I can feel it. He feels threatened by them, even more so than by the Babylonians. But why?

"But, sir, to drive a species to extinction before we've had a chance to fully study them—"

"We have studied them, Captain. Trust me, we know all we need to know concerning this plague on our world. And they were headed toward extinction long before we arrived. Their numbers had been dwindling steadily for centuries; we have only accelerated their fate. The only large population remaining exists far to the north, and we hope to deal with them shortly. They are a dying race, Captain, long on the road to oblivion."

"Race? That seems a strange word to for a species of animal."

It seemed that for an instant something flashed across Jacob's face. Fear? Self-reproach? He had let his guard down and said more than he wished.

But then it was gone, and his expression became rigid once more.

"Species, then," he said with a shrug. "But tell me, why art thou so concerned with this animal?"

"I simply find exo-biology fascinating."

"I see. Well, thou wilt find many other interesting animals on Ararat to study if that is thy interest. Now, I know thou wishes to return to thy ship, but it would be wrong for thee to leave so soon after so long a journey. Stay awhile. Tomorrow is the Festival of Martyrs, and there will be a joyous celebration. I would be honored to have thee attend as the guest of the council." He stood before her and extended his hand.

Jeena rose and offered hers automatically. She found herself agreeing to stay then kicked herself. *I have to get back to Samson. I know now I can't let these people find him. They've already condemned the entire race. Whatever perceived threat this Jacob feels from the tigras, how much worse would it be if he discovered Samson's sentience?*

Jacob clapped his hands, and from a shadowy corner Serug reappeared.

"Serug, the captain will be staying as our guest for a few days. Do I understand that thy brother has been her escort and guide?"

"Daniel. Yes, K'laq."

"Daniel, of course. Perhaps we can impose on his kindness for a while longer, yes?"

Serug bowed. "I am sure he would be most happy to oblige, K'laq."

The members of the council rose and bowed to Jeena, who returned the gesture before being escorted out by Serug.

"THE TIMETABLE WILL HAVE TO BE MOVED FORWARD," SAID ZACHARIAH WHEN SHE WAS gone. "We cannot risk Union involvement."

"It is no matter. We are ready," Jacob answered.

"What of her interest in the tigras?" asked Jabril. "Did thou not find it most unusual?"

"Indeed, I did. But let us not make overmuch of that. It may be no more than idle curiosity, as she claimed. Still, I shall be interested in hearing from Uriah upon his return."

"And the Apostates?" Harun asked. "Now more than ever they must be found."

"And they will be. The dark witch of Uruk knows their location and will share that knowledge with me—with her dying breath."

Chapter 10

And God said to the angels: "I am placing one that shall rule as My deputy," and they replied: "Will You put there one that will do evil and shed blood, when we have for so long sung Your praises and sanctified Your name?"

Proverbs 9:18
Arian Christian Bible

SERUG SEEMED PREOCCUPIED AND SAID LITTLE AS THEY RODE BACK TO HER TEMPORARY quarters. They arrived to find Daniel sitting on the doorstep, the reins of his kytar in his hands. He stood and smiled warmly to them both as they approached.

"Greetings, Serug, Captain Garza. All went well with thy meeting, I hope."

"Yes, Daniel, the council was most gracious," Jeena replied.

"The k'laq has persuaded the captain to stay for a few more days," said Serug. "She is to be the guest of the council at the festival. Jacob has asked me to convey his wish that thou continue as her escort for her time in our city."

Daniel grinned. "I would be most pleased to do so, Serug, most pleased. And perhaps thou wouldst care to join us tonight for the evening meal?"

But Serug had already turned his mount around.

"I have no time, Daniel. The remainder of the cleansing parties will be returning over the next several days, and I must meet with them. My duties doth occupy all my time, brother, as should thine own." Without bidding goodbye, he rode away.

"There is some distance between you," Jeena observed.

Daniel nodded sadly as he watched his brother leave. "He is Rosh-dan. His heart belongs to Jacob." He sighed. "So, what wouldst thou like to see today, Captain?"

"Please, call me Jeena. And I am completely in your hands, Daniel of the Maudrian."

Daniel laughed as he mounted his kytar, his humor returning.

"I am only an initiate, Jeena, and so the title is not yet mine, but..." There was a twinkle in his eye. "...it has a nice ring to it, does it not?"

They rode slowly along the cobbled streets, heading westward toward the residential district, eventually coming to a row of single homes. One stood out from the rest. It had a fresh coat of whitewash, and there were colorful bows and ribbons tied around the fence and the trees. It was the first decoration she had seen in the city.

"It is a marriage-house," Daniel explained. "It is given by the bride's father as part of the dowry, and decorated for the wedding."

As if on cue, bells rang from a nearby temple and a procession appeared in the street. It was led by a young boy dressed in white robes. At his side was a girl, also in white, her face covered by a veil. The couple walked somberly down the street toward their new home, while behind them people chanted and sang.

"They're so young," Jeena said.

"It is our way. A boy becomes a man at thirteen, and a girl may marry even younger if her father approves. But all their lives their family and friends will be there for them, helping and nurturing them."

They continued farther to the south until they came onto a busy, bustling place Daniel identified as the merchant quarter. The streets were lined with shops—bakeries, tailors, cobblers and butchers. There was light industry as well, and Jeena saw mills and granaries, carpentry works and forges, all turning out goods to be delivered in waiting wagons. The streets were crammed with shoppers and street vendors bartering their wares.

There was also the Rosh-dan. On every street corner she saw them, watching the men and women as they worked and shopped. Daniel explained they were there to prevent infractions of religious law. It seemed to Jeena they took great pleasure in their work.

Across from where they stood, two soldiers had stopped a young woman shopper and were berating her. They were shouting and pulling at her chador, apparently finding fault with her dress. As they continued their verbal assault, a crowd began to form.

They're intentionally humiliating her in public, Jeena thought, and felt the blood rushing to her face.

Daniel tried to move her along.

"Come, Jeena, we cannot interfere." Like the rest of the people she had met, he held the Rosh-dan in fear and awe.

She held no such views.

One of the guards, apparently displeased with the girl's answers, slapped her with the back of his hand, knocking her to the ground. Jeena was across the street before Daniel could move. She stopped before the largest and most brutish-looking of the soldiers.

"Leave her alone."

The man gaped at her. "Stand aside. This is none of thy affair."

"I said *leave her alone*," she repeated.

Daniel had worked his way through the crowed and now stood sweating and panting near her.

"Jeena, let us go. Thou cannot interfere." He spoke to the soldier. "She is a stranger to our city and is unknowing of our ways."

"Then best she learn quickly. Remove her—and cover her, lest I arrest her as well. She shows her face like a whore."

Daniel reached for her arm, but she pulled it away.

"And you're a sadistic bastard. You want to arrest me? Try it."

Enraged, the man reached for her—and never saw her move. In an instant, he was on the ground with his wrist held tightly in her grasp. She twisted it harder as he squirmed.

"How does it feel to be helpless?" she hissed.

The second soldier rushed toward them, grabbing Jeena's shoulder. The heel of her foot found his leg. There was a loud crack of bone, and he flew sprawling back into the street, screaming and grasping his knee.

Daniel, stunned into silence by the violence, suddenly rediscovered his voice.

"Stop this!" he shouted.

Two more soldiers had seen the commotion and were moving hastily toward Jeena, swords drawn. Daniel stepped between them and their quarry.

"Enough! This woman is under the personal protection of the k'laq!"

The soldiers halted in their tracks.

"Now," said Daniel, "this has been a regrettable misunderstanding."

There was a loud groan from the soldier still in Jeena's grip.

"Jeena, please," Daniel pleaded, "let him go."

She looked around at the startled faces of the crowd. The young girl was nowhere in sight. She released her grip on the prostrate soldier, who leapt up rubbing his wrist, red-faced and angry.

"As I was saying," Daniel continued, "this has all been a misunderstanding. This woman is a stranger to our city and a guest of Jacob and the council. Any further action against her will be reported directly to the council—do I make my meaning clear?" He pointed to the Rosh-dan still lying in the street gripping his shattered knee. "Thy man there is in need of medical attention. I suggest thou see to him."

The first soldier lifted the fallen man up, supporting him as he limped on his remaining good leg.

"The k'laq shall hear of this outrage," he said as they passed.

"Give him my regards when you see him," Jeena replied.

The disturbance over, the crowd began to disperse. Many flashed angry stares at Jeena, but she observed that not all the faces were unfriendly.

Daniel shook his head. "Thou art quite a mischief-maker, Jeena Garza, but do not worry overmuch. I will smooth things over with Jacob through Serug."

"I'm not worried at all, Daniel. And don't bother Serug. If Jacob has any problems with me he can tell me to my face."

He stared at her. "Art thou always so fearless?"

"Only when I'm hungry. What do you say about lunch?"

DANIEL OBTAINED A BASKET FROM ONE OF THE FOOD HOUSES, AND THEY MADE A PICNIC ON the western wall. They ate in silence as, far below them, farmers and merchants entered and left the city. There was much commerce between the various cities of the Afridi, Daniel explained, the rest of which lay to the east of New Jerusalem.

Jeena finished an apple and tossed the core to the ground below. She looked up to find Daniel staring at her intently.

"That was quite a display earlier," he said.

"I'm well-trained."

"So I observed. How long hast thou been a soldier?"

"Fourteen standard years, since I was sixteen."

Daniel made the mental calculations, converting the time into Ararat's shorter year.

"Truly? I would not have guessed thee for so old," he said, and then reddened. "I am sorry, perhaps that did not sound as it should have."

Jeena laughed. "No, that's all right. I always thought thirty was old, too. You may change your attitude once you get there. Anyway, years spent in zero gravity tend to mask some of the outward signs of aging—and I have no complaints about that."

"Thou hast traveled so far, and I have rarely been beyond the walls of my own city. Tell me, Jeena, what is thy home world?"

"I was born on Earth, if that's what you mean. I'm not really sure I'd call it home, though. Mostly, I've lived on starbases. I haven't been to Earth in almost ten years."

"No family?"

"No."

"I see. Friends, then?"

She shrugged.

Daniel looked away at a wagon train rumbling through the city gates, a cloud of fine dust blowing up behind them.

"I would find such a life...lonely," he said.

Jeena did not reply, and they ate in silence while watching the comings and goings below them.

"Why the desert?" she asked finally

"What?"

"The Afridi were the first chartered colony on Ararat. You had the whole planet to choose from. The southern hemisphere is temperate, almost a paradise. Even the north is more comfortable, if a little cold in the winter. Why did your people choose the desert as your home?"

"Caleb made the decision. He worried that a life of ease would give rise to sloth and licentiousness. As in the ancient days on Earth, the desert tests men's strength and resolve. It is a harsh life, but its very harshness preserves the purity of our purpose."

"And your only purpose is to spread the word of your religion?"

"Yes, of course. What else?"

"I don't know. I simply got the impression today that Jacob might have other motives in mind."

Daniel did not reply, but his expression was troubled.

"You have issues with Jacob, don't you?" she guessed.

"I have no issues."

"But something about him worries you. I can see it in your face."

"Jacob is K'laq of the Rosh-dan. Who am I to know his mind, or question his actions?" he asked irritably. "I am not a soldier like thee, Jeena. I do as I am told. I am not brave."

"I don't know about that, but I sense you care deeply for your people. I think you could be very brave if you thought you were preventing them from coming to harm."

Daniel stood. "We must go."

They took the steps down the wall to the waiting kytars and remounted. They rode slowly along the narrow road that ran beside the city wall, Daniel pausing frequently and biting his lower lip.

"Are you lost?" Jeena asked, smiling.

"Hmm? Nay, it is just...there is a shortcut."

"To where?"

He didn't seem to hear her.

"This way," he said.

Presently, the road came to an intersection and abruptly ended. A high stone barrier had been erected across it, running east. Jeena looked down the cross-street. The barrier seemed to run for many city blocks.

"What's behind this wall?" she asked.

"Come," Daniel said.

He led her east along the stone barrier; there was a strong scent of animals coming from the other side. They rode for two blocks before he stopped. The wall continued for a long way, but here it was in disrepair and part of it had crumbled away, leaving a jagged hole just large enough to peer through.

Daniel dismounted, looking nervously up and down the street.

"We should rest the kytars."

"But, Daniel, we haven't gone very far."

He pretended not to hear her.

"There is a watering trough on the other side of the street. You stay here. I will water the animals. Thou...thou may wish to stretch thy legs."

He took the reins of the animals and walked slowly to the trough across the street. Jeena waited until he had turned his back then peered through the hole, since he had obviously brought her here for just that purpose.

Her curiosity gave way to disbelief.

There were kytars—thousands upon thousands of kytars—snorting and stomping and kicking up dust and sand. Beyond their corrals she could make out rows and rows of low buildings, stretching back until they were lost on the horizon. Barracks—enough for an army of immense size.

Between the barracks and towering over them were wooden structures she had only seen as drawings in ancient texts—siege engines, catapults and rams, hundreds and hundreds.

Daniel returned with the kytars. "We must leave now."

"Daniel..."

"Now, Jeena," he said sternly, handing her the reins of her kytar. He leapt up on his own mount and hurried toward the center of the city.

Jeena followed, her mind reeling. Those armaments weren't defensive. *Jacob is preparing to go to war with the Babylonians. He must be mad! To attack another chartered colony is grounds for immediate revocation of charter.* The Union could strip Ararat from them, not to mention the criminal charges.

She caught up to Daniel.

"You can't let him do this, whatever his reasons. Even if he's successful, your people will lose everything."

He halted, reining his kytar to face her.

"Dost think I do not know this? The law concerning charter is well known, even on Ararat. But he is k'laq. I can do nothing."

"Then why did you show me?"

"I...I do not know. Perhaps so thou wouldst understand the forces that have been set into motion and steer clear of them. Thou art a soldier of the Union, but thou canst not stop this, Jeena, any more than I, and I...I would not see thee harmed trying," he said, blushing.

Jeena smiled. "Thank you, Daniel, but you don't have to worry about me. My days of battle are over. Jacob is a fool if he thinks he can get away with this, but I won't get in his way. This isn't my war."

The afternoon was slipping away, so they rode to a nearby meal-house, reaching it as the evening meal bells rang. They ate in silence, ignoring the stares and whispers of the other diners. When they were done Daniel escorted her back to her apartment.

"Please say nothing of what thou hast seen to anyone," he begged.

"Of course not." She gazed at the families shuffling along the street as they made their way back to their homes. "The people don't know, do they?"

"Nay. They believe all the preparations are simply for our defense. When the time comes, Jacob will no doubt convince them that war is necessary, and they will no doubt believe him. Then they will send the Rosh-dan off in glory." He sighed. "And yet still I pray. I pray that this madness will somehow be averted and all that we have accomplished will not be lost.

"But come, let us not dwell on these matters. Tomorrow is the Festival of Martyrs. Join with us as we celebrate and give thanks and perhaps thou wilt not judge us so harshly."

"I don't judge *you*, Daniel, except to judge that you are a decent and honorable man. I look forward to seeing you in the morning."

She stepped into her apartment as he rode away, collapsing wearily onto the bed. *One more day. One more day and I can leave these people to their petty war and fanaticism. I'm sorry, Daniel, but I can't help you or the Babylonians. It's selfish, I know, but all I want is to be left alone.*

Chapter 11

Wisdom is better than war.

Arian Christian proverb

JEENA HAD JUST FINISHED LACING UP HER MOCCASINS WHEN THERE WAS A KNOCK ON THE door. The morning had broken clear and bright, and already she could hear voices outside her window of people preparing for the festival. She rushed to the door and opened it.

"Serug," she said, startled. "I was expecting Daniel."

"I am commanded by the k'laq to bring thee to the council hall at once," he said tersely.

He had four guards behind him.

"Surely, this can't be about the incident in the street yesterday."

"No questions. Thou wilt come at once." There was no warmth in his voice.

She glanced at the duffel bag containing the MAAD.

"Of course. Let me get my bag."

Serug snatched it from the floor.

"I will take it," he said, and gently but firmly escorted her to a kytar.

He threw the bag on his mount and rode beside her, with two guards in front and two behind. Questions crowded her mind, but she didn't think it wise to speak—Serug seemed in no mood for conversation.

The five men escorted her into the council hall. Jacob sat alone at the council table, his head bowed as if he were lost in deep meditation. He did not rise as they brought her before him, and for a moment she thought he was sleeping.

Finally, he lifted his head.

"I apologize for the abruptness of this meeting, Captain," he said, "but certain…incredible matters have arisen which require thy assistance." He paused, knitting his brow. "Time alone, away from others, can be a blessing, for it can cleanse the mind and bring us closer to God. But too much time away from others is unhealthy. Prolonged solitude can often twist our perceptions, and puzzle the soul. Would thou not agree?"

"I suppose so."

"Thou crashed on Ararat almost two years ago, and during that entire time thou has had no other contact with thy fellow man. It may be that such isolation caused thy mind to become perplexed, so that thou hesitated to convey certain information to me at our first meeting. Think on this, now. Is there not something else of import thou would like to share with me?"

"Information?"

"Yes, something that thou didst not mention at our last meeting, that thou would like to add now. It was, after all, a short meeting, and I may have ended it prematurely. Or perhaps these were matters thou did feel were best heard by my ears alone.

"Yes, yes," he went on, his voice rising excitedly, "such a thing is perfectly understandable and would in no way reflect poorly upon thee. Indeed, it shows wisdom not unexpected in an officer. It is why I have brought thee here now, so that thou might open thyself to me alone, without fear. Come, reveal what thou hast so far kept hidden. I will believe thee."

He still wants my help, and so he's offering me a way out. But out of what? Samson? He's two hundred miles to the east. The war? Have they somehow made contact with the Union? Or the Coalition?

With no more information to guide her, she could only play out her hand to the end.

"I'm sorry, K'laq," she said, "I don't know what you mean."

His face sagged, and he slumped back into his chair.

"I was hoping for so much more from thee," he said wearily. "Bind her."

The men grabbed her before she could move, dragging her to a chair and lashing her tightly with rope as she struggled and shouted, "Jacob, are you mad? I am an officer in the Union Star Corps! Release me!"

"Leave us," Jacob said to Serug.

"But, K'laq…"

"Take your men and wait in the outer hall. Close the doors behind thee, but be ready to return on my command. Go now." He accompanied his words with a subtle hand gesture.

Serug slapped his arm across his chest and spun on his heels, leading his men from the hall. When they had closed the outer doors, Jacob signaled with a flick of his wrist to two guards who had been waiting silently in a darkened side room. They entered carrying a heavy wooden pole, and hanging from that pole, bound and gagged, was a tigra.

"Samson!" Jeena cried, fighting her bonds.

"Samson," muttered Jacob. "Even his name is a sacrilege."

"Jacob, let him go!" she shouted, still fighting to break free.

He nodded, and the men lowered the great cat to the floor. He appeared dazed, and there was a large knot above his right eye.

Jacob spoke to one of the guards. "Explain how thee came upon this animal, Uriah."

The man bowed. "Through the will of God, my cleansing party met Serug's in the desert. He told me of finding the woman and her ship. He confided that he had heard noises coming from the woman's ship and was suspicious that there was another whom she was hiding. He asked that we return to her camp and investigate."

"Which thou didst do."

"Yes, my lord."

Jacob turned his eyes to Jeena. "And what found thee there? Another pilot perhaps?"

"Nay, my lord. We came upon the camp unawares and discovered only this animal. We thought to destroy the beast as our law commands and search the ship, but when we had it trapped and roped, it...it..."

"Fear not, Uriah. Thou speaketh no blasphemy. Have I not seen its hideous form lo, these many years in my dreams, the beast of prophecy? It spoke to thee, did it not? As a man, it spoke, with all a man's guile?"

Uriah nodded, visibly shaking. "Yea, my lord, it spoke. First pleading in a voice fawning and compliant, as though to turn us with flattery, then spitting foul curses at us when we refused to hear more lies and bound and gagged him. Many of his words I do admit, lord, I did not understand, though I deemed them curses by the venom of his tongue."

"Did he speak no more to thee on thy journey through the desert?"

"Nay, my lord. Such was our fear of this demon that we kept him gagged, releasing him only to eat and drink, and then on penalty of death at his first word."

"Who else knows of this creature?"

"Only my men and I. We did not dare strike it whilst in the desert lest it unleash some power and consume us. We brought it with all speed to thee and thee alone, K'laq, for surely, thou wouldst know how to deal with one such as this."

"I do, indeed, Uriah. Thou hast done well. Speak of this to no one. Go not to your homes at present, but thee and thy men retire rather to the council hall guardhouse. Wait there until I send word."

Uriah bowed low, risking one last glance at Samson before leaving the hall.

"What say thee to this?" Jacob asked Jeena, his voice strangely calm.

"What do you want me to say? Of course, I didn't tell you about him. You people kill tigras on sight. I didn't think you'd take the time to find out what he really is."

"And what is he, pray tell?"

"Intelligent. Look, I don't pretend to know how it happened, but he's not anything like other tigras. He's sentient. Talk with him, and you'll see. He's different from all the rest. He's amazing."

"Amazing, yes, of that I have no doubt," Jacob replied.

Jeena regarded him curiously. *Why is he taking this so calmly? He doesn't seem the least bit surprised that Samson can talk. It's almost as if...*

"As if you were waiting for him," she said aloud.

"Waiting for him? I would not put it so. Let us say rather that his coming is not a complete surprise."

"What are you talking about?"

"Come now, Captain, even an Arian Christian could solve this riddle." He closed his eyes and began to recite. "'...and the beast will come among thee and all will be amazed. And they will shout, "Who is like the beast?" and all will fall before him and worship him.'" He looked sternly at Jeena.

"I've read the book you quote."

"And yet, you do not believe?"

"In what? That Samson is some prophesized demon? No, I don't believe it, and I don't think you do, either."

"Do not presume to know what it is I believe!" Jacob said angrily. "It is here, on Ararat, that the first battle in the final war against evil shall be fought. This we have always known. The prophecies must be fulfilled. The beast must not awaken. Ararat is ours!"

He raised a bony hand to point at her, his voice calmer, his anger, for the moment, in check. "This is a local matter, Captain, one that does not require the Union's involvement. I have no quarrel with thee, in spite of thy actions. I ask only that thee turn from this creature. Thou wouldst not even have to raise thy hand against him. Only deny him, and all will be forgotten."

Jeena looked pityingly at Samson lying bound, a leather gag strapped over his mouth. *What can I do for him anyway? I can't fight this entire city and this army alone. And even if I could, what then? Eventually, I'll have to go back to the Union. What future could he possibly have when I leave, alone on this desolate world? The sad truth is, he was doomed from the beginning.*

"I'm tired, Jacob. I'm so damn tired of war," she said wearily. "I don't want to fight you. I don't want to fight anyone ever again." She lifted her gaze to him. "But you're mad. Didn't you hear a word I said? He isn't a demon from some moldy old myth. Look at him. Look at him! He's alive and aware and intelligent, and probably scared out his mind. How can you even think of killing him now?"

"Now? What dost thou think has changed? Nay, his intelligence matters not. He is altogether evil, as is his entire species."

"Why, Jacob, why? Why are you so intent on killing him and his kind? And what did you mean, 'the beast must not awaken?'" Awaken from what? Why the hell are you so afraid of them?"

"We fear nothing," he said, but she knew it was a lie. "I see now that thou art already under his spell. Or perhaps thou, too, are part of the prophecy, the Whore foretold—she who would aid the Beast against her own kind. I had plans for thee, Captain. It is not my will that thou should come to this end, but alas, thy salvation is beyond me."

He clapped his hands twice, and Serug and his men reappeared, Serug now carrying Jeena's bag.

"Serug, have thy men take her to the prison."

They untied her and dragged her away as she fought.

"Jacob! Jacob, let him go! Don't you touch him, you son of a bitch!" she shouted as they took her from the hall.

"I SEARCHED HER BAGS AS THY HAND SIGNAL COMMANDED, K'LAQ, AND DISCOVERED THIS," said Serug.

Jacob looked at the object closely. It was some sort of rifle, that was obvious, but of a kind he had never seen. It was heavy, yet well balanced, with a strange tube underneath the barrel. He turned it over in his hands several times.

"A weapon of their science, no doubt," he said scornfully. "We have no use for such toys. Remove it to the armory."

"Yes, K'laq." Serug suddenly gripped his sword as he beheld the tigra.

"Peace, Serug. The beast is bound well. It is to be our final sacrifice tonight at the ceremony. I wish it to be a surprise for the people. Have it brought to the Nolstradium at the proper time."

He watched Serug leave the hall before turning his attention to the tigra. The beast was fully awake now and lay trembling on the cold marble floor.

Jacob went to him, studying him dispassionately.

"Well, now, demon, it is just the two of us. Shall I keep thee gagged, or test my soul against thy serpent's tongue?" With a cackling laugh, he pulled the blade from beneath his robes and, with a flick, cut the gag from the creature's mouth.

"NIZERAH, WE HAVE A NEW GUEST FOR THEE," ONE OF THE GUARDS SHOUTED INTO THE JAIL.

They had bound Jeena once they left the hall, and now he pushed her off the kytar. She fell to the ground with a thud. A squat bearded man answered the call and came out from the prison into the street. He bent down to take a closer look at her. He was dirty and had a foul odor. An ugly scar started at his brow and descended diagonally across his face. At the point where the scar and his left eye met there was a useless white orb.

He examined her with his working eye. "An outsider, yes?"

"Yes," answered the guard. "Arrest ordered by the k'laq himself."

"Ahh, an important prisoner. Thou binds her strongly for one so small," he said, grinning.

The guard stiffened at the implied insult.

"Do not let her size fool thee. She fights like ten cats," he said, wiping a trail of blood from his face.

"Yes? Well, perhaps a few days without food and water will soften her purr, eh?"

SAMSON CHOKED AND COUGHED AS THE GAG FELL AWAY.

"Better, demon?" the man named Jacob asked.

"I'm...I'm not a demon," he said hoarsely. If he could just remain calm perhaps he could reason with this man. After all, humans were intelligent and reasonable. But never in his life had he felt so afraid.

"Yes, I know," replied Jacob, smiling.

"You know? But you told Jeena I was the Beast. I don't understand. If you know I'm not your enemy..."

"I said thou art no demon, but thou art surely mine enemy. Thou art more dangerous to me than any ten demons. Now, answer me well, for I will know if thou art false. Are there any more like unto thee? Can any other of thy race speak? Answer!"

Samson paused. How many nights had he lain awake asking that same question? He had only seen one other living tigra, and that had been at the cliffs years ago. And yet, if he was here, wasn't it possible there were others?

No, there would have been some sign by now, some evidence of intelligence in all these years. *I'm a freak, that's all.*

"I don't think so," he said.

Jacob seemed visibly relieved by the answer. "That is good, very good. Well, then, it seems we have run out of conversation." He reached for the gag.

"Wait, please. You don't need to do this. I'm no threat to you or to anyone. I would never hurt your people. I admire man. Jeena and I—"

"Jeena? Ah, yes, the captain. Thou hast some sort of feelings for her, and she thee, strange as that seems to me. And how wouldst thou describe that?"

"Our relationship? Well, I guess we're friends," he replied uncertainly.

Jacob laughed. "Friends? Friendship implies a bond of equals. Though she is little better than an animal herself, blind to the will of God, she is still human. Dost thou truly consider thyself her equal?"

"Yes. No. I mean...I don't know. It's just..."

"Confused beast. Can it be that she has never explained what thou art to her? Then I shall. Here is the truth of it—thou art her pet and nothing more, just an animal she discovered in the wilderness and to whom she taught some simple tricks to help pass the time. Canst thou truly believe she has some deep feelings for thee, thou who art no more than a beast? Do not delude thyself. Doubtless she will feel some small grief at thy passing—we humans have a soft spot for our pets, after all—but she will soon enough find a replacement. A turtle, perhaps."

Samson glared at him, his retractable fangs descending involuntarily into view.

"Ah, now the true nature of the beast is revealed," Jacob mocked.

Samson cursed himself as he tried to will the teeth back to their resting position. They were a constant reminder of who and what he was and he hated them, but they were an autonomic response to his anger.

"I've done nothing to you. Why do you hate me so much?" he asked. The fangs slurred his speech slightly, further humiliating him.

"Because thou art an abomination. Man alone was made in God's image. Thy very existence makes mockery of that. But even were it not so, still would I desire your destruction and that of all your kind. Thou wilt not take this world from us, not thee nor thy entire race, low and bestial."

"Take the planet from you? Jacob, my species are just animals. How could we take it from you?"

Jacob did not answer, only moved quickly and pulled the leather gag into Samson's mouth before he could react, wrapping it even more tightly than before. Satisfied the tigra could not speak, he sat back in his chair and shook his head in mock sympathy.

"Poor stupid animal, ignorant even of thine own nature. Alas, that thou shall die with no answers to thy questions. And rest assured that this very night will thee die—and soon, the last of thy damned race."

Chapter 12

> Trust no one, not even your fellow prisoners. The enemy will have spies and traitors among them. Be guarded with all offers of help. Above all, remember your training and trust your instincts.
>
> excerpt from *SAG Survival Manual*

JEENA TESTED HER CHAINS. THEY RAN FROM THE MANACLES AROUND HER WRISTS TO A large iron ring imbedded in a heavy stone in the center of the round cell. It allowed her to approach the door, but not quite reach it.

There were several narrow windows cut high in the wall, and a few slivers of light dimly illuminated the area around her. She saw a second chain linked to the iron ring and followed it across the cell, almost stumbling over a man lying deep in the shadows. Pale and emaciated, he wore a tunic of what once must have been fine, glimmering cloth, but which was now soiled and tattered. On his face and arms were deep scars and blisters that had been left untreated and which were now festering.

She squatted near him and pressed her fingers gently to his neck in search of a pulse. He opened his eyes slowly.

"I am still alive," he said. His voice was weak, and there was a rattle to his breathing she had heard many times before. It was the sound of one near death. "I am Touloc, of the city of Uruk."

"I'm Jeena Garza."

His gaze fell on her flight suit. "You are an outsider?"

"Yes. I'm from the Union."

His eyes widened. "The Union is here? Ishtar be blessed."

Jeena shook her head. "No, Touloc, I'm sorry. I'm here alone, marooned on Ararat. The Union has not returned." She watched as hope faded from his eyes. "Who are you? Why have they done this to you?"

He took several labored breaths before attempting an answer.

"I am a messenger from the leaders of the Babylonian Confederacy. I was sent to seek help from Mordachi of the city of Pyros. The Rosh-dan intend war upon us, there can be no doubt now. I have seen their army, long hidden in their western lands. We cannot stand against such might. Almost a half-million they number." He coughed, spraying blood. "I have failed."

"Where is this Mordachi?"

He stared up at her with a look that was both pleading yet suspicious.

"Touloc, I am not in league with the Rosh-dan. I don't know if I can escape from here, but I'm going to try."

His eyes are clouding. It's almost over.

"Pyros lies hidden deep in the Azulz. Find Mordachi...please..."

He wheezed and was gone.

Jeena closed his eyelids gently. *A half-a-million-man army, on a zed-tech world. Jacob obviously means not just to defeat the Babylonians but to wipe out all trace of their existence.*

She leapt up. *Of course, he does! That's how he intends to get away with it. Manifest Destiny—who would be left to challenge it? They would have to get rid of me, of course, and this Mordachi and his people...and Samson.*

Samson!

She tugged viciously at her chains. Her immediate problem was escape. She had to get out and stop Jacob from sacrificing Samson. *And what if I'm already too late?*

Her hands balled into fists, and her eyes began to sting. *Then, Jacob, you will die. I'll kill you on your own altar. I swear it.*

THE DAY WAS SLIPPING INTO DUSK, AND THE FEW RAYS OF LIGHT THAT HAD EARLIER LIT THE cell were fading. She had worked steadily, using the edge of her shackles to chip away at the stone holding the iron ring. It was a painfully slow process, and time was precious; but if she could just work the ring loose...

There was coarse laughter from outside the cell, and she jumped up, dispersing the broken bits of stone and dust with her foot. She heard a loud crack followed by a heavy thud, and then the sound of keys being tried in the lock. The cell door flew open.

"Daniel!" she cried in surprise.

"Shhh!" He fumbled with the large ring of keys in his hand until he located the correct one and released her from her shackles. "I am committing a great crime, but I will not have thy death on my conscience. I have a kytar outside. Take it and fly with all speed from New Jerusalem." He grasped her shoulders and looked sternly into her eyes. "Go not south. Thou art right, this is not thy war, yet war will come and I would have thee far from it."

"Thank you, Daniel," she said, rubbing her wrists. "But what about you? You can't stay here now—Jacob will have your head. Come with me."

He smiled. "I am most flattered, but I cannot leave. This city is my home, Jeena, these people, my people. They are not evil, only misled. I would not wish to live elsewhere."

"Very well, then. I thank you for all you've done for me, but I need one last favor. Serug had a weapon of mine..."

He nodded. "When I heard they had arrested thee, I went to him to plead for thy release. He would not hear me, and ordered me gone, but I overheard somewhat of his conversation with his men. Much of it was of no concern to me and I paid little heed—a tigra, I gather, of some special worth is to be sacrificed tonight at the festival—but then I heard him speak thy name and my ears grew quicker. He spoke of a weapon that had been found in thy bags, and he ordered it to the armory."

"Thank you again, Daniel. And you were wrong in what you said before—you are a very brave man," she said and kissed him.

He reddened to the ears. "Thou art most welcome. But, Jeena, I am not a traitor and these are my people. I would not have thee harm them."

"All I want is to leave, Daniel. I promise I'll try not to hurt anyone, but one way or another, I leave New Jerusalem tonight."

FOLLOWING DANIEL'S DIRECTIONS SHE MADE HER WAY BACK TO THE WALL WHERE THEY HAD ridden yesterday. She continued along the road past the place where she had seen the barracks and the herd of kytars until she came to a large two-story brick building occupying almost the entire block.

She dismounted in an alley that ran alongside the building and peered around the corner. A door lamp illuminated the entrance. A lone soldier guarded the way, his hand resting on the hilt of his sword. She retreated back into the alley and found a discarded piece of cloth among the trash bins. Ignoring the foul odor, she threw it over her head and shoulders. Hunched over and affecting a heavy limp, she stepped out onto the street.

The guard observed her closely but did not move from his post. As she passed him she stumbled, falling towards him. Reflexively, he held out his arms to catch her. Jeena threw her elbow, slamming it into his chest. As he slumped forward she caught him, twisting his neck expertly. There was a sharp crack, and he fell lifeless to the ground.

She untied the keys from his belt and opened the armory doors. Taking the lamp from its hook, she stepped inside.

The light revealed a cavernous room and an immense store of weapons. Swords and spears, bows and pikes were stacked throughout, row after row after row.

She searched each row, swinging the lamp at the stacks of weapons, until she stumbled on the MAAD lying in a pile of swords. Setting the lamp down, she reached for the weapon.

A blow struck her from behind, and she fell to the ground. She rolled onto her back as a heavy weight landed on her chest. In the flickering light of the lamp, she could just make out the face of her attacker.

Esau.

"Bitch!" he cursed, and struck her across the mouth. He thrust the edge of his knife against her throat. "Thou should have shown me greater kindness on our journey together. No doubt thou wishes to be my friend now, eh?" His eyes flirted over her body.

"Yes," she said calmly

"Eh?"

"You're right. I do wish I had been kinder to you. Perhaps we can still be friends. I mean, I'm hardly in a position to stop you, am I?"

He pressed the knife more firmly, and eyed her suspiciously. With his free hand, he grasped the zipper of her flight suit and slowly pulled it down, exposing her breasts. He grinned. His hand wrapped around the flesh and squeezed. She moaned. Startled, he momentarily relaxed his blade hand.

Though Jeena had feigned resignation, she had actually been tense, waiting for this chance. Her hand shot out, and she grabbed his wrist as her left foot swung in a compact arc to come crashing against his face. He tumbled off her, and she leapt up, snapping the wrist in the same movement.

With an agonized howl, he dropped the blade. She snatched it up and loomed over him, fiery rage in her eyes.

JACOB STOOD ON THE DAIS, THE ALTAR BEHIND HIM STILL DRIPPING WITH THE BLOOD OF recent sacrifices. He gazed out over the throng of the faithful that packed the amphitheater and looked on from windows and roofs of the higher buildings, cheering and waving. There were religious banners and flags, and everywhere was the green-and-black of the Rosh-dan.

The sun was setting. The prayers had been read and the sacrifices performed. Soon, it would be time for the feast itself.

It had gone well, even though that fool Daniel had not shown to do his readings. Jacob would remember to speak to the Maudrian about him. It was a shame he was Serug's brother.

An explosion like a loud clap of thunder rolled out from the western edge of the city, accompanied by a great gust of blowing sand, forcing worshipers to cover their eyes.

"Nathaniel!" Jacob cried as the wind whipped around him, knocking his hat from his head.

A soldier ran up to him.

"Take a unit of the Rosh-dan and find the cause of that disturbance." He raised his arms to the crowd, calming the murmurs of the confused masses. "Peace, peace," he shouted. "Be not alarmed. We shall discover the source of the noise. For now let us not allow it to interfere with the festival."

The murmuring stilled.

"We have one last sacrifice to make, a gift I have saved for thee. It has been our duty and our privilege to prepare the way for the coming of the new order and the exaltation of Judaslam throughout the universe.

"It has not been an easy path. We have striven to make this place holy, to rid our world of the evil that infests it. We have not been idle.

"Long ago, our forefathers wisely decreed that the beast known as tigra should be driven from our world, and we have labored hard toward that end. Almost, our work is done. I have brought one of the few remaining creatures here, to be offered to God as a sign that our blessed Ararat will soon be cleansed of this plague."

He strode to the edge of the dais, his dark eyes bearing down on the awed crowd.

"Other evils there are, but their time, too, is at an end. For too long have we endured the blasphemies and wickedness of those who would turn from the Word. So, let us steel ourselves to our duties and, with this sacrifice, once again commit our lives to purifying our world for the greater glory of God!"

The crowd erupted in a frenzy of wild cheers. At his signal two guards appeared on the podium behind him, carrying the animal as before. They laid it on the altar and quickly slipped a rope around its neck, pulling its jaw back and exposing its throat. The beast trembled uncontrollably on the cold, slick altar, eyes white with fear. Jacob walked slowly toward it, knife raised high above his head.

"Jacob, please," it rasped, "don't do this."

A tug on the rope, and its pleas were silenced. Jacob murmured a prayer and laid the blade on the exposed throat.

"Jacob!"

THE MAN ON THE PODIUM WHEELED, KNIFE IN HIS UPRAISED HAND. JEENA HAD COME UP from the rear of the Nolstradium, riding a kytar, Esau mounted before her. His hands were bound, and she had the barrel of the MAAD shoved under his chin.

"Let him go, Jacob! Now!" She jumped off the mount, dragging Esau down with her and forcing the kytar down onto its flanks. Keeping Esau before her, she moved carefully toward the dais, spinning and turning so the wall archers could not get a bead on her.

Jacob shook with rage as he glared down at her from the podium, his dark eyes now blazing with a red fire.

"Corrupt and immoral whore! Put down thy weapon. Thou stands before the altar of God!"

She fired a single shot at his feet, sending stone splinters flying up at him.

"Don't lecture me, you bastard!" she shouted, pointing the barrel back at Esau. "I'm a soldier, Jacob. I have killed more men then you can possibly imagine. I won't hesitate to kill again. Or do you need a demonstration of my resolve?"

She lowered the barrel to Esau's crotch.

"Father!" shouted Esau. He had a large gash above his left eye, and his jaw was swollen.

"Hold! Do not shoot!" He spun around to the soldiers holding Samson. "Release the beast!" he hissed.

The guards hastened to cut Samson's restraints, and he leapt from the podium to stand shaking and wide-eyed at Jeena's side.

"Can you run?" she asked him.

Not yet able to speak, he nodded.

"Run?" Jacob railed, "And where wilt thou run to? Can thou truly believe that in all of Ararat there is a place we will not find thee?" He raised his arms to the massed men who were slowly inching their way toward her. "Behold the Army of God!"

Once Samson was released, she had hit the primer for the concussion cannon. A high whine emanated from the weapon, steadily increasing in pitch.

Now, the sound abruptly stopped.

"Jacob," she said, "behold this."

Pushing Esau to the ground, she leveled the weapon away from the amphitheater toward the city gates behind her and fired, throwing herself on top of Samson as she did.

The cannon erupted with a deafening roar. The blast ripped through the air, the massive energy wave striking the wall and exploding it into cloud of dust. The recoil wave instantly hurled back—a hurricane level wind that flattened everything before it.

As it passed over, she leapt up, pulling the kytar up with her. Everything was gone—the gate, the wall, the archers. All that remained was a gaping hole a hundred yards wide, ringed on either side by a pile of rubble. Her ears rang painfully, and a fine black mist fell over the plaza.

"C'mon, let's move!" she shouted to Samson.

Disorientated from the blast, he stumbled twice but quickly recovered and raced for the opening in the wall. Jeena took one last look behind her. Bodies littered the plaza, most knocked unconscious by the force of the recoil wave. On the dais, Jacob knelt clutching his head, his face twisted in pain and rage, a trail of blood running from his ears.

They raced well into the night, until the kytar was foaming and stumbling and even Samson was beginning to breathe hard.

"Okay," she said, dismounting, "let's take a rest." They were deep into the desert but still days from her ship.

Samson looked back in panic. "No! We can't stop. They're right behind us!"

She knelt and grasped his shoulders, feeling him tremble under her fingers.

"Samson, the kytar can't go any further. Not even you can run forever."

"No! We have to go! They'll come for me. I–I..." And suddenly he pressed his face against her. He had not cried since he was a cub, and Jeena could do nothing more than hold him tightly and let the fear flow through him.

When his body had stopped shaking, she pushed him away and held his tear-streaked face in her hands.

"I'm sorry," he said softly.

"Sorry for what? You don't ever have to apologize for being scared."

"You weren't scared."

"Like hell. My heart was in my mouth the whole time I was in the plaza. I'm just used to fighting in fear. Hopefully, it's a skill you'll never have to learn."

He reached up and touched her face.

"The skin under your eyes is turning black."

Jeena touched her face. "Probably from the concussion cannon. I must not have gotten down quick enough. I told you it's a dangerous weapon."

He gazed warily back west.

"Jacob won't come after us tonight, not after seeing the power of the MAAD. If he comes at all it will be with his army, and that will take a while to gather, especially since he no longer has any weapons."

"I heard a sound like thunder before you arrived at the plaza."

"That was his armory being turned into dust. Jacob is going to be busy rebuilding for some time." She rose and began removing supplies from her mount. "Let's make camp. I want to give the kytar a break from the saddle."

There was not much wood to be found, and the fire was small and gave little warmth. They sat side by side and ate some of the dried meat she had found in the armory. Samson was unusually quiet, and she didn't press the conversation.

He's lost his utopian view of mankind, and that's going to take a while for him to sort out. I suppose it's a good thing. Maybe he'll think better of his own race now that he's seen the cruelty man is capable of.

But she knew something else had been lost on that altar as well—his innocence—and the thought saddened her.

"Why do they hate me?" he asked finally.

"Don't dwell on it, Samson. Jacob is mad."

"It wasn't just Jacob. I heard them all screaming for my blood. Those people didn't even know me, but they all wanted to see me die."

"Religion can make people do crazy things. Jacob has them all convinced you and your kind are evil, and that killing you is necessary."

"Why? Why does he want the tigras dead?"

"I'm not sure, but I sense there's more than religion involved. There has to be something else, something besides just a quick pass into heaven."

"Heaven—isn't that where humans go after they die?"

"That's what some people believe."

"Do you?"

"Not really. I haven't any proof that God doesn't exist, but then again, no one's ever been able to prove to me that He does."

"I'm not sure if I believe in God or heaven, either, but…" He stopped and stared into the fire.

"But what?"

"Nothing. I mean, I know I'm not human, but I mean, if there were a God do you think…you know…" He sighed in frustration. "Never mind, it's stupid."

Jeena fought the lump that had suddenly appeared in her throat. She waited until she was sure of her voice before she spoke.

"It's not stupid. And if any God would keep you out of heaven, He wouldn't deserve to be God."

They were both exhausted, and although she knew they should set watches she wanted them rested. The desert night was chill, and she shivered as she lay down on the bedroll she had taken from the armory.

"You can lie next to me if you want," Samson said. "I know how you get cold outdoors."

"I thought you said I made you too hot."

"Well, I wouldn't mind tonight, if you don't."

She hesitated then scooted across the bedroll, curling up against him. Her exhaustion overtook her, and she was quietly snoring in just a few minutes.

IT WAS A DREAM. SHE WAS FLYING, SOARING ABOVE A STRANGE PLANET. THE GROUND BELOW was black and charred, the air thick with smoke and the smell of death. A great war had been fought here, beyond anything she had seen before. The entire planet was nothing but ash and cinder.

The image faded. Now she was on another world, but the scene was the same—everywhere the land was scorched and blotted, the sky dark and evil. This world too fell away, and a new one appeared, then another, and another. From planet to planet she leapt, finding only ruin and the silence of death.

Finally, on the last world, she saw a dim light and flew to it. There, amid the waste and destruction, stood a dark throne, and upon the throne sat a figure bathed in a golden light. His head was bowed in weariness or sorrow, and on it was a crown of many stars. She looked closely at the throne. It was crafted from the bones of the dead.

She flew nearer to the crowned figure, and as she did so he raised his head. Tears steamed down his face. He was trying to speak—it was a warning, she knew, though she did not know how she knew; she could not hear his words.

Then, the light around him faded, and darkness surrounded her. Still, she had recognized the face of the being who sat upon that terrible throne of death. It was the face of a tigra.

It was Samson.

SHE AWOKE WITH A GASP.

"Whoa, whoa," said Samson, holding her gently as she struggled. "Bad dream?"

"What? Yes. Yes, I guess so," she stammered, unsure.

"Want to tell me about it?"

She looked up at the golden face barely illuminated by the dying fire.

"I…" What was it? Something about Samson and a crown? But the dream was already gone. "It's nothing. I can't remember it now." She closed her eyes and drew herself closer to him and had no more dreams.

THEY MADE IT BACK TO THEIR CAMP AFTER A WEEK OF FORCED MARCHES AND FOUND IT IN ruins. The tent had been slashed to pieces and the firepit broken. Their provisions were scattered, and there were dents and scratches on the ship

"I guess I should have kept my mouth shut," said Samson. "I thought that if I explained who I was they would leave me alone. Instead, when they found out I had been living here with you, they went berserk, tearing the place up and trying to get inside the ship. Luckily, I had sealed it up after you left."

"Talking is the only reason you're still alive. A normal tigra they would have killed on the spot. Besides, it's just a camp. No real loss."

But in truth, she felt a great deal of loss. This camp had been her only home since coming to Ararat, and its destruction emphasized the point that they were truly on the run.

"I guess we can't stay here, can we?" Samson said wistfully.

"No. Jacob intends to destroy the Babylonians, but there's no guarantee he won't come by here first to deal with us."

"I suppose you're right. Do you really think we can find this guy Mordachi?"

She had told him of her encounter with Touloc in the prison during their run from New Jerusalem.

"We're going to try. We know he's somewhere in the Azulz. We'll just head north toward the mountains and hope we find a trail."

He looked skeptical. "Just head north? You call that a plan?"

She stooped down and began collecting supplies for the trip.

"No, you're right. We should just stay here and wait for the Rosh-dan to come by. I'm sure they'll be reasonable."

He grumbled an obscenity and began helping her gather provisions.

"I don't know if anyone has ever told you this before, but sarcasm is very unattractive in you."

They packed as much food and supplies as the kytar could carry, including the binoculars and the communicators. There was a small tent as part of the ship's standard provisions, and although it would be a tight fit for them both, they brought it as well.

Jeena strapped the handgun to her side and slung the MAAD over her shoulder. With the kytar already burdened, she would have to walk. She grasped the reins and, taking one last look at the place she and Samson had called home, began the journey north.

It was almost autumn, and the knee-high grass had returned to its golden color, the blades blending perfectly with Samson's coat. His movements were graceful, though Jeena knew his was not as fluid as that of other tigras. She had tried to get him to embrace the skills his species possessed, but he bristled at learning the ways of "those animals." Still, several million years of evolution could not be completely denied, and he moved through the grass stealthily, his footfalls so silent she occasionally looked down just to make sure he was still there.

The heat of summer was just a memory, and the air was warm but not stifling. The walk was pleasant, and she puffed easily on one of her last remaining cigars, Samson padding silently by her side.

"So, I guess there's definitely going to be a war soon, huh?" he asked.

"Looks like it," she replied, not taking the cigar from her mouth.

"What's war like?"

She removed the cigar and gazed down at him. "Noisy. As loud and chaotic as a thunderstorm and just as unpredictable."

"You've been in a lot of wars. Have you…have you killed a lot of people?"

She said nothing.

"I'm sorry, I shouldn't have asked that. I'm just worried."

"You don't need to worry. We're not going to war. We're headed in the opposite direction."

"I know, but what if Jacob wins?"

She gnawed on the cigar. "Touloc seemed to put a lot of stock in this Mordachi and his people. Between them and the Babylonians I'm sure they'll be more than a match for the Rosh-dan."

She smiled, but she was far from confident. Touloc had only learned of the true size of the Afridi army before his death, and the shock of that knowledge had been easy to read on his face. It was obvious he hadn't expected anything close to that number.

"Well, that's good," Samson said.

They walked in silence for a while.

"Do you think this Mordachi will be okay—about me, I mean? I used to think I'd like to meet more people, but now I'm not sure. In the books humans all seem so smart and brave and nice."

"Some are like that," she said, tossing the butt of the dead cigar away, "and some are like the Rosh-dan. And you can't tell which is which until you get to know them. I'm sure he'll be okay."

Actually, I'm not sure at all, but I intend to find out before I put you in danger.

"I'm just sorry your first experience with other humans was so bad."

"Yeah, well, I guess it was still better than running into a bunch of tigras." He pulled a piece of grass and stuck it in his mouth, his mood for conversation over.

Chapter 13

Battle at altitude presents one of the toughest conditions a soldier can face. It should be avoided if possible. If you do find yourself in such a situation remember that your two worse enemies are cold and thin air. Cold saps the will to do anything but get warm. Hypoxemia reduces your ability to think and to move. A cold, slow, confused soldier is of no use to the Union.

excerpt from *SAG Survival Manual*

J EENA LEANED CLOSE TO THE FIRE, LOOKING OVER THE MAP VICKI HAD PROVIDED THEM prior to leaving the ship. They were only five days out, but the air was already cooler. The smaller size of the planet meant that they would continue to encounter steadily colder temperatures with every mile north.

Samson sat quietly near her. She had hoped his reticence would improve as they increased the distance between themselves and the Rosh-dan, but his mood did not recover. There was an air of melancholy around him, and he seldom initiated conversation.

She put the map away and rubbed her hands briskly.

"Wish we had some marshmallows," she said.

Samson did not respond.

"What are marshmallows?" she continued rhetorically. "Glad you asked. They're outrageously sweet blocks of foamy sugar. It's an old Earth custom to burn them on the end of sticks. I have no idea why, but they taste wonderful."

Samson nodded silently.

"C'mon, Samson, you have to snap out of this funk. I know you've been through a lot, but you can't let it consume you. Are you still worried about Jacob?"

"No, not exactly."

"What, then? I wish you'd tell me whatever it is that's bothering you."

He continued to stare into the fire.

"What am I to you, Jeena?" he asked, in a voice that was little more than a whisper.

"What do you mean?"

"What is our relationship? Am I your pet?"

"*What?*" She was startled and shocked at the question. "Where the hell did you get a crazy idea like that? Of course, you're not my pet."

He turned to her. "Jacob said you only took me in because you were bored, and that you taught me tricks just to pass the time. He said you could never really like me, not the way people like each other, because I'm just an animal. Is that true?"

Jacob, you bastard! "Dammit, no, it is not true. Jacob is a sadist. It wasn't enough for him just to kill you; he wanted to hurt you. They're lies, Samson. Put them out of your head."

"I've tried, but I can't. I keep wondering—if I were a man and not a tigra, would you like me different?"

Jeena was lost for an answer. She stuttered for a second then blurted, "I don't know what you mean. I like you fine."

Samson looked away sadly.

"Oh, c'mon, don't do that. Dammit, Samson, I don't know how to answer that. You're not a man, you're a tigra. I don't know, maybe in the beginning I did think of you as some sort of pet, but that was before I really knew you, before I found out what you really are."

"And now?" he asked.

"And now? Well, *and now* I don't think of you any different than I do humans."

"But I thought you didn't like most humans?"

Jeena stared at the innocent expression on his face and broke out in laughter, shaking her head.

"You just won't let me off the hook, will you? No, I suppose I don't. So, I guess that means I must like you better then most, doesn't it?"

He considered that.

"I guess so." He shifted nervously, looking away. "Was it hard for you, Jeena, being out there all alone with only someone like me for company?"

"Someone like you? There's no one I would have rather been with than you."

He lifted his head, and for an instant their eyes met. She had looked into his eyes countless times, but now something different was happening. Holding his gaze in hers, she felt something—something she did not have a name for, but which made her instantly uncomfortable. She turned away quickly.

"Thank you," he said.

She pushed the strange emotion away until it was gone.

"Don't mention it—ever. If anyone in my old unit ever heard me talking like this they'd think I'd gone space mad. I'm not the kind of person other people come to for comfort."

Samson smiled. "Yeah, well, that would explain why you're so bad at it."

THE FLAT, OPEN LAND THEY HAD BEEN CROSSING SLOWLY TURNED INTO WOODS AS THEY approached the mountain. Within a few days, the woods had thickened into a dense forest.

The going was hard, picking narrow paths through the trees and struggling with the underbrush, but they finally reached the foot of the mountain and began to ascend. With the increase in elevation the temperature dropped. Jeena expected this, but was unprepared for its effect on her. The cold seemed to sap her strength in a way she could not understand. By the end of the second day on the mountainside, she was shivering and weak.

Although the climb was difficult, she had regained all of the muscle mass she had lost in the prison, so it should not have been as much of an effort it was. The cold might be biting, but no worse than on Mizar 3, and she had adapted to that quickly. Now, her limbs felt heavy, and breathing was work.

Then the snow began to fall.

JEENA STIRRED THE COOKING POT AS SHE LOOKED OVER THE MAP. ALTHOUGH THE AZULZ Range was clearly indicated, it covered a large area. Vicki had found no mention of a colony in this area, and she had no idea where this Mordachi might be. They were groping blindly in a hostile environment, and she knew that often spelled disaster.

"This is a sign of worse things ahead," said Samson, eating his stew.

"The snow?" Jeena asked, watching it fall.

"No, your cooking."

She gaped at him until she saw the gleam in his eye. Then they were both laughing, and with the laughter the pall that had settled over them the last few days was lifted.

"Ha-ha...oh, that was a good one," she said. "But seriously—you're an asshole."

The laughter began again. They huddled close around the fire as the falling snow grew heavier. Jeena shivered. Lately, the tips of her fingers stayed blue even after she was warm. She did not know what this indicated, exactly, but she knew enough field medicine to be worried.

"Brrr...I wish I had your fur."

"Still trying to make a coat out of me, huh?" He gazed up at the mountains still looming over them. "We can't be more than halfway up. I don't think we can keep going without more specific directions."

"I know. I was hoping to find a settlement by now, or at least a sign of one. I can't imagine there are any colonies above this elevation." She pulled the map from her pocket. "Look here. There's only one area of passable ground anywhere around here. Any colony in this area would have to use it. If we head through it we should find some sign of them."

Samson studied the map. "That's a good three days from here."

She caught the meaning in his look. "Don't worry about me. It's just taking me a while to get used to the cold. You'd be shivering, too, if you weren't such a fur ball. Now, let's get into the tent and get some sleep. We've got to get an early start tomorrow."

SAMSON STIRRED RESTLESSLY IN HIS SLEEP. A SHADOW WAS COMING TOWARDS HIM, A THING without shape. He could not see it, but he knew it was alive. It was not searching for him but for food, and he could almost feel the raging hunger that drove it.

Suddenly, the shadow sensed his presence and leapt on him with a roar.

He awoke with a cry, arousing Jeena in the too-small tent.

"What's wrong?" she asked, instantly alert.

"I don't know. There was something..." He shook his head to clear it. "I thought I heard something."

They both lay still, listening to the howling wind.

"I don't hear anything. Maybe it was the wind," Jeena said.

"Yeah, maybe."

She shivered and curled up next to him. Samson lay with his eyes open, staring out into the blackness of the tent. *It wasn't the wind, and it wasn't a dream. Someone or something was calling to me.*

They awoke the next morning to strong winds and heavy snows. Jeena had developed a cough during the night and was irritable, complaining of a headache. They ate sparingly of their dried food and broke camp quickly, working through the deep snow toward the pass.

The terrain continued to rise, and the going was arduous and slow. They made little ground that day and had to pitch the tent only a few miles from their previous camp. The wind had not let up and starting a fire proved impossible. Cradled inside the tiny tent, they ate the last of their dried meat. Jeena fell asleep immediately after eating, and Samson lay over her gently, trying to warm her body with his.

Her cough had become worse, and there was a blue tint around her lips and eyes. She had stopped shivering, but that did not comfort him. The wind howled throughout the night.

They awoke to a blizzard. Jeena was difficult to rouse and seemed lethargic even after waking. Samson saw that the blueness of her face had deepened to an almost purple hue. She spoke little and seemed clumsy trying to break camp. He took the tent down himself and threw it on the kytar. Bending against the wind and blinding snow, they made for the pass.

They had only gone a short distance before he halted. Jeena was stumbling and falling repeatedly; it was clear she was unable to walk farther. She did not protest as he lifted her onto the kytar. Grabbing the reins, he pushed on.

He walked throughout the long morning, fighting the roaring winds and snow and using the tree line as a guide. He trudged on until even he was near exhaustion. The sun was lost behind the great gray clouds and swirling snow, but he felt it had to be late afternoon.

He halted and looked around in dismay. He could not identify the terrain. He pored over the map he had taken from Jeena, but it was no use. Almost snow-blind and unable to determine their position, he stopped. They would have to wait out the storm.

He worked alone in the high winds to pitch the tent then eased Jeena gently off the kytar and carried her inside. She was cold and pale. She opened her eyes weakly and coughed, and he saw blood on her lips.

"Where...are we?" she asked, her voice wheezy.

"I'm not sure. Close to the pass, I think, but the storm is too bad. We'll have to wait it out."

She looked up at him for a long moment before speaking. Her words came in gasps.

"When the storm clears...head for the pass. Follow it...to the other side...of the mountain. The other colony...must be there."

"We'll get there," he replied.

"No, not...we. You. I can't...make it."

"Don't say that! You'll be all right, you're just cold. I'll warm you." He tried to cover her with his body, rubbing her limbs with his paws.

"It's not...the cold, it's...the altitude. I'm such an...idiot. Ararat...is so much smaller...than Earth. I never...considered that...the air would thin out...so much faster. We can't be at more than...five thousand feet, but the air...feels like twenty thousand." She coughed and wiped her mouth, holding the blood up for him to see. "Pulmonary edema. My lungs are...swelling. I'm dying."

Samson began grabbing their gear. "Then we'll go back down the mountain. I'll get you to more air!"

She grasped his arm. "It's too late for that. Even...without the storm you couldn't...get me down in time. I'm sorry...didn't mean...to leave you alone." She took several great, heaving breaths, her eyes beginning to glaze. "I wish..." She touched his face with pale fingers. "You asked me once...what you meant to me. No one has ever...meant more. Whatever happens always remember...I..."

"Jeena," he whispered, but her eyes had closed. He picked up her limp body and held her against his chest. "Nooo..." he sobbed. "Wake up. Please don't leave me, Jeena."

Not even on the altar of the Rosh-dan had he felt such utter despair and hopelessness. Alone and afraid, unable to do anything for her, he rocked her gently in his arms as the wind howled and his tears flowed.

Chapter 14

"To learn the secrets of the Universe in an instant, one need only to die. All other ways require patience."

> Favorite saying of Nanor, kho'pan of the Intawa, as quoted by Jeena Garza

H<small>E COULD BARELY SEPARATE THE SOUND FROM THE OTHER NOISES OF THE STORM. I<small>T</small></small> was faint, like a distant tinkling of metal, almost lost in the roaring maelstrom blowing around them.

He heard it again. Samson opened his bleary eyes—it was the sound of tinkling bells.

He laid Jeena down and rushed from the tent, fighting the wind and scanning the blindingly white landscape for the source of the sound. There, in the distant tree line, was a kytar. On its back rode a man covered in heavy furs.

With a roar greater than the wind, he leapt through the high snow, racing toward the rider. The startled figure turned toward the sound and saw Samson barreling toward him, his golden eyes wild. With a cry the rider spurred his mount, only to have it rear and throw him onto the ground.

Samson was on him in an instant, panting heavily, his fangs descended. The man scrambled to extract himself from the snow and drew his knife. His eyes were wide with fright as he backed up to a tree, the blade shaking in his hand.

"No," Samson panted. "You don't need that. I won't hurt you. I need your help."

He could feel his fangs projecting and cursed them.

The man froze.

"I need your help," Samson repeated. "There is a woman…"

The man let the knife drop from his hand and fell on his knees, lifting his arms to the sky.

"Listen to me, please. There is a woman…"

The man began chanting in a strange tongue, oblivious to Samson's pleas.

"Dammit, listen to me!" Samson roared. Rising onto his hind legs, he lifted the man easily in his powerful arms and shook him. "I have no time for this! A woman in the tent—up there—she is sick, very sick. Can you understand me?"

The man nodded.

Samson set him back down and backed away, dropping back to four legs.

"I know you're confused and scared, but I won't hurt you. Please help her. You can do what you want with me, but please…please help her."

The stunned man nodded again. "I help you, Shahaiya, yes."

Although Samson did not grasp the meaning of the word, it was obvious this man understood him. He bounded through the snow and retrieved the kytar, handing the reins back to the owner.

"She's just above us, on the hill. Follow me."

He took off at a run up the small elevation. He looked back once but saw that the man was right behind him. At the tent, he held the kytar's reins as the man dismounted and went warily inside. He came out in a rush a moment later, quickly removing furs from his mount.

"Woman very bad, very sick. Die maybe. No time." He hurried back in the tent with the furs, exiting a moment later carrying Jeena, bundled up, over his shoulder. He laid her gently across the kytar. "I go to village. Bring her to Nanor."

"May I come?" Samson asked.

The man looked at him oddly.

"Intawa welcome Shahaiya always, yes." He grabbed the reins of Jeena's kytar and leapt up on his own animal. He set a course through the trees, moving as fast as the two animals could go in the high snow. In spite of the continuing blizzard, he seemed to have no difficulty finding his way.

Samson followed close behind but soon began to lag as the blizzard and deepening snow worsened. Once or twice he thought he lost them, only to hear the bells on the kytar's reins. The labor took its toll on the big cat, and soon he was struggling, his head bent down and covered in frost and ice.

When at last he looked up again, both the kytars and the rider were gone, and he had stumbled into a clearing. Panting hard, searching for Jeena, he watched as a group of hooded men converged on and encircled him. He tried to speak but found he couldn't catch his breath.

A great weariness came over him, and the strength of his legs gave out. He fell gasping into the snow as the hooded figures closed in on him, spears in hand. They began to blur and waver, and the world went black.

THE SCENT OF FOOD PRODDED JEENA'S UNCONSCIOUS MIND, TEMPTING IT BACK TO wakefulness. She opened her eyes to a flickering fire, crackling and popping. She could no longer hear the storm. And she was warm.

A naked man danced around the fire to the beat of a drum, his body painted entirely blue except for yellow stripes under his eyes. His only adornment was a necklace of feathers and stones.

The drumming stopped. The man leaned close to her face and smiled. Even his eyes were a bright blue.

"Oha, Shahaiya semata," he said, grinning. A bowl of broth and herbs appeared, and he fed her several mouthfuls.

"Thank you," she whispered hoarsely before slipping back into an easy sleep.

"JEENA."

She sighed and stirred. The dream had been so real—the white-walled city and the palace, the old woman. A shame about the young soldier, though.

"Jeena," the voice repeated softly.

She awoke and opened her eyes. A large golden face smiled at her.

"Samson," she whispered, her voice still hoarse and raspy.

"Well, look who's finally awake," he said.

"What happened? Where are we?" She was lying on a pile of soft furs and covered in blankets. Her eyes were still having trouble focusing, but she could see they were in a long oval building that looked to be made of logs and branches. A fire burned in a center pit with many people around it.

"Among friends. They call themselves the Intawa. Ewar, a hunter of their people found us."

"Found us? Are we still on the mountain? How long have we been here?"

"Hey, answering all your questions at once is going to take the fun out of making you guess. Yes, we are still on the mountain, in a cove just the other side of the pass. You've been out for five days."

"Five days? I don't understand. I should be long dead by now."

"Are you complaining? The one named Nanor, the kho'pan—medicine man—has been caring for you since we got here, sticking some kind of herb under your tongue. He seemed to know what was wrong with you. Said some of his people had gotten sick like that when they first came to the mountain. He calls it 'bad air.' Whatever it is, he knows what he's doing. Your color got better almost immediately."

Jeena looked around the room. The people she saw were almost all tall and blonde, the men wearing their hair as long as the women. Both men and women wore loose leather breeches, and neither wore an upper garment. She noticed they all seemed to have blue eyes, bright and shiny against their ruddy complexions. They were a handsome race.

"One of them spoke to me earlier. Strange words."

"Yes, they seem to have their own language, but have no difficulty understanding Standard Galactic."

"Their own language? Humans haven't used anything but SG for centuries."

A group of naked children ran by, laughing.

"Can these really be the people Touloc sent us to find?" she asked skeptically.

"No—I asked about that already. But they know this Mordachi and the way to his city. Apparently, there is some trade between them. It isn't far from here, but the hunters say the snow makes the way impassable for now. They've promised to guide us when it clears."

The blue-faced man Jeena had seen earlier left the fire and came to them. To her bewilderment, he knelt before Samson and touched his forehead to the ground. He sat up and smiled at her.

"You strong semata. Get more strong soon. Shahaiya watch over you."

"This is Nanor, the kho'pan," Samson explained.

"Thank you, Nanor. Samson says you saved my life."

"Nanor is kho'pan. Know much. But Shahaiya know more. Shahaiya give life." Nanor bowed again to Samson before leaving them.

"Uh, Samson...?"

He sighed. "I know, I know. I'm not sure how it happened, exactly, but...um..."

She pressed him. "Go on."

"Well, I know it's silly, but I, uh... I seem to be one of their gods," he said sheepishly.

Jeena laughed as his ears fell flat to his head in embarrassment. She recognized his discomfort and stifled her mirth, placing a hand on his paw.

"I'm sorry. That was inappropriate. Thanks to you I'm alive when by all rights I should be dead. Maybe they're right. Maybe you are a god and I'm your first miracle." Her face remained serious for a second more before the laughter returned.

Samson growled something unintelligible and stalked away, shaking his head.

AS NANOR PREDICTED, JEENA GAINED STRENGTH RAPIDLY OVER THE NEXT FEW DAYS AND WAS soon walking around. He still forbade her from going outside so she stayed in the hut, a communal dwelling the Intawa called a *j'led.*

It was a warm and comfortable place. Animal hides lashed to the outside walls kept out the cold and wind, and the fire burned night and day, usually with a steaming pot over it. Ringed along the floor were sleeping mats of thick animal furs and blankets, separated from each other by only a few feet. This, she learned, was the extent of an Intawa's "personal space."

The men were gone much of the time hunting so she spent her days talking with the women. She discovered they were not the only Intawa on Ararat. This was just one of a group of tribes who lived along the northeast corridor of the continent. It was an existence eked out in the main with the use of Stone Age tools, although Jeena did see a few metal implements she was told were obtained through trade.

Living was communal in the most primitive sense of the word, with all work divided and all food shared. Each tribe considered themselves an extended family, and for that reason marriage partners could only come from outside the village, from other tribes. Once a year, at the height of the summer, the various tribes would meet at one of the villages for a week of celebration and games known as the *keppi.* It was during these gatherings that Intawa men would attempt to take a bride. There were always more men than women and the competition, while friendly, was intense.

The women explained that each prospective suitor would try to impress the girl's tribe with his ability as a hunter. This was accomplished through a series of competitions involving foraging, tracking, hunting and riding. The final choice of a mate was left up to the girl, but it was common for other members of the tribe to offer their opinions.

It often happened that many young men would return home from the keppi brideless, particularly in years of famine or disease. This was seen as a terrible omen. Without new blood there could be no children. With the birth rate of most tribes just barely keeping up with mortality, a few unsuccessful keppis could cause the tribe's population to decrease precipitously. It had even happened that a tribe had died out completely.

To help ease the strain, the Intawa practiced wife-sharing. Cultural norms dictated that the husband present the request to his wife on behalf of his "brother"—since the tribes considered themselves a family, all males of the same approximate age were brothers. The woman had final approval, and her word was the last say in the matter. If the request was denied, it could not be made again. The women of the j'led found this to be a most excellent arrangement, and those with a second husband were looked upon with envy.

Ewar, the hunter who had rescued Jeena and Samson, lived in just such a union. His wife had died in childbirth four years earlier, and he'd had no luck at the keppis, although the women confided to her that his heart was never really in it—he had loved his wife dearly. So, he now shared Anok's wife Ienta. Ienta admitted she thoroughly enjoyed the arrangement and would miss Ewar if he ever again took a wife of his own.

If Jeena was interested in the Intawa living arrangements, they were just as curious about hers. The women were intrigued by her relationship with Samson—Shahaiya, as they called him—a being they all considered a god. Jeena was shocked to discover they assumed an intimacy between them that didn't exist, and she fervently tried to correct this surprising—and, in her mind, rather bizarre—misconception. Her explanations were met with winks and giggles, as well as a few envious looks that made her scratch her head in wonder.

As a people, the Intawa were happy and engaging, quick to laughter and possessed of an easy demeanor; and Jeena was drawn to them and their simple way of life.

When she had fully recovered, Samson related the events leading up to her awakening in the j'led. He told her about being found by Ewar and the journey to the village.

"I guess the cold and the exhaustion must have affected me more than I thought. I no sooner walked into the village than I passed out. Ewar had already taken you in to Nanor. You were almost gone by then.

"Nanor was very worried. He said some of his people had gotten sick like that in the distant past when they first came to this land, and that his ancestors had discovered a cure, but that it had been lost in the mists of time. He started and stopped several times before finally mixing a combination of herbs that he put under your tongue. Whatever it was, it began working immediately. He sat by your side for days, giving you a small dose every hour.

"The hunters had surrounded me outside. They thought I was a wild tigra that had followed Ewar back to the village and would have killed me if he hadn't come looking for me. When I came to, I was here in the j'led with you. I tried to thank them for saving you, but they all fell to their knees crying, 'Shahaiya.'"

"A god."

"Right. They practice a kind of shamanism here, and apparently Shahaiya is one of their principal gods. The more I tried to explain who I was…"

"The more convinced they were that you *were* a god," she finished.

"Yeah."

Jeena surveyed the people as they moved about the j'led performing their daily activities. Men sat in small groups sharpening their spears; young women fried strips of meat in animal fat while others worked the large, two-handed mortar, their breasts swaying rhythmically as they beat the club into a large stone bowl. Old women were tanning and stretching hides as naked children ran about.

"They seem pretty calm for having a god in the house," she observed.

"They say I'm always with them. They just feel honored they can see me now."

She gazed up at him. "You took a great risk confronting Ewar, after what you went through in New Jerusalem."

Samson looked away. "I wasn't afraid of Ewar, or even dying. The only thing I was afraid of was losing you."

"Well, you haven't lost me yet, thanks to you."

A young girl brought a plate of meat and nuts, setting it before them and bowing to each in turn.

"By the way," Jeena said, "if you're a god, what am I supposed to be?"

"My semata, my concubine," he said and winced.

DAMN! HE HADN'T MEANT TO TELL HER THAT.

"Your what?" she asked icily.

"It was their idea, not mine," he protested, his ears lying flat on his head. "They just figure that since you're with me…I mean, they just naturally assumed…"

Her face began to contort.

"Now, Jeena," he said, backing away, "stay calm. It's really very funny when you think about it. Don't you think? Jeena?"

The Intawa glanced curiously at them as her laughter filled the j'led.

EWAR RETURNED FROM HIS HUNTING EXPEDITION AND WAS FORMALLY INTRODUCED TO Jeena. She thanked him warmly for his help.

"My heart glad to see you well, semata-who-lie-with-Shahaiya," he said.

"Um...please, just call me Jeena," she replied, giving Samson a sidelong glance. "Was your hunting trip successful?"

Ewar shook his head. "No, spirits of the animals are frightened and will not come to our lands." There was worry and sadness in his voice.

He excused himself, saying he would see them later that night at the celebration to honor Shahaiya and the return to health of his semata. He hinted with scarcely hidden hope that perhaps Shahaiya could bring the animals back.

"It's been like that since we came here," said Samson after he had gone. "All the hunting parties have returned empty-handed. They say it's been like that for weeks."

Jeena looked down at the plate of food they had been offered.

"This is probably a good portion of their food stores. Looks like they want Shahaiya well-fed before they ask him to solve their hunting problem."

Samson looked mournful. "I wonder what they think I can do?"

THE DRUMS BEAT IN A SLOW, REGULAR RHYTHM. A GROUP OF INTAWA MEN, LED BY NANOR, danced near the fire. One of the women explained to Jeena that it was a symbolic interpretation of a hunt.

Nanor's body was painted yellow, and he wore only a small loincloth that, Jeena noted with amusement, covered little. The old shaman crawled about the fire, obviously portraying a tigra. As he approached the other animals, portrayed by equally decorated Intawa men, they would scatter, leaving the hunters confused and saddened.

The dance ended, and a group of young women set trays of food before her and Samson. Nanor, his body glistening with sweat, bowed low before them.

"Shahaiya, praise to you and your semata," he said in his high singsong voice. "You great hunter, great god of tigra, you know all animals. Intawa always honor Shahaiya. All tribes give dance to you. All tribes sing your name."

Samson bowed clumsily, unsure of what was expected of him.

"Shahaiya thanks you, Nanor," said Jeena on his behalf.

Nanor nodded vigorously and smiled.

"Intawa now ask for help. Shahaiya go to brother. Shahaiya tell him Intawa good people. He no bother Intawa no more."

Samson looked at her in despair.

"Nanor, Shahaiya wants to help the Intawa, but he doesn't know what you want him to do," she said.

"Only ask brother to leave. Shahaiya lead him to tigra home beyond fire-mountain. Then animals return to Intawa hunting grounds."

"Are you getting this?" she asked Samson.

"I think so," he replied. "Apparently, there's another tigra stalking their hunting grounds and scaring away the game."

"Exactly. And guess which god they want to shoo him off?"

SAMSON SAT CROUCHED BEHIND A SNOWDRIFT, SNIFFING THE AIR. JEENA KNELT NEXT TO him, searching the wooded area beyond through the binoculars.

"I can't see him. Are you sure he's out there?"

"Positive. I can smell him."

"Hold on. Yeah, there he is. About half a klick west. Look." She handed him the glasses.

Samson looked. The tigra was pacing in the snow just beyond the tree line. He raised his head and sniffed warily.

Then he felt it—the same sense of being touched, of being probed he had felt that night on the mountainside.

He slid back behind the drift. "He knows I'm here."

"I doubt it. We're downwind."

He handed her the binoculars. "It's not my scent. I can't explain it, but he knows. I can sense it."

Jeena raised the pulse rifle. "It doesn't matter, I can bring him down from here."

Samson grabbed her arm. "No!"

She placed her hand over his paw. "Samson, I don't want to do this, either. I wish we had a tranquilizer gun, but we don't. If we don't do this the Intawa hunters will, and how many of them will die in the attempt? What else can we do?"

"I don't know. Just let me think for a minute, will you?" His whiskers twitched, and his ears were flat against his head. "We can't do this, Jeena, not like this. I know he's just an animal, but this is wrong. He doesn't know he's hurting the Intawa, he's just lost and hungry." He glanced back over the snow at the pacing tigra. "I'm going to try and communicate with him. Don't look at me like that—I don't know how. But I can't let you just kill him."

Before she could protest, he slipped out from the snowbank and made his way to the tree line. Once he had the protection of the woods he carefully moved toward the tigra, using the trees as cover.

But the tigra was wary; its ears were pricked, and it sniffed the air suspiciously.

Samson had made it almost to his quarry now—only a few trees and a few dozen feet separated them. The feeling of being touched grew as he neared, and he closed his eyes for a moment to focus. He felt dizzy, and suddenly, he saw himself as though through another's eyes. He was partially hidden, crouching behind a tree, his eyes closed.

His eyes flew open, and he crouched deeper in the snow, panting. *It was the tigra! I was seeing myself through his eyes! How is that possible?* Could this be some kind of communication?

His heart leapt at the idea. Maybe it was possible. Maybe his kind was more than brute beasts after all. *But Jeena is still out there. If she thinks I'm in trouble she won't hesitate to kill him.*

Taking a steadying breath, he stepped out from behind the tree.

The tigra was waiting. The hair on its neck bristled, and its lips were pulled back in a snarl. The fangs snapped down, dripping with saliva. Samson approached cautiously, keeping his head down and his ears flat against his head in a sign of submissiveness. The animal stood its ground, its muscles visibly tense under its fur.

He stopped a few feet from it and slowly lifted his head until their eyes met. For the space of a heartbeat, they stood unmoving.

Then, without warning, the big animal sprang. Samson fell back, a ribbon of bright blood spurting from his neck and arcing high in the air.

Jeena screamed. She bolted over the drift and ran towards them, then dropped to the snow on one knee and took aim.

Samson staggered to his feet, holding a paw to his bloody neck.

"No, Jeena, don't! I'm all right," he yelled, but his voice was weak.

"Get out of the way, Samson! Now!"

He stood his ground, putting himself between the cat and Jeena.

"No, I won't let you do it."

He was steadier now, and faced the tigra. The animal was ready to attack again, but its attention flitted between Samson and the woman behind him.

Samson dropped down on all fours, again assuming a submissive stance. His neck throbbed and his heart was racing, but he had to try again. He could feel the contact with the other tigra growing in him, but whatever it was, he did not have the skill to use it.

"Go away," he said. "You must leave this place. Danger here."

He repeated the phrases again and again, hoping to soothe the tigra; but it remained tense, poised to strike again. In an unconscious reflex, he began mentally picturing the events he was describing, visualizing the tigra running far away to the north of the Intawa village.

JEENA COULD NOT GET A BEAD ON THE ANIMAL WITH SAMSON IN THE WAY, AND BEGAN moving in an arc, cursing him as she circled to the left. Despite his protests, she intended to take the first clear shot.

Suddenly, the tigra made as though to lunge then stumbled and shrank back. It withdrew from Samson and turned toward the north, sniffing the air uncertainly. With one final glance back at him, it began moving away quickly, heading north along the pass out of the Intawa lands.

Jeena had just taken a position at the tree line and stifled a cry when the cat started to pounce. It halted and paced nervously as if unsure. Now it was turning away, but she kept it in her sights until it disappeared from view.

When she was sure it was gone, she ran up to where Samson sat in the snow. She tossed the gun down and examined the wound on his neck.

"Are you all right?" she demanded, her face stiff with worry.

The gash ran from his left ear to his sternum, but did not appear deep.

"Yes, I'm okay, just a little shaken up."

"*You're* shaken up?" she yelled. "What the hell did you think you were doing out there?"

"Jeena…"

"Don't Jeena me! And don't you ever come between me and a target again. He almost killed you. You can't reason with him, Samson, he's just an animal."

"Maybe he is, and maybe I am different from all the rest. But Nanor is right—I'm still one of them, I'm still a tigra. I couldn't just let you kill him in cold blood. Please try to understand."

She nodded, running a hand over her eyes, surprised to find them moist. "Yeah, I guess I understand." She picked up the rifle and slung it over her shoulder. "But don't ever do that to me again. I didn't save your furry ass just so one of your relatives could tear it up."

She turned and began trudging toward the j'led.

Samson followed closely behind her. "Yes, Jeena."

THE J'LED CELEBRATED THAT NIGHT. UNLIKE THE FORMAL CEREMONY THE NIGHT BEFORE, this was a full-blown party. Gourds of *kuse*, a potent drink made from the fermentation of a local tuber, were passed around. Soon Jeena and, to the delight of the Intawa, Samson joined in the impromptu dance around the fire.

Jeena had tended to Samson's wound, and between her ministrations and the kuse, he was feeling no pain. The women of the tribe stripped her to the waist, and Nanor presented her with an impe, the tribal necklace worn by all, thus making her a clanswoman of the tribe. The necklace was a string of smooth metallic stones of irregular shape the Intawa called *p'toc*. Nanor explained that they were very valuable and contained great power. As one of their gods, Samson did not need a necklace but was given the thanks and undying love of the entire tribe.

Earlier in the evening, he had tried to relate to Jeena the contact he had experienced with the other tigra, but she could make nothing of it. As the kuse flowed, he began to doubt the whole affair himself.

The party continued well into the night, with some of the tribesmen dancing until they dropped of exhaustion the next morning. He and Jeena quit somewhat earlier to the furs and blankets that made up their sleeping area. Others had already retired, and the j'led was alive with the noise of soft snores and other, more amorous sounds.

"You did good out there," Jeena said, gingerly touching his wound. "I'm proud of you. Shahaiya himself couldn't have done better."

"Yeah?" He grinned lopsidedly. "So, does that mean I can keep you as my concubine?"

Her smile disappeared for an instant before she forced it back.

"Don't press it," she replied.

He laughed, and she allowed him to wrap his big arms around her.

HANGOVERS WERE THE ORDER OF THE DAY THE NEXT MORNING, AND EVERYONE BUT JEENA seemed to suffer. Samson had to excuse himself twice to run outside and be sick. The drinking exploits of SAG commandoes were legendary in the Union, and Jeena's tolerance was phenomenal even by those lofty standards; so she spent most of the day assisting those other unaffected few in preparing meals. She also managed to speak with Ewar and some of the other hunters about Mordachi and the Mountain people.

"Here, try this," she said, pushing a bowl of hot broth at Samson. He was moaning softly and, in spite of the fur over his face, looked a little green.

"Oh, please, no food," he whined.

"Yeah, you never forget your first good drunk. But trust me, this will make you feel better."

He sat up slowly and sipped at the hot liquid. He saw that she was drinking from the kuse gourd.

"I hate you," he moaned.

"I just have a lot more experience with alcohol than you. You'll learn."

He peered at her over the bowl. "I'll die first."

"No, that would be bad form for a god. Besides, I need you alive and healthy. I spoke with Ewar and the other hunters. They say the pass will be open in five days. Looks like we're finally going to meet this Mordachi."

Chapter 15

The enemy of my enemy is my friend.

> Popular saying of the Intawa, most probably derived from an older Earth proverb

With the wild tigra gone the game returned, and with it the peace and contentment of the tribe. Jeena showed interest in their medicine and this pleased Nanor, who took her as his student. Her first lesson was that medicine and religion were deeply entwined. Her own recovery had shown that the herbs and roots the Intawa used had potent bioactivity, and she was anxious to study them. She was less excited about having to learn the chants and spells that went with their use.

Nanor had just explained the value of a certain tree bark in the treatment of skin infections, and was having her recite the prayer that went with its application. Once again, she flubbed the recitation.

"Nanor, do I really have to learn the prayer?" she asked. "The bark will work just as well without it."

He looked at her queerly. "Bark no work without prayer. Spirit in bark make work. Must make tree-spirit come out."

"Maybe my tree doesn't have a spirit," she muttered.

"All trees have spirit. How tree grow if no spirit?"

"Trees come from seeds and water and light. It's actually very simple."

"Ahh...so you can make tree?"

"If I had a seed I could, sure."

The old man nodded, his long locks falling around his face.

"You can make seed then?"

"Well, no..."

He grinned. "Not so simple, yes?"

Jeena frowned. It was impossible to disprove a negative—that is, that spirits didn't exist—so she let it drop.

"Okay, Nanor," she sighed, "you win. Teach me the prayer again."

NANOR HAD BEEN TESTING JEENA ON HER RECENT KNOWLEDGE AND NOW SAT BACK, PLEASED with her progress. "You good student. Learn much," he told her.

"You good teacher," she answered.

He leaned forward and studied her closely, his expression serious.

"Nanor old. Soon tribe need new kho'pan. You strong. Have much power."

Maintaining the tribe's health and enlarging its population was of paramount importance to a culture where infant mortality was high, and to the Intawa nothing was more blessed than the birth of a child. High value was therefore placed on fertility, and much of Nanor's work involved obtaining the gods' assistance in helping couples conceive.

As his unofficial assistant, Jeena had aided him in many of these rituals, and the couples were delighted to have the concubine of Shahaiya, a god with legendary sexual prowess, perform in the ceremonies.

"BUT I CAN'T STAY, NANOR. SAMSON—I MEAN SHAHAIYA—AND I MUST LEAVE SOON. You know this."

"Yes," he replied, grinning and nodding. "Semata stay with Shahaiya." He bumped his fists together. "Mate. Have tigra-child. He live with Intawa. Be strong kho'pan for tribe."

Jeena blanched. She was saved from having to explain the absurdity of this remarkable—and genetically impossible—request by Samson's timely arrival.

"Jeena, Ewar wants to meet with us. The pass is open," he said.

He looked curiously at her silent and stunned expression. Nanor sat nodding and smiling.

"What? Did I miss something?"

EWAR SQUATTED BY THE FIRE WITH SEVERAL OTHER HUNTERS.

"Can we make it through the pass now?" Jeena asked.

"Yes. We take you to Mor-da-chi now. Must go before more snow comes."

"How long to get to Mordachi, Ewar?" Samson wanted to know.

"Leave now, reach home of Mountain People when Little Ka-ta still in sky."

The Intawa referred to the two moons of Ararat as Big and Little Ka-ta, after the fireflies that frequented their lands every summer. If the small moon was still visible, then they should reach the mountain before midnight.

Jeena dressed in the skins and furs of the Intawa, and she and Samson packed what little supplies they had on their kytar. They met Ewar and the others on the outskirts of the village where they were waiting. The Intawa were sad to see them go but not too surprised—apparently, gods were not expected to stick around forever.

Nanor gave a blessing for their travels then performed a second rite Samson didn't understand, patting Jeena's belly and his rump, all the while grinning.

"What the hell was that all about?" he asked her as the hunters led them away.

She muttered something unintelligible and picked up her pace, a blush warming her face.

THE SNOW HAD MELTED CONSIDERABLY OVER THE LAST FEW DAYS, AND TRAVELING WAS EASY. In several places the trail narrowed so that they had to dismount and move in single file. Ewar said it was these narrows that made traversing the pass in winter so difficult—the snow here often reached the height of two men.

They finally left the constricted pass and entered a wide valley, beyond which Ewar said lay the mountain of Mordachi and his people. The snow was somewhat deeper, but showed signs of recent melting, and they made good time, the hard crust crunching under them as they went.

"Ewar, what are the Mountain People like?" Jeena asked, pulling her fur collar tight. Although she had fully recovered from her sickness, cold would continue to bother her the rest of her life.

Ewar shrugged. "They friends with Intawa, but they strange. Know much, but have no gods."

"Do they actually live in a mountain?" Samson asked.

"Yes. Live in belly of Pakahaita, Fire Mountain." He pointed to the horizon ahead.

Jeena halted and looked through the binoculars, gazing for a time before handing them to Samson. There was a high peak in the range that was conspicuous for its lack of snow cover. A heavy mist surrounded it, appearing to rise from the mountain itself.

He handed the glasses back to her. "What do you think?"

"Ararat is rich in thermal energy. I suppose they could have found a way to channel heat through the mountain."

Samson looked back at the mist-shrouded peak. "I thought that kind of technology was forbidden on a zed-tech world."

Jeena considered that. The equipment needed to pump natural heat through the interior of a mountain was far beyond anything even remotely allowed on a zed-designated world. Hell, even the machinery necessary to carve out the mountain would be prohibited.

"You're right," she said. "It is."

They stopped for a meal just as the sun was going down. Ewar had a faggot of sticks tied to the back of his kytar and made a small fire for them. They ate dried meat and flour cakes as Jeena questioned him and the other hunters about matters that had been puzzling her.

"Ewar, where did the Mountain People come from?"

Vicki had only mentioned two chartered colonies, and none of her maps showed any human habitation anywhere near here.

Ewar pointed west. "Many seasons past they come. People of A-free-dee."

She choked. Samson stopped in mid-bite and stared wide-eyed at the hunter.

"Do you mean," Jeena asked slowly, "that the people of the mountain came from the west, from the Afridi?"

He nodded. "It is so, yes."

Her mind spun. *It makes no sense.* Why would Touloc, an avowed enemy of the Rosh-dan, send them to seek the help of other Afridi? But maybe Ewar had it wrong. Maybe there were other colonies west of here.

"How do you know this?" she asked.

He looked at her coolly. "Intawa know many things. Story of coming of Mountain People told to Ewar by father's father. Intawa know this. Intawa here before people of mountain, before people of A-free-dee."

Jeena did a quick calculation. Three generations would put the story back about sixty years. So, this group was at least half a century removed from the people of New Jerusalem.

Daniel had said that the Afridi's influence did not extend east, so maybe this was a breakaway sect, unconnected to their distant cousins.

But there was no way to determine that now. Touloc had been on the edge of death when he spoke. Maybe he had been delusional, or had meant something entirely different. Either way, one thing was certain—they couldn't go back. There was nothing to go back to.

She murmured to Samson, "For the time being we better not let those people know about your, uh...unique talents."

"What if they don't wait to find out?" he asked nervously. "The Rosh-dan were ready to kill me before I said a word."

"I can't imagine these people are as brutal. The fact that Touloc sent us to find them, and that they are friends of the Intawa, speaks volumes. But we won't take any chances. I'll keep the MAAD close and the pistol in my coat. At the first sign of trouble we'll hightail it back to Ewar's people."

Samson tossed more wood on the fire.

"So, why can't I talk?" he asked glumly.

He doesn't want to have to act like an animal, but for now it's the safest course.

"Look, they may not feel one way or another about an ordinary tigra, but you? To the Intawa you're a god. To another culture you could be something completely different."

"I should have just stayed in the j'led," he groused.

"Maybe. But we didn't have this information until now." She pointed at Ewar and the other hunters, who were engaged in their own conversation. "Besides, look how meeting the Intawa turned out. People deserve a chance to prove themselves."

SAMSON LOOKED AT EWAR, WHO SMILED BACK. JEENA WAS RIGHT. IF HE HADN'T BEEN SO desperate he never would have made contact with the Intawa. After the episode in New Jerusalem, he would have avoided all humans like packs of hungry usks, and yet now he was one of them. He was a tigra, and still he was their brother and clansman, the god Shahaiya. No matter what these new humans might think of him he always had that—a place to belong.

"Okay," he grumbled, "so I won't talk. But I'm telling you, I see one bearded nut with a knife and..." He made a sliding motion of one paw over the other. "...I'm outta there."

JEENA HAD SOME DIFFICULTY EXPLAINING TO EWAR AND THE OTHERS WHY SHE DIDN'T WANT the Mountain People to know Samson could talk. She finally convinced them it was a joke she was playing. Ewar agreed it would be a very good joke on the Mountain People, and he agreed only to tell them that Samson was Jeena's pet—a statement she made sure Samson did not hear.

With that settled, she was left to puzzle on another statement Ewar had made. He had said the Intawa were on Ararat before the Afridi. *But how can that be?* The Afridi were the first colony chartered, immediately after the Five-Year Survey. The Intawa weren't even mentioned on the profile report, and there was no way the survey could have missed them.

When she could come to no logical answer, she asked him.

"Ewar, you said the mountain people came from the west. Where did the Intawa come from?"

He glanced at her and Samson then shot his arm straight up in the air, his finger pointing to the star-filled sky.

They finished their meal and began again toward the mountain Ewar called Pakahaita—the place Touloc had called Pyros. The peak now towered above them, and the mist was heavier, creating a ground fog that was disorienting. Even Ewar seemed uncomfortable riding through it.

At the base of the mountain he led them in a wide circle, seemingly searching for a landmark of some kind.

"How do we get inside?" Samson asked, staring apprehensively at the steaming rock.

"Ring bell," Ewar answered.

They continued through the dense fog, the sounds of their movements muffled as they made their way around the mountain. Presently, Ewar halted. He looked behind then ahead, as though uncertain of his location. He signaled the others to wait and spurred his kytar, disappearing into the shadows of the rock.

"Friendly looking place, isn't it?" Samson commented. He was sniffing the air and peering through the fog nervously. "What do you think he's looking for?"

Jeena dismounted and stretched her legs.

"I guess like he said—a bell."

Suddenly, the tolling of a deep sonorous gong resounded through the fog.

"Looks like he found it."

Leading their kytars, they headed in the direction of the sound and found Ewar standing in front of a huge bell suspended from a heavy wooden beam. He held a large mallet in his hands. Lifting the mallet, he struck the bell again. The low, resonant sound carried only a short distance before being swallowed up in the dense mist.

They waited in the silence that followed until Ewar lifted the mallet to strike again. Then, from the fog, came the sound of approaching kytars.

"Oha!" Ewar called in the direction of the sound.

"Oha, Intawa. Hello," came the reply, and two riders were suddenly before them, as if materializing from the fog itself. Jeena sensed Samson tense.

The two men dismounted and greeted Ewar warmly. They bore little resemblance to the Afridi, she noted hopefully. There were no black robes but rather clothing of more-or-less modern cut, with the loose-draped pants and double-breasted shirts that were only slightly out of style in the Union.

One of the men carried a synlamp, and again Jeena wondered at the advanced technology on this supposedly zed-tech world. Synlamps were basic energy wells, absorbing electromagnetic waves in all forms then releasing them back as light.

They spoke with Ewar in the Intawa language, occasionally flashing the light in Samson's direction and speaking excitedly. Ewar seemed to be explaining something and trying to calm them. They appeared only slightly mollified as they redirected the light to Jeena and the conversation continued.

Finally, they walked over and introduced themselves.

"I am Paul Byron, assistant to the Prime Minister of Pyros," said the holder of the lamp. He was a dark-haired young man of average height—Jeena guessed his age at mid-twenties. "This is David Proverst, commander of our armed forces," he continued.

He gestured to the slightly older, taller man by his side, whom Jeena noted was carrying an old, outdated carbine. Both men seemed wary of Samson, keeping their distance and eying him nervously.

"Ewar informs us that you have tamed this tigra," said David Proverst. "I must tell you I find that unlikely. We have studied this species for years and have never been able to domesticate them."

"Nevertheless, he is quite tame and you are in no danger," she assured him.

Samson remained silent, but the fur on his neck bristled, and he watched them closely through unfriendly eyes.

The armed man seemed unconvinced and anxious to have the meeting over.

"Very well. Ewar tells me you have a message for us. May we ask what it is?"

Jeena hesitated. "I was told to deliver it to a man named Mordachi."

David nodded. "Mordachi is the Prime Minister of Pyros. We will see the message gets to him."

Despite the differences in appearance, Jeena was not ready to trust in the descendents of Afridi.

"Mr. Proverst, my message was to be delivered to Mordachi himself. If this not possible, then just say so and I will be on my way."

Paul Byron answered. "I'm sorry, but it is our law that no strangers be allowed into our city. Ewar has shown great temerity in bringing you here without first contacting us. As for being on your way, until we clear this matter up you will not be allowed to leave. My apologies, but we cannot jeopardize the security of the city."

Jeena smiled. "Apology accepted. But we'll leave when we're damned good and ready. Like now."

Before the armed man could move she spun around, kicking him in the chest and sending him sprawling on his back in the snow. The pistol materialized in her hand, and she grabbed the second man, twisting his arm in a hold and pointing the gun to his head.

David Proverst leapt up, the carbine pointed in her direction.

"Don't do it!" she screamed. "Not unless you're willing to shoot through your own man."

Ewar began yelling at the armed man. As they exchanged words, the Intawa gathered around, their hands slipping stealthily into their coats.

Jeena scanned the area quickly, looking for an escape. *Damn! This was just what I most feared. I'm a stranger in a hostile environment with no clue as to my enemy's strength. For all I know the mists could be crawling with troops. And they're armed! How in Rigel's rings did they get projectile weapons?*

She knew without looking that Samson's fangs and claws had projected.

If we make a run for it now we could probably get back to the village, but that will mean killing these two.

The armed man's gaze darted from Ewar to Jeena.

"Ewar says that you are from off-world. Is this true?"

Now! Her mind said. If she was going to do it, it had to be now when his guard was relaxed.

But she knew she couldn't. Whatever changes had happened to her since her capture and escape, they had been deep. Not long ago these men would have already been dead.

"Yes, I am Captain Jeena Garza of the Union Star Corps. My ship suffered a navigation failure, and I was forced to make an emergency landing on your planet."

The man in her grasp glanced sidelong at her, his expression startled.

"The Union?" asked David, obviously impressed as well. His resolve seemed to waver, and he licked his lips nervously. He appeared to be trying to come to some decision. "I need to know more. At least tell me who sent you with this message."

Ewar brought me to these people. I have to trust them at least this far. If I don't, I'd better be prepared to kill them in cold blood.

"His name was Touloc, of the city of Uruk. He was trying to deliver the message himself but died before he could do so. He sent me in his stead."

"Touloc is dead?" cried David. She heard anguish in his voice.

The man in her grasp sagged as though the wind had been knocked from him.

"Give her the gun, David," he said, his voice resigned.

"Don't be hasty, Paul," he replied. "All we have is this woman's word."

Paul sighed. "Do you really believe the Rosh-dan would have made up a story like this, or sent a woman? No, David, I have no doubt she could have killed us both by now if that was her intention. Give her the gun."

Reluctantly, David clicked the safety on the carbine and tossed it at her feet. For a moment, no one moved

"All right," he said. "So, what do you intend to do now?"

Jeena released Paul then shoved the handgun back into her coat. She picked up the rifle and tossed it back to a surprised David Proverst.

"Same as when I came here. Deliver a message to Mordachi."

Ewar, who had watched the whole encounter with tense interest, now relaxed. He and his hunters slipped their knives back under their parkas unseen.

"All good now?" he asked.

David turned the carbine slowly in his hands.

"Yes, Ewar, all good. Just a little misunderstanding."

Ewar pointed to Jeena. "She clanswoman of tribe. She semata. You see?"

"Semata?" David asked in surprise. "I'm sorry. I didn't know. Do not worry, Ewar, she will come to no harm, I promise."

Ewar seemed satisfied and said his farewells to the two men. Turning to Samson and Jeena he wished them well, asking them to return to the j'led whenever they wished. Then, mounting his kytar, he led his men away into the mists. They could hear his laughter long after he had disappeared, apparently feeling the joke on the Mountain People had gone well, indeed.

"If you would care to remount, we can be on our way," Paul said to Jeena. "I suppose we can find a place for you to tie up the tigra outside the city gates."

"He comes with me," she said sternly.

David balked. "You can't be serious? Captain Garza, a city is no place for a wild animal, even a trained one."

Jeena looked down at Samson. His ears were laid back on his head and his expression was sour. *He's angry and ashamed.*

"I am being reasonable, Mr. Proverst. I don't expect you to understand, but I do expect you to trust me on this. He is gentle and intelligent. I would trust him with my life—in fact, I have. You have taken responsibility for bringing me into your city. I take full responsibility for him. If he cannot accompany me then I'm afraid I must decline to come as well."

David groaned, turning his kytar toward the southern entrance of the mountain.

"Very well, Captain, have it your way. But I certainly hope he's housebroken."

David and Paul had already turned their mounts and so did not see Samson's gesture. It was something he had picked up from her, a flipping of the finger that was a universal human sign of disrespect dating back centuries.

They had gone a short distance when Paul dropped back to ride next to her.

"I'm sorry about what happened back there, Captain, but if you had simply told us you were Ewar's semata it would have saved a lot of unpleasantness." He could not hide his bemused expression. "Forgive me. I suppose my surprise is evident. But I have to admit I'm curious as to how such a, uh...relationship developed between a star pilot and an Intawa hunter."

"You are mistaken, Mr. Byron. Ewar said only that I was semata, not that I was his. In point of fact, I am concubine to a god." She rode ahead, leaving Paul to puzzle over her answer.

They rode only a short distance before reaching a projecting overhang of rock, just high enough for a man to walk under. Jeena dismounted and, with Samson at her side, followed them through a guarded gateway into the heart of Pyros, mountain of fire.

Chapter 16

Into the wilderness we fled, leaving the city of our birth. There we discovered a new home. Only time will tell if we can re-discover ourselves.

> Jeruel an-Nur
> First Prime Minister of Pyros

THE GATEWAY LED INTO A DARK CAVERN, SO DARK JEENA WAS MOMENTARILY BLINDED. AS her eyes adjusted she saw the cavern was actually a short tunnel that ran from the gate to the interior of the mountain. The stones beneath her were smooth and flat, and the footfalls of the kytars echoed against the damp, cool walls.

A large iron door blocked the end of the tunnel and was guarded by two armed soldiers, an image of a mountain emblazed in silver on the chest of their uniforms. They looked in astonishment at Samson but otherwise made no move.

David gave an order, and they unbolted the doors, opening them onto a cavernous, brightly lit hall.

"We will leave the kytars here," David said. "Someone will come for them shortly."

Jeena removed her pack from her mount and swung it over her shoulder, the weight of the MAAD reassuring. With Samson close to her side, she entered the gleaming hall.

The room was carved out of the white rock of the mountain, the walls smooth and glossy and climbed in a gentle arch to meet in a high, vaulted ceiling. This was supported by thick, intricately carved pillars that rose from the polished floor. A beautiful but strange design was laid out in colored tiles in the center of the room.

Jeena gazed at the impressive work of engineering it represented.

It's as though giant sculptors simply carved out the parts of the mountain that were not wanted. The machinery to do this would have to be enormous. Someone is playing fast and loose with the rules of planetary designation.

"Welcome to Pyros," David said, though with little warmth, she noted. "Make yourself comfortable. Paul will locate Mordachi."

Paul excused himself while David took up a position near the guards. His behavior was polite but stiff, and she realized she had probably wounded his ego earlier.

She wished the first encounter with these people had gone better. If they were going to aid the Babylonians—and therefore, her and Samson—then resentment must not be allowed to smolder.

As Samson sat tense and alert, she paced the large hall, studying the detail of the interior. Whereas her initial impression had been one of opulent grandeur, closer inspection revealed evidence of extensive repair. There were large cracks in the walls that had been expertly sealed but were still visible, new tiles had been set in the floor design, the colors and textures not quite matching the original; and in many places the high-relief carvings in the columns had eroded away, restored with what appeared to be a kind of plaster.

It was clear that time and neglect had taken its toll on the great hall. It seemed to her it had been allowed to fall into considerable disrepair before restorations were initiated, and she wondered at the reason.

Her attention was drawn to the light sources illuminating the room. They were not synlamps, as she had assumed, but glowing orbs in translucent globes set at regular intervals around the walls. There was something familiar about them, and it took her a moment to place a name to the devices— electric light bulbs. Another riddle. Why would a culture with synlamp technology use antiquated, wasteful electric light for illumination?

And speaking of electric, how are they generating their heat?

"Mr. Proverst, the Intawa call this the fire mountain. Is Pyros volcanic?" she asked.

"No, not volcanic. Pyros sits over a natural geothermic reservoir. It is the source of our heat and electrical power. Because of thermal radiation, no snow accumulates on the mountain, as I'm sure you observed."

"It *is* remarkable. I can't imagine what it must have taken to build it."

"Neither can I."

She was about to ask him to elaborate on that statement when Paul returned with a bespectacled, rotund man at his side.

"Captain Garza, may I present Mordachi Robsaleum, Prime Minister of Pyros."

Jeena guessed him to be about sixty, of average height and somewhat more than average girth. His hair was silver, falling in curls to his shoulders. He wore trousers and a rumpled jacket, giving him the appearance of an elderly scholar.

She extended her hand. "Mr. Prime Minister, thank you for seeing me."

"Please, call me Mordachi, everyone else does," he said, shaking her hand. "Mine is more of a figurehead position, anyway, but I do get to make all the official noises and wear this nice pin."

A silver brooch in the shape of a mountain was fixed to his jacket.

He looked down at Samson, sitting quietly at her side.

"So, this is the ferocious animal Paul was telling me about, eh? Magnificent specimen. They tell me you have domesticated him. Absolutely remarkable. I have never been this close to one that wasn't sedated. Looks like you've been in a fight recently, eh, big fellow?" Samson remained mute. Mordachi smiled. "My, but you're a good boy."

He turned his attention to Jeena. "So. I understand you are a Union star pilot, marooned here on Ararat."

"Yes, that's correct. I crashed in your desert."

"I'm glad to see you escaped uninjured. You'll have to fill us in on what's happening in the rest of the wide galaxy. What you've done with the tigra is nothing short of amazing, by the way. I'm anxious to learn how you managed to tame him. We've never had any luck with them ourselves—too savage. But first, there is an important matter to discuss." He gestured to his right. "There is a small office we can use. Please, follow me."

The room they entered was carved from the same living rock as the hall. It had low ceilings and no windows, the light supplied by the archaic electric bulbs. In the center of the room was a round wooden table with surrounding benches carved from the stone floor. Thick cushions were scattered on the benches.

Mordachi motioned for Jeena to sit, and was amused to see Samson settle next to her, his hindquarters on the floor and his forefeet on the bench.

He chuckled. "He certainly is protective of you. Now, I am told you have a message for me from Touloc of Uruk, is that so?"

"Yes."

"Well? May I hear it?"

Jeena hesitated. "First, may I ask a question of you, sir? I was told there was a connection between Pyros and New Jerusalem. I'd like to know about that before I say anything more."

David spoke up, his irritation evident.

"Look here, Captain, we have gone out of our way to accommodate you. If you cannot—"

"No, David, it's all right. I'll answer the question. Yes, Captain, there is a connection, of sorts. We in Pyros are the descendants of a group who fled New Jerusalem almost eighty years ago. Scientists and their families, mostly. They had renounced Judaslam, and escaped from the city during the night, wandering in the wilderness before eventually founding Pyros. To the Rosh-dan, we are traitors, betrayers of the faith, and they have been searching for us unceasingly."

A word Jeena had heard in New Jerusalem suddenly came to her.

"So, you are the Apostates?"

Mordachi smiled. "That is a word I have not heard since my youth. Where did you learn it?"

"In New Jerusalem."

David looked at her suspiciously. "You have been in New Jerusalem?"

"Yes, it was in the city prison that I met Touloc and was asked to deliver his message."

"May I inquire why you were held in the prison?" asked Mordachi.

"For aiding a friend."

"That isn't a crime even among the Afridi. Surely, there's more to the story," Mordachi prodded.

"Let's just say my friend and Jacob didn't see eye-to-eye. Jacob ordered his execution, and I had a problem with that. I managed to escape from the prison and rescue him, and now I'm a fugitive, the same as the rest of you, apparently."

"Are you asking us to believe you escaped from the prison of New Jerusalem all on your own?" David asked, his anger rising. "Did it ever occur to you you may have been allowed to escape to lead the Rosh-dan to us?"

Jeena held her own anger in check, though she could feel Samson tensing next to her.

"I was not followed, Mr. Proverst. And if you remember, coming here was not my idea. I am here only as a favor to a dying man."

"Dying?" Mordachi asked, stunned. "Touloc is dead?"

"Yes, sir, I'm sorry. He died soon after passing his information on to me."

"I'm sorry, Mordachi," Paul whispered. "There was no time to tell you."

"Touloc dead," Mordachi repeated, shaking his head. "He was a good man. What a great loss to both our cities. Tell me, Captain, what is this message he felt was so urgent he would risk both his life and our discovery?"

"This: the Rosh-dan have amassed an army of over half a million men, keeping them sequestered and hidden in their western lands. They are preparing to march on Uruk. The city cannot withstand such a force, and Touloc sent me to ask for your help."

"A half-million men! That isn't possible. We'd have seen some sign," protested Paul.

"It's more than possible," said Jeena. "I've seen them."

"*You* have seen them?" David said sarcastically. "You have seen the army hidden from all eyes? But, of course—you escaped from the notorious prison of New Jerusalem, didn't you? And, oh, let us not forget your rescue of a friend from the very hand of the Rosh-dan. Quite a succession of adventures for a marooned fighter pilot, wouldn't you say?

"So, tell me, where is this friend? I would love to speak to someone who witnessed such daring feats."

Samson stood up.

"Then speak to me," he growled.

"Samson!" Jeena cried. She slid her hand quickly into her pack, her fingers gripping the MAAD.

The three men froze, their mouths gaping.

"What?" peeped Paul.

"I said talk to me. I was the friend she saved. I was bound on the altar of the Rosh-dan and would have been sacrificed if not for her. She saved my life, just as she escaped from the prison." He stared hard at David. "She has been through more than you can imagine, and if you think she is lying, then you are an even bigger fool than you look."

His mouth still gaping, his body trembling, David raised the carbine that had been resting in his hands.

Jeena ripped the MAAD from her pack and leapt up.

"Put it down!" she screamed.

Mordachi, who had been struck dumb and slack-jawed, now found his voice.

"No, David! Put that away. Put it away!"

David lowered the weapon.

Mordachi spoke directly to Samson.

"You can speak," he said, his voice filled with awe.

"How very observant of you. Good boy, big fellow."

An almost childlike smile appeared on the prime minister's face, accompanied by a nervous laugh.

"But...but how?" was all he could manage.

Jeena still held the MAAD, switching her aim among the three men. Adrenaline rushed through her, and she could hear the pounding of her heart in her ears. She grabbed her pack and began to slowly back up toward the door of the office.

"Everyone just stay where you are. We've delivered our message and we're going now. Don't anyone try to stop us. Believe me, you don't want to know what this weapon can do."

She moved with Samson out into the entrance hall, the three men following cautiously.

"Captain...Jeena, wait, please don't go," pleaded Mordachi. "We mean you no harm." He turned quickly to David. "Give me your weapon," he said urgently.

David hesitated.

"Now, David! That is an order."

Reluctantly, David obeyed.

Jeena tensed. "Don't try me."

Mordachi stopped in mid-reach.

"Please, Captain, trust me." Taking the rifle he released the clip, letting it clatter to the floor. Then he pulled the bolt back, and the chamber bullet flew out. He tossed the weapon at her feet. "David, order the gate guards away. *Do it.*"

David moved toward the tunnel door, his eyes never leaving Jeena or Samson. Jeena trailed his movements with the MAAD. He reached the door and shouted the order to the guards in the tunnel. They could hear footsteps fading, and then all was silent.

"There is no one between you and the outside world," Mordachi said. "You have us as prisoners, if you wish." His voice turned pleading again. "But I beg you not to go. I'm sorry if we have frightened you, but our reactions were simply those of astonishment. Perhaps, though, your animal's appearance is not the complete shock it should be," he added cryptically.

"I am not her animal!' Samson snapped. "I am my own person and my name is Samson."

"I'm sorry. Forgive me…Samson, I meant no offense." He turned to Jeena. "You trusted Touloc enough to search us out. I'm asking you to trust me now. Stay. Let us talk. If at the end of our conversation you and your animal still want to leave, I give you my word I will personally lead you to wherever you wish to go. Please, will you stay?"

Jeena kept the weapon aimed. "I can't think of a single reason why we should."

David stepped forward. "Then I'll give you a reason—you have nowhere to go. If what you say is true, the Afridi are set on all-out war. You think you can hide among the Intawa? How long do you think they'd last against the Rosh-dan?"

"There is another reason—Samson," Mordachi added. "I don't know how Samson has come to be— and unless I am mistaken, you don't either— but it may very well we be that we can shed some light on this…miracle. We mean no harm to either of you, Captain, and it just may very well be that we can help you."

Jeena was now at the door, but Samson had stopped. He sat unmoving, staring into the pleading eyes of the Prime Minister.

"Let's go, Samson," she ordered.

"I think we should stay."

"*What?*"

"I believe him, Jeena, or at least, I want to believe him. Maybe I even need to believe him. And they're right. We have nowhere to run but to the Intawa, and I won't lead the Rosh-dan to them."

"Are you forgetting who these people are descended from?'

"No. But then, look at what I'm descended from." He walked cautiously up to Mordachi and held out his paw. "Let's try this again. My name is Samson. I am a tigra, but I will not harm you. In fact, I would like to be your friend."

The old man gripped the proffered paw warily in his two trembling hands.

"And I your friend, Samson," he said, grinning. "And I yours."

It took some coaxing, but Samson finally convinced her to lower the weapon and at least answer the obvious questions concerning him. She told of finding him alone as a cub, and of those first few months together. She described the incident that led to his first word, and the months of learning that followed. Then she told of being discovered by the Rosh-dan and of Samson's near death at the hand of Jacob.

Mordachi shook his head sadly.

"I am sorry. The genocide of the tigra race is a terrible crime that should have been halted long ago. We have not done as much as we should have to halt the Rosh-dan, to our shame."

"It has not been for a lack of sympathy to the tigra's plight," Paul added. "We have been aware of this butchery, but we simply have not had the strength to challenge New Jerusalem."

"If Touloc's message is correct then it appears we no longer have any choice," Mordachi said. "Jeena, I understand your distrust of us, but we are not Afridi. If Samson spoke too soon then consider it an act of providence. Knowing what we do now, we cannot allow the Rosh-dan to continue the slaughter. Even if Uruk were not threatened we would fight now to protect Samson and the other tigras—as we should have done from the beginning."

SAMSON WAS GENUINELY TOUCHED BY THE OLD MAN'S WORDS. "THANK YOU, MORDACHI, but I can't blame you for not risking war with the Rosh-dan for the sake of...well, for the sake of some wild animals," he said.

Mordachi and Paul exchanged uncomfortable looks and diverted their eyes.

"Samson, I wish it were as simple as that," said the old man, his voice tinged with sadness. "Please believe me when I tell you it was not our intention, but our people were indirectly responsible not only for the creation of the Rosh-dan, but for the genocidal campaign against the tigras as well."

Paul spoke to their confusion.

"I realize the questions you must have for us, no less then we have for you. But explanations take time and it is already late. Mordachi, with your permission, I say let's leave this tonight. We can pick it up in the morning when we can give these matters the time and consideration they deserve."

There was general agreement, and although Jeena still seemed unsettled by the idea of spending the night in Pyros, they had little choice but to trust in Mordachi's integrity until the morning.

Mordachi instructed Paul to find them an apartment on the second level.

"Or would you rather sleep outdoors?" he asked Samson.

Samson's ears went flat. "No, I sleep indoors. Just like you," he added pointedly.

"Good, then please stay as our guests," he said, missing Samson's meaning. He paused, scratching his chin. "No, I suppose that is incorrect. Actually, I guess we're here as *your* guests. Well, at any rate, we will see you in the morning."

PAUL GUIDED THEM THROUGH THE INTERIOR OF THE MOUNTAIN, ALTHOUGH AS FAR AS JEENA was concerned it could have been on another world. Pyros was impossibly complex, a labyrinth of hallways and corridors that made her dizzy. She stopped even trying to remember all the turns they made en route to what Paul had called the Central Ramp—a spiral walkway that corkscrewed up from the lowest level to the top of the mountain. He explained there were four additional ramps located peripherally around the mountain.

"Interesting design feature," Jeena observed. "I'm curious, though—why no steps?"

Paul shrugged. "I guess the builders felt this was more convenient."

The apartment they were shown to had three rooms—a sitting room furnished with the same low tables and chairs as they had seen in the office, a bedroom with one large, low bed and a small water closet. As with the meeting room, there were no windows and all light came from incandescent bulbs, an oddity that still puzzled her. She wished she had remembered to ask Mordachi about it.

Samson sniffed around the bedroom.

"Only one bed," he called out as she was undressing in the outer room. "Guess we're bunking up again."

She entered the room and flopped on the bed. "It's big enough."

He lay down next to her.

"Is it always going to be so hard?" he asked wearily.

She knew what he meant.

"It's hard for them, too, and will be for everyone who meets you. Mankind is the only intelligent species in the galaxy—that's been our mantra for four hundred years. You shatter a very old belief."

"I know. I'm just tired of the looks and the insults, intentional or not." He sighed. "I wish I had a home."

"We'll find one."

Samson turned his head so he was staring into her eyes, their noses almost touching.

"We? You have a home, Jeena. Ararat is your home, Earth is your home, a hundred planets are your home. I forget sometimes that you're one of them, part of this incredible mass of mankind spread throughout the galaxy. It's funny. Mordachi called me your animal, but I always think of you as my human." He gently moved a strand of hair from her face. "You've never said it, and I try not to think about it, but you can't stay here with me forever, can you? I mean, eventually, you'll have to go back to the Union, won't you?"

Jeena rolled over and closed her eyes.

"It's all right if you do, really it is. All I've ever been is trouble for you. More than anything I want you to find a place where you're happy."

"Go to sleep, Samson," she said, and wondered at the change that had come over her, that tears now came so easily.

Chapter 17

A colony, having determined by popular vote that it wishes to join with a second chartered colony, may request such absorption provided it gives up all legal rights and claims to its charter. These rights and claims shall then pass to the government of the absorbing colony.

> Section 842, chapter 59, paragraph 44, CAIO
> directive concerning manifest destiny

THE NEXT DAY FOUND THEM SEATED AROUND A LARGE TABLE IN WHAT WAS THE MAIN government conference room. It was oval in shape and surrounded by high-back chairs. In the center sat a holo-projector, another unauthorized piece of high technology.

Besides David, Mordachi and Paul, three others were seated at the table. Mordachi introduced them as Kathryn Humboldt, elective representative and Secretary of the Interior; Jason Peters, Director of Archeological Research; and Levi Dubrey, Chief Historian and librarian of the Pyros library. It was clear by the awed stares he had informed them of Samson's abilities.

Jeena took a seat cautiously, Samson preferring to sit on the floor by her side.

"You didn't tell us there would be others," she said.

"I'm sorry, but there are matters of great importance to discuss and decisions to be made. The information concerning Samson and your news of the Rosh-dan will be released later today, but for now I thought it best to involve as few others as necessary. All those present know the situation and the news concerning you, Samson, but I wonder if you wouldn't mind saying a few words, just to prove I haven't lost my mind." Mordachi smiled.

Samson's ears flattened against his head.

"I'm not sure what you want me to say. I'm not a parrot or a trained animal. I am who I am, but I cannot tell you why I am."

The three newcomers sucked in their breath. Even David seemed as unsettled as he had been the previous night.

"It is possible, Samson," said Mordachi, "that we may be able to assist in answering that question. Captain Garza, I spoke somewhat cryptically last night about our involvement with the Rosh-dan's creation and genocide of the tigras. I think it is important for you to know the entire story. To that end I have asked Levi Dubrey to begin this conference, so that you might better understand how our present situation developed."

Levi was a thin, ancient man who wore the high-collared, rigid-cut clothes that had been out of fashion in the Union for a century. His beard was snow-white and neatly trimmed, coming to a point below his chin. He wore large round glasses with thick lenses that gave him a slightly owl-like appearance. He looked every bit the librarian he was.

He tore his gaze from Samson and stood.

"Mordachi has asked me to give you a brief history of Ararat and its colonies. Much of this will be old information to the rest of you, but the full story is known only to a few, so please bear with me." He glanced through the loose pages before him. "To understand the present political realities of Ararat, it is necessary to begin back at the end of the First Migration. As you are all aware, that era began with the discovery of the Hawking Drive and exploded into the first extraterrestrial exodus of mankind a few years later.

"For twenty years prior to this expansion, Judaslam had been growing as a major religious movement on Earth, and its adherents held sway over most Earth politics. With the First Migration, it underwent a steady decline. There are many social-psychological reasons for this I won't go into here. It's enough to know that by the time of the Obsidian Plague they had been reduced to little more than a fringe sect."

The Obsidian Plague—Jeena shuddered. *We tried to play God and almost destroyed ourselves in the process.* Fear of plague had ended the First Migration. It had taken humanity a hundred years to recover sufficiently to venture out to the stars again. By that time the Earth was united under a single government, and a detailed study of each planet was required prior to any colonization—the Five-Year Survey.

Levi continued. "The century between the First and Second migrations was a boom time for the Judaslamics. The horror of the plague turned into condemnation of the science and technology that had brought it to mankind. I'm sure you have all seen holos of mobs burning the universities and research centers during this time.

"Judaslam offered a return to primitivism, and a religious code that attracted huge numbers during this period of uncertainty and instability. Once again it became the greatest religious and political power on Earth. It is for this reason that the plague is referred to by the Afridi as 'the Great Intervention'—a punishment brought upon man by God for his blasphemous ways."

"That's repugnant," Jeena said. "Can they really believe their God sent eight billion people to a horrible death just to revitalize their religion?"

Mordachi nodded. "Unfortunately, that is exactly what they believe."

"They were very successful in restricting scientific knowledge for more than a century," Levi went on, "but eventually, mankind rediscovered the secrets to interstellar flight and the Second Migration began.

"Their leader during this time was a charismatic man known only as Caleb. It was he who first understood that with star travel once again a reality Judaslam's days as a major power were numbered. He began searching for a world on which to relocate his followers, and used his still-considerable power to pressure the Union and CAIO to accelerate the process."

"Levi, I have heard rumors that more than a little pressure was involved. Weren't there whispers of blackmail?" Jeena asked.

"Yes, and although they were never proven, the rumors were probably true. It was never divulged to the public, but six of the nine members of CAIO during that time were Afridi. Judaslam requires its believers to confess all transgressions to the Maudrian. It is entirely probable that Caleb used this sensitive information as leverage to push through the Afridi's charter on Ararat."

He paused, placing his fingertips on the table and peering into each face. "Now, the information I am about to tell you is known only to a few, but I am convinced that the Five-Year Survey of this planet was falsified."

Jeena's jaw dropped. Falsified? The Survey was mankind's only guarantee against something like the Obsidian Plague ever happening again. It was sacrosanct—above politics or even question. If the public ever suspected that a Survey was fraudulent she had no doubt it could bring down CAIO, perhaps even the Union itself, such was the fear of another plague.

"Levi, I'm sure you understand the danger of even speaking that charge aloud," she said.

"I would not even whisper it if I was not sure of my evidence. In fact, you have seen some of it yourself—the Intawa."

David frowned. "You've lost me. What do the Intawa have to do with the FYS?"

"Haven't you wondered where the Intawa came from?" the old scholar asked.

David shrugged. "I assumed they received charter, same as the others."

Levi turned to Jeena. "Does the Union record any charter to the Intawa?"

"No. The only chartered colonies are the Afridi and the Babylonians."

"Okay, so they settled illegally without charter. Happened a lot back then. Probably still does," David said.

"But from where, David?" Levi asked. "You know them. The FYS was completed more than two hundred years ago. What culture was that primitive even then? And if they were so primitive, how did they afford the cost of interstellar transport to get here?"

"I'm guessing you know the answer to that," Jeena said.

"Let's just say I have a very strong hunch. I believe the Intawa came here during the First Migration. I think I can prove they've been here for better than four hundred years."

"And there is no mention of them on the FYS." She was beginning to see his line of reasoning.

"Exactly, and there is no way the survey could have missed them. It involves some five thousand probes and covers every inch of the planet for a period of five years. All life is investigated, from viruses to the largest mammals. If the Intawa aren't mentioned on the official report, then the knowledge must have been squelched."

"But why?" asked Kathryn Humboldt.

"Caleb knew he had to get the Afridi off Earth while he still had a large enough following to create a viable colony," Levi explained. "Judaslam's numbers were already dwindling, and as one of the most austere sects, the Afridi were taking a particularly hard hit, especially among the young. Caleb remembered what happened during the First Migration and knew that the longer they stayed on Earth the more rapid their decline would be. He had his people in power and the financial means to pull it off—it was now or never.

"So, then Ararat is found, and it seems perfect—habitable, but off the regular shipping route so homesick colonists can't go running back to Earth aboard stray freighters. There's just one small problem—it's already inhabited. Not only inhabited, but the FYS determined what we have—namely, that the Intawa are from the era of the First Migration, probably one of the many lost colonies they had back then."

Kathryn Humboldt frowned. "I suppose I should know my Union history better, but why would that matter?"

"The First Migration occurred during a time of independent governments on Earth," Mordachi explained. "When the Union was formed a compromise was reached—all planets colonized prior to the formation of the Union would be treated as independent entities. They could elect to join the Union or not, and any further colonization of their planets would be entirely at their discretion."

Jeena shook her head. "What a mess."

"For Caleb, yes," Levi answered. "The Intawa had been isolated for so long they had regressed back to a primitive culture. They have no record of country of origin, no understanding of charter or even government in the modern sense of the word. The legal entanglements would have taken decades."

"And Caleb didn't have decades," Jeena deduced. "So, he used his influence in CAIO to have the information of their existence suppressed, then pushed for a zed designation to keep interest in Ararat low."

"Exactly," Levi replied.

"And you can prove this?" Kathryn asked.

"Well, I'd say the Intawa themselves are pretty substantial proof, but if you want more there may be some tantalizing evidence in New Jerusalem. My grandfather was curator of the archives there and told me he found papers mentioning an archeological dig northwest of the city. It supposedly held the remains of an ancient starship with a first-generation Hawking Drive."

Jason Peters, the archeologist, whistled. "Wouldn't that be something? Any chance someone could get in and investigate?"

Mordachi shook his head. "Not a chance. We could never get close. I wouldn't be a bit surprised if the Rosh-dan haven't already destroyed the evidence."

"So, if I understand this right, the Intawa are really the owners of Ararat?" asked Samson.

All eyes turned toward the big cat, and he dropped his gaze. He hated being stared at, especially by those he knew thought of him as little more than a curiosity.

"Uh, well, no, not exactly," said Jason. "The ownership of Ararat is a much more complicated matter."

"Yes," Levi agreed, "and a good place for you to step in, Jason." The old man sat down.

The Chief Archeologist of Pyros stood. He wore a shaggy beard and had the rugged good looks of a man who had spent a good portion of his life outdoors.

"Yes, well, all right. Let's see. In order to understand the issues involved, we need to go back to the first Afridi colony on Ararat. Caleb decided in the beginning that he wanted his main city to be in the desert for a number of religious reasons, but he also wanted to build large, imposing structures—as I'm sure you appreciated if you were there. This caused a problem because the shifting quality of the soil meant they often had to dig all the way to bedrock. It was during these early digs that the first troublesome artifacts were found.

"At first they were just some chipped stones, but it was enough for the Union to become interested. They immediately sent in some of their own archeologists and were soon sifting through everything the Afridi were digging up. There was a huge debate as to whether the artifacts were the work of natural forces or evidence of primitive tools. The Afridi vigorously defended the former interpretation, insisting there was no reason for the archeologists to be here."

"Sure, the last thing they wanted was a bunch of Union scientists poking around with the Intawa just a few hundred miles away," Jeena said.

"Precisely. Yet after a few years with no substantial findings, Caleb managed to convince CAIO to allow his own scientists to continue the investigations," Jason replied. "I've often wondered why he kept the digs up after the Union had left. My own theory is that he really didn't think they'd find anything—the rocks they'd been dredging up dated back more than ten thousand years, and nothing more recent than that had ever been found.

"Caleb was old by now—he had to be over seventy. Seth, his son, had taken on most of his duties and was preparing to terminate the project when the more sophisticated artifacts began to appear. As they dug deeper, the question as to the origin of these artifacts could no longer be debated—they were obviously the work of an intelligent race."

"Jason, nothing like what you're telling us has ever reached the rest of the Union," Jeena said.

"No, and with good reason. By this time, the Civil War was raging, and all contact between Ararat and the rest of mankind had been severed. But war or not, I doubt anyone else would have ever learned of this. Even disregarding the fact that the Union would have been all over this planet with teams of archeologists, consider what proof of an alien sentient race would have meant to the very basis of Judaslamic belief.

"Caleb and his people had worked too hard to allow that to happen. Seth couldn't quite bring himself to stop the work altogether—he was intelligent enough to appreciate what those artifacts meant—but he had to prevent knowledge of their existence from getting out. His answer was the Rosh-dan."

"The Keepers of the Faith," Jeena said snidely.

"Yes, and they had their work cut out for them. These new artifacts weren't just chipped stones, but tools and machinery dating back tens of thousands of years. Eventually, they had to isolate the entire research team and all the support staff to prevent 'contamination' from blasphemous ideas."

"I can't believe they kept the greatest scientific find in history from the rest of mankind. This is what we have been looking for since the first space flights. This is what sent us to the stars in the first place."

"I know. It weighed heavily on the men and women involved in the project as well. They began to openly debate not only the Rosh-dan's strong-arm tactics, but also the basic dogmas of the church. What they found buried under the sands of Ararat shook their faith until they reached the point where they could no longer remain. One night under cover of dark, the entire group fled."

"To this place," Jeena said. "How in the world did you build it?"

"Build it? Build Pyros?" Mordachi answered. "Good heavens, we have nothing near sophisticated enough to build this place. No, Jeena, we discovered Pyros, fell into it by accident, in fact. Pyros had been here long before man, buried under the snow for twenty thousand years. From what we have been able to discover, it appears that this was the ancient race's last great city."

Samson glanced around the large room they were in.

"They must have been pretty advanced. What have you learned about them?"

"At first, not much," Jason admitted. "We had scattered pieces of technology—and Pyros, of course. And we uncovered examples of their writing, but no one could decipher it so all we could do was catalogue and store it. What we did know was that their culture flourished throughout the planet, peaking around five thousand years ago at the advanced industrial stage. At that point, all evidence of writing ceases, and a rapid decline begins. Within a thousand years they are back to stone tools, then nothing.

"We took the information with us from New Jerusalem and continued our work here, hoping for a breakthrough. Finally, around fifty years ago, a genius named Jonas Gardner deciphered the code, and for the first time we could read the lost language. It gave us our first real look at who these aliens were."

"And what did you discover?" Jeena asked. "Who were they?"

Jason looked around awkwardly and sat down, his eyes downcast.

"Tigras," Mordachi said, his eyes on Samson. "The builders of Pyros were tigras."

"That can't be possible," Jeena whispered.

"Trust us, Captain. We have investigated this for many years. There can be no doubt. The brute animals you see today are the descendents of Ararat's ruling race."

IT WAS AS THOUGH THE FLOOR HAD DROPPED OUT FROM UNDER SAMSON'S FEET. HIS HEAD was spinning, and he felt faint. He took a step back and fell, trembling. He realized he was panting but was unable to stop it. Everything became blurry.

Jeena was instantly at his side.

"It's okay, take it easy. Samson, look at me. That's it, slow it down. Nice easy breaths."

He saw her fuzzy form sharpen and allowed her to help him sit up. The others stood around the table, worried expressions directed at him.

"It's all right," Jeena said, "he was just hyperventilating. You okay now?" she asked him.

"Yes…Yes, I'm all right." He grabbed her shoulders. "But, Jeena, did you hear? We weren't always animals. We were like you. We were just like you!"

She grinned. "Yes, I heard. It's incredible and wonderful."

"Yes, the discovery was incredible, but deadly," Mordachi said. "We were so excited by what we had found we made a huge blunder. Remember that our people were only recently departed from New Jerusalem. Many felt that this new information would vindicate us in the eyes of our brethren. Without revealing the location of our new home, a courier was dispatched with our evidence to Seth."

"Oh, Mordachi, no," Jeena groaned.

"I'm sorry. We had no idea their reaction would be so ruthless."

"That's why they're killing us?" Samson asked. "Because we were here first?"

"That would be enough. If the Union ever got wind that the descendents of the only other intelligent race ever discovered still existed, there is no doubt they would quarantine the entire planet. They might even remove us all from here. Jacob knows this, as have all the k'laqs since Seth.

"But they aren't killing your people just for real estate," Levi added. "We had proved that another sentient race had existed, as old as mankind and perhaps even older. It was an unraveling of all they believed. Seth became enraged. He executed the courier, labeled us Apostates and ordered a fatwa against us all. They have been searching for us ever since. The tigras...well, you know what he did to them."

Samson balled his paws into fists but said nothing.

"But what happened to the tigras?" Jeena asked. "How in the world did they go from being able to build this..." She gestured at the room. "...to the animals we see today?"

Mordachi answered. "We've been working on that puzzle for years, and haven't a clue. All we know for sure is that they seem to have progressed along a course fairly parallel to man's. The first signs of real civilization begin around ten thousand years ago and advance steadily for five thousand years. At that point all writing ceases and the decline begins. Whatever happened, it was rapid and universal."

Jason worked the holo projector, and a silvery leaf of metal appeared in the air above the table. It was covered in a delicate script, intricately carved.

"This is an early example of their writing. Beautiful, isn't it?"

"What is it written on?" Jeena asked.

"It's a kind of foil. We've found thousands of these pages. We haven't been able to identify the alloy, but they've survived the eons virtually unscathed. Apparently, they felt it was important to leave some proof they had been here."

Samson leaned close to the phantom image, drawn to the language of his race. "What does it say?" he asked.

"Its part of a story, a legend concerning one of their first kings. We think his name was Rorthra-Orr, or at least that's as close to a pronunciation as we can get. It is one of the very last examples of this type of script we have found."

He touched the projector again; and the leaf disappeared, replaced by a sandy-colored stone. Rough hatch marks were cut into one side.

"This is dated two hundred years later. Note how crude the letters have become. We've found almost nothing after this—nothing of their writing, that is to say. We continue to find evidence of technology for at least another three hundred years before the artifacts begin showing the same devolution."

Jeena frowned. "Wait. Three hundred years after writing stops, and they're still producing technology? You mean to tell me they lost their ability to write three centuries before they lost science, metallurgy? That's impossible. How did they communicate?"

"We honestly don't know, but the pattern has remained the same in every site we've excavated. We see the rapid degeneration of their script and then suddenly it vanishes, but we continue to find advanced artifacts for several hundred years more until that, too, disappears."

"How could they have lost so much?" Samson asked to no one in particular.

"I wish I knew," Jason replied. "Several theories have been advanced—genetic mutation, war, plague, even alien invasion—but nothing has ever held up to investigation. All we know is that it seems to have affected the entire species more or less at the same time, and that it resulted in loss of their written, and perhaps even spoken, language first. I'm sorry. I wish I had more answers for you."

"But you give hope that an answer may at last be found, Samson," Mordachi said. "We have always assumed that whatever happened was irreversible, but that is obviously not the case. The fact that you exist means there must be some way to reverse the damage."

Samson gazed at the faces around him. "I wish I could help you, but I don't have any answers. I honestly don't know why I came to be this way. And I know even less about my own species than you do." His ears slowly flattened against his head.

"I think this would be a good time for us all to take a break," Mordachi said. "We'll reconvene in thirty minutes. We still have the problem of the Rosh-dan and Babylon to discuss."

JEENA LED SAMSON TO A QUIET CORNER OF THE CORRIDOR. SHE TRIED TO GET HIM TO SIT, but he refused, standing with his paws clenched in fists and staring blankly at the stone wall.

"Are you all right?" she asked

His lower lip began to quiver. Then, suddenly, he was hitting the wall, slamming his fists again and again into the stone.

"Samson, stop it!" she cried. "Stop it, you're hurting yourself!"

Panting, his fangs partially projecting, he stopped and collapsed to his knees onto the cold stone floor. He held his bloody paws against his chest, trembling.

"What the hell is wrong with you?" she asked, thoroughly confused by his actions. "I thought you'd be excited, proud. Why are you so angry?"

"Proud? I don't have any reason to feel proud," he replied bitterly. "I'm worse than the Rosh-dan."

"Don't say that."

"It's true. They hate my species out of fear, but I've hated who I was, what I was. Oh, and how I hated, Jeena. I hated them so much, hated that I was born from the... the womb of an animal."

Jeena knelt and wiped away the tears from his fur. "Don't do this to yourself."

"No, let me finish. When I was young I used to wish that they would all disappear—that they would die— all of them but me, so no one would see me and be reminded of them." He raised his head to look into her eyes. "So you wouldn't be reminded of them.

"And now I find that they weren't always this way. They were once like me. Something happened, and they're...they're just lost. Like the one near the Intawa village, they're just lost and dying and... and I feel so ashamed."

He turned away. "How can you look at me?"

JEENA FELT THE HEARTACHE AND PAIN POURING OUT FROM SAMSON AS IF IT WERE HER OWN. She was engulfed by feelings she barely had words for—compassion, pity...and perhaps something more. Almost unaware of what she was doing, she took his head in her hands and leaned close, so their lips almost touched, but then abruptly pulled back, her face reddening.

"You, uh...you're too hard on yourself," she said, regaining her composure. "And you have done nothing to be ashamed of. We can't control our feelings, Samson, only our actions. You have a lot to work through, I know, but give it time. Right now, I want you to let one of the Pyros doctors see to your paws."

He flexed them. "I'm all right. I think I'd like to go back to the apartment, though. I don't really need to be at this meeting, anyway. I can't help them much against the Rosh-dan."

"You sure you want to be alone?"

He nodded and walked slowly toward the central ramp, his head hung low. Jeena stood and found Kathryn Humboldt staring at her oddly from across the hallway.

"I'm Kathryn," she re-introduced herself, approaching and extending her hand.

"Yes, I remember," Jeena replied, taking the hand.

"You and the tigra are...very close."

"Samson. Yes, we are."

"It's...so different," she said, laughing nervously. "I mean, it's so strange seeing an animal act like a person."

"Samson doesn't act," Jeena replied. "He is what he is. If you'll excuse me."

She brushed past the woman and met Mordachi in the corridor.

"I saw Samson leaving. Is he all right?"

"He's had quite a shock. It was a lot for him to digest. He just needs some time." She gazed down the corridor. "What a piece of work this mountain is. You know, I wondered about the electric lights."

"That was as far as their technology had advanced. They tapped the geothermal energy from the fissures below the mountain to drive huge generators located in the lowest level. They had long ago turned to dust, of course, but we were able to replace them. We've tried our best to reconstruct the city as it was then. It was our way of honoring those who built it."

She shook her head. "I'm still having a hard time imagining the entire species as sentient. What are their numbers now? Any idea how many are left?"

"Yes, we've been keeping track. The FYS estimated their total population at three million two hundred years ago. Our latest count put them at just over thirty thousand, with most of those north of here. The Rosh-dan have been very busy."

"And they're going to get busier. Jacob knows the Union will be back soon and he wants everyone out of the way—you, me, Babylon, the tigras. I'm convinced he wants to claim manifest destiny."

"I'm sure you're right. They've had scouts searching for us since we fled, but luckily only the Intawa know where we are and they know not to divulge our location. Jacob wants all the evidence we've accumulated destroyed."

"Can you defend yourself?"

"Against the numbers you've seen? No. We have mostly cavalry—less than ten thousand—but we do have more sophisticated weapons."

"Yes, I noticed. I don't suppose you want to tell me who delivers carbines to a zed-tech planet?"

Mordachi chuckled. "I'm sure you can guess."

"Smugglers."

"Yes. They had always been in the area, using the confusion of the war to ply their goods, but the Afridi and Babylon had no interest. I'm afraid we were not so noble. We've been able to buy something like fifteen thousand rifles, but mostly we've used them to acquire building materials and medical technology."

"And that's how you were able to rebuild Pyros."

"Correct."

Paul began redirecting everyone back into the conference room. "I think we should begin. Are you ready, Captain?"

"Yes, let's get it over with."

Mordachi began the second half of their meeting by having Jeena relate all she had seen and heard while in New Jerusalem, including her use of the MAAD on the gates and the armory.

"The armory was good work," David said. "That will slow down their timetable and give us a chance to muster our forces."

"Does anyone see any other option except to do as Touloc asked, to send our people to Uruk to aid the Babylonians?" Mordachi asked.

There was no comment.

"What are the Babylonians like?" Jeena asked.

"Primitive, like the Afridi," Mordachi answered. "But that is all they have in common. Uruk is their principle city, a beautiful, sprawling place headed by an elected regent. Unless things have changed recently, she must still be the same woman I remember, though she must be older than me by now.

"Theirs is an extremely open society, one that has to be seen to be appreciated. I visited there a few times in my younger days when we first established relations with them. Marvelous place. Levi, I seem to recall that you accompanied me there once or twice," Mordachi said, his eyes twinkling.

"I'm sure I can't recall," sniffed the old scholar.

"Really? Pity. I can recall it quite well." He saw Kathryn frowning and coughed. "But, we can save the reminiscing for another day."

"Any idea as to their military strength?" Jeena asked.

"The Babylonian confederacy is large," David replied, "but not so large as the Afridi. They are made up of many independent city-states, the largest of which is Uruk. All told, I would put their combined military strength at maybe one hundred thousand."

"That's quite a disparity in numbers, even with Pyros's more modern weaponry," Jeena said.

"Are we sure there is no other way?" Kathryn asked. "Shouldn't we at least try diplomacy with the Afridi?"

"Kathryn," said Mordachi patiently, "are you forgetting the fatwa against us? That encompasses not only those who left, but their descendents as well."

"That silly decree was issued almost a century ago. Who knows if they're even looking for us anymore? We've been hiding like thieves all these years and we don't even know if it's necessary. We could at least make the offer."

"What offer?" asked David.

"To stay out of their affairs with the Babylonians, of course."

"Stay out?" protested Levi, aghast. "You can't be serious."

"I am only thinking about what is best for Pyros," she replied. "Going to war with New Jerusalem is suicide, that much is obvious. What are we fighting for, anyway—to save a colony of sexual degenerates and a few wild animals? Yes, yes, I know, we owe Pyros to the ancient tigras, but for heaven's sake that was ten millennia ago. What's left of them is certainly not worth dying for."

Jeena, who was sitting next to Mordachi, started to rise but felt his hand on her shoulder. He stood, his face red and stern.

"I can't believe I have heard you right. You're willing to turn your back on our friends and the tigras? After what you have heard today? Not worth dying for? You couldn't be more wrong. They are both worth dying for, the tigras no less than the Babylonians.

"My God, Kathryn, these poor creatures are innocent. Maybe we have used the fact that they were 'just animals' as an excuse to overlook their slaughter in the past, but how can we do so now, after hearing Samson?"

"Mordachi is right," David agreed, standing with him. "Even if we weren't threatened, we couldn't just sit by and let the Rosh-dan destroy Uruk. But make no mistake—we are threatened. If Jacob destroys the Babylonians, he will have broken his Union charter. That opens the entire Afridi colony up to deportation. His only recourse then is to wipe them out so utterly he can declare manifest destiny—claiming that they freely elected to be absorbed by the Afridi.

"To do that he has to eliminate any witnesses. With the Babylonians out of the way, how long do you think it will take him to discover Pyros? No, either we join up with the Babylonians and fight him there, or we sit in our little mountain and wait for him to destroy us as well."

"A decision like this can't be made by the military—you don't have the authority. It is a matter for Parliament," Kathryn sniffed.

"Agreed," Mordachi replied. "That is why I have ordered an emergency meeting of the full Parliament tonight. I have no doubt they will follow my recommendations." He turned to Jeena. "Captain Garza, I want to thank you on behalf of Pyros for all you have done. Please except our hospitality and enjoy our city for as long as you like. Word of Samson should be spreading, though, and you may find privacy hard to come by."

"Thank you, Mordachi, and the rest of you for your kindness. I wish I could be more help, but..."

Mordachi shook his head. "No, my dear. You have done much for us already. This is not your war. If we should fail, then I would like someone left to tell the tale—someone the Union would believe. I have a feeling they would believe you."

SHE FOUND SAMSON IN THEIR APARTMENT, SITTING AND STARING VACANTLY INTO SPACE.
"You all right?" she asked. "How are your hands?"
"Paws, Jeena, I have paws, remember?" he said, flexing them. "They're fine."
"Okay, okay, paws, then, Mister Grouchy. But you still don't look right to me. Maybe you should let one of the Pyros doctors take a look at you."
"It's not necessary, I'm fine. Besides, everywhere I've gone people come up and stare at me."
"Have they been bothering you?"
"No, nothing like that. They've all been very kind, just curious and, to be honest, a little awe-struck, I think."
"Can't blame them for that," she said. She sat near him on one of the low seats. "So, what have you been thinking about?"
"Me. Well, tigras in general, really. Do you realize I know next to nothing about my race?"
"So, maybe this would be a good time to study up. Mordachi said the scientists in Pyros have been studying tigras for years. They have a wealth of data I'm sure they'd be more than happy to share with you. He's invited us to stay for as long as we like."
"I'd like that, but what about the Babylonians? Are they going to help them?"
"Yes, but they won't be leaving for several weeks yet. David tells me that most of the population doesn't actually live in the mountain, but in surrounding farming communities. It will take some time to gather their forces and arm them."
Samson sighed. "There has to be an answer. There has to be a reason why they came to be the way they are, and why I'm not."
"Yep, I'd say that's probably right. So, what do you say we start tomorrow looking for an answer?"

MORDACHI WAS PLEASED TO GRANT SAMSON ACCESS TO ALL THE INFORMATION ON THE tigras they had accumulated over the years. Jeena aided him at first, but was often called away to help David with the formation of a battle plan.
Although he had studied war and was the commander of the Pyros forces,

in truth, neither he nor anyone on Ararat had any real experience in warfare. Jeena was tapped for her extensive knowledge of battle tactics and assisted in the training of the troops, and soon Samson was alone in his studies.

He pored over all the data the Pyros scientists had collected and spent long hours in discussion with Jason and the other archeologists; but like them, he could find nothing to explain the tigras' downfall. He even went on safari to observe tigras in the wild but discovered little. They were too wary, and their senses too keen, for the men to get close.

After three weeks he knew what he had to do, and wondered how Jeena would take his decision.

"What are you reading?" she asked. They had just finished eating and were relaxing in the sitting room.

"It's a partial translation from the tigra histories."

"Have you learned anything?"

"Yes, but nothing helpful. I will say this about my ancestors—they weren't a peaceful race. Everything I've read indicates they were warlike and bloodthirsty. It's a wonder they didn't kill themselves off long before their civilization declined."

"Anything on the reason for their present state?" Jeena asked.

"No. At least, nothing in what they've translated. There are tens of thousands of pages that have yet to be deciphered, but it will take years to interpret them all. I'm never going to find out what happened to them here in Pyros."

"I'm sorry, Samson, I really am. But where does that leave you?"

"I've been thinking about that. I don't see any other choice but to go out there. I need to study them myself and hopefully find something the Pyros scientists have missed."

He read the doubt in her expression.

"All right, so I'm not a scientist. Then again, they've never had anything else to compare to the wild tigras. I have me. Maybe I can discover what makes us different."

"It's the longest of long shots, but if that's what you want I'm ready whenever you are."

He smiled. "You'd do that, wouldn't you? You'd follow me into the wastes, guarding me and covering my back for as I long as I needed. Why?"

She stared silently back. *Please don't ask me that. I don't know the answer myself. Or maybe I do, but I'm too much of a coward to face it.*

Samson chuckled softly. "Well, go ahead and be inscrutable if you want. Anyway, thanks for the offer, but the fact is you can't come with me. No one can. I have to go alone."

"Samson, don't be ridiculous. You can't go alone. How will you survive? And what do you think will happen if something goes wrong? You're no match for one of them."

"Thanks for the vote of confidence. But I don't have a choice—I have to go alone. I've tried getting close with the scientists, but they won't let a human get anywhere near them. The only way I'm going to be able to do this is alone. You've protected me all my life and I love you for it, but it's time for this cub to grow up. Besides, I'll only be gone a couple of weeks at first. I promise I'll come back before the army moves out." He rubbed the back of his paw against her face. "Please don't fight me on this. I've made up my mind."

She wasn't about to give up that easily and argued against his going well into the night, but in the end she could not dissuade him from leaving. When the arguments were over he fell into an easy slumber, but she was restless. The one argument she had not used was her own irrational fear—that if they ever split up, she would never see him again.

It was long into the night before she finally fell asleep, and when she did it was a sleep filled with dreams of war, of tall battlements and a dark enemy, of thunder and flood and death on a massive scale. And through all the death and destruction the only emotion she could feel was a sense of utter loss.

Chapter 18

Si vis pacem, para bellum.
(If you want peace, prepare for war.)

Ancient Earth saying

J EENA STOOD UNDER THE ROCK OVERHANG IN THE EARLY DAWN, SAMSON BY HER SIDE.
"David says the army will move out in two weeks. I want your word you'll be back by then," she said, her breath visible in the cold morning air.

"You have it. Besides, this is just an initial contact. I may stay out longer as I get more comfortable with them and they with me, but for now all I want to do is establish some kind of connection."

"You keep saying that, but just what kind of connection do you think you can make with these animals?"

"I'm not sure. I have an idea, but I'd rather not say anything just yet."

She gazed at him with a face drawn and somber. "You're an idiot."

Laughing, Samson stood and wrapped his large forelegs around her.

"Your pep talks kill me." He drew her close, his muzzle brushing her ear. "I will be back, I promise." Dropping down on all fours, he headed north across the frozen ground.

Jeena sat on a rock and watched in silence until he disappeared from view. A cough from behind startled her.

Kathryn Humboldt stood outside the gateway. "I'm sorry, Captain Garza, I didn't mean to disturb you."

"It's all right."

"I didn't mean to eavesdrop. I was looking for you. I wanted to explain my resistance to the war. Please understand that I am only looking out for the safety of my people."

"You don't have to explain yourself to me, Kathryn, I'm just a visitor here," Jeena replied wearily. She had been deep in thought and had no wish for company.

But Kathryn showed no sign of leaving. "Well, you have been a most welcome visitor. I never thought I would see someone from the Union back on Ararat in my lifetime. And what you have accomplished with that animal—amazing."

"Animal? Please don't call him that. His name is Samson, Miss Humboldt, Samson—it's really a very simple name."

"Samson, of course. I must say, you certainly have an interesting...relationship with him."

It was obvious the woman had more to say.

Jeena stood, frowning. "Go on."

"Well, I only mean that one could get the wrong idea, seeing you two together. Understand that I would never indulge in gossip, but you should know there are people whispering all sorts of things."

"Really? I would love to hear them."

She shook her head vigorously. "Oh, no, I couldn't, but they involve the animal. Of course, I don't believe a word of it, but it might be wise to take greater care with your reputation."

Jeena laughed.

"My reputation? Hell, Kathryn, I've been called a bitch, a murderer, a heretic and a whore—and they're all true. Any name you people could give me would be a compliment." She became grave. "And I've warned you once about calling him an animal. I won't warn you again."

"There is no need to take offense. I'm only trying to help you," Kathryn said indignantly. "And tigras *are* animals, whatever you may think. Good heavens, the way you defend him, you'd think the rumors were true."

Jeena shook her head sadly then struck the woman without warning, sending her sprawling onto the hard snow.

Kathryn sat up slowly, her hand holding her rapidly swollen jaw, an expression of shock on her face.

"You have it backward, Kathryn. You see, I'm the animal. It's Samson who is civilized. Oh, and by the way, call him that again and you'll be the one walking on all fours."

She tightened her collar around her neck and strolled back into the mountain, for some reason feeling slightly better than she had just a moment before.

Samson was walking at a comfortable pace when he heard hoofbeats behind him. He turned to see a rider coming from Pyros and stopped to wait for him.

It was David, and he dismounted as he reached him. He carried something in his hand.

"Hello, Samson, I was hoping to catch you before you left."

"Is something wrong?"

"No, nothing like that," David said, shuffling his feet. "Look, you and I got off on the wrong foot, I think. I wasn't very friendly to either you or Captain Garza at our first meeting, and I haven't extended as much courtesy to you as I should have. It took me a while longer for the shock to wear off, I suppose. Anyway, I wanted to apologize."

"You don't have to, David. I think I understand. And I heard about your defense of my people in Parliament. Thank you for that."

"I meant every word," he said, and held out the object in his hand.

"What is it?"

"It's a kind of vest, specially made for a tigra. Captain Garza gave me the idea when she told me about your leaving. I had one of our tailors make it up. I filled the pockets with maps of the locations of all the tigra populations we've been able to identify over the years. I thought it might come in handy."

Samson took the black leather garment. "David, thank you. I don't know what to say."

"You've already said it. Here, stand up, let me see if it fits."

Samson stood and allowed David to snap the vest over his chest and upper arms. It was thin and small enough not to interfere with his movement, either on two legs or four, and it had many pockets stuffed with maps.

"There," said David. "You'll be the best-dressed tigra in the wastes."

Samson offered his paw, and David took it.

"Jeena says you'll be back before I lead the troops south. I hope to see you then."

"You will. And thank you again, David. For your friendship as well as the gift."

David nodded awkwardly and leapt on his kytar, looking back only once to see the black-and-gold tigra quickly evaporate into the mists. He returned to his military headquarters to find Jeena poring over old maps with his officers.

"I'm worried about the delay in getting your men off," she said. "My destruction of the Rosh-dan arsenal must have set them back, but that was over a month ago. I imagine Jacob has been driving them night and day to rebuild."

"I know, but to depart any sooner would mean leaving men behind, and we are already greatly outnumbered."

"True. I suppose you have no choice, then. What do you know of the Babylonian military? How well trained are they?"

"Very well, I should think. I have never been to Uruk myself, but I know they have a standing army—they've had to with the Rosh-dan breathing down their necks—and that they are followers of Anil, the god of war in their culture. I understand their training is very intensive, but only in the use of swords and the like."

"Do they know what's coming?"

"Riders went out three days ago. They'll be told of Touloc's death and your activities in New Jerusalem. I can't imagine they'll glean much hope from it all."

"No, neither can I. But maybe this will help their spirits." She reached under the table and picked up her pack, removing the MAAD.

"Quite a weapon, from what you've said," David commented.

"Yes, it is. It can't fight off half a million men by itself, but it can help." She tossed it to him.

"But this is yours."

"I have no use for it, David. You do. It is my gift to you. Now come outside and let me show you what it's capable of."

It was late afternoon and the sun was beginning to set when they had finished. David was shaken by the power the weapon represented and was reluctant to touch it, even under Jeena's tutelage.

In token of thanks for the gift as well as the extensive military knowledge she had imparted during her stay, he offered her dinner at one of the many cafes located throughout the mountain city. They went high into the mountain, to an area she had never seen before.

Although Jeena soon became lost, David navigated the turning, twisting corridors that ran lattice-like throughout the mountain with familiarity.

"We know from our studies that tigras have a phenomenal sense of spatial vision," he told her. "Taken as a whole, the layout of Pyros is a work of artistic beauty that is difficult for the human mind to grasp."

"You seem to do pretty well," she observed.

"Being a native helps, of course, but I doubt I perceive the subtleties in the same way they did."

The cafe he led her to was in the uppermost level of the mountain, in what was the equivalent of a park. Here, shafts had been bored through the rock to allow natural sunlight into the interior. Trees and grass grew here, and they sat at a small table beneath a canopy of leaves.

"It's absolutely remarkable," Jeena said.

"It took a generation of hard work to restore the miles of plumbing and irrigation systems, but well worth the effort, I think."

They ordered their meal and ate while speaking of many things. David was genuinely interested in everything she had experienced, and she told him of the many battles she had witnessed—of the carnage and death, of whole planets under attack by legions of starfighters.

"I wish you were going with me to Uruk. I could really use someone with your experience."

"I'm sorry, David. I wouldn't be much use to you, anyway. I'm sick of war," she said. "I'm sick of the death, and the noise, and the stench of it. I wish I could help you and your people, but there is no more war left in me."

"I understand, and there's no reason to be sorry. I'm sure I'll feel the same when this is over."

"You've never been in battle?"

"No. Pyros has had a militia since its founding, but we've never had a large enough population to even consider confronting the Rosh-dan. We train, of course, but if ever attacked we'd mostly depend on the mountain for our defense."

"It's a good defense. An army would have a hard time penetrating this place."

"Yes, I suppose we could last a while, but not forever. Eventually, the food would run out or they'd find a way to block the incoming water and then it would be over."

They finished their meal, and David explained there was someplace special he wanted to show her. They continued their conversation as they made their way up the central ramp.

"You're all descendents of Afridi, but I haven't seen any temples," Jeena observed.

"There aren't any. It's hard to rediscover your faith once it's been lost. Don't get me wrong, many still have faith in a supreme being, but not in any organized manner. The disillusionment of the Rosh-dan stripped away what we thought we understood, and we're still grappling to find new answers. What about you? Do you practice a religion?"

"No. I was raised by Arian Christians, but I've never had much use for religion. Most of those I've seen are either messianic and therefore inherently dangerous, or hollow disseminators of empty platitudes like brotherhood and love and the general goodness of man."

David winced. "Ouch, that's a bit cynical, don't you think? Surely, you're not so jaded as to completely discount the possibility of some benign guiding force?"

"Oh, I don't know. I suppose I'd like to think of the universe as something other than just a random series of essentially pointless events, but I'm not sure I have the capacity anymore."

They ascended the rampway, passing openings on either side, halls leading out to the periphery like spokes of a wheel. Some passageways were straight, while others ascended or descended with no apparent order or regularity. These would then intersect with levels of other pathways and halls circling the mountain's interior. It created an almost innumerable number of intersections, yet there was no sense of randomness. Unlike the streets of New Jerusalem, the halls of Pyros appeared to have been laid out according to a single vision, alien though it was.

They reached the uppermost level, and David swung open a pair of heavy wooden doors. They stepped onto a stone balcony jutting out from the mountainside. Below them was only darkness, while above a kaleidoscope of stars shone bright.

"We call this platform the *halel*. It's my favorite spot in all of Pyros, and well worth the walk, I think," David said.

"It's beautiful," Jeena admitted, rubbing her hands over her arms. The air was brisk, but not biting.

"We're not sure what the tigras used it for. Was it just a viewing area for stargazing, or did it have some special significance for them, maybe even religious significance." He shook his head. "It's so frustrating. Here they are walking among us and yet they can tell us nothing, not even the answer to the one riddle that has puzzled our people for decades: What happened to you?"

Jeena shivered slightly as she gazed up at the cover of stars. Somewhere under these same twinkling lights, Samson was looking for the answer to that very question.

Chapter 19

Ever has it been said that love knows not its own depth until the hour of separation.

>Kahlil Gabran, 20th Century Earth Poet
>*Encyclopedic History of the Union,* 22nd ed.

Samson lay comfortably in the cool snow. In the week since he had left Pyros he had yet to find any tigras, but he was learning to live off the land. In an effort to gain a greater understanding of his people, he had finally forced himself to hunt wild game as a tigra. At first he was unable to stomach the meal, but eventually hunger won out; and on the second day he closed his eyes and choked down the still-warm flesh of a wolla.

He had made three kills since then. The raw meat was beginning to taste sweet, and hunting was becoming an enjoyable exercise. He felt his body growing sleeker and firmer, and he moved with a graceful fluidity that had only been hinted at earlier. He was amazed at how quickly he was adapting to the wilds, and found that the life he had left behind was becoming less important with each passing day.

How easily instinct takes command when its skills are needed, he thought. Remove the barriers that civilization sets up to control it, and instinct will rise to consume the whole. In time, genes will always claim mastery over the reasoning mind.

How long, he wondered idly, before he'd revert back to the ways of the beast? How long before comprehension gave way to reflex, and speech degenerated into grunts and snarls? *How tight is the hold that reason has on me?*

The urge to give into that primal instinct, to shed the complex cares of the thinking mind, was powerful and tempting. He could live out his life here in ease, hunting and sleeping—perhaps even mating. Worry could be left to those others, to those humans.

But then the image of Jeena appeared, and those thoughts withered and died. That way led to the past and to ultimate destruction. His way lay ahead, to the hope of a better future for him and his kind. With effort he roused himself, standing and shaking vigorously before continuing on his journey north.

TROOPS BEGAN TO POUR INTO PYROS; THEY WERE HOUSED IN BARRACKS LOCATED NORTH OF the mountain. A gymnasium was part of the complex, and David took Jeena to observe the soldiers in training.

A large crowd was gathered around a sparring ring, shouting encouragement to the participants, who were competing with short swords.

"We want them to become as adept as possible with primitive weapons," David explained. "Although we have enough guns to go around, our ammo is somewhat limited, and there's no telling how we'll be forced to fight before it's all over."

"Good thinking," Jeena agreed. "I see you have a co-ed military. Pretty progressive for a bunch of ex-Afridi."

"We like to think so, but wait till we get to Uruk. I'm told that not only is their commander a woman, but so are many of their elite fighters. They're supposed to be very good."

Jeena shrugged. "No one knows how good they are until they're tested in war. In a contest of raw troops on both sides, I'd rather have men."

"Really? You surprise me, Captain. As a woman yourself…"

"As a woman I know what it takes to turn us into hardened soldiers. Men have a genetic predisposition toward aggression that few women do. Sure, you can instill it, but that takes time and training. Even then, it's the rare woman who ever develops the taste for killing that men do. I'm speaking here in generalities, of course. Some men are pacifists by nature, while some women are naturally violent."

"And you?" he asked.

Jeena laughed. "I was one mean dog in my day, but I'm just a puppy now, David. I don't bite anymore, and I bark very little."

The contest in the ring ended with the larger man winning. He leaned over the ropes and signaled to David.

"Afternoon, Commander."

"Afternoon, Bernd," David replied. "You looked good in there."

"These guys are too easy," he said with a grin. "I'm looking for better competition. What do you say, Captain? Rumor has it that SAG commandos are tougher than nails. Want to prove it?"

There were cheers and laughs from all.

"The captain is just here as an advisor, Bernd," David told him. "She doesn't have to prove anything."

"Thanks for the offer, soldier, but I think I'll pass this time around," Jeena said. She allowed David to lead her through the crowd that had gathered around the ring.

"Sure, no problem," the big man called after her. "I wasn't going to hurt you, though. I just wanted to give you a few love taps."

He made a grinding motion with his hips, and the crowd laughed.

Jeena halted, her face reddening.

"Don't let him provoke you," David warned. "He's just young."

"That's the best time to learn a lesson," she replied, and turned to face her taunter. "You sure this is what you want?"

He laughed. "Aw, I'm just teasing you, Captain. You don't want to spar with me—I've never been beaten. No disrespect, but I eat bigger meals than you."

Jeena smiled thinly. "Is that right? Well, you might find me a little harder to swallow than you think."

She pushed through the laughing crowd to the weapons area, pulling a protective helmet and vest from the far wall and donning them as David tried to talk her out of it.

"This is ridiculous. He's the biggest man in the whole force."

"We have a saying in the Corps, David—mean and nasty beats big and stupid any day."

"He may fit the latter description, but you're hardly the former. Besides, I thought you said you were done with fighting."

The trousers she wore were far too loose and she made some adjustments with her belt, leaving a large loop on her right side, then she picked up a short sword and tested the weight in her hand.

"This isn't war, David," she said, grinning. "This is fun."

She leapt into the ring, and they presented their swords in a sign of mutual respect. Separating, they began slowly circling one another.

Jeena had not practiced sword combat since her academy days, and was content at first to stay on the defensive, feeling out her opponent's skill level.

He moved well for a big man, she thought, and had the confident look of someone used to winning.

He made a few testing jabs to her midsection, which she easily parried, then advanced more powerfully, forcing her to retreat. She felt the ropes at her back and feigned a thrust to the right, spinning left to escape the trap. He turned and faced her again, using the sword point to push her back. Jeena tried to go on the offense, but his long reach made that impossible, and she soon found herself back against the ropes.

This time she ducked and rolled, just missing the blow that swept over her. He was back on her in a flash, sweeping the blade in large arcs. Jeena timed his swing as she backed away as though intimidated by the assault.

When the right moment came, she leapt at him feet first, catching him in the chest and sending him sprawling to the mat. There were shouts and cheers from the onlookers who had gathered around the ring.

The big man jumped back to his feet red-faced and immediately came after her again, this time keeping his thrusts short and controlled. The blows were powerful, and it took all of her strength to turn them aside. He was cutting off the fighting surface skillfully, limiting her room to maneuver.

One swipe of his blade drove her sword arm back, and he reached in swiftly with his left hand, lifted her easily and slammed her hard on the mat. The crowd shouted encouragement as he swaggered around the ring.

"I'm going to stop this, Jeena," David shouted from her corner.

"My ass! I'm not through yet," she yelled back.

Rising to her feet, she repositioned herself to meet his attack. Again he came after her, driving and thrusting and forcing her to take a weak defense position. The crowd was egging him on. He had her cornered now, and towered over her, grinning and preparing to end the match.

As he opened up to deliver the final blow, Jeena made a quick feint to the left, shifting her hips slightly and catching the belt loop with the hilt of her sword. When she swung the sword the belt untied, with the result that her trousers dropped, revealing that she was naked underneath.

The shouting crowd gasped, and for in instant her opponent hesitated, his attention diverted to her bare pelvis. In that moment of hesitation, Jeena drove in, catching him in the sternum with the hilt of her sword. As he jackknifed forward, she struck him again on the back of the neck, and he crashed limp to the floor.

The gathered crowd of soldiers, stunned initially into silence, started to laugh and then to cheer as Jeena calmly pulled up her pants and readjusted her belt. They were still cheering when she went to help the dazed and blinking man off the mat.

"Lesson number one," she whispered in his ear, "is to never take your eye off your opponent's weapon, even if she's a naked woman."

Jeena strode defiantly over to David, who was holding his hand over his eyes and shaking his head.

"Mean and nasty, David," she said. "Mean and nasty."

SAMSON HAD TREKKED FAR INTO TIGRA TERRITORY WITH LITTLE LUCK. HE HAD COME INTO contact with lone tigras on several occasions, and each time he had sensed that familiar stirring—a connection of sorts that felt as though it was emanating from the animal. Yet each time he tried to speak, the animal withdrew.

It was no use. Whatever the sensation was, it was too alien for him to understand. He was tired and miserable and was heading back to Pyros in defeat.

He was now less than a day's walk from the mountain and lay in a state of half-sleep, worn out from hunger and frustration. As he rested in the snow, he became aware of primitive images flashing in his mind. He had experienced this visual aura before, but always in close proximity to another tigra; and always they had faded away when he tried to focus on them. Now he relaxed and let the images come and go as they would, without any effort to decipher them.

They were too brief and too diverse for him to try and comprehend, yet soon he became aware of certain primitive feelings and desires that seemed to accompany the flashes. Hunger he felt, and fear. Desire, too—not in the conscious sense of desiring a mate but only the base need to join. He felt confident these images and feelings were flowing from the minds of tigras, but he could not fathom how.

He was content just to listen at first, then tried to project his own simple idea into the mental maelstrom.

Come, he thought, and *friend*, and repeated those two simple concepts again and again.

Suddenly, he heard a sound and opened his eyes—and his heart jumped. Standing before him was a tigra.

Samson bolted upright, his pulse racing. The animal, a male, seemed anything but friendly. His lips were drawn back in a snarl, and his fangs were descended, dripping saliva. The images in Samson's mind evaporated, and he found himself reverting back to his human conditioning, speaking softly to the animal as he slowly backed away.

"Easy, boy, easy now. I'm not going to hurt you." He had only retreated a few spaces when his right leg gave out and he tumbled to the ground. With a roar, the animal leapt.

JEENA STOOD NEAR THE CORRAL FEELING IRRITABLE AND ANXIOUS. THE ARMY WAS SET TO leave in two days, and she had still not heard from Samson. She would wait until they rode out then go look for him herself.

David appeared, leading two saddled mounts.

"I hoped I'd find you. I thought you might like to take a ride around the city with me," he said. "I want to take one last look at the old place before I go."

Jeena took the reins of the offered kytar, stroking its neck. "You really love Pyros, don't you?"

"Yes, I do. In one thing only do Kathryn Humboldt and I agree—I would do anything to save this city and my people. I love it even more knowing that the old race built it. Did you know this was their last great work? Mordachi says it was built right at the end of their civilization."

"Makes you wonder why they would go through all the trouble," Jeena said. "They couldn't have been hard up for space by then."

"No, and this is the only structure of its kind, as far as we know. Before this they apparently lived in sprawling, single-story homes."

"Just one of many unanswered questions about them, I suppose," Jeena said. "How did your people find Pyros, anyway?"

"The Intawa pointed it out. When our people first came here from the west, the tribe befriended us. The mountain had been dead for millennia, of course, but the heat still rose through the corridors and kept most of the snow off. They showed us the 'fire-mountain,' and being scientists, our people naturally investigated."

"It must have been quite a shock to find this."

"So I've been told. Here they get thrown out of New Jerusalem for studying an alien culture only to land in its last, greatest city."

"That's one hell of a coincidence."

"Yes, my grandfather said it made him believe in a higher power again."

A rider approached at a full gallop and leapt from his mount, pulling David aside and whispering to him excitedly in hushed tones. When David turned back to Jeena, his face was pale.

"What is it?" she asked. "What's happened?"

"A scout has returned from the north. He has discovered a body. It's a tigra."

Jeena pushed past him and grabbed the scout, spinning him around.

"Where? Where did you find him?"

"A few miles to the north. On the ridge west of the northern road."

She leapt on the kytar.

David grabbed at her boot. "No, Jeena, you shouldn't go. Stay here, I'll investigate."

She pulled away and set off at a gallop. He quickly mounted his animal and followed.

Jeena rode fast, pushing her kytar until it was foaming, with David right on her heels. At the top of the ridge she jumped off and began a mad search over the snow-covered ground, with David joining her. A few minutes later, he called her to where he stood.

At his feet lay the remains of a horribly mangled animal, the ground beneath it red with blood. Only the general outline of its body made it identifiable as a tigra.

Jeena fell to her knees.

"Don't jump to conclusions. We see many tigras here in the north."

She began to weep. David knelt next her.

"Jeena, we don't know—" he began, but stopped abruptly.

Clutched in her hands, she held the bloody and tattered remnants of a leather vest. A small map was still inside.

SAMSON FELL BACK WITH A HOWL. THE SWIPE OF THE TIGRA'S CLAWS HAD RIPPED HIS VEST from him and cut a slash across his chest. His own fangs and claws had automatically snapped into position, and he was preparing to defend himself when the animal leapt again—this time over him. Samson spun around and saw a second tigra behind him, this one just as rabid and vicious-appearing as the first.

Ignored for now, he clutched his chest in pain as the two flew into each other. They attacked with a ferocity he had never seen in the holos. A fight between tigras was usually a slow, cautious affair as the animals circled each other looking for a sign of weakness. When the fighting did begin it was more often than not short-lived, with the weaker animal retreating, wounded but alive.

These tigras charged one another then reared up on their hind legs. For the next several horrifying minutes, they stood toe-to-toe, slashing and tearing at each other, neither willing to give ground. Soon both were covered in blood, their razor-sharp claws ripping away chunks of flesh, and yet still they would not back down.

Finally, the first animal struck a lethal blow, cutting across the other's neck. Even then it refused to halt its attack, and continued to tear at the corpse in rage.

Samson slunk away from the sight, sickened and trembling at the carnage he had witnessed. Only when he was sure he was safe did he allow himself to collapse unconscious in the snow.

Chapter 20

And ye shall hear of wars and rumors of wars: see that ye be not troubled: for all [these things] must come to pass, but the end is not yet.

Matthew 24:6
Arian Christian Bible

THE TROOPS WERE ASSEMBLED; TEN THOUSAND CAVALRY TROOPS STOOD READY TO MAKE the long journey to Uruk and help defend their endangered friends. David stood near his mount, speaking with Mordachi one last time before leaving.

"I hate to leave her like this," he said, "but we can't delay any longer."

It had been two days since the discovery of Samson's body. David had dragged Jeena away and brought her back to Pyros on his mount; he sent two men to bury the remains. Since then she had remained in her apartment, refusing to speak even to Mordachi.

"There is no more you can do for her," Mordachi replied. "We'll care for her and help her as best we can."

"I know you will. Listen, if anything happens…I mean, if I don't return…tell her…tell her how terribly sorry I am for her loss."

"I will, my friend. But you will be back, and you can tell her yourself."

David had put his foot in the stirrup to mount when a disturbance caught his attention. There was murmuring and shifting in the ranks.

"My God," gasped Mordachi.

Coming up alongside the array of mounted kytars was a lone rider. She wore the helmet and arms of the Pyros military, but there was no mistaking her identity.

"Jeena, what the hell are you doing?" David asked when she stopped before them.

"I'm coming with you."

"No, absolutely not," Mordachi said sternly. "It's out of the question."

"Mordachi's right," David said. "This isn't your war, you said so yourself."

"Does that matter?" She leaned forward in her saddle, gazing hard at him. "I've seen what you're up against. You need me. I'm the most experienced soldier on this planet. With me your chances of victory increase. Leave me here, and more of your people will die. You said you wanted me—well, here I am. You want to save Pyros? Then take me with you."

David hesitated, looking back at the columns of men and women he was leading into war. *Yes, I need you. Haven't I lain awake for nights in fear of this day? I have trained as a soldier, played as a soldier, but I am no killer of men.*

He looked up at her drawn face glaring down at him, her jaw set so tight surely her teeth must soon grind into dust.

Not like you.

"All right," he said finally. "If you're willing, then, yes, I want you."

Mordachi pulled him aside.

"Are you mad?" he said in a hushed voice.

"No, I'm desperate. She's right, I need her. I need all the help I can get. Mordachi, we both know I have never led men into battle. She has. And that weapon of hers scares the hell out of me. I'd much rather she wield it."

"I understand, but she is not a machine. She is emotionally broken. Even if what you say is true, at best you have a fragile and unstable soldier. And don't think she's coming with you to win a war. Look in her eyes, David. That woman is going into battle for one reason—to die."

"You think I don't understand that?" he answered angrily. "I know what she's been through, but I have a war to win. If bringing her along means fewer of my people die, than so be it. I can't afford compassion right now. I will use everything I can to save Pyros—even her."

Mordachi patted him gently on the arm, sighing. "All right, son, you must do what you think is necessary, but take this as a warning—that weapon of hers is more powerful than anything you or I have ever seen. If her fragility should shatter while it is in her hands, the danger may not just be to the enemy—and you may not be able to control her."

Jeena nudged her mount toward the whispering men. "Let's get going."

"Please reconsider, Jeena," Mordachi pleaded gently. "Stay here with us.

You need time to heal."

She ignored him and spoke to David.

"Are the troops ready?"

"Yes."

"Then let's go. It's four weeks to Uruk, and Jacob has already set out."

The two men exchanged worried glances.

"No, gentlemen, I'm not having visions. I know he's marching because he has to. In less than two months the rainy season begins. He has half a million men and tons of machinery to move and a lot of distance to cover—he has to have left by now." She turned grim. "Now, if there are no more questions concerning my sanity, I suggest we get moving."

She sat silently on her kytar as David addressed the troops and started them off. Their route would take them over flat country for most of their journey, and he had hoped to use the time to work with them before reaching Uruk. All were good riders, but as a part-time army, they had little experience working as a unit.

Jeena had helped him devise several training exercises, including close-order drills, sweeps and cavalry charges they could practice while still moving swiftly toward Uruk. The first day, however, he wanted them to get used to hard riding, and moved them steadily and swiftly well into the night.

The two moons had already set before he finally gave the order to halt. The men and women were tired and sore, but there was little grumbling as they made camp. Soon, tiny fires dotted the hillside as they ate a late meal before turning in.

He sat across from Jeena at their own small fire. She had said nothing during the meal, and now sat staring into the flames.

"I'm all right," she said suddenly.

"What?" He was almost startled to hear her voice.

"I know Mordachi thinks I should have stayed in Pyros, but I'm all right. I'd like to take over the training in the morning, if you don't mind."

"No, not at all. I'd very much appreciate it. But are you sure you're up to it? I mean, after all you've been through?"

"Been through? You mean Samson's death? David, I've seen thousands die. Poor little Maggie died right at my feet. And those women in the prison—I watched them die one by one. You don't have to worry about me; Death and I are old friends. It doesn't affect me anymore."

Her voice was steady and unbroken and her face composed, yet he could feel the lie in her words. That she would go to such lengths to shut down her emotions told him all he needed to know about the depth of her loss.

He watched the fire reflecting in her eyes. There was so much pain buried behind those eyes, and anger, too. *Forgive me, Jeena, but I need that pain, and that anger. I need all that you have. I need you to save my people.*

They broke camp before dawn. Although there were a few mishaps, including a runaway kytar, David was pleased with their speed and professionalism.

His first task was to get them proficient in riding in formation. As Jeena had pointed out, a cavalry's greatest asset was its mass, and was best utilized by driving into an enemy as a single unyielding unit. Separately, each animal and its rider could be overcome, but as part of a cohesive group they became a powerful and effective force.

Under her direction, he divided them into three groups and assigned captains to each. They practiced charges and sweeps under Jeena's scrutiny. As she had warned him, while they were all capable riders, they were woefully inept at synchronized movement.

They kept at it the entire day, all the while moving steadily south. They took orders without complaint and enthusiastically, knowing the skills they were learning could very well save their lives.

David allowed them only a few short rests during the march, to rest and water the kytars. They needed toughening up before facing the army of the Rosh-dan, and he wanted them to get used to putting long days in the saddle. Even Jeena complained she was a little stiff and sore by the end of the second day.

She sat near him at their campfire, smoking a cigar and stretching her legs. She had been more talkative today and less somber, though he had been careful to avoid any unsettling topics.

"You ride like you've been on a kytar your whole life," he commented.

"I'd never even heard of a kytar before landing on Ararat, but we have similar animals on Earth. I spent a lot of time in my youth riding them at the Home."

David remembered she had mentioned something about the Home before. It was a sort of orphanage, he recalled, and the memory had seemed unpleasant to her, so he let it drop.

There was some playful shouting and laughter from one of the nearby tents.

Jeena shook her head.

"They're dedicated, if not particularly skilled yet, but they're too lighthearted, too confident."

"I think that is mostly your doing. You don't know how pleased they all were that you're coming with us. They feel your training and expertise gives them a great advantage. They have a lot of confidence in you."

"I'm glad they have faith in me, but over-confidence will get them killed. This war will be brutal, maybe more so than you understand. In the morning, I want you to take a good hard look at your troops. My guess is that, even if we win, half of them won't be coming back."

David grew somber. Pyros being the relatively small community it was, he knew most of the men and women under his command by name. He had tried not to think too much in terms of losses. Now he let her words sink in. How many would die?

He glanced back at Jeena, who now sat back, her eyes closed. She has seen so much death and destruction in her life. *Is that why she keeps everyone at arms-length, why she resists letting anyone get close? Except Samson, of course, and now he is dead as well. Maybe that is the only way to survive war. Will I be the same, when this is all over?*

THE WORK CONTINUED OVER THE COURSE OF THE MARCH, AS JEENA FOUGHT TO WELD THE troops into a single fighting unit. Although David was technically the commanding officer, he turned most of the instruction over to her, bowing to her greater experience.

She was a natural leader who knew the subtleties of command. Praise, when earned, was given publicly and within earshot of all. Criticism was always constructive and directed in private. She pushed them and pushed them again, but in a way that earned respect, not resentment. She was the first to rise and the last to bed, and if she drove them hard, she drove herself harder.

He was learning, too. Although he had taken command some years before, he had no practical experience in leading an army. The Pyros military, composed as it was of mostly volunteer, part-time soldiers, was far too democratic a group, in Jeena's estimation. Battle was no time to try and forge a consensus. Orders needed to be given and immediately followed, or lost lives were the usual result.

David had a tendency to give suggestions rather than orders, and to explain his reasoning in detail. Jeena slowly broke him of this, and to his surprise—but not hers—the company admired him more for it.

EVEN WITH THE TIME NEEDED FOR TRAINING, THE COMPANY MOVED QUICKLY, COVERING more than half the distance by the seventeenth day. On that day, their maneuvers came to an abrupt halt.

"You've done wonders with them in such a short time," David observed. They were watching as the company practiced spearheading into an enemy line, driving a wedge to separate them then sweeping around to attack the flanks. They carried out the move with fluid precision.

"They've done it themselves," Jeena said. "You should be proud. Your people have worked hard and done all that I've asked of them."

"I notice we've only been practicing with swords and spears. Are you just trying to save ammunition, or do you have other plans in mind?"

"Both. As well as your people have performed, I've been thinking we'd be better off using them as pure cavalry. Carbines shot from charging mounts aren't particularly effective. It would make more sense to create a separate rifle unit out of some of Uruk's foot soldiers. You think your people would mind parting with their rifles?"

He smiled. "I doubt most of these people have ever fired a gun. We only recently acquired them, and ammunition has always been in short supply. They're comfortable with sword fighting; you won't have any trouble getting them to give up their rifles."

"Good. And by the way, you need to find better smugglers. These weapons have to be fifty years old, at least."

"No, really? But we were assured they were practically state of the art."

A scout came galloping hard from the west. David had sent outriders soon after leaving Pyros—he had taken Jeena at her word that Jacob was moving and did not want to run into the Rosh-dan accidentally. He had no delusions about who would win that encounter.

"Riders!" the girl gasped, pointing back to from where she had come.

"It's okay, Sarah, calm down," he said. "How many were there?"

"Three. Heading south."

"And you're sure they were Rosh-dan?" Jeena asked.

"Positive. There's no mistaking those dark clothes and long beards. I saw no sign of an army. They were moving quickly but not galloping."

Jeena leapt up on her kytar.

"It's a point patrol. The main army can't be more than a day behind them. David, assemble the company. The race has begun."

When the troops were mounted and assembled, she addressed them.

"Our timetable has been moved up. I'm sorry, I realize you could use more training but that will have to wait. If we ride hard we can make Uruk in ten days. It will mean few rests and little sleep. Both you and the kytars will be exhausted by the time we arrive, but we must reach the city before the Rosh-dan. So, gird yourselves, and let's ride."

SAMSON CLOSED HIS EYES. THE WOUND TO HIS CHEST WAS NO LONGER PAINFUL, BUT HE would carry the evidence of his folly for the rest of his life.

He had roamed the wastes for days following the attack, trying to determine what had gone wrong. That his species was telepathic could no longer be denied, as was his certainty that it was his attempt at communication that had somehow caused the rage he had witnessed.

But why? He had only been sending a message of friendship.

The realization slowly dawned on him that perhaps it was the nature of the message, and not the message itself, that was the problem.

I'm too human. I'm not sure even Jeena realizes how much. I can connect with them, but my mind is not like theirs. Language, reason—they've wired my brain in a human pattern. I was trying to project an idea, but like humans, I can't form an idea without putting words to it. Even though they, too, were once aware, cognizant thought is beyond them for now.

But something had to set them off. If they can't grasp the complexity in my cortex, what could they understand?

The answer was quick in coming—the limbus. In his attempts to establish the telepathic link, the tigras had been unable to interpret the ideas of his higher prefrontal brain centers, and so had followed the pathway to the complex group of interconnected structures controlling his emotions—the limbic system.

It must have been overwhelming, the complex emotions so alien to them yet so powerful: love, empathy, longing. Yet some they must have understood. Fear? Yes. Anger, too, after a fashion.

And hate? Can an animal hate? Perhaps not, but I can, and hate fuels my anger. How much hate for the Rosh-dan do I have? More than I will admit. And self-hatred? Yes, that, too. No wonder they went mad.

Into the depths of this emotional maelstrom, unfiltered by his reasoning centers, the tigras had fallen. Fear, pain and hunger had fairly defined the extent of tigra emotional capacity for millennia, and they were unable to process this flood of information. So, they latched onto what was familiar—anger, aggression, rage.

All the ugly emotions I try to suppress, and it possessed them. They fought not as animals but as men would fight—to the death.

He realized now that if there was any hope in reaching the tigras through this telepathic link, he would have to find a way to control and negate his negative feelings, even those buried deep in his subconscious.

He worked mentally through all the information he had studied on Jeena's ship and was pleased to recall many techniques in what was called *self-hypnosis*. Humans had apparently been very interested in controlling this aspect of themselves as well. But would any of the methods work well enough? And if not, could he survive another failed attempt?

He did not ponder the question for long.

Either I find a way to reach them in this way, or I return to Pyros in defeat and leave them to their doom.

For days he practiced the remembered lessons, slowly working through the panoply of emotions that churned within him. He did not try to suppress the negative feelings, for that would take them out of his control. Rather he learned to separate them. Those he wished to keep from the tigras he set aside, mentally locking them away in a place only he could open with a specific thought—a keyword.

He felt his mood lightening as the dark thoughts were contained, and his confidence grew. But it was one thing to have power over his own mind. Would he be strong enough to prevent another from reaching into what he held hidden?

There was only one way to find out.

HE SAT IN A CLEARING NEAR THE FOREST EDGE, HIS EYES CLOSED. HE DID NOT TRY TO SEND a message this time, not yet. For now he simply allowed himself to feel at peace. He pictured himself and another tigra, sitting together in the grass. The morning came and went, yet he was in no hurry.

Suddenly, he heard a rustle and opened his eyes with a start. Near him lay a tigra male, his eyes half-closed, resting lazily in the noonday sun.

Chapter 21

> Ibru: *n.* Term describing the bonding ceremony between members of the Babylonian cult. The actual nature of this bond, or its legality in the union, has not been firmly established.
>
> *Encyclopedic History of the Union,* 22nd ed.

O NCE MORE JEENA WAS AMAZED AT THE WILLINGNESS AND DISCIPLINE OF THE PYROS army. These were for the most part farmers and tradesmen, not soldiers, and yet they rode as hard and uncomplaining as any veteran troops.

David was equally impressive. He rode throughout the ranks, helping and encouraging them in any way he could. It seemed to her he was thinner than at the outset of their journey, and yet he appeared harder and stronger, his once-pale skin now shining with a healthy glow.

On the afternoon of the tenth day of their breakneck ride, the walls of Uruk rose before them. Jeena slowed the galloping cavalry and had them ride in formation as they reached the open field before the city gates. They would enter Uruk as an army, not a mob.

The walls of the city gleamed in the rays of the setting sun. They were built of shimmering white stone and were not as high as those of New Jerusalem. In the center of the wall was a large iron gate, with two smaller entrances on either side. Flanking the main gate were two huge stone tigras, their right paws raised in benevolent welcome.

The roofs of several ornate buildings could be seen beyond the wall—churches perhaps, or temples of some kind. To the east lay a thick wood of birch-like trees, and to the west she could just make out the reflection off a large lake.

Horns sounded from the walls as they approached. The center gate was opened, and they entered to the cheers and garlands of a gathered crowd. People were lined up in the plaza, shouting and screaming encouragement as they passed. Some threw confetti from balconies of nearby buildings.

Jeena was grim as they led the army into the plaza, but David smiled and waved to the ecstatic crowd, obviously enjoying the adulation.

"I didn't expect this kind of welcome," he shouted over the noise. "It's quite remarkable, isn't it?"

"Don't let it go to your head," she shouted back. "We haven't done anything yet."

She observed that clothing in the city of Uruk came in two styles—little or none. She had heard from Mordachi of the Babylonians' penchant for nudity but was unprepared for the reality of the sea of bare flesh that pressed around her.

A clear area had been kept in the center of the plaza, where a small greeting party awaited them at the far end of a red carpet. In the forefront stood an aged woman, silver-haired and lined of face but dressed in a shimmering gown of translucent material that flowed around her like water. On her head she wore a thin band of silver, a red stone set in its center, and in her hands she carried a golden scepter in the form of a nude woman.

Jeena and David dismounted and walked along the carpet to the waiting dignitaries as the crowd continued to cheer. Behind the elderly woman were several men and a woman, in stances that made it clear they were military. They all wore a kind of kilt made of many leather straps, and sandals laced to their knees, but were naked from the waist up.

As she approached them, Jeena saw that the left nipple of both the men and the woman was pierced by a ring, from which hung a small golden sword.

The older woman stepped forward.

"I am Elaina, Regent of the city of Uruk of the Babylonian Confederacy. Welcome to our city, and thank you for heeding our call."

David stepped forward and bowed. "I am David Proverst, commander of the Pyros military. This is Captain Jeena Garza of the Union Star Corps."

"Yes, we received word of the captain and her activities. I was not aware you would be accompanying the army, Captain Garza, but we are most grateful for your presence."

"I hope I can be of some help, Regent," she said, bowing.

Although the woman before her was old, her face was uncorrupted and her smile broad and inviting. She carries the mouth-lines formed from a lifetime of smiles, Jeena thought, and for an instant she hated her.

The regent's hair was the same hue of silver as the band that encircled her head, and was long and flowing. Her body, though showing age, was still hale, without sign of disease or corruption, and she carried herself with erect dignity.

"All aid is welcome in this time of conflict." The regent turned to David. "You and your army have ridden far and are in need of rest. We have made quarters ready, and if you wish, I can have your people taken to them. If you and the captain are not too weary from your journey, though, perhaps later you would join the leaders of the Confederacy and the military high command for a small reception in your honor."

"We would be honored, Regent."

Orders were given for the bivouacking of the troops, and they were led to their quarters. Seeing they were comfortably housed and assured they would be taken to mess shortly, David thanked them all for their hard work and dedication. Promising to see them in the morning, he and Jeena followed their guide to their own quarters.

They were led to the Temple of Ishtar, the regent's official residence. Their escort explained that, besides her duties as regent, Elaina was also head priestess of the temple and leader of the cult of Ishtar. Apartments had been prepared for them in the temple.

It was situated just north of the plaza and was a large building, octagonal in shape and built of lustrous blue stone. The domed roof was gilded and shone almost red in the sun's dying rays. They were directed up white stone steps to large brass doors that swung open as they approached, revealing a marble interior.

The foyer was large and airy; in the center was a larger-than-life statue of a reclining woman, her right hand caressing her breast. This, they were told, was Ishtar, goddess of pleasure and sexual union. Before the statue were scattered flowers and small coins—offerings to the goddess for favors requested and received.

Their escort continued past the foyer to one of two stairways located on either side of the room. Along the well of the stairway were statues set in niches depicting couples and groups in various sexual acts. By the time they reached their accommodations, David was sporting a bright crimson blush.

They were given connecting rooms, the guard explaining that a *shimhatu*, or priestess of the temple, would arrive later to escort them to the reception.

Jeena opened the connecting door and found David on the balcony, looking out over the city.

"So, what do you think of Uruk now that you've seen it?" she asked.

He shook his head, grinning. "It's incredible. I had dreams of this place when I was an adolescent, I think."

"They certainly live up to their reputation so far. Let's hope their military also lives up to what you've heard."

"I wouldn't be a bit surprised," he said. "Did you see those physical specimens behind the regent? I swear that woman was as big as the men. But you seem to handle all this exposed flesh better than I do. I can't seem to decide where to look."

"I'm used to it. The Corps is not a place for modesty. Look where you want, just try not to gawk. If these people are followers of Ishtar, I doubt they'll have many rules on that type of thing. Still, when in a strange land, it's best to let the natives lead then follow appropriately."

"Well, you've certainly traveled more than I so I'll take your advice. But what do you make of this Ishtar? I know I've read about her, but I can't really recall much."

"I only know about her from legends and history books. The cult of Ishtar dates back to the first cities on Earth and probably predates the written word. She was not only the goddess of procreation but of sex itself, and the patron of prostitutes."

David laughed. "You're joking, of course."

"I'm serious. Prostitution is the world's oldest profession, and Ishtar one of its oldest goddesses. In ancient times, the cult of Ishtar used prostitution as a way to raise money for the temple."

"Really? You don't think they still...do you?"

She grinned. "I wouldn't be a bit surprised."

David whistled. "This is some goddess."

"You don't know the half of it. According to legend, Ishtar had innumerable lovers, both men and gods—a horse and a lion, too, I believe."

"Well, then it seems you two have something in common," David teased, then turned ashen. "Oh, Jeena, I didn't mean that," he stammered. "Please forgive me. It just...it just came out."

"It's all right, David." She went to the railing and looked out over the city as the sun set. "Actually, Ishtar and I don't have as much in common as you might think. The rumors you heard about Samson and I are false." She turned to face him. "But I won't defend myself on a technicality. I won't defend myself at all. It's true I cared for him—deeply—and if that offends people then let them be offended. My mistake wasn't in becoming emotionally involved with an alien, but in becoming involved at all.

"Take this advice from one soldier to another: never let anyone get close. In the end, one of you will be left alone."

"I don't think I can live that way."

"You'll learn. And don't look so stricken—you haven't hurt me or insulted me. I'd rather, though, that you didn't mention Samson to the Babylonians. I'm tired of explaining him to people."

"Of course, I won't. And I am sorry, Jeena," he repeated, with sincere regret.

"I know, but don't be. Come on, let's get ready for the reception."

DAVID WAS ON THE BALCONY, STILL KICKING HIMSELF FOR HIS INSENSITIVE REMARK, WHEN A temple priestess arrived with clothes for them both. She was young and pretty and, he noticed, virtually naked.

The clothes were one-piece tunics, which to his dismay were just as sheer as the one the regent had been wearing. He walked through the adjoining doors to Jeena's apartment, calling to her.

"In here," came the reply from another room.

He entered the bathroom just as she stepped out of the tub.

"Oops, sorry," he said, turning away.

"It's okay. Like I said, I stopped being shy in the Corps. What are those?"

"Clothes sent to us by the regent. Not much to them, though. You'd better look." He handed one blindly behind his back.

"Wow. I've heard of sheer, but this is about invisible. Still, when in Rome..." There was slight rustling. "Well, how do I look?"

He turned around. "Naked."

"I think that's the whole idea. Now, let's see how you look in yours."

He raised his hand to stop her. "I rather think not—I'm not quite as open as you. I'll just wear what I have on, thank you."

"The regent sent these specifically for us," she reminded him. "You'll be insulting her if you refuse."

"But..."

"Not only that, but everyone else there will be wearing this, or less. If you go fully clothed people may think you're only there to gawk. I certainly hope that's not true," she added, mischief in her eyes.

"Of course not!"

"Well, then, you could just hide in your room. I suppose I could make an excuse for you—inform the regent you've taken ill, or some such ridiculous reason for your absence. She doesn't appear stupid, though, and I'm sure she'll see right through it. Can't imagine that would do much for your image, or for Pyros."

"All right, all right, enough." He looked at the thin cloth in his arms. "So I'll wear the damn thing, but I swear I'm sitting down at the first opportunity."

THE RECEPTION WAS HELD IN THE GRAND BALLROOM OF THE TEMPLE, AND WAS ATTENDED by the leaders of the various city-states that made up the Confederacy as well as by their military commanders. The most striking of these was the woman who had stood in guard of the regent on their arrival in Uruk. Elaina introduced her as Selanja, Commander of the Army of Uruk and head of the joint Babylonian military force.

"Each city has its own military," the regent explained, "but for this crisis they have all agreed to combine them under Selanja's command."

"It's a pleasure, Commander," Jeena said, shaking hands. She was struck by the power of the woman's grip, as well as by the intensity in her green eyes.

"The pleasure is mine, Captain," she replied. "I was delighted to learn that an officer from the Star Corps had joined us. I am most anxious to discuss strategy with you. There is a war council scheduled for tomorrow, but I hope we may find time to speak some tonight."

"I look forward to it, Commander," Jeena replied before moving along the reception line.

With the formal introductions over, she wandered the reception hall making small talk and pleasant conversation with the various dignitaries. She eventually found David seated at one of the tables, alone and looking uncomfortable.

"Still self-conscious?" she asked, sitting next to him.

"Yes."

"You should drink more. It works for me." When he didn't smile she rolled her eyes. "You are going to have to get over this unnatural phobia about nudity."

"I do not have a phobia about nudity. And I don't see how simple modesty can be considered unnatural."

"Simple? David, the regulations society places on proper dress and conduct are some of the most complex social rules human beings have. I watched a woman in New Jerusalem beaten in public just for showing her nose, or her toe, or whatever it was. Modesty is in the eye of the beholder."

"Well...I suppose you're right, but it's not just the nudity. It's the sexual overtones that go along with it. Haven't you noticed how these people all seem to rub and touch each other at every opportunity?"

"Yes, I have, and that's an entirely different matter," she said grimly. "If you're being groped, I'll speak to the regent at once. You don't have to put up with that."

"No, not me," he said in exasperation. "Did I say it was me? I said they grope each other. No one has touched me."

Jeena smiled. "That's what I figured. Well, they don't seem to mind, so what's your problem?"

David slumped. "I don't know. Really, I don't. Maybe I've just discovered what a prude I am and I don't like it."

She downed her drink. "Don't label yourself just yet. You've been cloistered in that mountain your whole life. New ideas take time. I have a feeling you'll be a proper little nudist in no time at all. Now, if you'll excuse me, I need another drink."

Before long a gong sounded, and servants directed the crowd to the prepared dining area. Jeena and David were seated at the center table with the regent and other dignitaries.

The regent stood and raised her glass. The hall became still.

"Ladies and gentlemen, dignitaries of the Confederacy, friends, we gather here tonight in the darkest hour of our union, in a spirit of cooperation and brotherhood, to defend our land and our way of life. In that spirit, and in keeping with our mutual alliance, the city of Pyros has sent an army of her sons and daughters to aid us in this, our time of greatest need. Please join me in honoring them."

The rest of the guests stood and raised their glasses, Jeena and David bowing in return.

"And now, although the next days may be dark and dangerous, let us celebrate in this spirit and forget for a time our troubles."

She rang a small glass bell, and servants came forward with food-laden platters as music filled the hall.

DAVID SAT BETWEEN THE REGENT AND SELANJA, AND WAS UNABLE TO KEEP HIS GAZE FROM wandering to the charm dangling from the large woman's breast.

"It is the badge of the Temple of Anil," Selanja said proudly, noticing his interest. "It is given to those who have trained in the military arts and passed the prescribed tests."

"I see," he replied, embarrassed to be caught staring. "The training is thorough, I imagine."

"Yes, the tests are extremely challenging, both physically and mentally. Many try, but few receive the sword. I was one of only three in my class to do so, and the youngest at fourteen."

"That is quite young. I don't mean to pry, but is that procedure painful?" he asked, pointing to the sword.

"Somewhat," she answered, smiling. "The entire induction ceremony is highly ritualized and contains elements of both pain and pleasure, as does life itself."

He smiled awkwardly. "How…interesting." He finished his drink in a gulp and became engrossed in his meal.

JEENA SAT TO THE REGENT'S RIGHT, THE OLD WOMAN REGARDING HER ODDLY.

"Forgive me for staring, Captain, but there is something strangely familiar about you. Although I know it is not possible, I feel we have met before."

"I don't see how."

"Nor do I. Well, perhaps the answer will come to me in time."

At the end of the meal the tables were cleared, and the regent once again rang the glass bell. Now the music changed from the soothing melodic tones that had been playing to a more exotic, sensual rhythm. From each end of the hall a dancer entered, one man and one woman, naked and advancing toward each other in slow choreographed movements.

"As you know, Ishtar is the goddess of passion," the regent explained. "This is a dance in her honor. It is a representation of the sex act, from initial attraction to climax."

The dancers slowly circled each other, the tempo of the music increasing as the arc of their movements grew smaller, their nude, undulating bodies projecting a steadily increasing sensuality. Jeena was mesmerized, her gaze fixed on the couple. As the tempo of the music climbed, she felt her own pulse quicken. The rest of the room seemed to fade away, and she was aware of only the dancers.

Faster and faster they moved, limbs flowing around each other in complex rhythms, their faces masks of ecstasy. The tempo of the music climbed. Jeena's lips parted, and her breathing became shallow, her body glistening with sweat.

Suddenly, the music stopped as the dancing couple fell into each other's arms. A soft cry escaped Jeena's lips. The room came back into focus, and she saw that the regent was smiling at her.

"I'm sorry. I, uh…" She felt her face flushing.

"You needn't explain yourself, my dear," the old woman said. "The Dance of Ishtar has that effect. Its rhythms are as old as mankind and are meant to evoke the deep passion that lies in us all."

The music changed, and the guests began filling the dance floor, moving in slower but still sensual steps. Excusing herself, Jeena escaped to the balcony, the cool air refreshing her.

She sensed someone else and turned around to see Selanja watching her.

"Forgive me, Captain, I did not mean to intrude."

"No, it's all right. I just needed some air."

"I understand. The music of Ishtar can be intoxicating, especially to outsiders."

"So I've discovered."

"Do not feel embarrassed. To feel the passion of the goddess is a good omen. It bodes well for our endeavors."

"Does it? Well, in that case I'm glad. We need all the help we can get."

Selanja nodded. "I feel that way as well. My people are well trained, but we face a vastly superior enemy, and fanatics at that."

"Exactly. And from what I've seen of the terrain and what I know of Jacob, my guess is he will hurl those fanatics at us in a massive frontal attack."

Selanja moved closer, obviously excited. "I have come to the same conclusion and have looked forward to discussing the matter with you. Even with the assistance of Pyros and their guns we could be overwhelmed by sheer numbers. I do not believe Jacob will be overly concerned by heavy casualties. But do I understand rightly that you have with you a weapon that may turn the odds in our favor?"

"Possibly," Jeena said. She explained the nature of the MAAD, and her use of it against the walls of New Jerusalem. "But it was not designed as a defensive weapon, and against an onrushing horde of suicidal zealots its use may be limited."

"I will not pretend to understand your explanation of how it works, but from its effect on New Jerusalem I believe we could devise a plan utilizing it."

They both smiled.

"Selanja, would it be possible to go somewhere and discuss this further tonight without offending the regent?" Jeena asked.

"The council meeting is scheduled for tomorrow morning, but I told Elaina of my hope to steal you away. She expects it and will not be offended. Come, the war room has already been prepared."

SARGON LEANED OVER THE TABLE, SCRUTINIZING THE CONTOUR MAP UNDER HIM.

"That is quite a plan," he said. He straightened, his flowing brown hair falling back over his broad shoulders. "The Rosh-dan are in for a few surprises."

"So we hope," Jeena replied.

She and Selanja had worked on defense strategy long into the night, and had only left to freshen up after the sun had risen. They had just explained their plan to the other commanders.

Sargon smiled, his blue eyes gleaming. He was, as Jeena had noted earlier, a perfect physical specimen, as were the other commanders, Ghannon and Halamesh. All wore the Sword of Anil.

"Undoubtedly, the Rosh-dan will have a few surprises for us as well," Selanja warned. "In war nothing is certain, victory least of all. We all have extensive military training, but only Captain Garza has ever fought in a war of this scale. This is not a time for egos—the most experienced should lead. For that reason, I have asked the captain to temporarily take over general command of the defense of Uruk, and she has agreed. I sent word of my decision to the regent last night and received her approval this morning.

"Captain Garza will take command as General of the Army. Under her, I will command the Babylonian forces and David the cavalry of Pyros. Ghannon, you will lead the first rifle line."

Ghannon frowned. He carried a scar that ran from his neck to his stomach, a souvenir of his capture and torture by the Rosh-dan. He had been on a scouting mission three years before, and they had come upon him unawares. For two weeks he had endured their methods of extracting information—methods, Jeena noted darkly, little different from those she had suffered at the hands of the Coalition.

In the end he had feigned unconsciousness. As they dragged him to his cell he made his escape, killing both guards in the process. He was the toughest of all the Babylonian warriors, and his hatred of the Rosh-dan ran deep.

"I mean no offense, Captain, but I am against this. One of our own should lead."

"No offense taken," Jeena replied.

"I do not doubt your military expertise, but you are not one of us. You cannot know the depth of feeling we have for our home, or the hatred for those who would destroy us. Hard decisions will soon have to be made, sacrifices you may not be willing to make. We in this room would gladly die for Uruk. Can you say the same?"

Jeena looked at the other commanders, who stood silent, also waiting for her reply.

"It's true I'm an outsider. I know almost nothing of your city or your people," she answered slowly, "but my hatred of the Rosh-dan runs as deep as yours. I don't give a damn about glory or command. All I care about is destroying Jacob and his army. For me, this is personal. If defeating the Rosh-dan means giving up my life, then I will do so—gladly."

"The decision is made, Ghannon," Selanja said. "General Garza will command."

He nodded curtly.

David studied the map.

"I still don't like the idea of my cavalry having to come all the way from the east wall. That's a lot of ground to cover in the heat of battle. What about using this thick wooded area here on the eastern flank?"

"We discussed that, but the underbrush is too heavy. The kytars would become entangled," Jeena answered.

"Couldn't we clear out an area behind the trees, large enough to hold the cavalry? Halamesh, what do you think?"

Halamesh scratched his chin. "It could be done. We have the manpower. It would certainly bring you closer to the main battle site."

"But can you keep the kytars from bolting once I start firing the MAAD?" Jeena asked. "There will be a lot of noise and wind."

"Yes, I believe so," David replied. "We'll have the riders dismount and hold the animals down on their flanks. They should be less affected by the blasts and easier to handle that way."

"Then let it be done," Selanja said. "Are you all comfortable with the signals? Remember to listen closely to the communicators that Captain—I mean General—Garza will supply. We need to time our movements carefully, particularly when her weapon is firing."

Jeena had given them all a graphic description of what the blast from a MAAD would do to human flesh, and none of them wanted to make the mistake of being in the way when it went off.

Their plan depended on precise timing. They would face the enemy initially from behind a barricaded front a mile from the city gates. Here they would place ten thousand rifles under Ghannon's command to soften up the anticipated charge of Rosh-dan and hold them off for as long as possible.

When they could do no more, Selanja would order a slow retreat to the second line. Once Ghannon's men were safely past, Jeena and the second line of five thousand artillerymen would open up. This, Jeena hoped, would be the deciding period. If, between the rifles and the MAAD, she could inflict enough casualties it might trigger a panic. In that case, they would push forward, driving the enemy back, with David's cavalry squeezing them from the east and Sargon's main army coming up from behind.

If resistance turned out to be greater than anticipated, the second line would also retreat, while Sargon's forces surged forward into battle. At that point David's cavalry would be called out to drive a wedge into the mass of Rosh-dan, breaking them up and allowing the foot soldiers to penetrate the enemy lines. If the worst came to pass then Ghannon's riflemen, now on the city walls, would provide covering fire for Sargon and his retreating army.

When all were safely behind the walls, Halamesh would spring their surprise.

Although she had helped Jeena devise the plan, Selanja was least happy with it, for it called on her to remain on the wall and direct the battle below by way of the communicators.

She argued one more time to be allowed to lead an army division.

"I am a soldier," she said again. "I wish to fight, not observe."

"You will not be observing, you will be ordering the movement of all the troops," Jeena reiterated. "I need someone up there who can gauge the flow of battle and make critical decisions at crucial moments. If you do your job right you'll save more of your own men then you would take of the enemy—or doesn't that matter to you?"

Selanja's face reddened.

All right, so it was a rotten thing to say, but it made her see how important her job is. The truth is, I should be directing the fighting, but I don't trust anyone else to wield the MAAD. She has a brilliant head for strategy. I need her up there.

"Very well then," Selanja agreed. "It will be as you say...General. Our scouts should be returning soon with the enemy's exact location. Until then, let the commanders go and prepare their troops. We will reconvene at a later time."

The men saluted and left, leaving Jeena and Selanja to go over some small logistical matters. Selanja noticed Jeena fingering her impe and asked her about it.

"It was given to me as part of my initiation into the Intawa tribe," she replied. "Are you familiar with them?"

"In name only, from the people of Pyros. It is beautiful." She looked closely at the small metallic stones in the necklace. "These are the p'toc, the trading stones, are they not?"

"Trading stones?"

"Yes. At least, they fit the description from the Pyros traders. They came to us searching for them, but we have never found any in this area. Apparently, they trade with the Intawa for them and use them to pay the smugglers for the items they need."

Jeena looked again at the silvery stones around her neck. Of what material were they that smugglers would want them? She decided she would ask David about it when she got the chance.

TWO DAYS PASSED, AND THERE WAS STILL NO WORD FROM THE SCOUTS. SELANJA HAD invited David and Jeena to review the Babylonian troops with her, and both were impressed by their skill at arms and their general physical conditioning. Selanja explained that athleticism was highly encouraged in Babylonian society. Those children who showed interest and ability in the military were given more specific training and allowed to join the Temple of Anil on a trial basis.

As they reviewed the troops, Selanja explained the philosophy on which Babylonian life was based.

The lives of the Babylonians, they learned, revolved around the temples. These were religious houses dedicated to the veneration of a particular deity, as well as a kind of social club for people with similar interests and aptitudes. There were many temples, reflecting the pantheism of Babylonian culture; each god represented a particular facet of human life. Shamash was the God of Wisdom, and his followers included scientists and diplomats. Bacchus was the God of Wine for whom the fields before the city gates were named, and to whom the vintners looked to protect their crops. Anil represented physical strength and skill in battle, and those who earned the right to wear the sword were considered masters of the military arts.

There were many others, some with large followings and some composed only of a few individuals, yet each was given honor and respect.

Above all, however, stood Ishtar. Her temple set the tone and pace of the entire Confederacy, and she was the patron of the city of Uruk.

"Specifically, Ishtar is the personification of sex and passion, and yet in a larger sense she is representative of all human relations," Selanja explained. "The way in which we Babylonians relate to each other, as well as to the world at large, is directly influenced by the teachings of her temple. We place little emphasis on possession in our society, either in material things or in our relationships with others, something you may have already observed."

David blushed. "Yes, I've noticed. Yours is certainly a very open society. I take it you don't believe in marriage, then?"

"Most couples who choose to bond do so in the *ibru* ceremony. I'm sorry, but there is no adequate translation. Marriage, however, is not uncommon among us, though in neither case do we practice monogamy in your sense of the word."

"My sense of the word? Is there another sense?"

"We think so," she replied, smiling. "To us it is far more important to bond as soul-mates. Once one has become *ibru* to another, the bond is lifelong—more so, since it transcends death. To us sex is not the same as love. It is simply a gift, one we may share with friends—our word is *tappu*—as we wish, openly and freely."

When the review was over, they excused themselves and headed for the mess. David shook his head as they made their way. While Jeena had lived and worked in the loose moral code of the Corps, he was finding it difficult to abandon a lifetime of more rigid social rules.

The Babylonians had welcomed the Pyros army with open arms—in some cases literally—and many had responded in kind. Much of his company had enthusiastically taken up the local customs, and went about in various stages of undress, something Jeena pointed out.

"Really? I hadn't noticed," he replied. "Oh, all right, so I've noticed," he admitted, catching her look. "As long as they're correctly outfitted when the battle call comes I'm allowing them to dress—or not—as they like."

"Very forward-thinking of you."

"Don't be patronizing. I know you consider me one step beyond a Neanderthal." He glanced at the men and women of his command, who were milling around in the mess. "But they have hard days ahead of them. I won't interfere with any happiness and pleasure they can find until then. Some have even begun to make noises about wanting to stay after this is all over—assuming there is an after, of course. If the Babylonians have no objections, I'll leave the choice of returning to them."

"Not bad for a caveman. I think you're evolving."

"You think so? Well, then, what about you? Any thought to what you'll do when this is all over?"

"Not really," she said. "I still don't have a way to safely contact the Union. If and when I do I imagine I'll be placed back on active status, once they've determined I'm healthy enough to still fight. Not that anyone seriously expects to see me again."

"I can understand why, from what you've told me about the prison. By the way, I've been meaning to ask you—how did you ever manage to escape?"

"A Union commando squad raided Mizar 3. I still don't know why. We don't attack prison planets—not important enough. Maybe they thought it was a fuel depot or some other strategic target. They seemed pretty intent on destroying the whole place. Anyway, one of the explosions ripped a hole in my cell."

David grinned. "And knowing you, you were out before the rubble had even settled."

Her eyes glazed over at the memory. "No, not really. I was so weak and...lost in my mind. I just lay there in the mud looking through the hole, not even considering escape. Then something inside of me snapped. I don't know where I got the strength, but suddenly I was clawing at the wall toward the opening. Supply ships had landed just before the raid and were still on the tarmac waiting to lift off."

"I see. And so you borrowed one?" he said.

"Not right away. No, first I had to find the guard-sergeant."

He nodded. She had told him something of the sadistic guard who had been her tormentor, and it had enraged him.

"I hope you found him."

"Yes, I did."

She could still see him beneath her, the knife plunging into his chest again and again...

"Whatever he got he deserved," David said. "I can't imagine the horrors you must have lived through."

Jeena stared silently into her coffee.

"I had a child," she whispered finally.

He felt his blood go cold.

"A girl. I only got a glimpse before..." She closed her eyes.

"Oh, Jeena..."

"Stupid. I was so stupid not to take the permanent contraceptive the Union offered. I don't even know if they buried her."

He could do nothing but stare at her in pity.

After several minutes she took a deep breath and looked up, glancing around the mess.

"It looks like your people are leaving."

"What? Yes. Well, I, uh…I'm going over to the barracks to give them a little pep talk. Care to join me?"

"No, David, you go. I'll catch up with you later. Go on, I'll be fine," she added, seeing him hesitate.

THE MESS WAS EMPTY. SHE ALTERNATED BETWEEN THE COFFEE AND THE CIGAR UNTIL BOTH were gone then laid her head in her hands. Hers was more than just the strain of the last few weeks; it was a weariness beyond the body.

I'm so tired. I just want to go home.

The strangeness of the desire took her by surprise. By any definition of the word, she had never had a home, nor could she ever recall wanting one. A soldier's only home was whatever base she was presently assigned to. That was the way the Union wanted it, and it was pounded into the soldier's psyche from the first day of recruitment. A home, any home, led to thoughts of return, and that led to distractions; distractions led to mistakes; mistakes ultimately led to fatalities. Having never had a real home, distractions were something Jeena never had to worry about.

No, no distractions ever encroached on my life. No memories of family or friends haunted my dreams, softening me, making me lose my edge. Never let them get close, wasn't that my motto? Don't learn their names; don't look into their eyes; don't feel.

Suddenly, an image appeared in her mind unwanted, a golden face with large gold-speckled eyes. Jeena shut her own eyes tight, her hands balling into fists. *No! Go away. Just go away!*

The image slowly faded.

She opened her eyes and frantically wiped away tears she hadn't been aware she was shedding.

"Stay out of my head, dammit," she muttered. "You're dead. You're dead, and there's nothing I can do for you now."

SHE RETURNED TO HER APARTMENT AND WAS RESTING WHEN THE CALL CAME THAT SELANJA wanted to see them all in the war room. Halamesh was the last to enter and took his seat around the map-table.

"I will make this brief," the muscular woman began. "Two of the scouts have returned. The third has not, and we fear the worst. David, she was one of yours, was she not?"

"Yes, Sarah," he answered, and Jeena saw his eyes were red and swollen. Sarah was his first casualty as a commander. There would be many more.

"I am sorry," Selanja said, and then grew stern. "It is as we feared. The scouts report that the army of the Rosh-dan will reach the Bacchian Fields in two days. General, it seems your estimation of their numbers was wholly accurate. Half a million men are marching on Uruk."

The commanders exchanged anxious glances.

"Is there anything you would like to add?" she asked Jeena.

"Just this," she said, standing. "I have always found that the hardest part of war is the waiting. Keep active with your people. Let the troops see you. Our plans are drawn and we are well prepared. That is all."

She pulled David aside as they left.

"I'm sorry about Sarah."

"We were...we knew each other. I know her family."

"Your men will want to speak with you. You need to go to them now."

He straightened, nodding stiffly, and strode out to meet his company.

Selanja stopped her in the hallway.

"The regent left a message asking that you see her in the palace. She wishes to speak with you."

"Did she remember where we met before?" she joked.

"Do not underestimate her, Jeena. She is more than she seems. She is the head priestess and chief shimhatu of the Temple of Ishtar. That means little to you, I know, but she has power and abilities that may surprise you."

"Jacob called her a witch."

"So I have heard," she said. "Well, you will have to make up your own mind. Go to her and listen closely to what she says."

Jeena found the regent in her private apartments in the temple; she lay on a cushioned table as two shimhatu massaged her with scented oils. She smiled on seeing Jeena enter and motioned for her to sit near her.

"If my timing is inconvenient..."

"No, not at all," she replied. She sat up and dismissed the two women then led Jeena to the balcony overlooking the city. "Ours is a beautiful city, is it not?"

"Yes, it is. Very beautiful."

"And yet a city is more than buildings of stone and mortar. A city is a reflection of the people in it, a statement of their way of life and the commonality that binds them. Uruk is not its temples or its paved streets of marble, it is its people. It is their way of life that we defend against the Roshdan."

"I understand, Regent."

"Do you? I wonder if one who has never set down roots can truly understand the depth of love we feel for Uruk."

"Why do you say that?" she asked defensively.

"My dear, I mean no disrespect, but that much of your past would be obvious even to a priestess of the first rank. You carry the mark of a loner on your soul like a scar. But I will not deceive you. Most of what I know concerning you was in the communiqué from Mordachi in Pyros."

"I see. Well, as I'm leading your army, I suppose you're entitled to know a certain amount about me.'

Elaina smiled. "I'm sorry, but I find the reticence of the young quite amusing."

"I'm not so young anymore."

"I was born more than seventy standard years ago. My daughter Aramis is two decades your senior. You seem still a child to these old eyes, but then, age, as in all things, is relative. You have experiences beyond my reckoning, and in the art of war no one on Ararat is as adept, I feel. It is why I agreed to place you in charge of our defense.

"So tell me, as general of our newly combined forces, do you think we will be successful against those who would destroy us?"

Jeena hesitated. She had been in too many battles to ever feel comfortable predicting their outcome.

"It will be difficult. We are vastly outnumbered, and they have had a long time to prepare, but with a little luck I think we can make Jacob regret his decision to attack Uruk."

"Good, for I am a firm believer in luck, General Garza—or perhaps *fate* is a better word. You see, I believe it was fate that brought you to us." She sat on a bench and motioned for Jeena to sit next to her.

"Fate?"

"Yes, for I recall now why you seem so familiar. I have seen you before, many times. I have seen your face in my visions."

Jeena smiled.

"You do not believe in visions? But of course not, you are a Union soldier, a pilot, a woman of science. You have no time for such nonsense."

"Something like that."

The regent laughed. "You are blunt, that is good. Time is too short for banter, and your arrival here, at this time, begs many questions."

Jeena shrugged. "Ask me anything."

"In truth, I know quite a bit about you already. I know you were raised in an orphanage, and that you joined the Union Star Corp at a young age. I know something of your military career, and of your escape from the Coalition prison world."

"Then you've pretty much got my whole life right there."

"No. What I have is a scaffolding, a structure that frames a life. I have placed the very survival of Uruk, and perhaps of the entire Confederacy, in your hands. Before I can feel comfortable with that decision, I need to know what that scaffolding holds."

"I suppose I can understand that, but what more can I tell you?"

"The information I am looking for I do not believe you could supply," she replied cryptically. "However, there is a method that would tell me much, if you will allow it."

"What method?"

"Do not be alarmed. It is a skill developed long ago and passed from mother to daughter through the long ages. All events in our lives leave patterns, emotional imprints on our subconscious. For those who have the ability, these can be read almost as a series of vignettes, and their emotional importance understood."

"Jacob warned me you could read minds." *But I'd hoped he was crazy and you weren't. I still hope that's the case.*

"Did he? I would call that too grandiose a claim. Let us say, rather, that I would be viewing brief glimpses of the important events of your life."

She's serious. She really thinks she can read my mind. How do I answer that? I suppose it wouldn't hurt to humor her—after all, she is the head of government here. Still, I don't really have time for this silliness.

"Think of it as humoring an old woman, if that makes it more palatable. I promise not to keep you long," the regent added, as though already reading her thoughts.

Jeena sighed. "Very well. What is it you need me to do?"

The old woman placed a bony hand on the back of her head, at the base of her skull.

"Only relax. Close your eyes and allow your thoughts to wander freely."

Jeena complied, anxious for the whole thing to be over. Why were these people so worried about religious omens when there was a war to be fought?

Presently, she became aware of a slight tingling at the point of contact between her and the regent. It was not an unpleasant feeling, and she felt herself relax more fully in the old woman's grip.

ELAINA CLOSED HER EYES AND CONCENTRATED INTENTLY. THE TECHNIQUE WAS unpredictable, and no two people responded exactly the same. It was best to simply open oneself completely, although that often held its own dangers.

Soon, she felt Jeena slump in her arms. A moment later, she became aware of dim images, shadows that seemed to flitter across her internal vision.

But they did not come easily. It was as though, even in her unconscious state, Jeena's mind was fighting the intrusion. Elaina pressed further. The first fuzzy images flitted into view.

A vague birth memory, distorted and fleeting. No answers there. Wait. Here was something—no sign of a mother-bond. How unusual. Was she abandoned? Did the mother die during the birth? Frustratingly, the images vanished, and new ones appeared. Her first, early years. No, far too fragmented to be useful. Shame—they often yield so much information.

Now she was in the Union Home. There were children—many children—coming and going, and Elaina could sense their separation from Jeena. A horse she saw. Yes, Noah. Noah was his name.

She caught glimpses of men and women—lovers, and yet she knew Jeena felt no love for them. There was her first taste of battle, and Elaina relived the terrible beauty of an enemy destroyer exploding in a phased plasma field.

She pressed her fingers more firmly against Jeena's spine. There was an explosion, and suddenly she was floating in a great ocean. A ship. Horror and death. Then she was on a planet, cold and dim. Distorted faces laughed and mocked her. Pain. Humiliation. Rapes and beatings that seemed to go on forever. There was the cry of a newborn infant, and Elaina knew the terrible truth.

The old woman sighed. So much pain. So much suffering in a single lifetime. *The desire for the sleep of death is strong in this one. It is a wonder she is still sane.*

She girded herself and pressed on.

She was in another ship now. Fire and flames. Fear as she plunged into an alien atmosphere. Then a new sun rose, and she looked upon it. Ararat, yes. The images began to fade. A last figure, unclear and flickering, suddenly appeared, wavered for an instant and was gone.

Her heart leapt. It was not the image of a man she saw, but of an animal—

and the animal had a name.

Samson.

Excited by her discovery, the old woman had begun to withdraw and end the session of the Nihn-Psi when she became aware of a locked chamber in Jeena's mind. It was as though the girl had barricaded some part of herself from the rest of her subconscious, in a place so deep Elaina doubted even Jeena herself could access its contents. It was a mental defense—a wall—of a kind the regent had never encountered in all the minds she had touched, and she could not resist the temptation to glimpse what lay behind.

She bent her will on the barrier, using all her strength against it until slowly the wall began to crumble. Sweat poured from her as Jeena's unconscious mind fought the intrusion. Finally, a tiny crack appeared. Elaina gazed into the opening...

...and screamed.

Chapter 22

The goal of the Shimhatu training is nothing less than the absolute control of the mind. To control the mind is to control the body. The body will do what such a mind commands, even to its own destruction.

Introduction
Shinhatu Training Manual

J<small>EENA AWOKE AND BLINKED</small>. "I'<small>M SORRY, DID</small> I <small>FALL ASLEEP</small>?"

Elaina nodded. "It often happens during the Nihn-Psi."

"I feel woozy."

"It will pass."

She bowed her head and took several cleansing breaths.

"That's better. So, did you find out what you wanted?" she asked with a smirk.

"I am not sure."

"Regent…"

"Thank you, General. I know you find this all very foolish, and it was good of you to take the time. You have many duties pressing upon you, and I will not keep you further."

Jeena stood. "Very well. I'm sorry if I sound like I'm belittling your religious beliefs. I mean no disrespect." She nodded politely and left.

A <small>SHIMHATU CAME TO</small> E<small>LAINA AFTER</small> J<small>EENA HAD GONE AND FOUND HER DEEP IN THOUGHT</small>.

"Are you all right, Mother?" Aramis asked.

The old woman nodded.

"Did you perform the Nihn-Psi?"

"Yes." Elaina rose and went to the railing, looking out over the city. "For so long have I awaited her arrival, her face haunting my visions. Yet as the years passed, and she did not come, I began to doubt she would appear in my lifetime, and I almost did not recognize her when first we met. But I doubt no more." She turned grimly to her daughter. "She is the one, Aramis. Jeena Garza is the Deliverer."

Aramis trembled, sinking unsteadily onto a bench near her mother.

"And there is more. She has awoken the Beast. I have seen him in her thoughts."

The younger woman grasped her hand. "Are they one?"

"I do not know. She has buried all thought of him deep within herself. I caught a glimpse, no more. Her heart is a mystery to me, as is the reason he is not here with her now."

"Then we remain ignorant still, and stumble blindly to our fate. Mother, why must this time come now, with the Rosh-dan beating at the gates?"

"Why? Who can say. The birth of an age comes when it will, and cares not if it is inconvenient. It is not for us to question its timing but only to assist in its delivery. For my part, I would not have it so, but if this new age of Ishtar be suckled on the ashes of war then so be it. Gird yourself. We knew this day would come."

"Yes, and I have feared it all my adult life. You yourself have spoken of the darkness which surrounds her, and of the evil which will be unleashed, if she and the Beast are not one."

She laid a gentle hand on the younger woman's shoulder. "It is true, there is darkness in her, which even the Nihn-Psi could not pierce. But there is also power, power enough to change the course of the universe, I think.

"You ask why. It is clear she is to play some part in this war, for good or ill, something not shown to me in my visions. We must let events play themselves out, and stay to the path we have set ourselves. If we can control her, guide her, then all our plans will come to fruition, and the glory of the goddess will spread throughout the galaxy."

"Yes, Mother." Aramis's gaze was stern. "And if we cannot, what then? You know the answer, for you have seen it—an eternity of slavery for mankind. You risk too much. I beg you, destroy her now. We will fight the Rosh-dan without her and take our chances. If we fail, then we fall, but it will be Ararat alone that we doom, not the whole of mankind."

Elaina snapped her hand away. "Foolish woman! There is no turning back.

Do you not understand? The old age is dying; the new age is upon us. It will come whether we wish it or no. The dragon of change is here, now, and our only hope of survival is to ride its wings. Destroy her! You know not what you ask. I alone have seen the power we both fear. I barely grazed its surface, yet it almost consumed me." She raised her right hand. Where her fingertips had touched Jeena, black blisters had formed. "It was like touching the sun."

SAMSON STOOD ON THE HILL AND GAZED OUT OVER THE MOONLIT VALLEY BELOW, THE snowy fields a sea of pale gold. He had called to them, not with words but with mental images laden with emotional meaning. From all corners of the wastes he had called them, and they had come. They stood now before him—all that remained of his race—an army of forty thousand tigras.

The process of learning to communicate through the mind link had proved daunting; but he would not give up, and over the last few weeks had gained in his ability until now he could direct his thoughts into it with ease. Being sentient, his mind was stronger than those of the others, and like a beacon of light in their dim world; they were drawn to him, drawn to the power of his thoughts. Although the nature of the light was beyond their understanding, they felt the need to be near it, and to follow it.

Once he had gained confidence in his abilities, Samson gently probed the reaches of those minds. On the surface, there were only the base hungers of beasts; but deep within, on a level just below conscious thought, he found that they were aware of their world slipping away, of their long age coming to an end.

It terrified them.

So, he tried to instill a concept in their minds they had long ago forgotten. He tried to give them hope.

He had called them together, and now it was time. He closed his eyes and projected a new image into their minds, then quickly turned south. They followed, moving fast, picking up speed until they were racing with the wind across the snowy land.

Perhaps we are damned, as Jacob said, but we will not fade quietly from our world. We will not pass gently into night.

For this one brief moment, at least, they were no longer a lost and dying race. By the strength of his will they were made a people once again, if only for a short time.

There was another concept Samson had formed, but which he kept locked away for now—he would release it into the link when the time was right. For he would not leave the fate of his race to others entirely. If they were destined for extinction, then at least they would end their days fighting for themselves, and not as sheep for slaughter. The concept was one the ancient race had once known well, and for which humans had a word.

The word was *war*.

JEENA STEPPED OUT OF THE TEMPLE INTO THE BRIGHT SUN OF EARLY MORNING. THE CITY around her was clean and gleaming. Across from the temple gardens, the open-air market was just beginning to stir. The smells of flowers and fresh foods floated through the plaza.

Ghannon walked toward her carrying a round yellow object in his hand.

"Selanja asked that I escort you to the Temple of Anil," he said. "She is coordinating the evacuation of the city."

"Thank you, Ghannon."

He handed her the object in his hand. "In case you are hungry. It is a kaba fruit."

She sniffed; it had a slight peachlike aroma. Biting into it she was rewarded with a mouthful of juicy pulp, somewhat like a strawberry in flavor. She ate it hungrily as they walked.

"Mmmm, it's wonderful," she said, wiping her hands on the handkerchief Ghannon provided. "Thank you."

"It is nothing. They grow in my garden," he replied flatly.

"If the kaba is any indication, then you'd have made a good gardener."

He frowned. "I am a soldier. I wish to be nothing else."

"You still disapprove of Selanja's decision to place me in command?"

"As I said, Captain, I am a soldier. I obey my orders."

"I see," Jeena replied, and noted that he alone among the commanders did not address her as "general."

They headed south along the main avenue in silence. People were packing up their belongings and locking their homes. There was no sense of panic Jeena could see, and everyone seemed to be working together to make the move as easy as possible for all involved.

"Your people seem calm, considering the uncertainty they're facing," she observed.

"That is because they know that everything that can be done is being done, and that panic will not help. You will find we are a stoic society."

"So I've noticed. There is also a great sense of community here. I'm surprised they feel the need to lock their doors."

For the first time, she saw a slight smile appear on the soldier's lips.

"We are not a city of saints. We well understand the weakness of our fellow man. Why tempt people unnecessarily? Given a strong enough enticement, even the most noble can be lured into doing something he might later regret. Though, in truth, there is very little theft in Uruk. We have little true wealth here to steal, for one reason. If it is one's goal to amass a fortune, this would be a poor city to choose."

Jeena looked around at the marble buildings and immaculate lawns on either side of the street.

"It seems wealthy enough to me."

"Most of what you see is the result of public works. Little is privately owned."

"And these are paid from city taxes?"

Ghannon looked horrified.

"Great God Anil, no. We would be taxed to death if that were so. No, most work is accomplished through the temples. Some will collect money outright through donations, while others call upon the skill and talents of their congregations. It is a better method than taxing, I think, for here the people give freely, as opposed to it being taken from them."

"It's a wonderful system," Jeena agreed.

"It is simply our way, but it does limit one. Most of our people belong to more than one temple, and that requires devoting much time to community service, time unavailable for the accumulation of wealth. But then, people choose to live in Uruk because of the quality of life, not material possessions."

"And what about those people who refuse to contribute, or are destructive or break the laws? Are all your citizens so altruistic?"

Ghannon shrugged. "There are disagreeable people here as elsewhere, of course. But they are few in number. We have discovered that most antisocial problems arise in childhood, and we devote much time and love in the raising of our children. We try to identify such patterns early, so that we have a better chance of correcting them.

"We have a flexible legal system and will work with lawbreakers as much as possible to come to a mutually agreeable resolution. If one continues to be a burden to the community, then, yes, there are punishments, including imprisonment and banishment, but these are seldom used.

"In point of fact, Uruk has few laws. We expect people to act like adults and take responsibility for their actions. At the very least, we ask that they not bother the rest of the citizens unduly. Other than that, how you wish to live your life is entirely up to you."

"You and your people have an enlightened philosophy, Ghannon."

"I think so. It is based on a strong sense of community and civic duty, tempered by our acceptance and love of individuality. I would not live any other way."

Jeena looked at the powerfully built man, the scars on his body clearly visible. He had withstood weeks of torture at the hands of his enemies and was now willing to die in battle, all for the city he loved. Touloc had done the same. These people had something special here, and they knew it.

Presently, they came to the Temple of Anil, the God of War. It was a rectangular building ringed by beautifully carved columns. The lawn was dotted with trees bursting with small white blossoms. Ghannon led her up a short flight of steps to a pair of wooden doors. They met Selanja in the foyer.

"Good morning, Ghannon, and thank you for escorting General Garza," Selanja said, then gave the man a long, passionate kiss. The greeting surprised Jeena, though not as much as when the muscular woman turned and greeted her in the same way.

Selanja broke the embrace and saw Jeena's stunned look.

"Forgive me, General, I did not mean to take liberties or to offend you. It is just our customary greeting at the temple."

"I'm not offended, I'm just a little surprised. It's not the greeting I would have expected in the temple dedicated to the God of War."

"It is a way to remind ourselves of what it is we fight for," Ghannon explained. "Also, we inflict quite a few bumps and bruises on each other in our training here. It helps balance out the pain."

Jeena smiled ruefully. Mordachi had been right—theirs was a vastly more open society than any she had seen, and yet they carried themselves with an openness and natural ease that made her feel comfortable.

"Well," she said, still feeling the kiss on her lips. "If the greetings are over, let's go see how the evacuations are going."

JEENA STOOD AT THE SOUTHERN GATES, WATCHING THE EXODUS FROM THE CITY. IT WAS AN orderly stream of humans and kytars, carts and wagons, as the civilian population headed for the relative safety of the southern cities. The evacuation would continue throughout the day.

"The last will be gone before nightfall," Selanja said. "They all have food and housing waiting for them in the other cities."

"Uruk will be quiet tonight," Ghannon said. "I do not think I will sleep well until her people are returned." He sighed. "I am going to pay a visit to the Temple of Ishtar. May I escort you back, Captain?"

Selanja made as if to correct him, but Jeena forestalled her.

"Yes, Ghannon, thank you. Selanja, will we see you later?"

"I have duties in the temple to attend, but I understand there is to be some kind of contest between the troops later and I was intending to watch. I will see you there."

Ghannon escorted Jeena back to the Temple of Ishtar.

"Are you coming inside?" she asked.

"Yes, I have an appointment with several of the shimhatu. Others may feel differently, but I find a night of their arts before battle actually increases my concentration."

Jeena grinned. He spoke without embarrassment or bravado. It was a simple pronouncement, both normal and healthy in his eyes.

"Well, you enjoy yourself, Ghannon."

"I shall."

Jeena continued on to her apartment and through the adjoining doors to David's room. He was wearing shorts and boots and was in the middle of stretching exercises.

"What are you doing?" she asked.

"I've set up an intra-company z-ball game. I'm taking your advice and trying to keep them loose until battle." He spoke in a light tone, but his eyes revealed the sorrow of losing Sarah.

"That's a good idea. You can cut the tension around here with a knife. So tell me, where does an ex-Afridi from a zed planet even learn about z-ball, let alone get one?"

"Smugglers. They're more than just a source of illicit trading, they keep us abreast of the latest Union fads."

"I see. That reminds me," she said, tapping her necklace, "what do you know about these stones?"

He looked closely at her impe.

"Intawa trading stones. Looks like a good set. The smugglers would pay dearly for them."

"Why? What are they?"

"They call it carborillium. Apparently, it's pretty valuable."

Jeena looked again at the stones around her neck. *Valuable? Rigel's rings, yeah, I'd say they're valuable! Carborillium is only the most precious commodity in the galaxy.*

As far as she knew it didn't even occur naturally but had to be created under immense heat and pressure in a lab. A layer only a few atoms thick lined the singularity cells that powered the newest Hawking Drives—it was the only substance able to withstand the tremendous forces involved, and a few grams cost a small fortune to produce.

I've been walking around with the price of a star cruiser around my neck!

David started on knee bends. "So, how did your meeting with the regent go?"

"What? Oh, that. I'm not sure. You know, she tried to read my mind."

"Really? I certainly hope you weren't entertaining any impure thoughts."

"I'm serious. For all their practicality, these are a very superstitious people. Elaina believes she has seen me in her visions."

"Really? Hmmm...so maybe she's the one with the impure thoughts."

"All right, that's it, get out of here. Go play your game. And I hope you get your bell rung!"

"Ishtar forbid," he said, and quickly dodged the shoe that came flying.

JEENA WENT IN SEARCH OF SELANJA AND FOUND HER SOMETIME LATER BEHIND THE barracks, excitedly watching the z-ball game from the sidelines. David had initially included only the Pyros company in the game, but the Babylonian soldiers had been so intrigued he began sending in many as substitutes when he saw they were catching on to the rules.

The field was plotted out in illuminated chalk and divided into a grid of sixty-four squares ten meters on a side. The teams consisted of twelve players each, positioned in various formations as set out by the team leader, or centerback. Each player's ability to move was dictated by his initial grid position, much as in the game of chess, a major difference being that, in z-ball, all players moved at once.

The ball was a zero-gravity device that operated on the same principle as the levitation jack, and was tuned to hover exactly seven feet above the ground. It could be thrown or kicked higher, or carried lower, but if left unmolested would always return to its idling height.

Play was initiated by the centerback and continued until the player holding the ball was "swamped'—wherein he became buried under a pile of opposing players—or a score was made. The latter was accomplished by throwing or kicking the ball through a circular loop known simply as the "hole." These were usually suspended in anti-g fields, but as none were available, David had them mounted on poles.

The plays could be simple or incredibly complex, depending upon the skill of the players. Coming in contact with the ball, either intentionally or accidentally, made that player suddenly "eligible," meaning any opposing player able to move into that position had carte blanche to pummel, gouge, kick, hit or otherwise inflict physical harm in an effort to obtain control of the ball. Advancing the ball along the ground required the player to constantly re-evaluate his own position in relation to the opposing players, in order to chart a path of least resistance. This required singular concentration and an iron will. For beginner players, then, the safest plays were passes, and Jeena noted that both sides in this game were relying heavily on that strategy.

"Enjoying the game?" she asked Selanja.

"Yes, it is very exciting. I think I have the basics down. I've asked David to put me in as a substitute on his side. They need the help."

She was right. Although the score was tied, David was losing players to some very determined and aggressive play by the other team—a team led by none other than Bernd Jimes, the same young man Jeena had sparred with in Pyros.

She watched the game for a few minutes then whispered in Selanja's ear.

"Yes, I understand. But will that work?" the blonde woman asked excitedly.

"Only one way to find out."

At the next break in play, Jeena met David as he limped in off the sidelines.

"Looks like you could use a hand out there," she said.

"You could say that," he replied, pouring water over his dirt-encrusted head. "You offering to help?"

"Just put us in for one play."

"Us? You and who else?"

"Selanja. I've been going over a play with her."

David looked skeptical. "I'll take you—you've played before. But I really don't need another rookie. Don't get me wrong. The Babylonians are tremendous athletes, they just don't have the experience."

"C'mon, just for one play. You need a couple of substitutes right now, and Selanja is very strong."

"Strong? The woman's a draft animal. Ouch! Okay, okay, you're both in on the next play. So, what's your plan?"

"Put me in at center attack, epsilon-beta position, and send Selanja in as a powerback. Position her in the gamma-deuce grid. Then just heave the ball to me."

"You're going to run from a beta grid?" he asked incredulously. "Have you looked at the size of your opponents, woman? You get swamped by those forwards, and we'll be looking for another general."

"Trust me, coach, I promise not to get hurt."

"Hmm...well, I suppose I'll have to take a shot. I'll set the offensive line in a Kasparov-six pattern. That should at least give you a running chance."

The bell sounded, and the teams retook the field, Jeena leading Selanja to her starting position grid.

"You know what to do?"

Selanja looked up-field, counting off the grids. "Yes."

"And you're sure you can make it?"

"Positive. On Ararat, it is not so far."

"Okay. Remember, timing is everything."

David called out an offensive formation he felt would give Jeena the best chance at an open run—at least for the first few grids. After that she would be on her own. Standing in the rear position, he prepared to jump at the ball hovering just over his head. He glanced at Jeena, who nodded.

Leaping up, he grabbed the ball and hurled it to her before his feet hit the ground. She caught it expertly and immediately took off on a diagonal run, heading to the left sidelines. As he had anticipated, she had little opposition for the first few grids and was just past the half-field mark when she saw Bernd and several other enormous defensemen converging on her.

Bernd was grinning evilly as he bore down full speed on the gamma-five grid, the only position still left open to her. She reached the spot first and threw herself to the ground, releasing the ball at the same moment. The defending players, suddenly seeing the ball float free, tried desperately to halt their forward momentum and grab it. They never had a chance.

As soon as Jeena began her run, Selanja had taken off straight down the field. She was a half-step behind her as Jeena reached the G-5 grid. As Jeena fell, Selanja leapt up and over the grid, catching the ball in mid-air and continuing onto the grid beyond, a grid that was presently occupied by a very surprised Bernd Jimes.

Selanja came down feet first, slamming into Bernd's chest and knocking him to the ground. Following Jeena's instructions, she raced down the now-empty backfield toward the goal. The sidelines exploded in cheers as she jumped up and tossed the ball in the hole.

The Babylonians went wild. Jeena ran downfield and embraced Selanja. The two were still clinging to each other as Bernd strode toward them, a referee in tow.

"That point doesn't count, General," he said.

"Oh? And why is that?" Jeena asked, grinning.

"Its a basic rule—two offensive players can't occupy the same grid. You two were both in G-5."

"Actually, you're wrong about that. Selanja was never in G-5, she leapt over it."

Bernd looked to the referee, who was scratching his head.

"Well, that's true. As far as I know there's no rule against leaping over an entire grid. Not sure why not."

"It's because z-ball is always played in Earth-normal gravity, not in the weaker gravity of good ol' Ararat," Jeena said.

"Sorry, Bernd," the ref said. "The general is right. The point stands. Game over."

Bernd stood crestfallen as the cheering crowd herded the teams into the barracks for an impromptu party. Jeena hooked her arm around his waist.

"Oh, c'mon, Bernd, cheer up. I'll buy you a drink to make it up to you."

"It'll take more than a drink, General," he replied, sulking.

"Then I will make it up to you, Bernd," Selanja said, eying the big man amorously.

JEENA SAT ASTRIDE THE KYTAR HITCHING POST OUTSIDE THE BARRACKS, SMOKING ONE OF her last cigars and nursing a bottle of Babylonian whiskey. It was late, and the party had broken up some hours earlier, leaving behind only a few diehard revelers whose occasional outbursts of drunken laughter wafted through the warm night to disrupt the chorus of insects serenading her. Selanja had left around that time as well with an obviously intoxicated Bernd, and Jeena had not seen either of them since.

She saw her now, though, walking toward her, naked but for a kilt, a slight smile on her lips.

"How's Bernd?" she asked, passing the bottle.

"Sleeping like a baby," Selanja answered, hopping up on the post and taking a drink.

"You didn't hurt him, did you?"

"No more than he wanted me to."

Jeena smiled and shook her head.

"You know, you could have joined us. Bernd certainly wouldn't have minded, and you don't strike me as the prudish type."

"Don't underestimate my prudery," Jeena said. "I thought we had a pretty tolerant sexual code in the Corps, but compared to you Babylonians I'm practically prudish."

Selanja laughed. "We are not so different. Most people accept that sex is a natural part of life. We believe that as well, and have simply removed the artificial restrictions set in place by other societies."

"So I've seen. Don't you people ever get jealous?"

"Jealousy is not unknown, but in truth, we are not a very possessive people. We understand that sexual attraction for others doesn't die just because you are in love. To pretend that it does just sets you up for disappointment and disillusionment."

"Sure, it sounds good in the abstract," said Jeena, taking another drink from the bottle, "but I doubt most people could handle it. You could leave yourself open to a lot of hurt that way."

"That is true. It takes a tremendous amount of trust and maturity. I mean no offense, but it seems to me that most of mankind has never gotten past the giggly adolescent stage of sexual development. If it's going to be a dirty little secret, snickered at behind closed doors, then there is no way it can advance to our kind of openness."

"That's just sex. What about love? Can love survive that kind of openness?"

"It can and it does."

"I have my doubts. Your system sounds logical, but I've seen love bring logic to its knees. Haven't you ever been in love?"

"Yes, I am in love with a wonderful man. He is my ibru. He is someone who loves and trusts me completely, and I feel the same towards him. It is an absolute and inviolable trust that gives us the confidence and freedom to be who we are. It brings me a joy I cannot imagine living without."

"An ibru is a soul-mate, something like a husband, isn't it? So you have an ibru, but you were just with Bernd. How does that work?"

"But, Jeena, that was just fun, like the game we played. I have no deep feelings for Bernd. My attraction was simply sexual. I made that clear to him in the beginning, and he accepted it. My ibru is certainly not going to worry about such a small matter. It takes nothing from him."

"You're going to tell him?"

"Naturally. There is no need for secrecy. It is a normal part of life for us." She looked quizzically at her. "And you? Have you ever been in love?"

She stared at the bottle in her hand. "No."

"That surprises me. Your eyes carry the pain of one who has suffered a loss of the heart—that much has been clear to all since you arrived. Forgive me.

Perhaps that is something too near yet to speak of."

Jeena tipped the bottle back and took a long drink before answering.

"You're wrong, Selanja. I don't know anything about love. I wouldn't know it if it hit me in the mouth. All I know is war."

They drank in silence, passing the bottle back and forth before Selanja hopped off the post, pulling Jeena down with her. She held her hand out.

Jeena grasped it. "Are we going somewhere?"

"Yes, to my home. If you would like."

Jeena hesitated only a moment before putting her arm around the other woman's waist and allowing herself to be led back toward the city.

"So, tell me Selanja, who is your ibru?" she asked.

"You have met him. He is Sargon."

"Hmm. I admire your taste."

"I am glad, for tonight I share him with you."

Chapter 23

Chaos theory clearly demonstrates that even infinitely small inputs into a system may, over time, create enormous results. A single pebble may start an avalanche; the beating of a butterfly's wings may signal the birth of a tornado.

The Butterfly Effect

MORDACHI PUFFED AND WHEEZED AS HE TRIED TO KEEP PACE WITH THE SPEEDY FEET OF the youth.

"Good heavens, young man, slow down. What is so important I have to rush to the gates like a startled wolla?"

"Hurry, Mordachi!" the young man called over his shoulder. "The Gate Master said you must come with all speed!"

Grumbling, the prime minister followed the page through the atrium and into the tunnel leading to the southern gate. He arrived gasping and shaking his head at the soldier on guard.

"This had better be important," he warned.

The soldier did not answer, just pointed a trembling finger to the open gate.

Mordachi's frown changed into a startled gasp as he beheld the figure sitting at the entrance to the city.

"Samson!"

"Hello, Mordachi."

"But...But we thought you were dead." He quickly told of finding the mangled body of the tigra by the northern road.

"No, it wasn't me, although it easily could have been. I'll have to tell you the story later, though, I'm pressed for time as it is. May I enter? I need to talk with Jeena."

"She isn't here," the old man replied sadly. "News of your death affected her gravely. She lost all hope, I think. She went with David and the army to Uruk weeks ago."

"I see. Then I must hurry. I'm going to Uruk myself, but I wanted to see her first. Goodbye, Mordachi, and thank you for all your help."

"Wait! Why are you going to Uruk?" he asked, following Samson through the gate.

As he stepped out into the midday sun, he shrieked. Behind Samson in the fields before the city, stood row after row of tigras, thousands upon thousands, and behind them thousands more, an expanse of gold that extended all the way to the hills beyond.

"Yes, Mordachi," Samson said, "the ancient race has awoken. To what end we will come I do not know, but we will sleep no more."

Turning, he sped the army of tigras off to the south, leaving Mordachi to stare in open-mouthed wonder.

IT WAS LATE THE NEXT MORNING WHEN JEENA FINALLY MADE IT BACK TO THE PALACE. SHE found David in his room, moving slowly and trying to work out the knocks he had taken in the game.

"So, there you are," he said. "I wondered where you had gotten off to so early, or did you even make it home from the party? You were hitting the bottle pretty hard." He stopped and gaped at her. "Good heavens, what's happened to you?"

"What?" she asked, startled.

"Your face."

She put her hand to her face. "What's the matter? What's wrong with my face?"

"You're smiling."

"Very funny."

"I'm serious. I haven't seen you smile like that in a long time. It's good to see. Can I ask what caused it?"

"I'm not sure, really—this place, these people. I think maybe I'm starting to heal." Her smile faded. "I loved him, David."

"Yes, I know," he replied, and he did not have to ask of whom they spoke.

"Did you? I didn't, or at least I wouldn't admit it. I told myself it was just compassion and friendship I felt, but the truth is I was ashamed. I was ashamed for loving him, for wanting him. Like everyone else, I was too damn shallow to see past the fur."

"Don't be so hard on yourself. Interspecies love is a taboo as old as mankind. You've had to fight emotions everything in your experience told you were wrong. At least you're finally working through your grief."

"I still have a long way to go, but if there is any place I can become whole again, then I think Uruk is it. I've decided that if we win this war I won't be going back to the Corps. I'm staying here."

A young shimhatu knocked and entered.

"I am sorry to disturb you, but Commander Selanja has asked that you both meet her immediately on the parapets above the city gates."

They found Selanja with Sargon and Halamesh looking out over the Bacchian Fields. Selanja handed Jeena the binoculars.

"Look to the horizon."

In the distance, she could see an enormous cloud of dust and smoke moving toward them.

"They're close. They should reach the fields by nightfall." She passed the binoculars to David.

"I have sent Ghannon to inform the regent and order the military on full alert," Selanja said. "All not on duty are to remain in their barracks."

"Are the preparations ready?"

"Yes. I have seen to the clearing and to the work at the lake," Halamesh answered. "The barricades are in place. All is prepared."

"Good. I want to be able to move at a moment's notice. Sargon, I want your rifle division ready to depart immediately. David, get your cavalry together but don't mount up just yet. Prepare to move to the clearing on my orders. Selanja, see to your commanders. Make sure that the main army is properly outfitted and armed."

They departed to their tasks, all but Sargon.

"You left early this morning, *licente*. Selanja and I worried that perhaps you had regretted your decision to join us."

"No, not at all," she said, smiling. "I just felt too good to sleep. I wanted to walk in the morning air and enjoy the day. I regret nothing about last night."

"Then I am glad. I will see to my duties."

"Wait. Licente—you called me that last night. What does it mean?"

Sargon grinned. "It means 'tigress' in the old language. It seemed…fitting somehow."

Jeena felt herself blushing. "I see. Well, we both have work to do."

"Yes, General," he replied, saluting.

Jeena stood alone on the parapet, gazing through the binoculars. *So, I've finally found a place to call home, and yet I still can't escape war. Am I still soldier enough to fight? And even if I am, and manage to survive this, then what will I do?*

She watched as the slowly approaching horde drew ever nearer the city. It was no use worrying about tomorrow now. Whatever future she had, it lay beyond that.

She went to the armory and donned the protective body armor of the Pyros military, the sign of the mountain prominently displayed on the chest guard. She looked closely at the black helmet but instead chose the highly stylized headdress of the Babylonian high command, with its flared nosepiece and long cheekguards. If it was slightly less utilitarian than the other, so be it—she was general of both armies and wanted her troops to recognize that fact.

Clasping a sword to her side, she picked up the MAAD and rode out to the barricades.

She found Sargon and Ghannon together, inspecting the rows of crossed pikes that ran the length of the Bacchian Fields.

"Is everything ready?" she asked, dismounting.

"Yes," Ghannon replied. "I am leaving now to position the ammo runners and messengers. If you will excuse me."

Jeena walked with Sargon along the barricade, speaking encouragement to the men as they went. The cloud of dust loomed dark and foreboding in the distance.

"Do you know, General, that I have never seen an Afridi? All I know of them I have gleaned from stories and from Ghannon, and his opinion is understandably biased. You have been among them. What sort of men are they?" Sargon asked.

"Determined," she said. "Convinced of the righteousness of their cause and certain that the way to their god lies through your destruction."

"Why does their god wish to destroy us? He would be welcome here, and treated with all the honor of the other gods."

"I'm sure he would, but the Rosh-dan will never allow it. To them, the belief in other gods is a great evil, one that must be abolished." She stopped and gazed through the pikes. "They don't just want Uruk, Sargon, or even the Confederacy, they want the entire planet, all of Ararat under their rule and under that of their God—and that's just for starters."

"I do not understand this. To kill in the name of a god is a great evil," he replied, "and to wish to enslave an entire world is madness. It is a city of madmen we fight."

"No, not all are mad or evil. I believe most are kind and decent. One, especially, took great risk to help me, and I still worry about what happened to him. Those people just want to live in peace, but that will never happen as long as the Rosh-dan rule."

Sargon looked back across the field. "I would not have my city ruled by such people, *tappu*."

"Neither would I."

A messenger came up to them, shouting and pointing west. "General, the enemy has halted. A rider is approaching."

Through the binoculars, Jeena saw that the juggernaut had stopped; the large cloud of dust was settling about a mile from the barricade. She could see men and kytars spread across the width of the plain and stretching all the way back to the low hills, where a city of tents and machinery was being erected. Between the barricades and the Rosh-dan, a single rider approached, a white flag in his hand.

"Looks like they want to parley," she said. "Will you join me for a ride, Sargon?"

They met the emissary of the Rosh-dan in the center of the field. Jeena recognized him at once—it was Serug. Her own face was hidden under the elaborate faceplate of the Babylonian helmet.

"The Holy Cities of the Afridi and the Elder Council of the Rosh-dan demand the immediate surrender of the Babylonian Confederacy and all of her people," he demanded.

"For what cause does the Rosh-dan make such an illegal request of a chartered colony?" Jeena asked.

SERUG PEERED QUIZZICALLY AT THE SPEAKER, HER VOICE STRANGELY FAMILIAR BUT HER face obscured by the gleaming helmet.

"We do not request, we command. Our cause is just. Babylon is an evil and debased society, wholly and irretrievably. Thy people defy the one true God and flaunt His laws. We have endured this moral outrage at our doors long enough. Thou wilt cede to our demands or fall utterly to the Army of God!"

"And what are your demands?" Jeena asked.

Serug smiled. It was as the k'laq had said—once the idolaters saw the power and might of the Rosh-dan they would quickly sue for peace. They were truly a corrupt people, completely devoid of honor.

"Thy army will surrender immediately and lay down all weapons. The leaders of the Confederacy will sign a Condition of Manifest Destiny, renouncing their Union Charter and turning all property, lands and right of rule over to the Council of the Rosh-dan."

"And what of our people, and our way of life?"

"Thy people have been corrupted by their leaders. Those who recant their pagan beliefs and accept the one true God will be sent for re-education and in time allowed to live as members of our community. Those who do not will be dealt with more severely. These are our conditions for peace."

Sargon stirred in his saddle but remained silent.

"Your demands are unjust, but it is not my place to accept or refuse them," the woman replied. "The Regent of Uruk leads the Confederacy, and it is her decision. We will take this to her for her consideration."

"Do as thou wilt," he replied tersely. "We will wait only until dawn. Thou hast until then." He turned his mount around.

"Wait. It might help to convince the regent if you could grant a small favor, a token of good faith."

"What token is this?" he asked, suspiciously.

"It is nothing. We have lost a scout, a young woman we believe you may be holding. If you would return her to us, it would go far in showing the regent the magnanimous nature of your superiors. Consider it an act of mercy."

"Yes, I know of this woman," he answered grimly. "Scout, thou says? Thou means spy. All spies face interrogation by the inquisitors of the Rosh-dan, and her questioning is not yet over. Thou wishes for her return? Accept the conditions of surrender and it may be. Thou hast until first light."

THEY RODE BACK TO THE BARRICADES, JEENA LEAVING SARGON TO SEE TO THE FINAL preparation while she went to the city to meet with the regent. She noticed that the older woman's right hand was bandaged.

"It is a trifle. Do not concern yourself," she said. "What news have you?"

Jeena repeated Serug's demands.

"He asks us to give up our entire civilization and all that we believe? Nothing else?"

"If we fight he may take all that anyway, as well as the lives of the people," Jeena reminded her.

"True. It seems we can either live as slaves or die as martyrs. Not much of a choice, is it?"

"No, it isn't."

"No. Well, we cannot give in to his demands, so all that is left to us is war."

"Yes, Regent. I will convey your answer to him."

"Good." She seemed hesitant, gently rubbing the bandages on her hand.

"Was there anything else?"

"I hoped we might speak a while."

"I'd be happy to, but with the enemy at our doorstep, I'm not sure this is the time."

"You are right, of course, but such is the precarious nature of our future that such a time might never occur."

"Very well. What did you want to talk about?"

A smile crept over the woman's face. "The nature of the universe, but as we are pressed for time, I'll focus on one subject—your birth. You were raised in an orphanage, I know, but do you have any information about your mother?"

Jeena was taken aback by the directness of the question. "No, not really. She never gave her name. 'Garza' was the surname of one of the sisters."

"So, nothing about where you were born? Your father? Any knowledge of siblings?"

"No. I'm sorry, Regent, but why are you asking? What difference does it make?"

"None, I'm sure, but you humored me once, humor me one more time. Relate to me anything you were told about your mother and your birth, even if it seems inconsequential." She motioned toward the chair.

Jeena sighed as she sat. "They never told me much, and after a while, you learn to just stop asking. It was a Saturday—visiting day for couples looking to adopt. The nuns said it was more hectic then usual. There had been a fire nearby the night before, and police and emergency crews were blocking the street."

"Go on."

"I know I was only a few days old when she showed up at the orphanage. No one knew how she got in—for the children's protection security is very tight."

"Did your mother mention anything to them about your birth, or why she was giving you to them?"

"No. She didn't say much, apparently, except that she couldn't keep me and had to leave very soon. As for my birth, the only thing they ever mentioned was that I had no marks of birth trauma, so they thought I may have been a c-section."

"And your mother—did they tell you anything concerning her?"

"Just that she was exhausted and dirty, as though she had traveled a long distance on foot. They said she had a slight accent, and thought she might have been born off-world. They took her to the kitchen in the basement and fed her, and offered to let her stay a while, but she refused. Sister Caroline, the one who accepted me from her, said she turned to refill my mother's plate and she was gone. No one ever saw her again. That's it. That's all I know."

"And she has never tried to contact you?"

"No. Regent, really..."

"All right. I'm done prying. Please return to your duties, and thank you again for indulging me."

AFTER JEENA LEFT, ELAINA STOOD AND SLOWLY PACED THE ROOM, HER HEAD BOWED IN thought. A solitary figure stepped out from behind a hidden panel.

"You heard?" the old woman asked.

"Yes," Aramis replied.

"You are a shimhatu of the sixth rank," the old woman said. "Use your training. What did you learn from her words?"

Aramis thought a moment before answering. "The mother was running from someone or something, that much is obvious. Yet I do not believe the unknown agents were after her—she seemed more afraid of the child being caught than herself. She chose the orphanage deliberately, so if she was trying to hide the infant, it is unlikely she had any connection to the Arian Christian religion that could be traced."

"Very good. Yet there is more. Consider: a woman has a child by surgery, yet almost immediately after the birth leaves on foot, carrying the infant. There is some strength there. After arriving in a strange city, she locates an orphanage in an area crawling with police, yet is able to slip past security and enter and leave silently and unseen. These are singular skills, are they not?"

Aramis frowned. "Military?"

"Just so. It seems the mother may have been a soldier like her daughter."

"Is that important?"

"Everything concerning her birth is important, if we are to lift the mists that surround her. But already intriguing possibilities arise." She lifted her hand against more questions. "No, daughter, not yet. Truly, I have more questions than answers still."

Aramis bowed. "As you wish. I must attend to my duties." At the door she turned. "It's a shame we know nothing about the father."

"Let us hope she has one," Elaina muttered when her daughter was gone.

THE COMMANDERS MET IN THE WAR ROOM TO DISCUSS THE ROSH-DAN'S DEMANDS AND THE regent's response. David had not yet dressed out in the Pyros body armor, but the Babylonian officers presented in full battle gear. They wore steel breastplates embossed in brass with a roaring tigra, and thick leather kilts made of overlapping straps. Heavy sandals laced up their legs, and each officer was armed with a long broadsword.

Jeena repeated what Serug had demanded, watching as David's face first registered hope at the news that Sarah still lived then collapsed when told of Jeena's failure to obtain her release.

"Is there nothing more we can do, Jeena? Couldn't we attempt a raid?"

"No, David. We don't have the manpower to try it, even if we knew she was still alive. I'm sorry. I tried."

It was decided that he and Selanja would go with Jeena in the morning to deliver the regent's answer. The meeting was adjourned, but David was still unwilling to let the subject of Sarah die.

"Let me go after her. I will take just a few men."

"No. I wish I could do more, but I can't risk it."

"But, Jeena..."

"Come, David," said Ghannon, putting a hand on David's shoulder. "There is nothing more she can do."

JEENA PACED HER ROOM ALONE. SHE COULD STILL HEAR DAVID'S PLEADING VOICE, STILL SEE the crushed looked on his face as she condemned Sarah to the torture of the Rosh-dan inquisitors. There was obviously more to his relationship with her than he had let on.

If only I weren't in command. A small raid might work, if they were quick and silent enough. If only...

But no. She *was* in command. She was commander-in-chief of an army facing enormously superior numbers. She could not risk more lives for one soldier who might already be dead. Her decision had been the right one. Yet that fact brought her no peace.

Dawn was still hours away when she mounted up and rode to the barricades. Halamesh greeted her. He seemed anxious and preoccupied.

"You are early. The sun will not rise for many hours yet," he said.

"I can't sleep. And you should be at the lake. I don't want to take any chances the Rosh-dan may not wait till dawn."

"My men are in position. I will join them shortly." He looked around nervously. "Come, there is coffee farther along the barricade. I will walk you to it."

"I don't need coffee, I'm tense enough. Where is Ghannon? He should be posted here."

"He is around, I am sure. Perhaps we can find him. I will walk with you."

"No, its all right. I—"

The noise of distant gunfire suddenly erupted from the direction of the Rosh-dan encampment.

"What the...? Halamesh, what the hell is going on here?"

He shrugged, but his face belied the attempt at innocence.

Jeena could now hear the hoofs of galloping kytars approaching. Through the barricade she saw dark shapes rushing towards them. Instinctively, she raised her pulse rifle.

"Don't shoot!' Halamesh cried, throwing himself in front of her.

A kytar suddenly leapt over the barricade, followed by a second, and then a third. Their riders wheeled the animals around as they reared and snorted, full of fire from the race. All the riders were clad in the coarse dark clothes of the Rosh-dan.

The lead rider spun his animal around and threw back his hood.

"Sargon!" Jeena cried.

The other two followed suit and Jeena stared in angry disbelief as she beheld David and Ghannon. She was about to curse them all when a figure sitting hitherto unseen behind David suddenly slumped and fell from the mount. Jeena rushed over as Halamesh brought a lamp to the rider's face. It was Sarah.

"Halamesh, bring up a cart. Now!" Jeena ordered.

In an instant, two men appeared and lifted Sarah onto a small wagon then raced with all speed to the hospital.

Jeena now turned her attention to her three commanders.

"I thought I gave specific orders not to attempt a raid." she snapped.

They stood silent with eyes downcast.

"I am to blame," confessed David. "I wouldn't let it go."

Sargon stepped forward. "No, we all agreed to this."

"Did you? And my orders meant nothing? Don't you think I wanted to rescue her?" she asked, looking from man to man. "But dammit, we can't risk the entire city! The whole war could have been compromised because of your actions. It killed me to leave her there, but...but..."

Her voice broke, and she turned away, her eyes stinging.

Sargon spoke. "Forgive us, General, but we knew you could not order the raid, although your heart may have wished it. David confided in me of his true relationship with Sarah, and for the sake of their love we formed our band. We knew that had you not had the burden of command you would have led us yourself."

"We have disobeyed a direct order, and that is inexcusable," Ghannon added, "but we do not leave our people to torment. That, perhaps, is different in the world from which you come."

He stood before her, chastened but firm. He alone among them had suffered the torture of the Rosh-dan inquisitors, and knew firsthand what they would do to the girl. He could not have allowed her to remain in their hands, even at the risk of his own life.

And Jeena knew Sargon was right as well. *How I wish I* had *led the raid myself!*

She looked sternly at them all.

"If any one of you had been killed, the defense of the whole Confederacy would have been compromised, perhaps fatally. Had any of you considered that?"

They diverted their eyes from her gaze, a clear indication that, in their haste to achieve their aim, that possibility had not crossed their minds. She let them stew uncomfortably for several minutes before speaking again.

"But you were not killed. Apparently, the gods of Babylon protect fools and heroes, for you are all both. What you did was rash, but brave. I'm proud of you all. But if you ever disobey an order of mine again..."

They all broke out in simultaneous and vigorous protest of the impossibility of such an event, swearing oaths of future obedience with such fervor she had to smile.

"And you," she said to David, "have a couple of hours till dawn. Go to her. Be with her while you can, since you've gone to so much trouble to bring her here."

Grinning broadly, he jumped on his mount and galloped into the city.

"As for you three," she said, turning back toward the others. "Let's find that coffee. I want to hear how the hell you managed to pull this off."

DAVID SAT WITH SARAH IN THE CITY HOSPITAL. HER BODY BORE TERRIBLE WOUNDS, BUT these had been treated and dressed. There were sophisticated instruments connected to her head and chest, medical equipment the Pyros physicians had obtained over the years from trade with smugglers. Although Uruk had fine healers, they did not have the benefit of the modern medical advances available to the Pyros physicians.

There had been some grumbling, but Jeena had placed the Pyros team in charge of the wounded. She wanted the best care her people could get—egos be damned.

"She is in shock," the doctor informed him. "She has suffered a mild concussion, superficial burns and several broken ribs, not to mention dehydration, but she should recover fully."

David thanked him profusely.

"The Babylonian physicians have an interesting salve made of local herbs we are using to treat the burns. Stinks to high heaven, but I've seen the results on others—very impressive."

With the doctor's consent, David sat for a time at her side, holding her hand and speaking softly to her. In time, her eyes fluttered open.

"David..." she said weakly.

"Yes, I'm here. You're safe now. You're in a hospital in Uruk. You'll be well soon."

"I thought it was a nightmare. I was in a horrible place. I called for you, but you weren't there. I thought you had forgotten me."

"Never."

"Then I had a dream you rescued me, but it wasn't a dream. I really am here with you, aren't I."

"Yes, Sarah," he said as her eyes closed. "And I swear I will never leave you again."

DAVID RODE BACK TO THE BARRICADES JUST BEFORE LIGHT AS JEENA WAS HANDING OUT THE communicators.

"They are old and simple devices, but they're the best we have."

Selanja studied hers curiously, turning it over in her hands. It looked like a thick black necklace.

"Put it around your neck like so," Jeena demonstrated, "and put this piece in your ear. Now touch this switch. These are voice-activated and have been tuned to the same frequency, so we'll all be able to hear one another. Once the battle begins there will be a lot of noise, so listen carefully, and don't everyone try to talk at once."

She watched as they each repeated her instructions, checking each instrument to ensure it worked.

"All right, everybody get into position. David, Selanja—let's mount up."

They rode out slowly, Jeena in the center and wearing the Babylonian headdress as before. Three riders met them at the parley site. Besides Esau, Jeena recognized a second man as a member of the Elder Council. Between them sat Jacob on his mount, menacing and grim.

They stared at each other in icy silence, finally broken by Jacob.

"I do not see the regent among thee," he observed dryly.

"The regent has business of state to attend, and sends her regrets," Selanja answered.

Jacob laughed mirthlessly. "Does she now? And so in her stead she sends her lackeys to face us. Very well. Thy witch may hide a bit longer behind her walls, for all the good it will do her." He looked over the three, his gaze settling on the silver mountain emblazed on David's chest plate. "Thou dost not wear the sign of Babylon."

"No."

Jacob squinted, studying David's face. Suddenly, his eyes widened.

"Apostate!"

David remained silent.

"I see. Well, well, so we find thee at last. The long years have not dimmed our memory of thy treachery. And now the prodigal children return at last only to wage war against their fathers. I should have expected no less of traitors. Perhaps it is better so, for now we will not have to go in search of thee after we have defeated the infidel."

"We fight against the tyranny of demagogues, who would use their beliefs to enslave others," David replied.

"Speak to me not of beliefs, thou who has none! Thou art of a banished people, lost from God. Pray tell me, after all these years, hast thou found what thou were looking for? Hast thee found comfort in thy cold science? I think not. But such is the fate of those who would turn from God. Thy science will not save thee, and thy destruction will be thy reward." He straightened in his saddle. "The time for speech is ended. How does the regent answer?"

"Her answer is this," Jeena replied. "You and all your army trespass on Babylonian soil. To raise an army of aggression is in violation of Union law, and of your charter. You are hereby ordered to remove yourselves to your own lands. Fail to do so, and you and all of your followers will be destroyed. Of your demands, we recognize none."

Jacob peered into the darkness of her helmet.

"So, thou art the leader here? I tell thee, thy threats are idle. Thou hast not the strength to withstand the Army of God. Why dost thee hide thy face? Thy voice is familiar to me. Show thyself, if thou be not afraid."

Jeena hesitated for just a moment, then reached up and removed her helmet.

Jacob reared back as though he had been struck, his face twisting into a snarl. Esau cried out and drew his sword, spurring his mount toward her.

She drew the pulse rifle.

"Do it, Esau! Come and meet your God as a cloud of dust!"

Jacob grabbed the reins of Esau's kytar, holding him back.

"Nay, stay thy wrath!" He glared at her. "So, thou hast found the idolaters. Surely, I spoke in truth—thou art now truly the Whore of Babylon."

"And where is thy Beast, whom thou didst live with in most unnatural wickedness?" asked Esau. "Be assured thou canst not hide him. He shall be found, and his death will not be quick."

Jeena gritted her teeth. "I know the truth about the tigras, Jacob. I know of their civilization that existed here, and of your people's tampering with CAIO and the Five-Year Survey. I know it all. It's over."

Jacob laughed. It was a high-pitched, maniacal cackle, frightening to hear.

"Pray tell me why so? Is it thy intention to report my activities to the Union? Oh, but wait, thou cannot. Not that it matters. Justice belongs to the just, and just is our cause. Or dost thou truly believe thy one weapon can defeat the Army of God?

"No, Captain, thou should have stayed in space, flying thy little ship. Thou hast entangled thyself in affairs beyond thy comprehension. I am afraid the Union will have to win its Civil War without any further assistance from thee. Thy time, and that of all of thee, has come to an end."

With a cry, he spurred his mount and, shouting to the others, galloped back to their encampment.

"Get back to the barricades!" Jeena cried. "David, get your cavalry to the clearing. Selanja, to the wall."

She spurred her mount and sped back to the first line. A section was moved aside as she and the others raced through then replaced.

"Are the men ready?" she asked Ghannon.

"Yes, all are in position."

"Good. Hold your fire until they are within range. Make them remember this day!"

She spun her kytar around and raced toward the city. At the second line she jumped off her mount and slapped its flanks, sending it galloping toward the walls. The second line was already kneeling in firing position. She donned her helmet and flipped the pulse rifle on.

"Stand ready!" she shouted down the line. "Hold your fire till my signal!" She spoke into the communicator. "Talk to me, Ghannon. What do you see?"

"An ocean," he said calmly. "And it is about to break upon us."

Jeena looked at the ground beneath her. The loose dirt trembled from the pounding of men and kytars as they rushed the front lines. She stared down the line. Her men could feel it, too. She could hear Ghannon shouting orders to his troops, his deep voice echoing in her ear.

"Hold your fire! Hold!"

The trembling increased as the sound of the approaching enemy grew loud in her ear.

"Steady now...steady!" Ghannon shouted.

Jeena involuntarily held her breath.

"Fire!" he screamed.

She jumped at the roar of ten thousand automatic rifles firing at once.

Although ammo was precious, she wanted the Rosh-dan's first experience with modern weapons to be memorable, so the front line had received the lion's share of the ammunition. Her line was to fire on semi-automatic only, but then, they had the MAAD.

Ten thousand guns rained bullets into the charging mass of the enemy, and she waited for a signal from Ghannon. The gunfire seemed to go on forever—a continuous thunder of weapons-fire. Through her earpiece, she could hear Ghannon shouting orders, firming up sections of his line and directing runners to distribute the ammunition.

Finally he spoke to her.

"They're pushing through! We'll have to..." His voice fizzled.

"Piece of shit," she cursed, and slammed her fist into the side of her helmet. The hissing stopped. "Say again, Ghannon."

"We are moving back. They are coming in fast...cutting down...not stopping them."

"Pull back," she ordered. "Keep it orderly. Continue to fire as you retreat."

"Understood."

Jeena shouted down her line. "All right, the first line is retreating. They'll be coming through in a hurry. No one fire until I give the signal—remember, those are your people out there."

In the distance, they saw the first of Ghannon's men appear over the ridge; the gunfire was now deafeningly close. Soon, the entire first line was before them; and coming up behind them, the main body of the Rosh-dan army, a sea of men spanning the width of the Bacchian Fields, a scant five hundred yards away. They were moving fast, their voices raised in a cry.

Jeena hit the switch on the butt of the MAAD and a high whine began.

"Let them through!" she ordered as the first of Ghannon's men ran past them. They would continue on to the city to take their place on the wall under Selanja's command. More and more ran by—almost ten thousand men—and behind them a host of almost half a million.

As the last stragglers ran past, she gave the command.

"Fire!"

A hail of bullets exploded into the wall of humanity before them. Men on kytars—the charging cavalry of the Rosh-dan—fell in a hideous mass, only to be overrun by the troops behind. The first line had decimated the Rosh-dan's first cavalry charge, and now Jeena's men finished the job. Still the main force of foot soldiers continued their suicidal advance.

Jeena sprayed the field with her pulse rifle, the high-velocity projectiles tearing through the body of the first victim before continuing on to strike a second, and sometimes a third. Yet nothing seemed to slow them—they ran over their dead comrades without so much as a look.

The whine of the MAAD stopped. Bracing herself, Jeena triggered the cannon. Once again the awesome power of the weapon was unleashed. The explosion ripped into the advancing line, obliterating the flesh of the charging wall of men.

Before her, where once had stood a thousand Rosh-dan, was now only an open swath of ground extending a hundred yards deep. Few bodies would ever be found in that space, and of those, none would ever be identified. Jeena's hands tingled and her ears rang. The whine began again.

The rushing mass hesitated at first, uncertain in the face of the power of the MAAD, then ran to fill the space left vacant by their dead brethren, advancing once again. The rifles cut down their ranks. The whine of the recharge stopped, and Jeena fired again, and again a thousand souls disappeared into a cloud of oily dust.

Still the enemy came.

Jeena was horrified at Jacob's disregard for the death she was inflicting on his men. Again and again she fired, and with each blast of the cannon, the shockwave turned thousands of Rosh-dan into a fine spray that splattered over the nearby survivors. Many of these soldiers were completely covered in the sticky brown liquid, yet still they came. Sargon had been right—they were fighting an army of madmen.

Amazingly, the Rosh-dan were able to hold the line despite the carnage around them, but slowly they began to waver. Some of the units had slowed their assault, unwilling to face this unknown and seemingly inhuman weapon. Others had stopped advancing altogether.

Then, just as Jeena thought they would turn back, disaster struck. She fired the cannon—and nothing happened. She pulled the trigger repeatedly without effect.

"Jeena, what is wrong?" asked Selanja's voice in her ear.

"The MAAD is down!" she screamed. She was covered in sweat and dirt, and both ears rang painfully. A trickle of blood ran from each. She examined the power meter on the weapon—it was low, but not empty. She flipped over to the pulse rifle. It, too, was inoperable.

The Rosh-dan army, on the brink of retreat a moment ago, now felt the tide turn. The unholy explosions, which had vaporized men like a blast of God's breath, had stopped. With a cry, they renewed their attack in earnest, throwing themselves against the spitting guns.

"Sargon, I have to pull back," Jeena shouted into the communicator. "Advance the main force." She turned to her men. "Pull back! Keep firing and retreat!"

"...again, General. Say again," came Sargon's voice.

"Advance! Advance!" she screamed, cursing the communicators, the smugglers and anyone who had helped build the antique junk.

Her retreat was rapid and organized, with Jeena able to do little but direct the line back to the wall. She continued to shake and prod the MAAD, cursing it as well. Behind them the main body of the Rosh-dan army came rushing forward.

"David, the MAAD is down. We've had to move the main force in early."

"Yes, I heard," he crackled in her ear. "How bad is it?"

"We hurt them, but not as much as I had hoped. The plan stays the same—be ready to move on Selanja's orders."

Selanja stood high on the city wall, monitoring the battle. She was to relay information to Sargon and David concerning the pitch of battle and advise them on where to best engage the enemy. When she had determined that the army had done all it could, she was to signal their retreat while at the same time releasing David and his cavalry from their hidden clearing.

Jeena's second rifle line raced toward the safety of the city walls as Sargon and his men rushed past to engage the Rosh-dan. She dropped to her knees and threw off her helmet. As the war raged in front of her, she broke down the MAAD as quickly as she could.

"Jeena, what are you doing?" asked Selanja. "Get back to the gates."

She could hear the clash of the two great armies and Sargon shouting commands. There was the ring of steel meeting steel and cries of agony as men attacked each other with swords and knives.

"We may still need the MAAD," she said. "I'm going to try and fix it."

"Get...ass...back," came the reply, and for once she was glad the damn communicator didn't work.

Pulling the power module from the butt of the gun, she saw the problem—dust had settled on the connectors. In her haste, she hadn't secured it tightly enough.

Cursing herself now, she spit-cleaned the connectors and rapidly reassembled the weapon. Flipping the power switch on, she was rewarded with the cannon's signature sound.

She was about to announce the news to Selanja when she heard the woman's cry in her ear.

"Sargon, your left flank is collapsing! They're encircling you. Get out! Jeena, the Rosh-dan are pouring in from the west. Sargon will be trapped."

Jeena whirled. A large force sweeping in from the west was rapidly surrounding Sargon's battalion—Jacob must have divided his forces before the attack. But where were they coming from? There was nothing to the west but the lake.

"Halamesh!" Jeena called suddenly. "Halamesh, answer me!" There was no response. "Selanja, look to the west. Can you see Halamesh's position?"

"Jeena, there is smoke coming from the lakeside."

So, they had come over the lake. They must have had rafts prepared and ready, swarming over Halamesh and his men. Jeena slumped. It meant that Halamesh was dead, and their plan was broken—there would be no surprise.

Her immediate concern, however, was getting Sargon and his army out.

"David, engage your cavalry," she barked into the communicator. "You're going to have to break it up. Get those men out of there!"

From her right, a charging stream of kytars burst from behind their protective screen and charged into the battle, David leading the way. They crashed into the enemy's eastern flank, slicing through them and trying to work their way west to Sargon and his beleaguered troops.

The force of the charge initially threw back the front line of the Rosh-dan, and much of the Babylonian army was able to pull back as the cavalry took on the enemy. The Rosh-dan soon regrouped, however, and their second cavalry now charged from behind the lines, bottling up the Pyros troops.

David's progress slowed to a crawl and finally stopped. He was not able to reach Sargon. Making their stand, they held the line bravely as the shadows of the afternoon lengthened, allowing what remained of the Babylonian army to break for the walls of the city.

"We can't hold them much longer," he shouted finally.

Jeena could see him, tall on his mount, his sword slashing, his body covered in blood.

"Sargon, can you fight your way back?" she asked. "David can't reach you."

She had never felt so impotent. The MAAD was useless now with the armies so entangled.

"I heard," Sargon replied. His words came in gasps. "David, get your men out. You've done all you can."

"I'm sorry, Sargon," David answered. "Retreat!" he shouted, and the riders began cutting their way back to the walls.

As the cavalry fell to the rear, the east flank collapsed. Between Jeena and Sargon stood the entire Army of God.

Jeena opened up with the pulse rifle, trying to create an opening for Sargon and his men. She could just see him in the distance, his bloody sword rising and falling. Her rifle was having no effect. Like ants, the Rosh-dan were swarming over his position.

"Fire the cannon, Jeena!" Sargon cried.

She looked at the weapon in her hands. From this distance it would kill him and all his men, and he knew it.

"I can't," she whispered numbly.

"Fire, damn you! You can't save us. They will overrun the city!"

Suddenly, the enemy rushed over him, and she could see him no more. A horde was descending toward her.

"Forgive me," she whispered and leveling the cannon, fired it into the battling mass of men. With the explosion, Sargon, his men and a host of the enemy disappeared from the face of the planet.

She stood unmoving. Blood ran in rivulets from her nose and ears.

"Jeena, get back!" shouted David. "Run to the gate."

But she did not run. She strode slowly back to the walls, firing the cannon repeatedly, her face cold and expressionless. In between blasts, she sprayed the enemy with the pulse rifle.

"David, where are you?" she asked, her voice eerily calm.

"On the wall. Jeena..."

"I need a kytar, a fast one. Meet me at the gate."

"Jeena, what…?"

"Do it now!" she screamed.

The rifle was finally empty. She fired the cannon one last time as she reached the city wall, the enemy at her heels. David was waiting for her, the reins of a kytar in his hands.

She leapt up on the animal.

"Get back inside. Halamesh is dead. I must get to the lake."

DAVID SHUDDERED. THE WOMAN BEFORE HIM WAS HARDLY RECOGNIZABLE. HER FACE WAS ghostly white and grotesquely swollen, with large black circles surrounding her eyes. As she spoke, her head twitched, first in one direction and then in another, as though debating both sides of some internal argument.

It was her eyes, however, that struck him hardest. They were dull and cold, and he had the sickening feeling he was not speaking to a living woman.

"Jeena…"

"Goodbye, David," she said and, kicking the animal in its flanks, raced off to the west.

The enemy was now at the walls, their numbers extending far back into the Bacchian Fields. Great battering rams were rolled to the gates. Ladders were thrown up, and men scurried up them.

There was no more ammunition for the rifles, and Ghannon was directing archers to fire at the host of men below. Selanja had collapsed after Sargon's death and lay oblivious.

The ram under them was covered with an iron roof the archers were unable to penetrate. The reverberations could be felt all along the wall as the heavy war machine was hurled against the gates.

"It will not hold long," Ghannon warned.

A Rosh-dan soldier made it over the wall, and he cut him down. More were scrambling over the parapets.

"Soon it won't matter," said David, rushing to his side. "They'll all be over the walls."

One enemy soldier had slipped over unseen and stood with his sword over the prostrate body of Selanja, ready to strike. He fell with a strangled cry, a blow from Bernd cutting him almost in half.

"Bernd!" called David, happily. "I didn't know you had made it."

"I was busy at the other end of the wall," he replied, driving his sword into another invader and tossing his body to the ground below, "but I wanted to see Selanja. I heard about Sargon," he added sadly.

Roused at last by the tumult around her, Selanja stirred and stood. Seeing the chaos at the walls, she picked up her dropped sword and strode to Bernd's side. She answered his questioning look.

"The time for mourning is not yet here. Now is not the time for tears. Now is the time for battle. Now is the time for revenge."

With a cry she threw herself into the melee, slashing and hewing everything before her, Bernd at her side. Together they drove back all who dared challenge them, until the stone beneath them flowed red with the blood of the enemy.

The battle raged on, with more of the Rosh-dan rushing over the walls, only to be driven back by the might of the defenders. But they could not hold out forever. Many had already breached the defenses, and there was fierce fighting in the plaza. The ram was taking a heavy toll on the gates. When those finally gave way, the entire army of the Rosh-dan would flood the city.

As if in echo to the steady pounding of the ram below them, a deafening thunderclap suddenly boomed from the west, followed a moment later by a great gale. Ghannon ran to the western wall, pointing towards the lake.

"There!" he cried. "Brace yourselves!"

Rushing toward the city was an enormous wall of water, thirty feet high and moving at great speed. Like an avalanche, it crushed everything in its path, snapping tall trees like kindling and driving huge boulders before it.

Too late, the Rosh-dan saw it as well. A terrible cry went up, and a desperate race toward the rear began. The gates and wall were forgotten as each man fought to climb over his comrade in an attempt to flee.

It was all in vain. The towering wall of water was on them, crushing them and hurling them against the walls. Those that did not die instantly drowned agonizingly in the rushing, churning water.

The defenders looked in awe at the carnage below. Corpses of men and kytars floated by as the raging flood carried them east. Where only moments ago the sound of battle had rung in their ears, there was now only the rush of water and, in the distance, the faint cries of despair from the remaining Rosh-dan army.

David spoke into his communicator.

"Jeena? Jeena, please answer me." He repeated his plea many times, but the only response was static.

Each in turn tried in vain to reach her, but it was no use. They all bowed their heads. Selanja, unable to hold back her grief, sank into a corner and wept.

Chapter 24

"No one ever won a war by dying for his country. You win a war by making some other poor, dumb bastard die for his country."

> Quote attributed to 20th Century
> General George S. Patton
> *Encyclopedic History of the Union*, 22nd ed.

DAVID LEANED AGAINST A PARAPET OF THE WESTERN WALL, GAZING OUT AT THE SUN DYING a bloody death on the horizon. He had tried throughout the day to reach Jeena, without success. He accepted now that, in destroying the dam that had released the flood, she had perished.

Ghannon had left the wall earlier to see to the troops and check on the casualties. They had tried to get Selanja to go to the hospital, but she refused and had just now retired to the barracks. David was to meet with Ghannon later in the war room, but first he wanted to stop at the hospital.

Looking once more at the settling water to the west, he said a quiet goodbye to his friend.

Sarah was sitting up when he entered the ward. The place was a center of activity now, with wounded in every bed and some waiting in the hallway. David greeted them all and saw that they were being well cared for. Only when he had ensured their needs were attended to did he allow himself to sit with her.

"How are you feeling?" he asked.

"I'm good. The doctors say they will release me tomorrow." Her limbs were still bandaged and the stench of the herb poultice was heavy. "I see you've gone native," she said, smiling.

David looked at himself. He was filthy, covered in dirt and grime and blood—none of it his. Such was his luck and skill at arms that he had made it through the fighting with only a few scratches. He took note that he was also quite naked.

As he stood on the wall after the battle, he had followed Ghannon's lead and removed his soiled and bloody clothes. He had simply forgotten to redress. In light of all that had happened, it seemed a ridiculous thing to worry about. He wished he could have told Jeena.

"I'm sorry, Sarah, I guess I forgot."

She squeezed his hand. "It isn't important."

He spent an hour with her before the doctor ushered him out, saying she needed rest not talk. Promising to see her in the morning, he went to his room to wash up. When he was clean, he left to meet with the regent, passing the open door to Jeena's room. Hesitating a moment, he went in.

It felt like going back in time, but it had only been a day ago they had sat here, and she had smiled and laughed, as though the sorrow of a lifetime might finally be lifting. He wondered what she had found that had given her hope.

He saw her impe on the table and picked it up, rolling the stones in his fingers. *I'm glad you found a moment of peace, my friend. I only wish it had been enough to save you.*

He put the necklace down, his eyes beginning to burn, and quickly left.

THE REGENT SLUMPED IN HER CHAIR, SHAKING HER HEAD.

"I do not believe it."

"I am sorry," Ghannon repeated, "but she is dead."

"It cannot be. She cannot die. Have I not seen her fate? Have I not looked into the eye of the beast and seen them enter this city?

Ghannon shook his head. "I do not understand your questions, Regent."

She did not hear him. "Yet, if she is truly gone, then the new age is stillborn. Hope is abandoned. Darkness will cover mankind, and all my visions are naught but an old woman's dreams," she whispered.

"We who remain will never abandon you, or our city, Regent," Ghannon said, misinterpreting her grief.

"What? What did you say, Ghannon?"

"Only that we are making new plans to defend the city. We will fight to the last man and woman."

"Fight? Then the war is not won?"

"No, Regent, not yet." He explained their present situation, informing her of the death of Halamash and Sargon. "It was thought the flood and the great loses they suffered would have been enough to drive them back to New Jerusalem, but it appears they still have some fight left in them. Jacob is mad. He is willing to exterminate his entire army to destroy us. He has them digging in, preparing to wait until the waters recede. At that time, I assume they will attack again."

"And can we withstand another attack?"

Ghannon paused, then answered truthfully. "No."

"I see. Well, then, we will do what we can, since we can do nothing else. I will inform the people and send word to the other cities so they may prepare in whatever way they can. And, Ghannon, please thank your men for me. Victory or no, their heroism and sacrifice shall not be forgotten."

He excused himself and began to leave.

"Has Selanja begun to grieve for Sargon?" Elaina asked.

"Yes."

"That is good. Give her tomorrow as well, then assign her some simple duties to keep her occupied."

"But, Regent, she in command now."

"I know, but she needs you to take on that responsibility for a time. Do not worry, she will do as you say. When she does not, then she will be well enough to assume command."

When he was gone she went to the window and looked out upon the city below. Her body began to shake, and she clutched at the drapery for support.

"Ishtar! Ishtar, why have you forsaken me!" she cried.

DAVID SAT DOWN WEARILY. HE HAD NOT SLEPT IN ALMOST TWO DAYS, AND HIS MIND FELT numb, his limbs heavy. Ghannon stood across the war table, reviewing the casualty list.

"Of the fifteen thousand rifles, twelve thousand are still able, though, of course, the ammunition is spent. They will be reassigned to the main army group. Of that we have many less than fifty thousand still able to bear arms."

"Half my cavalry was decimated," David said sadly. "I have maybe six thousand who can still ride a kytar or carry a sword."

"A total remaining force of less than sixty thousand, against how many remaining Rosh-dan?"

"I have been trying to estimate their losses. Our rifle lines and infantry must have accounted for a hundred thousand, at least. Add to that another fifty thousand that fell to the MAAD."

"And the flood," Ghannon said. "Great God Anil, but there must have been a hundred thousand men caught under the waters."

David shook his head at the numbers. Over a quarter-million dead, and yet still they stayed, preparing to fight again.

"David, there is something I need to confess," Ghannon said, his face pained.

He looked inquiringly at the grim soldier.

"Are you sure I'm the one to hear it?" he asked.

"Yes, for you were closest to her. I obeyed Captain Garza out of duty, but in my heart I never fully trusted her commitment to Uruk or to our cause. I never called her General. Yet in the end, she gave up her life for my city and my people and proved herself better than Ghannon. I was petty and wrong and I am shamed by my actions."

"It's all right, Ghannon, I'm sure she'd understand. Trusting people was hard for her, too. I don't think she ever really had much luck making friends, but I know that here in Uruk she had hoped to find a home." He laid his head in his hands.

"You are tired," Ghannon said. "I have had sentries posted on the walls, though I do not expect an attack until the waters have receded. Get some rest; we will not be needed for several days."

David nodded. "You, too."

"Later. First, I must go to the Temple of Anil and pray. I will pray for General Garza, and I will pray for myself. I will pray for forgiveness."

DAVID JOLTED AWAKE; THE WALLS OF HIS APARTMENT ECHOED WITH THE BLARE OF THE CITY horns. Jumping to his feet, he ran out into the hallway, encountering a shimhatu.

"What's happened? Why do the horns blow?"

"I do not know, Commander, but there is a great commotion at the gates," the girl answered.

Rushing past her, he leapt down the steps, racing out of the palace toward the city gates. Could the Rosh-dan already be attacking? But, no, the fields must still be flooded. *Or have I slept for days?*

Confused and disoriented, he pushed through the crowd that had gathered at the main gate.

"What's happened?" he asked a sentry. "Why do the horns blow?"

The man pointed at the waters lapping up against the gates.

"Look!" he cried.

In muddy water up to his waist walked Ghannon. In his arms, he carried the limp, unconscious body of Jeena Garza.

David leapt into the water with a cry, gently taking Jeena from him.

"Is she...?" He was unable to finish the question.

"She lives still," Ghannon answered. "She breathed several times as I carried her."

A litter arrived, and David placed her in it tenderly, ordering the bearers to take her with all speed to the hospital. He turned to Ghannon.

"How did you find her?"

"I could not sleep. Dreams troubled me. In them, I heard the general speaking to me, but with words kind and gentle that I did not deserve. I had come to the wall to find some peace and was looking upon the water when something caught my eye—a body draped over a piece of driftwood—and I turned the binoculars toward it. When I saw the emblem of Pyros on the armor, my heart jumped. I called to others and raced into the waters to retrieve her."

David turned toward the hospital, but Ghannon grabbed his arm.

"She called out to me in my dreams, David," he said, awe in his voice. "She called to *me*, the one who had believed in her the least."

The rumor of Jeena's return spread quickly, and a crowd was already forming in the street before the hospital entrance. David pushed through them up the steps. He was met by a very large woman wearing a nurse's uniform who did not move when he approached the door.

"Please, madam, I wish to enter."

"Yes, I know," she said sourly. "You have come to see the girl. I will tell you what I have told all these other people—no."

"But, you don't understand—"

"No, you don't understand. That woman is terribly injured. The doctors are working very hard to save her, and they need space to do that. Do you know what they don't need? A bunch of unnecessary people milling about, wringing their hands and getting all wet-eyed and standing in everyone's way."

David started to protest, but stopped. She was right. He could do nothing for Jeena now but stay out of the way and let the doctors do what they were trained to do.

Sadly, he turned and worked his way back through the crowd. Sarah had been transferred to the satellite clinic now housing those injured who were considered stable. He would sit with her while he waited for word about Jeena.

It was dusk when he left Sarah. He had received no word about Jeena and thought to pass by the hospital in hopes of hearing some news. The crowd was gone, and only the nurse remained, steady as a statue before the doors. Selanja paced in front of her.

"Selanja, have you heard anything?" he asked.

"No. I have been here for hours, but they won't tell me anything, and *she* won't move," she snarled. She glared at the nurse, who glared back.

The hospital door opened, and the chief physician of Pyros stepped out. His smock was damp with sweat, and he appeared bone-weary. He held up his hand as they both began speaking at once.

"Wait. Listen first. She is alive, but badly hurt. She has suffered massive internal injuries and multiple broken bones—effects, I assume, of that weapon. She had one collapsed lung when she arrived and the second was partially fluid-filled. She has second- and third-degree burns on her chest and hands. There is swelling of the brain." He ran his hand over his face. "I've never seen a body so broken."

"But will she live?" asked David

The physician began as to answer, then shook his head sadly. "No. She may live a day, three at the most, but her injuries are terminal. I'm sorry."

Selanja reached for the door.

"I want to see her."

The doctor blocked her way.

"I'm afraid I can't allow it."

She grabbed him by his smock and with one hand lifted him above her.

"I am in your debt for all you have done for her, but you will let me see her. And you will do so now."

"Uh...yes, yes. All right. For a moment," he stammered, suspended above her head.

They followed him to Jeena's room. She lay peacefully, her body connected to a dizzying array of instruments. On her head was a contraption like a small leather cap, humming audibly. Her face was no longer pale, David observed, but had turned a dark purple, the skin tense over her swollen and distorted features. Thick bandages covered her hands and chest.

Selanja stood over her, lightly stroking her hair.

"Can she hear me?" she asked.

"No. We are keeping her in an artificial neural sleep for now."

"Can you wake her? Just for a moment."

The doctor sighed, but went to the wall of instruments and adjusted the settings. The sound from the helmet changed in pitch. A moment later, Jeena's eyelids fluttered open, her eyes barely visible within the mass of swollen flesh.

Selanja leaned forward, her mouth brushing against Jeena's ear and whispered, "Listen to me, Jeena. I know the guilt that torments you, but you did not kill Sargon. I watched him fall to the swords of the Rosh-dan. He was already dead when you fired." Her eyes welled with tears. "Do you understand me, *tappu*? It was not your blast that killed Sargon."

Tears pooled in Jeena's eyes and ran down her face as her body was wracked by great silent sobs.

"Enough. She can take no more," the physician warned and reset the instruments.

They watched as Jeena's expression relaxed and she slipped back into unconsciousness.

The doctor turned to Selanja. "What did you say to her?"

She wiped her eyes. "What she needed to hear."

"I see. Well, then I hope it gave her some measure of comfort."

Aramis brought news of Jeena to her mother in the prayer room of the temple.

"But do not get your hopes up," she warned. "The doctors say she will not live long."

But Elaina was crying; then, to Aramis' astonishment, the tears turn to laughter. She stood and spun, clutching her arms about herself, the sound of her mirth echoing in the domed room.

"Hope? All hope left me at the news of her death, and all faith in the goddess." She turned to the marble statue set in the alcove of the room, candles flickering at its base. "Forgive me, Great One, forgive my moment of weakness. I shall not doubt again. Do not fear, daughter, Jeena shall live, you will see. She will recover and herald the dawn of a new age. Nothing will stop it now. Nothing *can* stop it."

Chapter 25

The plan, then, was for Halamesh to destroy the dam at Lake Bel, thereby flooding the Bacchian Fields and, with it, the Rosh-dan army swarming toward the city gates. Jacob, however, had sent a large mass of soldiers over the lake by raft, and these discovered Halamesh and his men and overcame them. It then fell to General Garza to release the waters, and this she did, though she herself was caught in the deluge. Her broken body washed up at the city gates the next day, and it is said that even the Gods wept to see such ruin.

> Excerpt from *The Battle of the Bacchian Field*
> As told by Ghannon of Uruk

It had been three days since Jeena's body was discovered in the waters yet her condition did not improve. Ghannon had cloistered himself in the Temple of Anil, offering hourly prayers to the god for her recovery. Selanja had not seen David in two days and went in search of him, finding him in the barracks gym.

"How long has he been here?" she asked.

"All day," Bernd replied. He was leaning against a hitching post just outside the gymnasium, looking in through the open doors. "I tried to speak to him, but he almost took my head off."

David swayed, exhausted, before the practice dummy, slashing and hacking with his sword, sweat pouring from him, his face a mask of anger and pain.

"He came in hours ago and ordered everyone out," the big man continued. "I thought he'd gone mad. I've been watching him to make sure he doesn't hurt himself. What happened?"

Selanja shook her head sadly. "Jeena is worse. The doctors do not believe she will survive the day."

She went inside to stand behind David. He was breathing raggedly, his chest rising and falling in great gasps.

"Any news?" he asked without turning around.

"No. The physicians look in on her from time to time, but…"

He lifted his sword with two hands and slashed again at the dummy, stumbling and falling to his knees. "What was the point of finding her? Why let her live, just so those who love her can watch her die? Your gods have a funny sense of humor."

"It is late. You need rest," she said. "And she may yet recover. The regent believes so."

"Dammit, Selanja, that's just the desperate prayer of a frightened old woman. Why do you cling to false hope? It will just be that much harder when she dies."

"False? Hope is never false, David. And do not tell me you lack hope as well as faith. What hope have we of defeating the Rosh-dan? And yet here you remain, still defiant, still ready to do battle against impossible odds."

He shook his head and ran his hand through his wet hair, pulling it from his face.

"No, I don't delude myself. I know we can't win this war. I'm in this final battle for revenge, Selanja—revenge for Jeena, revenge for what they have done to our people, and for what they will do to those left after I am gone."

A young Babylonian soldier ran in.

"Commander Selanja, Ghannon sent me to find you. He says to come with all speed to the hospital. The general is gone."

With a cry, David ran out of the gymnasium, Selanja, then Bernd, on his heels. He burst through the hospital doors and found Ghannon standing outside Jeena's room, his head bowed.

"What happened, Ghannon? Please tell me she did not die alone."

Ghannon raised his head. "Die? I do not know that she is dead at all, David. I do not know where she is. She is gone."

Puzzled, David and Selanja entered the room. The bed was empty, a shattered ewer lying in pieces on the floor.

A doctor sped into the room and spied the vacant bed.

"What's happened? What have you done with her?" he demanded.

"We have done nothing with her," Selanja answered, grinning. "She has awoken."

"Don't be absurd," he snapped. "That woman could not have walked away."

"Then she has flown," Selanja said.

"Dammit, flown or walked, where the hell did she go?" David asked.

Ghannon snapped his fingers. "I have been trying to answer that myself and it just came to me. The war room!"

The three commanders raced from the hospital to the Temple of Anil. They entered the war room cautiously, unsure of what they would find.

The room was dark, with only a single flickering candle for light. In the far corner sat Jeena, almost lost in the shadows. She was slumped in a chair gorging on fruit, a blanket wrapped around her.

"Anil be praised!" gasped Ghannon

"Tappu?" Selanja said.

Jeena lifted her head. Her face was pale in the dim light and covered in beads of sweat.

"Water...please," she said weakly.

Ghannon rushed from the room and returned with a ewer, kneeling as he handed it to her. Jeena put it to her lips and tilted the vessel, not stopping until she had drained it completely.

"Thank you, Ghannon," she gasped.

He caught the ceramic jar as it slipped from her bandaged hands.

"Jeena, you should be back at the hospital," David said worriedly.

"No, I'll be all right," she answered. Her voice was coarse and raspy. She looked around the room. "How did I get here?"

"But, tappu," Selanja explained gently, "you walked here yourself. Do you not remember?"

Jeena shook her head.

"What *do* you remember?" David asked.

"It's foggy. I remember bits and pieces of the battle and...then I was riding out to the earthen dike Halamesh and his men had constructed. They were all dead. There were four Rosh-dan soldiers. My pulse rifle was empty, so I drew my sword and attacked."

"You attacked all four alone? That was a brave feat," Ghannon said.

"No, Ghannon, not brave, more like madness. I don't remember the fight, just finding myself standing alone with their bodies at my feet.

"The device for releasing the trapped water of the lake was meant to be raised by six men, and although I tried, I couldn't budge it. The next thing I remember is standing in the gully in front of the dike and priming the cannon."

She surveyed the faces around her. "That's all I remember until you all arrived here."

"Ghannon found you floating in the flotsam the day after the battle and carried you to the city," David said.

"Did he? Thank you, Ghannon."

Ghannon still knelt before her, his lip trembling. Drawing his sword and bowing his head, he presented the hilt to her.

Jeena looked in confusion to Selanja.

"Place your hand on the hilt," she instructed.

Weakly, Jeena laid a bandaged hand on the hilt of the sword. In a choked voice, the old soldier spoke.

"I offer you my sword, I who have never called you general. For that I beg forgiveness and I say now that I am yours to command for as long as life flows through my body, if you will have me. This oath I swear to Anil, and to all the gods."

Jeena smiled. "You never have to bow to me, Ghannon, and I would gladly have you by my side, in war or in peace."

He stood, and though his eyes were moist, his face was set in a wide smile.

"You need rest now, tappu," Selanja said.

"What about the battle? Did the flood destroy the enemy?"

"No," David answered. "We did them great damage, but we believe half their army still remains. The flood waters have kept the rest at bay until now, but when the ground dries, we expect they will attack again."

Jeena stared silently at the map table.

"How much time do we have?" she asked at last.

"The water has already receded," Ghannon replied. "The ground should be passable in three more days. Come, General, Selanja is correct. You must rest."

"In three days I can rest for eternity. How are the gates?"

"They took quite a beating," David answered. "We've reinforced them, but they won't take much more."

"Don't seal them up too tight. I want us to be able to get out quickly when we have to. Selanja, I know you had organized fire-spotters and water brigades prior to the battle. Are they still on alert?"

"No, not since the battle ended, but they can be readily activated. Do you think we are at risk?"

She nodded. "They know we are trapped behind these walls. They may try to burn us out before attacking. Ghannon, where is the lowest point of land just in front of the walls?"

Ghannon lit another candle and held it above the contour map on the table.

"Here, just west of the main gate. There is a wide depression extending perhaps a hundred yards."

"That will be the last area of ground to dry," Jeena explained. "If they make it as far as the walls, we'll try to drive them into the lower ground and hope the mud slows them." She sagged forward.

"That is enough, Jeena. You're going back to the hospital. I want the doctor to examine you again," David insisted.

"And when the doctor is through with his examination, I will bring you to my apartment," Selanja offered. "You will stay with me while you recuperate, and I will make sure you get something more edible than that seaweed they were feeding you through your vein in the hospital."

Jeena allowed David to escort her back to the hospital, where they found the regent had just arrived. A team of Pyros physicians conducted a barrage of tests, halting them only when she made it clear she'd had enough.

David pulled the chief of staff aside, "Well?"

"Well, she's weak and dehydrated, but the internal injuries have just about healed. Don't even ask me how that is possible. It isn't."

Elaina joined the conversation.

David shook his head. "Maybe her injuries were not as severe as you had thought."

"Commander, you saw her. I worked on her for over six hours when they first brought her in. The burns to her hands went clear to the bone!"

David looked through the small window to where Jeena was dressing, slipping a tunic over her head. The palms of her hands were an ugly red, but nothing like the charred remains he had seen when he lifted her from Ghannon's arms.

"Then the answer is clear," Elaina said. "It is a miracle, a gift from the goddess."

The doctor coughed. "No offense, Your Highness, but I'm a physician, I don't believe in miracles. I may not be able to give you a detailed scientific explanation, but I'm sure one exists." He sighed. "I don't know, maybe it has something to do with that accelerated metabolic process we witnessed."

David gave him a look that made it clear he was in no mood for medical jargon.

"Sorry. Just prior to her disappearance from the hospital our instruments recorded an enormous increase in her metabolic rate. I've never seen anything like it. It's possible that all that energy was directed toward tissue repair—though don't ask me to explain how. It might also account for why she was so dehydrated and hungry following her recovery. I'm sorry, that's all I can tell you. One of our residents is doing further studies on her tissue samples. Maybe he can find some answer to this."

Elaina's face formed a thin smile. "Is he? I would be most interested in his findings.'

"Not me," David said. "No, honestly, I don't care how it happened. You say it's all science, the regent says it's a miracle. Either way, she's back and she's whole—and you know what? That's good enough for me."

Word of Jeena's recovery spread throughout the city. There were whispered rumors that she was Ishtar returned. Jeena tried her best to squelch the religious nonsense, although she was at a loss to shed any light on the nature of her recovery. The medical resident, however, had not given up searching for an answer.

IT WAS LATE. HE HAD OPENED A BOTTLE OF WINE TO CALM HIMSELF, AND HAD ALMOST finished it. He looked again at the collection of evidence, the tissue samples and test results, and closed the file case. Though it was still hours till dawn, he would not wait. This was far too important. He would wake the chief of staff now.

There was a noise in the doorway and he looked up to see an elderly woman.

"Excuse me. This area of the hospital is off limits," he informed her, his words slightly slurred.

The old woman smiled. "Forgive me. I am Elaina, regent of our city. I was just paying a visit to our wounded."

"Oh. Oh, Regent! I'm sorry. I didn't recognize you." He squinted at the clock on the wall. "It's kind of late, isn't it?"

"Yes, it is. I was going to say the same thing to you. Do all doctors work such long hours?"

He smiled. "I'm just a second-year resident."

"Well, you show great promise by your dedication. You must be working on something important. I shall leave you to it."

"Thank you. No, wait." He gazed at the file case by his hands.

She stepped into the lab. "You seem upset. Can I help you in any way?"

"I don't know...it's just...I performed some tests...on General Garza."

Elaina became grave. "I see. She has helped in our defense, and for that I am grateful, but I have been very leery about having her in the city. I can't put my finger on it, but there is something very strange about that woman, something...unnatural."

He sighed in relief. "Ma'am, you have no idea. You're the head of government here, right?'

"That is correct."

"Then I might as well tell you this now, since you're the one who's going to have to do something with her."

"Go on."

He opened the case and removed a sheet of paper.

"This is a detailed chemical analysis of her blood."

She smiled. "I'm afraid I would not know how to interpret it."

"Then let me explain. All known life, from the simplest viruses to man himself, is composed of various combinations of the same twenty amino acids—no more. It is a statement of scientific fact that holds true throughout the galaxy."

"I believe you."

He shook the paper in his hand. "General Jeena Garza carries the genetic coding for twenty-five separate amino acids."

The old woman frowned. "How is that possible?'

"It isn't. I mean, it isn't possible in nature."

"Young man, what exactly are you saying?"

He replaced the paper in the case and removed another. "I ran a chromosome scan on her. There's no easy way to say this. Her entire genetic code has been engineered. She's a horror."

The regent stepped back, her eyes widening.

"No! That is impossible!"

"Regent, I wish I was wrong."

"No. You are mistaken. You must be. She is a grown woman. If she was...There would have been another plague. She would not have been allowed to live to adulthood."

"I don't have an answer for that. Maybe she did cause a second plague in the Union and we never heard of it. Maybe she escaped somehow and that's how she ended up here."

"But who could have done such a thing? Why would they even try?"

"I don't know. But I've repeated the studies a dozen times and the results are the same. Apparently, whoever they were, they weren't happy repeating the work of Obsidia, they wanted to do them one better. These genes haven't just been tampered with, they're entirely artificial."

ELAINA SAT DOWN, HER MIND REELING. *So, this is the darkness I could not see; this is the evil she carries within.* Madmen! Weren't eight billion dead the first time enough? What possibly could have driven them to try it again? And who? With all the precautions in place throughout the galaxy, who could have done this?

The young doctor continued. "Twenty-three paired chromosomes, thirty thousand separate genes, three billion base pairs—all built from scratch. In effect, they've created an oxymoron—an alien human being. But don't ask me why."

"How is she different?" she asked numbly.

He shrugged. "There's no way of telling. Physically, she's no different from any other woman—a routine exam wouldn't show anything unusual. Although, if her recent recovery is any indication, then one thing is certain—she's very hard to kill."

"Who knows of this?"

"No one yet. I was just about to take my results and the tissue samples to the chief of staff. At the very least, she'll have to be totally quarantined, though who knows what damage she may have already done. We could all be infected by some virus and not even know it." His fear was evident.

"Yes," she agreed, "at the very least." *As with the horrors of old, you are blameless, yet that innocence will not save you. What would they do, even those who love you? Could they overcome the fear and loathing that even now stirs within me? Would they cast you out—or worse?*

Elaina stood, sighing deeply. "You were right to tell me of this. We must act swiftly. You have all the samples here?"

He nodded. "Yes, they're all in this case, along with the test results."

"Very good. Bring it. I will personally escort you to the temple hall, where you may present your finding to the medical staff and the commanders.'

"Uh...yes, ma'am."

He turned to lift the case and Elaina's hand shot out with practiced skill, grasping his neck at the first vertebrae. He turned in surprise and found that her foot had somehow become entangled in his. There was only the faintest expression of disbelief as he fell, his own bodyweight snapping his neck as she held him in her grip.

I am sorry, for you were only doing what you thought right. May your God embrace you.

Opening the case, she began the methodic destruction of all the samples. She would send shimhatu to dispose of the body.

Created by the insanity of man or the hand of the Goddess, you are the deliverer. You must bring forth the new age. I will allow nothing to prevent that from happening. Nothing.

THE NEXT DAYS WERE SPENT REVIEWING THE TROOPS AND EXAMINING THE DAMAGE TO THE city walls. The gates had taken a beating—they were bent and twisted, the center one worse than the others. Ghannon had ordered them strengthened with oak beams, but Jeena felt the changes would make the gate unusable, and modified the structure in order to make them serviceable to her own troops.

The force of the rushing water had created a wide crack in the wall that ran along the entire length of the north face. Even if it withstood another attack, it was now unstable and would have to be replaced.

They all agreed their best hope was to engage the enemy before the Rosh-dan could reach the weakened gates and wall; any retreat behind them would be left as a last resort. Jeena proposed a closed, three-line defense—archers, cavalry and infantry, all aligned west of the center gate, again in an effort to force the Rosh-dan to fight in the mire of the lower ground.

David would once again lead his Pyros cavalry—his leadership and sacrifice in the first battle had created such love and loyalty among the men and women of his command she felt certain they would follow him to the gates of hell itself. She elected to stand with Ghannon and Selanja and lead the Babylonian army. They all made it clear they felt she was still too weak to fight and tried to persuade her to remain in the rear, but she had stood firm.

"What would you have me do, sit on the wall and cheer? And if the battle is lost, then what? Do any of you really want to consider what Jacob would do to me if he captured me alive? I know I don't. No, if we win this final battle then I want to be a part of it. If we lose—well, better I die fighting with the people I love than at the hands of a madman."

On the third day of her recovery, Jeena was called to the regent's apartment. She found the old woman sitting alone on the balcony. She noticed that her hand was still bandaged.

"It is a slight wound," the older woman explained, "but for some reason it will not heal. But let us turn to more important matters." She sighed. "I wish we had more time together, Jeena. There is so much you must learn, and so many questions I still have concerning you.

"But our time together draws short, and I can do little to help you, I'm afraid, except perhaps to set you on the right path, for I have seen my death, and it is near."

She halted Jeena's protests.

"It shall be as I have seen. Do not trouble yourself. I have lived a long and happy life and have no regrets, save one—that I will not see the fruition of your destiny."

"And what is my destiny?"

"That lies beyond my sight. But there is a power in you, Jeena, such as I have never felt in all my life. You are unaware of it, for you have walled it off, buried it deep within your subconscious. But though sealed away, this power is not idle; it grows even as we speak. It will continue to gain in strength until finally a day will come when you can no longer contain it. On that day it may consume you, unless you first learn to control it."

Jeena shook her head. "I don't understand."

"You will. I cannot help you in this, but I may be able to help you help yourself. Am I right in assuming you wish to stay here in Uruk should we win this war?"

"Yes." *But how does she know that? I've only just decided myself.*

"Then it shall be. This morning I signed the necessary papers granting you citizenship."

"Regent...I don't know how to repay you. Thank you."

"I ask only a small favor in return. If we should pass through this dark time to days of happiness and light, promise me you will enter into the training of the Temple of Ishtar. In its teachings and disciplines, you will find the strength necessary to control the power inside you."

"How can I agree to that? I am not a believer."

"I do not ask for your faith. I ask only that you take the training of the shimhatu. Perhaps you think of them only as courtesans, and for those of the first rank you would not be so wrong. But do not take lightly the skills and strength of those of the upper ranks. From mother to daughter, we have kept alive knowledge lost to the rest of mankind through the ages. Take the training, Jeena—the rest will come in time."

She sighed. *Training as what—a palace prostitute? Can she be serious? But this is no joke to her, and she obviously means well for me. And yet I don't know what she thinks I can learn or what she believes my destiny is. But I do want to stay in Uruk, and taking the training would give me time to consider my next step. I suppose it wouldn't hurt anything. Then why do I feel like such a fraud?*

"Very well, Regent, since it means so much to you. I give you my word. If we defeat the Rosh-dan then I will take the training of the temple, but I don't promise to become a shimhatu, and I can't guarantee anything will come of it."

Elaina smiled. "Thank you. You have lifted a great worry from an old woman's heart. And as to what will come of it, who can tell? Still, in the training of the sisterhood you may find the strength to face the destiny that awaits you."

FOLLOWING HER MEETING WITH THE REGENT, JEENA WAS CALLED TO THE WALL ABOVE THE center gate. Selanja was there, watching as a lone rider below them came to a halt. A white flag hung limp in his left hand.

"I am sent by Jacob, K'laq of the Rosh-dan and Commander of the Army of God. The city of Uruk and all of Babylon stands in the face of utter destruction. If thou would not see all thy people slain, then lay down thy weapons and surrender at once. I am to await thy answer."

He yawned and looked away, as if bored with all this formality.

Jeena peered closely at the rider. Her vision was still cloudy, but she recognized the sneer and haughty manner immediately.

"Rhiannan, hurry. Under the cover of the wall, lend me your bow," she whispered to the archer at her side.

"Jeena, you cannot," Selanja protested. "He is a messenger, and under protection of the white flag."

The weapon in hand, Jeena notched the arrow swiftly and drew it back. The arrow flew, grazing the kytar's flank and causing it to rear, sending the rider flailing to the ground. The mount galloped away to the west as the rider stood, hobbling slightly and staring in fright at the women above him.

"Now that I have your attention, Esau," Jeena shouted, "you can have my answer. There will be no surrender—now or ever. To the last man and woman will the people of Babylon fight, not only in Uruk but in every city of the Confederacy. There can be no victory for you here, only more death for your men and more suffering for those waiting in New Jerusalem. Tell that to Jacob. Tell that to the madman who leads you. Now, go, and get out of bowshot as quickly as you can!"

Esau turned and began jogging back to his camp, a noticeable limp in his stride.

Selanja stared at her with disapproval.

"Oh, it's all right. He and I go way back," Jeena said. "Besides, now we have a little time."

David and Ghannon were informed, but Jeena told them to remain in the empty warehouses that had been converted into temporary barracks. Unlike the regular wooden barracks, these buildings were made of stone and offered better protection against the anticipated fires. The two women would remain on the wall to monitor the Rosh-dan's movements. They had two working communicators left, and David and Jeena wore them. The fire-spotters and water brigades were out and ready.

"If they start a ground attack we'll call you out," Jeena said to David through the communicators, "but if the aerial bombings begin I want you and your men inside. Selanja and I will make for the war room."

Selanja stood on a parapet, looking through the binoculars. "There's a lot of movement going on in the Rosh-dan camp, but I can't see much through the dust. Looks like they may be moving some of the large machines."

Several minutes of silence followed, broken suddenly by a roaring sound above them.

"Get down!" Jeena shouted.

A fiery blast exploded in the plaza behind them, sending burning shards in all directions. The two women were up and running in an instant, making for the war room just below the eastern wall. They reached the door as a second projectile burst against the stairs.

"David, it's begun," Jeena said.

"We're hearing it," David replied through the communicator.

"Selanja and I are in the war room. You and Ghannon keep your men inside. Let the fire brigades do their job."

"You won't have to tell us twice," he shouted over the roar of a large explosion.

For the next hour a thundering inferno fell over the city, with the army able to do nothing but wait it out. The bells and horns of the fire brigades could be heard as the Babylonians fought desperately to save their burning city. When at last the explosions halted, they were replaced by the sounds of boulders crashing into the city walls.

The two women stepped out into the plaza to see fires blazing all around them, and fire crews desperately dashing from one to the next. Jeena stopped one of the racing fire captains as behind her the city walls shuddered from the new attack. His face was dark with soot, and his clothes were soaked through.

"Can your people control the fires?" she asked.

"Yes, General, but much will be lost. The Temple of Ishtar is engulfed in flames."

Behind her, she heard a loud groan. She turned to see one of the graceful towers of the temple sway then topple to the ground with a thunderous crash. The fire-captain excused himself and, together with a water brigade, ran to the threatened building.

Another crash reverberated against the wall, then a second, and a third. Suddenly, the entire western half collapsed. Jeena and Selanja gazed out onto the Bacchian Fields.

"David, Ghannon, the wall is gone," she shouted into the communicator. "Get your men out now."

The barrage ended as the soldiers of Babylon began pouring into the plaza. Jeena ordered the gates open, and they rushed through, rapidly setting up the defensive line she had arranged. Dust rose in the distance as the Rosh-dan began their advance.

Jeena stood in the center of the archery line, only a hundred yards from the now-ruined walls. Fifty yards behind were David and what was left of his cavalry, the kytars stomping and snorting and ready for battle. At the ruined wall stood Ghannon and Selanja with the rest of the Babylonian army, the final defense of the city of Uruk.

Looking back, Jeena could just see Selanja, her long blond hair flowing in the wind. She thought again of Sargon and Halamesh and Samson, and gripped her sword hilt until a trickle of blood ran from her still-raw palm.

"Ready!" she shouted down the line.

The archers notched their arrows in their bows.

"Aim!"

Seven thousand arms extended, bowstrings drawn. The charging, screaming enemy came within range.

"Fire!"

The arrows sang, and seven thousand Rosh-dan fell dead.

The archers now fired at will, dropping men and kytars as they steadily retreated to the cavalry line. When the enemy had closed half the distance, Jeena gave the order for the charge. David and his troops flew by the archers and crashed into the advancing horde.

She immediately ordered the archers to the wall and called Selanja and her men up. The two women watched as David's cavalry drove into the center of the Rosh-dan's line, dividing them in half.

"Now!" Jeena shouted. "For Uruk! For Babylon! For freedom!"

Swinging her sword, she ran headlong into the mass of the enemy, Selanja and Ghannon beside her.

She avoided the thrust of the first soldier, driving her blade deep into his chest. Selanja swept her unit to the east as Ghannon and Jeena fought side-by-side, cutting a path into the attacking enemy. Bodies fell at their feet.

A Rosh-dan soldier armed with a pike thrust at Ghannon, missing. He fell back in agonized terror as a sword separated his spear arm from his body. Another wielding a two-handed axe swung at Jeena but misjudged, burying the blade into the back of a screaming comrade. He gaped in open-mouthed shock at his mistake before he, too, fell to the ground, headless.

They continued their relentless assault, hacking and thrusting through to the main body of the Rosh-dan army. Such was the ferocity of their attack that many of the enemy went around them rather than face the grim death they were delivering.

JEENA FINISHED HER MAN WITH A THRUST TO THE HEART AND WIPED THE SWEAT FROM HER brow. In the distance, she saw a Rosh-dan soldier drive a pike into David's kytar. The animal crashed to the ground with David pinned under him. With a cry, she ran to him. Her sword sang as she cut through the dense mass of attackers between them.

When she reached David he was standing but lame, fighting off two of the enemy that had pounced on him. Leaping to his side, she drew off one of them, a swarthy, evil-looking man whose hair and beard were as black as soot. He was skilled with a sword, and they slashed and parried, moving around each other as the larger battle raged about them.

Jeena saw an opening and dove inside his thrust but slipped on the wet ground, falling. Her adversary saw her error and swung his blade. Only her quick reflexes saved her life, but his blow cut a slash across her back. She leapt to her feet, and as she did, her steel breastplate fell away, the straps having been severed by the stroke.

Gaping for an instant at her bare breasts, the Rosh-dan gasped. Jeena flicked her sword, and he gasped again, this time grabbing at his throat as bright blood spurted from between his fingers. He fell dead to the ground.

"Bernd would've been proud!" David called out to her as he finished his man.

Jeena ran to his side, putting her arm around his waist to brace him.

"Can you walk?" she asked.

They scanned the chaos before them. The battle was going badly. The Rosh-dan were just too numerous. As many as they cut down, more came in from behind. The enemy had set wagons filled with pitch on fire, and were rolling them through the Babylonian line with soldiers following. Many of the wagons had fallen over, and fires blazed all around. The air was thick with oily smoke.

"Walk to where?" David asked.

She met his gaze in mutual understanding. "Good point. I suppose this is as good a place as any to make our stand."

He nodded. "That sounds good to me." He extended his hand to her. "Awful glad to have met you, Jeena Garza."

Jeena gripped his hand in her own.

"The feeling is mutual, David Proverst."

A unit of Rosh-dan rushed towards them.

"Till the end then."

"Till the end."

Chapter 26

At the genetic level, a species is nothing more than the accumulation of possibilities. As with any statistical causality, some possibilities occur more frequently than others; some are advantageous, others injurious. If all the best possibilities in the human genome were to be expressed in a single individual, he would be as far in advance of us as we ourselves are from our Neanderthal cousins.

> From a lecture given at the 20th annual Interplanetary Genetic Symposium

SELANJA SAW THE PYROS SOLDIER FALL TO THE BLOW, HIS HEAD BOWED FORWARD. THE Rosh-dan was about to deliver the fatal stroke when she swung, cutting through his abdomen and driving him screaming to the ground. A slash from her blade, and he was silent.

She lifted the fallen man up—it was Bernd. An ugly gash ran across his brow.

"Are you all right?" she asked.

"Hey, beautiful, good to see you again," he said, leering at her in spite of the wound.

"Yes, you are all right," she said, rolling her eyes.

Suddenly, from behind the enemy lines, came shrill screams, growing louder and repeating throughout the Rosh-dan. Selanja gripped her sword.

"What is happening?"

Bernd stood and looked back out over the battlefield, trying to peer through the smoke and mists. Deep within the main body of the Rosh-dan army something was moving, slicing through the enemy and scattering them.

"They're being attacked," he said, his voice filled with wonder, "from behind."

"Attacked? By whom?"

"I can't see," he said, still trying to make sense of the chaotic scene. "It looks like...No, it can't be! Look out!"

A large golden form flew between them, leaping onto a Rosh-dan soldier who had been set to strike at their backs. Five razor-sharp claws swept through the man's neck, and he fell lifeless to the ground.

"Tigras!" Selanja shouted.

Now they could see them all around, thousands of animals, racing wildly in all directions but attacking only the Rosh-dan. They were a yellow cyclone of death, hurling at the enemy, little more than a blur. They could only make out slashing claws and dripping fangs, and men dropping like unstrung puppets.

Unable to fight against this new and inhuman enemy, the Rosh-dan began to scatter, then to retreat. As the tigras continued their merciless attack, the retreat became a rout.

JEENA SWUNG HER SWORD AGAIN, CUTTING THROUGH THE MAN'S CHEST. TWO MORE CAME up behind him. There was no end to them, and both she and David were tiring, bleeding from wounds great and small.

It will soon be over, thought David. He hoped Sarah could make it to one of the southern cities. Jeena was right—the Babylonians would never surrender. Jacob would have to fight for every inch of the Confederacy, and eventually, they would defeat him.

The thought made him smile. He wished he could live to see that day.

He parried the blow from his man, catching sight of a yellow blur as he did. It moved too fast for him to make out clearly, but suddenly the Rosh-dan went down screaming. Then he saw why—a golden tigra had its fangs buried in the man's neck.

The man fighting Jeena saw it, too. With a cry, he dropped his sword and ran a few paces, only to be dragged down from behind by a second animal.

"My God!" David cried. There was a maelstrom of animals around them now, a slashing, swarming sea of yellow death. "Jeena, do you see it? Do you see it?"

She stood swaying, gripping her bloody sword. She had seen it, and looked in puzzlement at the action around her. Suddenly, she threw her sword to the ground and whirled about, desperately searching.

"Where do you think they came from? Jeena..."

But she did not hear him. Her arms limp at her side, her legs trembling, she began to walk toward a near hill. Her stride became faster until it was a trot, and then she was running, racing, blind through her tears, toward the top of the hill.

Through the mists of smoke and fire he had come over the crest of that hill, like a king from some ancient time. He stood, proud and erect, fire blazing in his gold-speckled eyes. Jeena reached the hill and flung herself on him, clinging to him and weeping like a child.

A moment later, David limped up behind her.

"I don't believe it."

"Hello, David."

"Samson? But we thought you were dead."

"I know, Mordachi told me. I'm afraid it was a case of mistaken identity—but just barely."

Jeena stuttered through her tears, still holding onto him, unwilling to let go.

"I th–thought I had lost you. All this time..all this..."

"I'm sorry, Jeena. I came as soon as I could, but as you can see, I've been busy."

David looked out over the army of tigras still fighting.

"That seems an understatement."

Jeena pulled her face from his neck and held his head in her hands; slowly, she leaned forward and pressed her lips against his. David grinned.

"What was that?" Samson gasped when she finally broke the embrace.

"A kiss...sort of."

"I know that, I just mean...why?"

"Because I love you, Samson. I love you so very much."

His mouth drew back in a wide smile. "You do? Really? But I'm not human."

Her laughter now mingled with her tears. "So what do you want me to do, grow a tail? Because if that's what it takes then I'll have one implanted. I don't care if you're human. I don't care if you have fur and paws. I don't care about any of that. Just please tell me that you love me, too."

With a roar, he stood and lifted her in his arms, holding her and spinning her around.

"Love you? I have loved you all of my life!" He lowered her to the ground and pressed his lips to hers, his eyes gleaming. "Is that how it's done?"

"We'll work on it," she said with a laugh.

"Ahem...I hate to break this up, but I think the Rosh-dan would like to go home now." David nodded to the fighting below.

The battlefield had become a slaughterhouse. Forty thousand tigras, with a speed and agility unmatched by any human, had fallen upon the desperate soldiers of the Rosh-dan with pitiless fury. Razor-sharp claws and projecting fangs tore into soft flesh, rending it in an instant before moving on to the next victim. Jeena watched as retreating men threw themselves to the ground in an act of complete surrender, only to be leapt upon by these terrible angels of death.

"Samson, please, it's over. Can't you stop this?" she begged.

"I'll try, but it's easier to start a thing than to stop it."

He sat down and held his head back, closing his eyes and humming softly. They watched as he visibly relaxed, his breathing becoming deep and regular. David and Jeena stared in puzzlement as he sank into a trance.

At first they could see no effect, but slowly the attack of the tigras began to grind to a halt. One charging animal sprang upon a screaming, fleeing soldier, dragging him to the ground, only to then walk away, leaving the hysterical man in the mud, unnerved but unharmed. Throughout the Bacchian Fields the tigras, apparently satisfied with their revenge on those who had sought to annihilate them, halted the massacre and began to move slowly to the north, toward the Rosh-dan camp.

Samson opened his eyes and shook himself, as though awakening from a dream.

"Telepathy?" David asked in wonder.

"Yes, though not in the way humans tend to think of it. I know, David. I know what happened to my people. I know why they lost their ability to speak and, over the centuries, their reason."

The tigras entered the area of the Rosh-dan camp and began encircling it.

"What are they doing?" David asked.

"They will not harm them, but neither will they allow them to leave," Samson explained. "Not until they give up Jacob. For his role in the genocide against my people, he will answer to me."

Ghannon ran up, followed closely by Selanja and Bernd. On seeing Samson, Ghannon drew his sword.

"It's all right, Ghannon," David said. "It will take some explaining, but this is an old friend."

Jeena motioned Selanja closer. "You asked me once if I had lost someone I loved, and I told you no. I lied. I had lost *him*, but now I've found him once again."

Selanja wrinkled her brow in confusion. "I do not understand, tappu."

"I think she means me," Samson said. He held out his paw to the astonished woman. "My name is Samson."

Selanja froze. Then slowly, like a child who, on returning home from school, discovers that her stuffed animal has come to life, she began to grin, then to giggle uncontrollably. She grasped his paw warily but warmly, still in disbelief.

"And this is Ghannon," Jeena said to Samson. "A brave soldier of Uruk and a great friend."

Ghannon stood rigid, his hand still on his sword.

"Great God Anil," he whispered. "You are truly Ishtar returned."

Bernd had turned ashen at the sound of Samson's voice.

"I heard rumors in Pyros, but I didn't believe..." He teetered and fell forward, landing with a thud.

"Is he hurt?" asked Samson, alarmed.

Selanja went to him and turned him over. His eyes rolled in his head.

"He is all right. Too much stimulation does this to him," she said, grinning.

She revived him, and they made their way back to the city.

The Babylonians, who had been overjoyed though shocked and puzzled at the unlooked-for aid of the tigras, now stared in wide-mouthed wonder at Samson and Jeena as they strode side-by-side into the city. Many dropped to their knees at the passing of the pair, a reaction that had them both scratching their heads.

A palace messenger met them at the crumbled walls.

"General, the regent lies dying. She has asked for you. Please hurry."

The messenger led them to the ruins of the Temple of Ishtar. The towers had fallen, and its once graceful dome lay in a heap of broken stone. Small fires still burned its ruined shell.

The regent lay on a cot at the foot of the broken steps, her head bandaged and her eyes dim. Jeena knelt before her, taking her hand.

"Please, Regent, allow them to take you to the hospital."

"No, my child, it is too late for that. My time is ended, but I go in peace. Uruk is safe, is it not?"

"Yes. It is just as you foresaw. There has been much damage, but we have won. The war is over."

"Then all is well." She gripped Jeena's hand tightly. "We are not responsible for how we enter this universe, only for our actions within it. Always remember that, child."

"I will," Jeena replied, puzzled.

The old woman spied Samson, her mouth gaping in wonder.

Jeena tried to explain. "It's all right, he won't harm you. His name is..."

"Samson."

"Yes, but how..."

"Bring him to me. Quickly!"

Jeena led Samson to the regent, introducing him. Elaina reached out, and Samson allowed her to gently touch his face.

"Do you love him, Jeena?" the old woman asked.

Jeena did not hesitate. "Yes, I do."

"Then all shall come to pass." She coughed weakly then crooked her finger to Samson. "Come closer."

He leaned near, until his ear brushed her lips. When at last he pulled away, her eyes were fixed and her breathing had stopped.

The commanders bowed their heads. The shimhatu in attendance wept openly and covered her body, then carried her away in reverence.

"What was it she said to you?" Jeena asked.

Samson looked puzzled. "I'm not sure. It didn't make a lot of sense. Let me think on it a while before I say anything."

Chapter 27

By this sign shall you know the Deliverer: she comes not alone.
The Beast walks with her, arm in her arm, heart in her heart.

From the *Tel-Marbuk*
Holy book of the Babylonians

G HANNON LED A FORCE OF URUK MILITARY IN FULL BATTLE GEAR TO THE BELEAGUERED camp of the Rosh-dan, demanding their immediate surrender. Esau had fled with a company of his men after witnessing the onslaught of the tigras, but Jacob and the Elder Council had not understood the danger until too late, and were now trapped.

With the army decimated and surrounded by a hostile and alien menace, the angry and rebellious survivors were quick to accept the terms and, after a brief internal skirmish, swiftly handed over their leaders. Jacob and the elders were taken to the city and imprisoned to await trial and sentencing.

Of the half-million men who had marched on Uruk, fewer than fifty thousand remained alive to return to New Jerusalem to tell the tale.

It was agreed that, with the regent gone, Selanja would temporarily assume control of the city, until such time as proper elections could be held. She immediately ordered repairs begun on the city walls as well as the temples and other public buildings destroyed in the war. Once news of the victory spread, masons and carpenters from all over Babylon poured into the city to offer their services.

David became distraught on discovering that the building housing Sarah and the other convalescing wounded had been destroyed, but breathed a sigh of relief when he learned all had been evacuated prior to the building's collapse. He and Sarah were now staying in a small vacant home near the hospital. Each day they would visit and speak with the injured, aiding them in any way they could.

Jeena and Samson were given temporary apartments in the Temple of Anil.

A week had passed since the death of the Regent, and they had not left their apartment in that time. Selanja had given strict instructions that they not be disturbed.

THEY LAY ON THE FLOOR, JEENA WRAPPED IN A BLANKET. SAMSON HELD HER CLOSE WITH HIS arm around her, her face nestled in the fur of his chest. The sun was just rising, the warm rays streaming through the window onto the carpet where they lay.

"Are you all right?" he whispered.

She stirred, but did not answer.

"Jeena?" He felt her tremble in his arms. "What's wrong? Are you crying? I'm sorry if I did something wrong. This is all very new to me. Jeena, please say something. I need to know what you're feeling."

She lifted her head from his chest. Her eyes were gleaming, and her lips were set tight in a wide smile. She seemed to be battling a wave of laughter that was threatening to burst from her. The effort proved too much, and the dam broke.

"Oh, I see. You're laughing, not crying," he said, relieved but confused. "Well, that's good. I mean, laughing is better than crying, isn't it?"

Jeena's efforts to still her mirth only made it worse.

"Actually, now that I think about it, I don't think you're supposed to be laughing, either."

She threw her hand over her mouth as the intensity of the laughter increased.

"Um...Yeah. Listen, maybe I should point out that I'm feeling extremely vulnerable and unsure of myself right now, and your laughing isn't helping. In fact, I'm real close to crawling into a fetal position. Could you at least stop laughing long enough to tell me if you're all right?"

Jeena finally got the fit of laughter under control enough to speak.

"No, I'm not all right. I am so much better than all right, and I'm laughing because I was just as nervous and unsure as you were."

"And now?" he asked gently.

She closed her eyes and laid her head against his chest.

"And now I am more sure than ever that here is where I belong, by your side."

They slept until late in the morning, then awoke to lie in the warmth of the sun and spoke of the events of the last few months.

"You said you would tell me what happened to you when we had time to be together," Jeena said. "Well, it looks like we have some time, so start talking."

Samson told her of the first time he had felt the mind-link, when they were lost in the snows of the Azulz.

"I felt it again when I tried to get the tigra to leave the Intawa's hunting grounds, but I couldn't seem to get a grip on what it was."

"Why didn't you say anything about this before?"

"Say what—that I thought my species was telepathic? I've read about the studies your people have performed over the years. Telepathy claims have a very sordid history in human science. You'd have laughed in my face."

Jeena smiled. "Yes, I suppose I would have."

He explained about the dead tigra she and David had found, and of his error in trying to contact the animal through conscious thought. He told of the days of trial and error until he had finally gained the ability to reach into the mind-link at will.

"What is it like?" she asked.

"Chaotic. It's a whirlwind of noise out there. If I relax, I can pick up the minds of every animal around but all at once, jumbled and incoherent. Only recently have I become adept enough to isolate an individual, though it isn't very informative, mostly just feral images—hunting and eating and mating, with no real thoughts other than those of want and need."

"This is incredible. What you've done is nothing short of remarkable."

"No, it's nothing. I can communicate, and they can understand me, after a fashion, but they cannot yet reason. I can control them, but I can't give them understanding. I can't return sentience to them."

She kissed him gently. "You realize you really are Shahaiya now, don't you? Lord of the Tigras."

"Lord of a dying race, perhaps," Samson replied. "They're still doomed, Jeena. Unless I can find a way to restore their sentience, they are still doomed to life as dumb beasts, stumbling blindly toward extinction on their own planet."

When all had been made ready, the trial of the Rosh-dan council began. The commanders assembled in the main hall of the Temple of Anil. Ghannon and

Bernd, who had made himself Selanja's unofficial aide-de-camp, brought in the prisoners and had them kneel before the tribunal. This consisted of Selanja for Uruk, as well as a representative from each city in the Confederacy. At the the end of the table sat Samson. It had been decided that Jeena, acting for the Union, would sit as adjudicator.

She stood and spoke to the prisoners, all of whom save Jacob trembled in fear.

"Before you sit the representatives of the Babylonian Confederacy, against whom you have waged an unjust war. It is they who shall determine your fate. It is just that they do this, for as an aggrieved people, they have both the right and the duty to judge their oppressors." She took a document from the table and read it. "These are the crimes of which you have been found guilty: of instigating an illegal and wrongful war in violation of your Union charter; of ordering the torture and murder of innocent people, guiltless of any crime; of direct interference with CIAO and the falsification of the Five-Year Survey. For all of these crimes the sentence on any world would be death."

The elders bowed their heads, some prostrating themselves on the floor. Only Jacob remained steady, staring defiantly at her, hatred still burning in his eyes.

Selanja stood.

"But it is not the way of the Confederacy to take life. Life—any life—is precious to us, and we will not violate our beliefs, even to avenge our dead. However, the power you have shown over your own people is too great to be allowed to continue. It was through your lies and propaganda that you were able to create an atmosphere of hatred between our nations, and we will not risk your return.

"Therefore, the sentence of this tribunal against the Elder Council of the Rosh-dan is imprisonment in the city of Umar, far to the south, there to live out the remainder of your lives."

Many of the elders saw the mercy in this sentence and thanked them profusely, their faces still pressed to the floor. Only Jacob still wore a sneer of distain on his lips.

Jeena moved to stand before him.

"In addition, you, Jacob, K'laq of the Rosh-dan, are held responsible for ordering the continued genocide of an innocent species, the native sentient race of Ararat—the tigras. For such a brutal and heartless crime no adequate punishment exists, but luckily your fate does not fall to me. You committed this atrocity against another race, and it is to them that you will answer."

Samson stood erect and walked slowly from the table, his steps measured, his eyes locked with Jacob's, until he stood only an arm's length from the kneeling man. Neither spoke as they beheld each other for the first time since the altar of New Jerusalem.

"So, it is thee who will sentence me, eh, beast?" Jacob finally spat.

Samson nodded once.

"And am I then to tremble before thee? Bah! I think not. Kill me if it be thy desire—I expect nothing less from an animal such as thee. But it changes nothing. Thy miserable race is doomed. My only regret is that my blade was not quicker at the altar. Do it, then, and be done! I did not hesitate to kill thy people, and I would kill thee now—thee and that whore who made thee what thou art."

Samson roared, the sound shaking the temple walls. His fangs snapped down, and his arm swept back. Five claws, sharper than razors, gleamed icy-white from his fingertips.

Jacob grinned, stretching out his neck to meet the blow.

Samson let his arm fall to his side. His fangs slowly retracted.

"No," he said, shaking his head. "No, Jacob, I will not kill you like this, unarmed and defenseless. I will not become like you and give in to my hate. I have grown beyond you. I give you back your life, and I give your fate back to the Babylonian people. Let them keep you in their prison, and may you live long and miserably in your confinement."

Turning his back, he went to Jeena and embraced her.

With a strangled cry, Jacob sprang, pushing aside a guard and grabbing his sword. He lunged at the embracing couple. Instinctively, Ghannon and Bernd drew their swords and swung, both blades meeting above Jacob's shoulders at the neck. The body fell headless to floor, the stolen sword clanging beside it.

Jeena ordered the shocked and horrified elders, some of whom had soiled themselves, away to begin their long journey to Umar. Jacob's body was removed, to be buried in an unmarked grave—none wished to make his final resting place a rallying point for the remaining Rosh-dan. To the surviving soldiers they offered amnesty and the opportunity to return home, provided they lay down their weapons and swear oaths never to take up arms again. The offer was readily accepted.

With the dispersion of the Rosh-dan, Samson sent the tigras back to their lands in the north.

"There is not enough game for them here, and it is too dangerous to have so many in close contact with man, though this was once their land, too."

Now that the matter of the enemy was resolved and the repairs to the city well under way, Jeena and Samson had time for each other. They used it to catch up on the months they had been separated.

She told Samson of the ride to Uruk and of the battle of the Bacchian Fields, describing the heroic deeds of all the commanders but saying little of her own activities. She spoke of all the people she had met and befriended in Uruk, and of the sorrow of losing Halamesh and Sargon. She did not shrink from relating the events of the night she had shared with Selanja and Sargon, and watched for his reaction, but he only smiled and said he was glad she had found happiness and healing. If tigras were prone to jealousy, she could see none in him.

"You know, there was a time when I didn't want you to meet other humans," he said. "I was so afraid of losing you. But now I see how much the time here has helped you. You are so much...I don't know—lighter. You almost glow."

She smiled. "I have a long way to go, but you're right, I'm happier than I've ever been. But what about you? Whatever happened to the frightened cub I once knew? You've grown, Samson. You've become a leader, strong and confident."

He moved next to her on the couch and put his arm around her.

"Oh, that cub is still here in some ways, but he's no longer afraid and ashamed. I've spent most of my life ashamed of what I was, and afraid I might never become more.

"I'm not ashamed anymore, Jeena. I'm a tigra, one of the last of an old and noble race. A terrible thing happened to my people, but it doesn't take away from what they were, or what they might become again. And I'm no longer afraid. If I never become more than they were, then I will consider myself lucky—and proud."

She nestled her head against his chest. She understood now what Selanja had felt for Sargon—Samson was her soul mate in a way no human could ever be. He was her *ibru*.

The funeral for the Regent was held in the sacred burial chamber of the Temple of Ishtar, the cleanup of which was now complete but the repairs just beginning. Several people spoke, including Aramis, her daughter and a shimhatu of high rank within the temple. She spoke of Elaina not as regent, but in her role as mother and teacher.

Jeena was also asked to speak.

"In the long life she lived, my time with her was only a moment, but it is one I will always cherish. She loved all of you, and made me see the beauty and splendor of your city and your culture. She made me a citizen of Uruk, and no greater gift could I have asked for."

There was little weeping and many smiles, for Elaina had lived a long and happy life and had died the way she had lived—in defense of the city she loved.

With the burial of the regent, the time for Jeena's training began.

JEENA SAT BACK ON HER HEELS, SLOWLY OPENING HER EYES AND STEADYING HERSELF WITH A few deep breaths. Across from her sat Aramis, also kneeling. She was much like her mother, with the same steel-gray eyes and dignified bearing.

"That was hard," Jeena said, stretching the muscles of her neck.

"Yes, you went very deep that time. You have made much progress in only a week. Your mind is as agile as it is strong."

They were kneeling on the bare ground of a cliff overlooking the southern outskirts of Uruk. A low rumble of thunder rolled lazily in the east; the rainy season would be here soon.

They had encamped here three weeks ago with few provisions and no tent. Aramis explained that the secrets of the temple could only be mastered by those who had first obtained true inner knowledge, something that required total concentration and no distractions. With Aramis as her guide, Jeena was exploring her own psychological makeup. It had been easy enough at first—she had undergone multiple psychological tests during her training in the Corps, and thought she knew herself pretty well. She accepted that her difficulty in forming close personal ties was due to her abandonment as a child, and that the adrenaline rush she so craved in her younger years was simply a substitute for the emotions she would not allow herself to feel.

Then, Aramis forced her to delve deeper, dredging up dark and brooding feelings she had not known she had—needs, dreams and desires that shocked her and caused her shame. Aramis patiently helped her through these feeling, explaining that they were present in everyone.

"There is a dark room in each of our minds, Jeena, a place where we lock away those feelings and images too vile and horrible to acknowledge, even to ourselves. But they are a part of who you are, as much as any part of you. To deny them gives them power. You must confront even the darkest part of yourself, for only then can you understand it and the processes that gave it birth. With understanding comes mastery, and with mastery comes freedom."

Aramis regarded the women before her. Hers had not been an idle compliment—Jeena had come impossibly far in only a few weeks, reaching places in her mind that few shimhatu had dared to face.

Yet, she knew there was a deeper place, a sealed room in Jeena's mind that held...something. *What was it Mother saw? Whatever it was, its power was truly frightening.* She could feel its radiating strength even from a distance. It was no wonder Jeena refused to look there.

But that day would come; the future was moving along the path her mother had set. However, the new age did not begin with the war's end. The war was immaterial, nothing more than an event to bring the Deliverer and the Beast to Uruk. These were simply the labor pains. The true birth of the age of Ishtar had yet to occur, and before it did, Jeena must be made strong enough to control the power within her.

Thunder rolled again. Today would be their last one here. It was time to return to Uruk and continue her training.

"We shall leave for Uruk in the morning. Selanja has given us permission to use one of the training rooms in the Temple of Anil until our own temple repairs are complete. You have only taken the first small step. The real work of training has not yet begun."

"Somehow, I knew you were going to say that. How long does the training take?" Jeena asked.

Aramis sighed. "You still cling to old concepts. What is time but a yardstick by which to measure the journey? If you begin walking now, you will reach so far in a year, and farther still a year hence. How far will you have traveled in a lifetime? So it is with Ishtar. The discovery has only begun."

"Well, you've certainly inherited your mother's gift of vagueness. And what, exactly, am I supposed to discover?"

"That is simple. The knowledge of who you are."

"I see. And what will I do once I've discovered that?"

"Master it."

Chapter 28

"As you know I have performed the Nihn-Psi, that art which allows us to feel the essence of another, and have touched the inner being of she who is called Jeena Garza. Let no other attempt this again, for in her lies a power beyond all imagining, a burning fire that has almost consumed me, and even now I am not free of the pain. She is not aware of, nor is she ready to believe in, this power. But she must be made to accept it and learn to control it. You must teach her. Do not fail, for the fate of two species rest in her hands."

> Last written instructions of Elaina, Regent of Uruk, to her daughter Ararmis

THE RAINY SEASON BEGAN, BUT THE CITYWIDE REPAIRS CONTINUED UNABATED, WITH skilled craftsmen from all over the Confederacy lending their services. They knew Uruk had suffered the wounds of war for them all. Soon, scaffolding and protective tarps blanketed the city, and the sounds of repairs could be heard on almost every street.

The basement levels of the Temple of Ishtar were found to be undamaged, much to the relief of the shimhatu, for it was here that the ancient texts and manuscripts of their religion were housed. These were removed and stored in temporary storage facilities in the Temple of Shamash.

Samson had become an instant celebrity among the Babylonians. The story of his youth with Jeena in the desert, together with his last-minute deliverance of Uruk, combined to create a tale of mythic proportions. Enthusiastic crowds greeted him wherever he went. Some even suggested building a temple in his honor, an idea he politely but firmly quashed. As the rains drizzled on, however, the novelty began to wear off; and eventually, he was able to stroll the sodden streets reasonably unmolested.

With Jeena immersed in the training of the shimhatu, he decided to continue his own studies. All of the temples were honored to open their libraries to him, and he was soon spending most of his days with his nose buried in some book. These were not holo-books but genuine paper-and-print tomes. He loved the feel and smell of the ancient volumes, but did miss the accompanying pictures the other format provided.

From the Temple of Ea he learned of the physical and mental development of the human child, and was pleased to find that it mirrored his own in many ways. In the Library of Shamash he studied the development of human law and logic, from Aristotle and Boole through to the latest works of Francis Saleen.

At the Temple of Anil he enlisted the help of Ghannon in studying military strategy. For the next week, Ghannon scratched his head in amazement as Samson breezed through the books he provided. He seemed to take in whole pages at a time, and remembered everything he read.

Samson arrived at the temple one day to find Ghannon before a table on which he had placed figures representing a primitive army. A small pile of identical pieces sat nearby.

"What's this?" he asked.

"A test. I have set my pieces in a battle formation. I wish to see how you would align your men in response."

Samson studied the display for a few minutes then began placing the foot soldiers, chariots and archers rapidly in position. When he finished, he looked up expectantly.

Ghannon frowned. "That is not the defense I would have expected from you."

"Sorry, I may have gotten it wrong. I thought you had your men up to represent the Athenians in the Battle of Marathon, 490 B.C. in the old Earth reckoning."

Ghannon looked up with a start. "Yes, that is correct. But yours is not the Persian response."

"Um...well, no. They lost that battle. I thought this might give them a better chance."

Ghannon stared at him a moment longer before studying the arrangement again.

"I see. Hmm…interesting."

Each day that week Samson arrived at the temple to find that Ghannon had prepared a new strategy problem for him to solve, representing battles from antiquity to the present. In each case, his solutions were unique, workable and very effective.

On the last day, Ghannon reviewed Samson's latest alignment, shaking his head over his solution to the problem of boson field generators.

"Your mind for strategy is remarkable. You seem to have the ability to see the entire battle as a whole. There is no more I can teach you, though General Garza could no doubt expand your knowledge." He looked wistfully at the tigra. "You know, you could earn the Sword of Anil in a short time if you so desired."

Samson glanced at the golden sword dangling from the man's left nipple. He had no such appendage himself, but all the alternative sites he could think of were equally sensitive.

"Ahh…thank you, Ghannon, but I really only took this up as an intellectual exercise."

IN A SEPARATE ROOM IN THE SAME TEMPLE, JEENA STOOD NAKED BEFORE THREE SHIMHATU of the sixth rank, Aramis among them.

"Very good, Jeena," said the eldest. "Let us try another. The third left intercostal muscle."

Jeena closed her eyes, concentrating. A short moment later the three examiners could see the small muscle between the two ribs contract.

For weeks she had been learning to control her body, using methods the followers of Ishtar had passed down for generations. Although she was nowhere near the skill level of the highest rank of shimhatu, she had progressed rapidly.

She also now understood how the shimhatu had gained their reputation for sexual prowess. She was certain some of the techniques she was mastering could bring a man to his knees in pleasure. The thought made her smile.

"I am happy to see you are enjoying your training," Aramis said.

She opened her eyes to see all three smiling back at her.

"I'm sorry. I was just thinking—"

"Yes, we know where your thoughts were," Aramis replied. "Remember, we were once novices ourselves. And you are correct, our training does give one a certain power over the men of our species—a power that should never be abused."

They all managed to retain an air of dignity for a few seconds before breaking out in riotous laughter.

AFTER THREE LONG MONTHS, THE RAINY SEASON FINALLY ENDED. SAMSON HAD WORKED HIS way through most of the temples and was now studying at the Temple of Ishtar. He had brought several books back to their apartment and was lying on the carpet reading them. Jeena lay next to him. Between her training and his studying, they had seen little of each other.

"Aramis tells me you're just about finished in the library," she said.

"I am. That's it," he replied, pointing to the small stack of volumes on the floor.

"So, what are you going to start on next?"

He closed the book he had been reading and rolled over.

"I've been thinking that it's time for me to leave. I still have to find a way to help my own people."

"Samson, I'm sorry. I've been so busy with my training I forgot all about the tigras. Do you know what you're going to do?"

"Not precisely. I need to talk to Mordachi and the scientists in Pyros. I know the tigras are telepathic, and that somehow that is connected with their downfall, but I need their help to fill in the details and, hopefully, find a solution."

"That's a big problem you're tackling," she said, "but I can't help but feel optimistic these days. The rains have stopped. I'm ready to head north whenever you are."

Samson smiled. "I don't remember inviting you. You still have your training with Aramis to finish—though for the life of me I don't know what she's trying to accomplish. Anyway, this problem doesn't require your presence, only the scientists in Pyros."

"Quit trying to give me the slip, fur ball. They've been pushing me hard these last few months. Even Aramis says I need a rest. Besides, this works out perfectly. The last of David's men has been released from the hospital, and they're making arrangements to return. We can all go back together."

David was thrilled to hear that Jeena and Samson would be accompanying him and his men, especially since he and Sarah had decided to marry on their return.

"David, that's wonderful," Jeena exclaimed. "She's a lucky girl."

"Thank you, but the luck is mine. I suppose I've known for some time how I feel about her, but I always hesitated in taking it further. The war kind of put things into perspective."

"War usually does." She leaned forward and kissed him.

"Hey, I'm almost a married man."

"Don't remind me. You know in a Babylonian ceremony the bride gets the groom last?"

"Really? Hmmm. No, stop, I'm joking! I wouldn't survive. No, I think we'd better make this an old-fashioned Pyros wedding."

On hearing the news of David's impending nuptials, Selanja decided to accompany them to Pyros with a contingent to honor the ceremony. Ghannon would remain to run the temporary government. Bernd, as always since the death of Sargon, elected to stay at Selanja's side.

Jeena questioned her concerning the new closeness of the pair.

"He is *tappu*—heart friend—and no more," she replied. "Sargon remains my ibru. Bernd understands this and is content."

The company was arrayed in full battle gear at the recently repaired gates; wagons held those too injured to ride. The people of Uruk had returned to their homes following the war's end and now stood gathered in final farewell.

Selanja spoke with Ghannon.

"I will return in three months. The palace should be completed by then and ready for the new regent's coronation."

He kissed her farewell. "We will await your return, tappu."

David gave the signal and the army of Pyros, now less than a third of those who had entered the city, marched in glorious array through the gates. People stood on the walls and leaned from the windows of nearby buildings and cheered, raining a downpour of confetti and flowers over them as they passed.

Jeena rode with Samson striding near her at the rear of the procession. Although she was sure he could learn to ride, he steadfastly refused the offer of a kytar.

"I'll leave the same way I came—walking," he said.

A great cheer went up as they passed through the gates. The legend of their deeds had only grown during their stay, and they were loved and respected by the people as much for their gentleness of spirit as for their heroic rescue of their city.

THE GROUP MADE ITS WAY AT A SLOW, STEADY PACE THROUGH THE FIELDS TO THE EDGE OF the western desert, filling the days talking and laughing and sharing tales of their adventures together. Two weeks out, they sat around a warm fire, discussing the future of Ararat and watching the light display in the night sky.

"It's so beautiful, and so much more lively than any aurora I've ever seen," Jeena said.

"I'm not surprised. It's Ararat's odd magnetic field," David explained. "I'm told it fluctuates in a very complicated pattern. I saw a tracing of it in school once. Damnedest thing—looked to me like a brainwave scan."

"Whatever the cause, it's just one more thing that makes Ararat so special," Jeena said. "Which reminds me, what will happen now that the Afridi are defeated? I don't mean to insinuate anything, but it has been my experience that power vacuums rarely last for long."

"If you mean do we in Pyros have any plans to take control of New Jerusalem or the other Afridi lands, the answer is no, but I cannot speak for Babylon."

Selanja frowned. "We have no claims on them, nor do we wish for more than we have."

"I understand, but your two governments may want to reconsider their policies. The Afridi have violated their Union charter. One or both of you could make legitimate claims on them."

"Yes, but why would we do that, Jeena?" David asked.

"Political and military stability, for one thing. Let's be frank—the Roshdan may be defeated, but none of us has any idea of who will be in charge when the remains of their army returns. I hate the idea of occupation as much as you do, but I'm not sure just leaving them alone is the best policy. What do you think, Samson? The tigras have claims as well. Samson?"

"Hmmm? What? Oh, I'm sorry, I wasn't really following the discussion. Whatever you decide is fine with me," he said, and returned to mulling over whatever it was that had engaged him.

THE FOLLOWING MORNING THEY CONTINUED NORTH, PASSING ONLY A FEW MILES FROM Jeena and Samson's old campsite. The two decided to take a detour and visit it again, telling the others they would catch up later.

They reached the crash site, and Jeena dismounted, standing next to Samson and staring at the broken remains of the windblown and overgrown camp.

"Can it really have been only a year? It seems like a lifetime ago," she said.

"In some ways it was." Samson stood and put his arm around her. "Do you know that in all the time we've known each other I've never thanked you for taking me in when I was lost and alone? Thank you, Jeena, thank you for everything." He felt her tremble in his grasp and turned to see a tear run down her cheek. "What's wrong?"

"There is something I have to tell you, but I am so afraid you will hate me after."

"You know that's not possible."

"Don't say that until you hear. Samson, you weren't lost, and you weren't abandoned. It was me."

"I know."

"No, you don't. Listen. I was the one—"

"Jeena, I *know*. I know it was you who killed her."

She looked up at him, and tears streamed her face. "You know? How?"

"I've known for a very long time. It was her scent that drew me to your camp, not the food. I could still smell it on the mound under the ship's wing for months. As I got older, it didn't take much to put it all together."

She laid her head against his chest. "I've lived in fear for so long of telling you the truth. Please forgive me," she whispered.

"I do, and I know you had no choice, and that you have been carrying around the burden of that guilt for too long. How could you have known? You were marooned on an alien planet, alone and scared. It wasn't your fault.

"Even after I reasoned what had happened, I never wanted to bring it up. I was ashamed of her, Jeena. I was ashamed of being born to an animal. But I'm not ashamed anymore. She did all she could for me in the only way she knew. I never really knew her, but I think I would like to say goodbye to her now."

Jeena watched as he sat beside the mound, now covered in green grass, with lowered head. He spoke soft words that she could not hear then kissed the ground.

"Are you okay?" she asked, when he returned.

"Yes. I've needed to say those words for a long time. You see, you're not the only one who has needed to be forgiven."

They turned to leave the camp when something from under the flapping remains of the tent caught Jeena's eye. She went over to it and picked up a reddish object and dusted it off. It was a small clay tablet with a handprint imbedded in it, and in the center of the hand was a tiny pawprint.

They caught up with the rest of the company before nightfall. They said little of their visit to the camp, but stayed close to each other near the fire; and Jeena's hand never left Samson's.

AFTER MANY DAYS RIDE, THEY FINALLY CAME TO THE PASS THAT HAD ALMOST CLAIMED

Jeena's life, and then onto the rich fields before the great mountain city of Pyros. A boy saw their approach and raced to the huge bell, swinging at it with the hammer. Again and again the bell tolled as people poured from the city gates, running to them and letting out a great cry, until they were surrounded by a cheering and shouting throng. Many a brave man who had not shed a tear throughout the sorrow and death of war now wept openly to be back among his family.

Mingled in with the shouts of joy were the tears and mourning of those whose loved ones would never return.

Mordachi stepped through the crowd and greeted David. He embraced him long, and when he released him there were tears in his eyes. He looked out over the men and women dismounting and celebrating with their families.

"So few?" he asked sadly.

"Yes," David replied. "Many gave all they had so that we might live free. They lie now in honor with the fallen of Uruk, in the hollowed ground of the Bacchian Fields."

"Then let them lie there in peace, where they sacrificed so much. Our people will wish to visit them, though, to pay tribute to their memories."

Selanja had been standing near David and now stepped forward.

"That they may do, sir, as many and as often as they wish. Your people will always be welcome in Uruk, where they are held as dear to us as our own."

"Mordachi, this is Selanja, commander of the Babylonian army and head of the interim government of Uruk," David said.

"It is an honor, Commander," Mordachi replied, bowing and taking her hand. "It has been too long since I last visited your fair city."

"The honor is mine, sir. For what your people sacrificed in our defense, there are no adequate words of thanks. Now that the need for secrecy is ended and the way between our cities safe, I hope there will be much visiting between our peoples."

Jeena had dismounted and stood near Samson. Mordachi saw them and smiled.

"I see you two have found each other again. I suppose there is more than luck in that, but I do not have the wisdom to put a name to it. I am glad to see you again, Samson. When I last saw you at the city gates, with an army of tigras behind you, I thought this old mind had finally snapped. Then, when they returned without you, I feared the worst. Tell me, did you find what you were looking for? Out there in the lands of your people?"

"I think so, Mordachi. It is because of them that I've returned to speak with you," he replied.

"We will be happy to assist you in any way we can. It seems your people have now had a chance to avenge themselves on those who sought to annihilate them. In that we have played a part, though at great cost. I hope our sacrifices have helped to wash away the stain of our indifference for so many years."

Samson stood and, to the surprise of the old man, embraced him warmly.

"That error is well paid for my friend, and I thank you with all my heart for those who cannot speak. Now, though, I think a new era has begun. I've come to ask for your help again. I believe I know what happened to my race, and I think I may have stumbled upon a way to reverse it."

Chapter 29

The electromagnetic field, while stable, fluctuates in an unusually dynamic but repetitive pattern (see graph 17). The cause of this phenomenon is unknown and warrants further study, should time permit.

> Detail from the Five-Year Survey report on the planet Ararat

SAMSON ROSE TO SPEAK. AT HIS REQUEST, MORDACHI HAD SET UP A MEETING WITH THEIR best scientists. Mordachi had introduced him, but in truth, there was none present who had not heard of the great tigra.

"I want to first thank you all for coming. I know that for most of you, this will your first experience in speaking with a non-human, but I hope that as we work together, the novelty will wear off."

He smiled warmly at the faces around the table, but only David and Mordachi grinned openly back.

"All of you here have worked for years on the problem that concerns us today, so I won't belabor you with a long introduction. The primary question is this: What caused the sudden decline of the tigra race? Specifically, why did they lose their ability to write before all other aspects of their culture? I believe I have at least a partial answer."

The scientists leaned forward intently. For many, this was a problem to which they had devoted their lives.

"What was it you discovered, Samson?" Jason prompted.

"Just this. The tigras do communicate, but not with words. They are telepathic."

There were murmurs and guffaws from the assembled scientists. Some openly laughed. Telepathy was the Flying Dutchman of science—claims had been made for centuries purporting its existence, but none had ever survived the light of scientific experimentation.

Samson waited until the commotion died down before continuing.

"Believe me, I am quite aware of the history of telepathic claims, but make no mistake—this is no theory. I have done it. I used this method of communication to control forty thousand tigras and lead them to war at the gates of Uruk." He leaned across the table, his golden eyes aglow. "And if my words are not enough to convince you, then there are a hundred thousand Rosh-dan lying dead by their paws in the Bacchian Fields as testament to its truth."

The laughter faded as they saw the grimness in his eyes.

"But, Samson, even assuming this is true, how does it explain the tigras' history?" Levi asked.

"That's the wonder of it, Levi, that such a potential boon could be so disastrous. How long has mankind searched for telepathy, dreaming of the great benefits that could be achieved if only ideas could be shared instantly and precisely, mind-to-mind?"

"True, we've always been seduced by the idea of telepathy. It would certainly improve communication. You would lose all the ambiguity inherent in words," Mordachi said. "I would imagine you could glean great insight by bringing together all the great minds of an age."

"Perhaps, and maybe that's the way it would begin. But consider—once telepathy became the preferred method of communication, why would a race even need speech? Were that to happen, how long would it take for language itself to fall into disuse, slowly to be forgotten? A thousand years? Five thousand?"

"I think I see what you mean," Mordachi said slowly. "Telepathy would be so much more efficient than speech that eventually it would supplant it completely."

Samson nodded. "And what is writing but the symbolic representation of the spoken word?"

"So, the art of writing disappears with the spoken word," Jason said, thinking aloud. "All right, I can buy that, but why would that cause the collapse of civilization? You're not eliminating communication, just improving the method."

"Unfortunately, it is the method that is the problem," Samson continued. "The sentient mind is incredibly complex, and utilizes concepts that we take for granted yet cannot even precisely define—consciousness and self-awareness, for example. What happens when the telepathic process within a species becomes so complete that all thoughts are shared instantly with every individual? Imagine a child born into such a society. Where does its mind begin and those of the others end?"

"I see," said Jason, beginning to grasp the line of reasoning. "They would essentially become one thinking organism—a collective individual."

"Correct. And I fear that is what happened to my people. The tigra civilization died out because it stopped being a civilization at all. Civilization implies plurality, individuality, yet this was the very thing they had lost."

"Interesting theory. And the slide into primitivism?" Mordachi asked.

"I believe that as their minds became more firmly fused, they began to connect at ever deeper and more primitive levels. I've joined with them. They are not self-aware. There is a tiny spark of conscious thought remaining in them, but they no longer have the ability to tap into it. Their thoughts are of only the most basic and primitive emotions. But primitive as it is, it is a powerful force, and it takes a strong, conscious effort to pull away from the whirling vortex of images and feelings.

"And therein lies the trap. The more deeply their minds melded, the more of their own individuality they lost. Without a strong individual psyche, none had the strength of will to separate from the group. It became a downward spiral, ultimately bringing them to what we see today—feral animals."

The room had become quiet.

"How terribly sad," Mordachi said.

"Yes, it is. I believe that once the process began the outcome was inevitable. I think any species would have succumbed, even man."

"Your hypothesis certainly answers a lot of questions. But what about you?" Jason asked. "Why weren't you affected?"

"Circumstance and luck. Remember that my mother had wandered far to the south of the last remaining tigra population left on Ararat. When she died my only mental link to the collective psyche of the tigras was broken, and at an early age. With no mental interference, I was able to develop my own individuality under Jeena's influence. Ironic, isn't it? Jacob's total elimination of my race in the south made it possible for me to become what I am, something that eventually led to his own destruction."

"But what caused these telepathic powers?" Jason asked. "The tigras had developed an advanced society long before this catastrophe, so it certainly wasn't something native to the species. Have you any idea what happened?"

"That is the question I have puzzled over since discovering the tigras' mental connection. Whatever it was, it had to have affected the entire planet more or less at the same time, or they would have simply moved out of its area of influence. No, it had to be both universal and unstoppable."

"And you know what that was, don't you?" Mordachi asked.

Samson smiled. "Actually, it was David who gave me the answer."

David looked startled "Me? I can't imagine how."

"You told me once that Ararat's magnetic field was very strange. You said it resembled a brainwave pattern."

"Well, yes...at least it did to me. But, Samson, I was only talking in generalities."

"Samson, I have studied the planet's magnetic field for many years," said a scientist. "They do have a cursory resemblance to neuro-fields, but they really aren't the same."

"Not the same as a *human's*, you mean. I'd be surprised if they were, considering man is not telepathic on Ararat. But tell me, have you ever recorded a tigra's neuro pattern?"

The room fell silent. Mordachi slapped the table.

"Of course! How stupid of us not to see it before. But is that possible?"

Samson shrugged. "You tell me. What are brainwaves but electromagnetic impulses? Is it possible to use one energy wave as a carrier for another?"

A scientist nodded. "Theoretically, yes, if they are in phase."

"That's what I thought. I think that if you look, you will find that tigras generate a neuro field virtually identical to Ararat's magnetic field, and in phase. I believe something caused a major disturbance in Ararat's magnetic field some five thousand years ago. I think that towards the end the tigras must have come to the same conclusion. This mountain, Pyros, must have been a last, desperate attempt to shield what was left of their unaffected population from the field's influence. Of course, in the end, it made no difference."

The table was silent. Mordachi looked at the faces of the astounded scientists, a slow smile appearing on his face.

"Samson, I think you've done it. You've solved the riddle."

The table exploded in a din of voices as each scientist began to propose experiments to verify Samson's theory.

He raised his paw. "You are all welcome to proceed with any experiments you see fit as long as they don't injure or endanger the tigras. For myself, I am satisfied that this is the answer. I did not come here to prove anything. What I am interested in is something a bit more tangible. I want nothing less than to find a way to eliminate the cause and bring the tigras back to sentience."

"You want to change Ararat's magnetic field?" asked one scientist in disbelief.

"Yes. The pattern is probably changing subtly over time anyway, but the process could take centuries to complete, and I can't wait that long. I am proof that once the mental connection is broken my species can regain what they have lost. My question, then, is a simple one—Can it be done?"

One of the senior scientists scratched his head.

"Planetary fields are always changing and evolving, but they do so in response to changes in the planet's core and solar forces. To deliberately alter one..." He whistled. "It would be an enormous undertaking."

Samson nodded. "I understand, but that is the project I intend to pursue. I don't expect miracles. I understand that to accomplish this—if it's possible at all—could take years."

"At least," the scientist mumbled, but he was already scratching out equations on a tablet.

Chapter 30

Carborillium: Metal synthesized in a complex process involving massive pressure and neutrino bombardment of osmium. Its main use is as a protective coating in the singularity cells of hyperdrives. It is not found in nature.

Encyclopedic History of the Union, 22nd ed.

THE PREPARATIONS FOR DAVID AND SARAH'S WEDDING PROCEEDED, WITH ALL OF PYROS anxiously awaiting the day. Jeena had become the unofficial coordinator of events and even threw Sarah's bachelorette party, the details of which David had the good sense not to inquire about. There were rumors she had instructed Sarah and several others in a few exotic temple pleasure secrets, but this was never proven.

Samson was equally mum concerning David's bachelor party, but was ill with a hangover for two days after.

The day of the ceremony broke bright and warm. Selanja and a phalanx of the Babylonian army in full battle dress led Sarah from the city gates to the top of a hill just beyond the mountain. There, among the wildflowers and in the presence of all the city, the two exchanged vows.

As the wedding ceremony ended, Mordachi pulled David aside.

"Congratulations, David, the two of you will be very happy, I know. I wonder, though, have you given any thought to your future? With the defeat of the Rosh-dan, the need for a fulltime military is questionable. There has been talk that Parliament may disband the army."

"Yes, so I've heard."

"Now that you're married, I imagine children will be coming soon?"

David smiled. "Sarah and I have discussed it, yes."

"And children don't exactly raise themselves, do they?"

"No, they don't. But what are you getting at?"

"Just this. I want to retire. Oh, I'll still work on Samson's project—I owe it to him, and besides, I love the challenge. It's the prime ministry I'm vacating, and I can't think of anyone I'd rather support to take my place, or who is more qualified for the job."

David thanked the old man many times. With his popularity among the people and Mordachi's support, he had an excellent chance of being elected.

Jeena was thrilled to hear of it.

"David, that's wonderful! Pyros couldn't have a better man leading it."

"Well, I haven't won yet, but with Mordachi's support it does look promising."

WORK CONTINUED IN EARNEST ON THE TIGRA PROJECT, AS IT WAS NOW CALLED, WITH ONLY minimal gains. The problem proved to be every bit as difficult as anticipated.

Like all planets, Ararat's magnetic field was a product of its spinning molten core. Ararat's field was so odd it had to imply an extremely unusual core composition, but what that might be, let alone how to change it, was beyond their knowledge and their science.

The only option that remained was to attempt an alteration of the existing magnetic field. As several of the scientists had pointed out, they needn't change it significantly, only enough to disrupt the wave pattern.

However, even this proved to be a daunting task. The field was enormous, encircling the planet and extending outward for thousands of miles. It was also immensely powerful. Little progress was made for many weeks; then one day Mordachi called Samson to meet with the project team.

Mordachi stood at the head of the table, looking tired. A holo-projector displayed a floating image of Ararat with a graphic depiction of its strangely oscillating magnetic field projecting from it like a web of thin, spidery hairs.

"The difficulty has always been the problem's magnitude," he began. "Attempting to change the configuration of a planet-wide phenomenon like a magnetic field requires thinking on a gigantic scale." He pointed to the image of Ararat. "Ideally, we'd like to attack it at its source, the molten core, but that is beyond our abilities at present. However, we think we've come up with a plan of altering it from space that would work."

Samson listened intently.

"What we propose is to place orbiting field generators around the planet, synchronized to generate a wave one hundred and eighty degrees out of phase with Ararat's present pattern." Mordachi worked the projector, and a multitude of tiny black dots appeared above the planet's surface.

"Excellent! And how long would it take to place enough generators to affect a change?" Samson asked excitedly.

Mordachi looked at the faces of the team but was offered no help. He looked down sadly.

"Well, that remains a problem. Even assuming we could get state-of-the-art generators at the power level we need, and assuming we could place them in orbit at the rate of one a week..." He spread his hands in a sign of futility. "Samson, we would need over fifteen hundred machines to effect any real change in the field."

SAMSON MADE A QUICK CALCULATION. AT ONE A WEEK, IT WOULD TAKE THIRTY YEARS. AND that was assuming not only an uninterrupted supply—difficult to guarantee against the backdrop of a civil war—but also the funds to pay for them. The cost would be astronomical.

He stood and addressed the table. "I want to thank you all for all the hard work you've put toward the project. It was a difficult problem, and your finding a solution was more than I dared hope for." He looked at Mordachi. "You've calculated the cost, of course."

The old man nodded. "As a percentage of Pyros's economy, it would require roughly seventy percent over the next thirty years."

"I thought it might be something like that."

The scientists around the table looked away, averting their eyes.

"Please, gentlemen, don't look so sad. You've solved a difficult problem elegantly; it is just beyond our means at present. The tigras have waited forty thousand years for their resurrection; they can wait a bit longer. From my heart, I give you my eternal gratitude for what you tried to do for them, and for me."

JEENA FOUND HIM SITTING IN THE HIGH GRASS NEAR THE WESTERN ENTRANCE OF THE CITY. The sun was sinking low, and his face was radiant in its rays. She sat next to him and ran her hand through the fur on his head.

His eyes shone as he spoke.

"They were wonderful, Jeena. They worked so hard, and all for a species that isn't even aware of their efforts. Of all the qualities I admire in man, it is that gift of empathy you feel toward others less fortunate that is the most remarkable."

"They worked so hard because of you," she said, "because they respect and admire you and all that you've done. I take it they didn't find an answer to your problem?"

"Oh, they found an answer. To help the tigras, all I have to do is ask them to give up two-thirds of all they have for the next thirty years."

At her insistence, he explained the details of the plan.

"Four generators a month—the equivalent of the cost of your transport ship every month—for thirty years," he concluded sadly.

"Or one a day for the next five years."

"Huh? Yeah, well, I guess the math almost works. Why are you grinning like that?"

She unhooked the impe from around her neck and handed it to him.

"Here is payment for your first four generators, my love."

"SAY THAT AGAIN," PAUL SAID. HE STOOD BEHIND HIS DESK, HIS HANDS BALLED IN FISTS.

"Paul, you've been getting robbed by the smugglers," Jeena repeated. "It's why they risk their lives cutting across battle lines to get here. You're trading carborillium for trinkets. Carborillium, Paul! A metal so rare a rock the size of my fist could outfit a frontline star fighter."

He continued to glow crimson. "But they said carborillium was only semi-precious. Barely worth the trip, they said. Just stopping by on the way to more profitable planets, they said."

"Paul, there is no more profitable planet. These space pirates would hyperdrive through an exploding nova to get their hands on these stones, and for a few hundred kilos they'll sell us as many field generators as we need and set them in orbit." She tossed her impe on the desk. "When can you contact them?"

"Pretty much any time I want. They left a narrow-band transmitter set to their frequency. We send a signal when we have stones to trade. But, Jeena, outside of yours, we have no other stones."

She smiled down on Samson sitting at her side. "Ah, but the *gods* are with us."

"ARE YOU SURE WE'RE NOT TAKING ADVANTAGE OF THEM?" SAMSON ASKED AS THEY MADE their way to the Intawa village.

Jeena led her kytar over the thick green grass of the pass.

"Samson, David and Mordachi have agreed to give the Intawa anything they want for the stones, and if they are anywhere near as plentiful as they seem to be, then the Intawa will still have the wealth of whole systems left. Besides, you know they would be happy to help Shahaiya in any way they can."

"And my semata," he added.

She puffed out her chest. "Hey, that's right. After all, I am Nanor's favorite."

"Uh-huh. So, you better have a good explanation for the old man as to why you still haven't produced a tigra-child for the tribe."

She groaned.

As they approached the village they were met by a cheering group of blond-haired children, laughing and singing. Soon the noise attracted the adults, who began pouring out from the j'led. On seeing Jeena and Samson, they joined the happy chorus of voices.

Ewar met them in the clearing, embracing Jeena and bowing to Samson.

"We have joke on mountain people, yes?" he asked, his blue eyes still dancing at the humor of it.

"Yes," Samson agreed. "A very good joke."

"Shahaiya come back to live with Intawa now, keep tigra brothers from hunting grounds?"

"Don't worry, Ewar," Jeena answered. "The tigras will not bother you anymore. Shahaiya will keep them in their own land in the north."

"Ah, this very good. You live with them?"

"Not right away," Samson said, "but I would like to help them, if the Intawa will assist me."

"Intawa always help Shahaiya," he replied. "You come in j'led. We talk."

They sat around the fire with Ewar and the other tribal leaders, including Nanor. He immediately wanted to know how progress on the tigra-child was coming, and was disappointed to learn Jeena was not yet pregnant.

"Shahaiya need Intawa help for tigra brothers," Ewar explained to the group.

"What Shahaiya need?" Anok asked.

Jeena removed her impe, handing it to Ewar. "We need more stones like these, more p'toc. The people of the mountain will give the Intawa anything they want for them."

There were confused looks on the faces of the men. Anok spoke for them.

"P'toc for mountain people, not for Shahaiya?"

Samson realized a more detailed explanation would be necessary.

"The mountain people can help me, but they must have the stones to do it."

"Then we give p'toc to Shahaiya," Anok replied.

The others nodded in agreement.

"But they are very valuable, Anok. The Intawa shouldn't just give them away. You should trade them for things you need."

The Intawa shook their heads. It was one thing to trade with the mountain people for the few metal tools and pots they needed, but they could not bring themselves to barter for something Shahaiya obviously wanted.

AS THE DISCUSSION CONTINUED, JEENA WATCHED NANOR RISE AND GO TO A SHADOWY corner of the j'led. Following him, she saw a small child in a crib, sallow of skin and coughing . Nanor spoke to the child gently, rubbing a bird feather across her brow and reciting a prayer.

"Is she ill?" Jeena asked.

The blue-eyed girl regarded her listlessly.

The old man nodded. "Roots no help. Spirits of plants no listen to old Nanor," he said sadly.

"And that is why you want a new kho'pan so badly, isn't it?"

He looked up at her with tired eyes. "Nanor old. Intawa get sick. No get well. Maybe soon, no more Intawa."

She understood that he felt the health of the tribe was entirely his responsibility. If they were sick, it meant his power was fading, and that put the people in dire danger. Such was the precarious nature of their existence that even a minor increase in the death rate or a drop in the birthrate could prove disastrous.

She touched the old man gently and returned to the fire.

SAMSON WAS FRUSTRATED. HE HAD GAINED NO GROUND IN GETTING THE CHIEFS TO ACCEPT payment for the stones, even from a third party like Pyros.

"Shahaiya need stones, Shahaiya take stones," Ewar insisted indignantly. "Intawa need nothing from mountain people."

Samson sighed as Jeena sat at his side.

"It's hopeless," he muttered.

"Just follow my lead," she whispered back, then focused on Ewar. "So, the chiefs need nothing from the mountain people?" she asked. "Then I guess the chiefs don't care about their people. The chiefs don't care if the Intawa die."

The chiefs exchanged shocked expressions.

Ewar spoke defiantly. "Why semata say this?"

"Because the Intawa people need a kho'pan. Nanor is old; he will not live forever. Why not use the stones to bring a kho'pan from the mountain?"

"What the hell are you doing?" Samson whispered.

Anok looked suspicious. "Mountain people have kho'pan? This is true?"

Jeena stood and addressed the men. "The mountain people have many powerful healers. They do not know the ways of the spirits, but Nanor can teach them, and then they will be kho'pan. But if the chiefs wait too long, then who will be left to teach?"

Nanor had overheard the conversation and came nearer the fire.

"Mountain healer come to village?" he asked excitedly. "Be student to old Nanor?"

"Well, I don't know," Jeena answered vaguely. "A powerful kho'pan is very valuable, yes?"

Ewar and the other chiefs nodded. A kho'pan who could wield his magic and keep the tribe healthy was invaluable.

"Maybe one come to village, maybe for many p'toc? If Shahaiya ask?" Anok ventured. He seemed skeptical that such a worthy could be had for nothing but stones.

"Quite possibly," Jeena answered. "Can you get more like these?" she asked, pointing to her necklace.

Ewar and the others studied them. "These good stones. Not many. Maybe some," Ewar said.

JEENA FELT HER HOPES FALL. MAYBE CARBORILLIUM WASN'T AS PLENTIFUL AS SHE HAD BEEN led to believe. If finding them turned out to be a lengthy process, it could set Samson's plan back many years.

There was more discussion. It was finally decided that Ewar would lead Samson and Jeena to the area known to have the most stones to see what the potential was.

Lying on their bed of carpets and furs later that night, she expressed her concerns.

"I'm worried. It's possible David and the others misunderstood the Intawa traders. Maybe carborillium isn't plentiful here. It may be extremely rare and hard to find."

"I'm almost as worried about what happens if it's not," he admitted. "You just promised these people a Pyros physician. How do you intend to get one to come here?"

"I never promised one would live here, exactly," she said. "All these people need is good medical care. I'm sure Mordachi can arrange for some kind of clinic to be based here. Think of all the illnesses these people suffer that modern medicine could cure. It would be an enormous boon for the tribe."

"It would certainly take away a lot of the uncertainty from their lives. But what was all that about the doctor having to learn from Nanor?"

"I don't want us to destroy their culture while healing their wounds," she explained. "Whoever comes here has to be willing to respect their ways and work within them."

"Assuming anyone comes at all. We haven't found any stones yet," he reminded her.

THEY WALKED STOOPED OVER IN THE AREA WEST OF THE VILLAGE FOR SEVERAL HOURS WITH little luck. Jeena found two very small stones; while they were valuable, they were not nearly enough for their needs.

She straightened her aching back, and watched as Ewar combed the ground. Only Samson felt comfortable, on all fours scanning the dirt between his paws; but he had found nothing yet.

"Okay, guys, let's take a break," she said.

She took a long drink from her canteen then splashed her face before leaning up against a large boulder. Ewar and Samson joined her, Samson sitting down looking dejected.

"I guess p'toc are harder to find than I thought," she said.

"Yes, very hard to find, very rare," Ewar replied.

"Don't get discouraged. Nothing in life comes easy. We'll just have to look a little harder, that's all." She bent to stroke Samson and spilled some of her water on the boulder. It washed away the dirt, revealing a metallic sparkle beneath.

Hey, what the...

Pouring more water over the spot, she rubbed away the dirt. A silver vein gleamed back at her.

"Ewar! Ewar!" She pointed at the spot.

He looked closely at the shiny rock and shrugged.

"But...but it's p'toc!" she exclaimed.

"No, not p'toc." He lifted the stones of her necklace. "P'toc very smooth, very pretty, see?" he asked, as though explaining to a small child. "This rock ugly. We look more." He resumed his search of the near ground.

Jeena slapped her forehead. *Idiot! P'toc isn't the Intawa name for carborillium, only for small weathered stones of the metal. They probably form from pieces that break off larger boulders like this one, and become slowly smoothed by wind and rain. No wonder they're so rare!*

Samson was up beside her now, dancing and laughing around the huge rock.

Ewar shook his head. It was hard to understand a god. Harder still to understand a semata.

Chapter 31

And the angel said to me, "Why do you wonder? I will tell you the mystery of the woman and of the beast that carries her."

Revelation 17:2-4
Arian Christian Bible

JEENA AND SAMSON STOOD BEHIND MORDACHI AS HE WORKED THE SENSORS ON THE DESK-sized monitor before him. The holo screen projected a slowly rotating image of Ararat. Suddenly, a small blinking light appeared above the planet, far in its northern hemisphere. A few minutes later, a second light materialized.

"Well, it's begun," Mordachi said. "They're distributing the generators."

Two months earlier, Paul had contacted the smugglers and started the negotiations. At first they balked about the size of the order and what he offered to pay them, but it soon became clear to them that, somehow, the man had learned the true value of carborillium. Paul made it clear that, for their previous dishonesty, he was ready to contact other smuggling operations if they were unwilling to tackle the project.

The deal was sealed when he presented them with a lump of metal weighing almost half a kilo—advance payment for the first thirty generators, with subsequent payments to be made on delivery. After that they practically fell over themselves agreeing to the conditions.

The industriousness of the black market never ceased to amaze Jeena. Here they were in the midst of a raging civil war, yet these smugglers were "finding" enough high-tech field generators to fill an order that would raise suspicion anywhere in the galaxy—they fell off a space freighter, one smuggler offered in way of explanation. It was true that for the right price anything could be had.

The monitor they were using to verify the generator placements was also provided by the smugglers, and was Paul's idea. Having dealt with these people, he wanted some way to supervise their work. Aware of their own reputation, the smugglers agreed.

After the fifth light appeared, Mordachi stepped aside.

"All right, Paul, it's all yours. Keep an eye on them and run the diagnostic tests as soon as the last one is in place. Oh—and good work."

Feeling somewhat vindicated for his previous fleecing, Paul grinned as he took control of the viewer.

"With a little luck we should have the last of the generators in place in five years," Mordachi told Samson.

"Thank you, Mordachi. None of this would have been possible without you."

"I'm just glad we were able to help." He scratched his chin thoughtfully. "I wonder, though, what we will unleash five years from now."

"I can't say for sure," Samson admitted. "They've been asleep for five thousand years. When the time comes, I'll be here to guide them back to wakefulness, and then we shall see."

"We went by the Intawa clinic last week," Jeena said. "It's wonderful. They've vaccinated the children and have set up health screenings. I even saw Nanor instructing one young doctor in the properties of certain roots. How did you ever talk them into becoming students to a shaman?"

"Oh, it wasn't that hard, really. I merely pointed out that there were undoubtedly plant extracts unique only to Ararat, and that they had a living expert on their use right next door. Throw in new knowledge and a chance to discover a cure for some disease to a group of doctors, and stand back. As if that weren't enough, there was also the added incentive of all the new equipment the extra carborillium was bringing in."

"So, it works out for everyone," Samson said. "That's good."

"Maybe not for everyone. I just received a report today of riots in New Jerusalem. I'm afraid those people are in for some tough times ahead."

"Couldn't happen to a more deserving group," Samson growled.

"They weren't all bad," Jeena said. "Most were just misled. I wonder sometimes what happened to Daniel, the young priest who aided me. I hope he's all right and things work out for him and his people."

"I suppose you're right," he agreed. "My revenge was aimed at the Rosh-dan. I'm satisfied with their destruction."

"So, I guess you two will be leaving soon?" Mordachi asked.

"Yes, Selanja needs to get back and turn over the government to the new regent, though I'll be shocked if she isn't elected," Jeena answered.

"And don't forget, you still have a lot of training to complete," Samson reminded her.

"Well, we will miss you both greatly. Jeena, you should know that I am introducing a bill in Parliament to make you commander-in-chief of the Pyros military—in absentia, of course. I believe Parliament will vote to disband the military, or at least reduce it to a skeleton force, and I would just feel better knowing there was someone to whip us into shape if the need ever arises."

"Mordachi, I would be honored, but I don't ever intend to lead soldiers into battle again."

JEENA WAS HELPING SELANJA AND BERND IN THE STABLES, PREPARING THE KYTARS FOR THE long ride back to Uruk. Samson had gone to visit the tigras three days earlier and was expected back today. The people of Pyros had been wonderful and gracious hosts, but all were anxious to return to their homes. Bernd had decided to go back to Uruk as well, and David had given him his blessing.

"Has Samson decided what he's going to do once we get back?" he asked.

"He's bringing along copies of all the translations of the tigra texts Mordachi and his people have found. He wants to learn the language and perhaps teach it to the others when they awaken," Jeena told him.

"Does he really think he can snap the tigras out of this mind-link?"

"That's the plan, but we won't know anything until the generators are activated."

Selanja was placing a bridle on a kytar when it suddenly began to stomp and whinny. Many of the other animals were acting likewise. They were trying to calm the steeds when Samson walked in.

"Hey, fur ball, nice to see you again," Jeena said, grinning. "You must have gotten a lot of wild tigra scent on you. You usually don't spook the kytars like that."

"Hello, Selanja, Bernd. Ah, Jeena, could I have a word with you outside?"

She followed him out of the stables and into the morning sun.

"So, what's the big secret? Omigod!"

Before her lay nine tigras, lazing in the grass.

"Calm down, calm down," Samson soothed. "I have them under very good control."

"But what are they doing here?"

"That's kind of what I want to talk to you about. I'd like to bring them back to Uruk with me."

She frowned. The animals looked peaceful enough, but...

"Why, Samson? I thought nothing could be done until the field was neutralized."

"To break the connection among *all* the tigras, yes. But I've learned enough to work with a small number, like these nine. I purposely chose only those who demonstrated a high degree of intelligence. If I can separate them from the larger group, I believe I can teach them."

"Why?"

He sighed. "Jeena, in five years I'm going to have more than forty thousand very confused tigras to deal with. I'll need help if I ever hope to help them."

"And you really think you can do this?"

"Yes. In five years I think I can have these nine at my level."

Jeena frowned, not completely convinced. "These guys look peaceful enough, but I don't know."

"Not guys—girls," he corrected. "They're all females."

She laughed. "Oh, I see. You sure you're not just setting up some kind of tigra harem for yourself?"

Samson's ears fell flat to his head and his whiskers bristled.

"Of course not! Females are just easier to control. Of all the...do you really think I would—"

"Oh, don't get your feathers in a ruffle, I'm only teasing. But why all the secrecy? Selanja is in the stable, why don't you just ask her?"

"Well, she *is* the head of Uruk's government for now, and she might have some reservations about having nine wild tigras living in her city. But I was thinking, or rather hoping, that since you were her best friend..." He let the thought trail off, looking up at her with hopeful eyes.

"I get it. You want me to butter her up for you."

He nodded enthusiastically.

"Oh, all right, I'll talk to her. But why do I feel like the madam of a tigra whorehouse?"

Samson closed his eyes and shook his head in exasperation, muttering obscenities under his breath.

As Jeena had expected, his fears were unfounded. Selanja was more than happy to do all she could for him and his people, and had no objection to his entourage.

They set out two days later and were given a rousing sendoff by the people of Pyros. David hugged Jeena long in goodbye.

"It will be quiet not having you around. Don't make it too long between visits."

"I won't, I promise. The way between the cities is safe now, so I expect to see you in Uruk as well. Bring Sarah and give me a chance to corrupt that young wife of yours," she said with a wink.

He turned to Samson. "I suppose you and I will be seeing more of each other."

"Yes, David, I'll be coming up frequently to check on the tigras and monitor the progress of the generator placements."

Selanja started them off. Waving to the assembled crowd, they began their journey back to Uruk. It was a slow and easy trek, with frequent stops. One of these resulted in an impromptu game of z-ball. Jeena and Selanja rolled with laughter as Samson, ball-in-mouth, raced toward the goal line, dragging a prostrate but determined Bernd the entire way.

During the evenings, Samson gathered the nine tigras by the fire to begin their education. As they drew farther from the mental noise of the north, his influence over them grew. The others watched in rapt fascination as he prodded them with his mind to mimic his facial motions, in preparation for the day they would learn to speak. It was a slow and laborious process, but Samson had patience; and soon they could all see improvement.

It was late summer when they finally reached the Bacchian Fields. The horns of the city blew, and a crowd met them at the gates, led by Ghannon.

He kissed Selanja.

"It is good to see you again, tappu," he said.

"Thank you, Ghannon, it is good to be home."

He was startled to see the wild tigras, but she explained their presence and the need to find housing for them. As part of their education, Samson wanted them to live indoors, in as civilized surroundings as possible.

"The final decision must be the regent's," he replied, "but I do not believe that will be a problem. Housing will be found."

He led them to the new palace to meet the newly elected regent, the identity of whom he refused to reveal.

"I will only tell you that she will be as surprised to meet you, as you will be to meet her," he answered cryptically.

The Temple of Ishtar had also been rebuilt, and as they passed they stopped to admire its splendor. It retained its original octagonal shape, but its walls were now of a shimmering red stone, the twin towers capped in ivory marble. The golden dome had been replaced and was now even larger and more glorious. The statue of Ishtar that had graced the foyer of the old temple had been destroyed in the fire, and a new one commissioned. It sat outside the temple in a small courtyard.

Jeena halted abruptly, gaping up at the large figure. As before, the woman representing Ishtar lay on her side propped up on her left elbow, her right hand caressing her breast. But whereas the previous figure had had a generic feminine face, this one was a perfect likeness of her.

It was not just the unexpected shock of seeing her own face on the carving that had struck her dumb, however. Lying behind the woman was a tigra, its paw draped seductively over her shoulder.

"Ghannon..." she began, then realized she had no idea what to say.

"It is as it was commanded by Elaina, General. There were instructions found after her death."

Jeena walked around the huge statue in awe.

"When did she find the time to draw this up?"

"The plans were not recent, General. As near as I could tell they were made almost thirty years ago."

Thirty years ago! I was just born. How did she know? Had she seen all this, even Samson and the destruction of the old temple? *Will the training of the shimhatu give me the power of her vision?*

Ghannon led them past the temple to the palace. The entranceway was alive with shafts of multicolored light radiating through glass panels. A stairway led to the second floor offices and apartments. The door of one large office was engraved with the word REGENT. Ghannon swung the door open.

It was a large, elegant room, finely appointed. On the far side, a highly polished desk sat in front of glass doors that opened onto a balcony. The room was empty.

"Isn't the regent going to meet us here?" Jeena asked.

Ghannon gave a hand signal, and the doors to a side room opened. A group of shimhatu, led by Aramis, entered the office. In her hands, Aramis carried the Scepter of Regency.

They stood before Jeena and bowed as one, even Selanja and Ghannon. Aramis straightened and presented the scepter to her.

Jeena felt the blood rush from her face. "I don't understand."

"Don't you? It is a simple thing," Aramis said. "You have been elected by the people of Uruk to be their regent."

"Elected? But...but I never ran for office."

"Run for office?" Ghannon huffed. "Who in their right mind would ever run for public office? No one runs for office here. They are thrown in kicking and screaming and are usually thankful to have the burden lifted."

She looked wide-eyed at Selanja. "You knew this?"

"Ghannon informed me when we embraced, but in truth, I expected it. There were murmurs among the people for many weeks before we left. You might have heard them yourself had you not been so involved in your studies."

Jeena looked around at the assembly with the expression of a trapped animal. Her gaze fell on Samson.

"Don't look at me, this is the first I've heard of it," he said, "but I like the idea. Let's face it, you're never going back to the Corps. You'll make a fine regent—and besides, you need the work."

"No one can be forced to serve, Jeena," Selanja said, "in spite of Ghannon's words. You may refuse if you wish. I should tell you, though, that this election was the closest we have ever had to a unanimous vote. Still, the decision is yours."

Jeena gazed again at the golden scepter in her arms, and when she raised her eyes, they were moist.

"I do accept, gratefully."

Aramis and Selanja came to stand beside her.

"You do not have to choose now, but it is customary to select a ceremonial name when elected. You may wish to consider what you would like to be called during your reign."

Jeena thought for only a moment.

"Licente," she said, her eyes capturing Selanja's.

Aramis smiled. "That is fitting. Then you shall be known as the Licente, Regent of Uruk."

Ghannon opened the balcony doors and led her out. Below were gathered the people of Uruk in the newly expanded palace gardens. A roar went up when they spied her holding the scepter cradled in her arms. Jeena could do little more than smile and wave through misty eyes as the cheers continued.

SAMSON ASKED SELANJA, "WHAT DOES *LICENTE* MEAN?"

"In the ancient language, it means 'tigress.'"

He stared in wonder at Jeena waving to the crowd, Elaina's last words echoing in his ears.

Guard the tigress well, Shahaiya, for by the blood of her hands will your people rule the stars.

The celebration lasted well into the night. All in the city slept late, and none slept later or better than Jeena Garza, the Licente, Regent of Uruk, and her ibru Samson, Shahaiya, Lord of the Tigras.

END

ABOUT THE AUTHOR

R.J. LEAHY WAS BORN IN 1960 IN ST. LOUIS, MISSOURI, WHERE HE spent "a blissfully unremarkable childhood." High School was followed by a short but adventurous period on the West Coast, slacking in the pre-slacker age. After running out of money and friendly confines, he reluctantly returned to the Midwest and enrolled in the University of Missouri School of Engineering.

"At that time CAD was still very crude, as apparently, was my ability with drafting instruments. At the recommendation of my teachers, I changed schools and majors the following year, eventually matriculating from Truman University with degrees in Chemistry and Physics. Not yet willing to suffer the indignity of work, I opted for continuing education, graduating four years later with a medical degree."

He is a practicing physician as well as a writer of fiction and collector of ancient medical texts. He remains in the Midwest, where he lives with his fiancée, a remarkable woman who indulges his love of scotch and fine cigars without complaint. No higher praise can a man give.

ABOUT THE ARTIST

BRIAN HAMNER IS A HIGHLY MOTIVATED, CREATIVE AND VERSATILE illustrator specializing in fantasy and dark fantasy artwork. A frequent exhibitor at art shows and competitions throughout the south, Brian calls upon his love of the fantasy universe to create his stunning images. His unique style of art has received praise from many different sources including artists, private collectors, and industry professionals.

Brian captures the fantasy universe like no other artist. His bold style and attention to detail reflect a fascination from which his work has continued to evolve. A complete online gallery and portfolio can be found by visiting www.brianhamner.com

Brian currently resides in Tuscaloosa, Alabama, with his beloved wife and two perfect children.

Printed in the United States
68920LVS00012B/149